NOAH
AND THE
HOLY
SCEPTER

THE WALLS OF JERICHO

Luke Elliott

ISBN 978-1-63814-180-8 (Paperback)
ISBN 978-1-63814-181-5 (Hardcover)
ISBN 978-1-63814-182-2 (Digital)

Covenant Books
11661 Hwy 707
Murrells Inlet, SC 29576
www.covenantbooks.com

To my awesome son Ethan and beautiful daughter Trinity.
Your excitement motivated me more than you know.
And for all the times I questioned, "Does that make sense to you?"
I say thank you!

And to the love of my life, Tammy.
Your encouragement from the beginning
means more to me than you know.
Thank you for always believing in me.
I may want a million things, but I only need one…you.

In Memoriam

Kash Jameson Delony
January 26, 2021–January 27, 2021

"For You formed my inward parts;
You wove me in my mother's womb.
I will give thanks to You,
For I am fearfully and wonderfully made;
Wonderful are Your works,
And my soul knows it very well."
—Psalms 139:13-14

Even though you were only with us for a brief 25 hours, you brought our family so much love and joy. We are sad that we did not get to see you grow up but are at peace that you're in heaven. We rejoice at the image of Jesus pushing you on a swing.

Forever in our hearts.

Preface

There are two things that every person in the world has that is unique to them, just two. The first is their heart. The *heart* is an overused, sometimes oversimplified word that can describe a myriad of ideas. For me, the heart encompasses a person's love, desire, pursuit, and soul. Each person is given a heart and the ability to project it in the world any way they wish.

The second part of a person that makes them unique is their story. The story of their life. Who you are, where you're from, what you have experienced, the people you meet, the trouble you have caused, those you have loved and hurt, etc.—each person has a story unique and beautiful all their own.

So that's it, each person receives a heart and a story. However, in the rarest of occasions, God so decides to bestow an additional story on a few chosen people. Like an extra slice of pizza for dinner, an extra piece of cake at a party, an extra thirty minutes of playtime at night. It's not as if the story makes the person better than those who did not receive one of their own; it's merely an added morsel in an already delicious life. But whatever the person chooses to do with the story, that's a different matter altogether.

I just so happen to be one who was doubly blessed with a story. A story that I can say with confidence can only be from God because I am nothing special, and the story I'm about to tell is too much for anyone to imagine on their own. Also, in my opinion, a story is only story if you share it with others.

Would it surprise you I can recall the day when it all happened… the day I received my second story? I was newly eighteen, ready to break free into adulthood. It was Sunday morning. Our familial pattern at this point in my life was set in stone. Sunday was church. Being a college kid, I no longer attended Youth Group. Instead, I sat next to my parents in "big" church. I can say up to this point in my churchgoing experience, I could not recall with any type of confidence a sermon that I heard.

Don't get me wrong, I grew up attending Sunday worship, Youth Group on Wednesdays, an occasional Bible study, weekend conferences, mission trips, etc. Sure, I knew some of the more common Bible stories like Daniel and the lion's den, Jesus turning water to wine, and David and Goliath. As for locating those stories in the Bible, good luck.

So there I am sitting next to my father, a former minister, listening to Pastor Bill Counts as he begins his sermon. Pastor was in his eighties, his health failing, so he sat on a stool as he spoke to a congregation of around a thousand. I liked listening to him speak. He had a soft, level tone. His words chosen intelligently not just to make a point but rather to help drive it home, so to say. A stranger could tell he was a well-educated ivy leaguer by the way he handled the English language.

There I was about to drift away in my thoughts like every other Sunday. You know what I mean, I'm sure. You're listening but not really listening. Your eyes are on the speaker, but your mind is three hundred miles away. Thinking about one-liner's from a movie, the next level in a video game, whether the Cowboys were going to make it to the playoffs, is that pretty girl two rows up across the aisle gonna look back at you again. Then in what can only be described as a flash, my mind focused like a laser to what Dr. Counts was speaking on: the story of Jericho.

Before I continue, let me say that as a child in Bible school and attending VBS, I could recall tidbits of the story. It was mainly the song children sing about the walls coming down. Don't ask me to sing it either…

Dr. Counts says Jericho, then Joshua, then the walls. I'm transfixed. My mind is off and racing. It's like I'm there in Jericho. I can see the gigantic city walls, I can hear the soldiers marching, I smell the stagnant air and feel the humid breeze. Okay, so here is where things get interesting. Now I told you that some of us receive an extra story. Well, for me, it did not come in a string of thoughts. The best way to describe it, and I'm sorry for lack of imagination in description, but the best example is a brain transplant. But rather than the entirety of the brain, let's call it a "story transplant."

Whereas once there was an empty spot on the bookshelf in my mind, now there was a novel, and not just the idea of a novel or a premise to a novel, but the whole story!

I could see the end, the beginning, the twists, characters, everything—it was suddenly just there. Some may describe it like lightning striking your mind. Mine was like a bolt of light striking my brain, leaving a scar that never healed. All this being said, this happened when I was eighteen years old…eighteen for goodness sakes! Just about to leave home, head back to college, find my wife, and start a life.

Now my mind had a guest, and let me just say that the guest wanted out. I tried a few times to write down what I saw, but for whatever reason—busyness at school, work stress, date nights, free time or the inability to describe with clarity what I saw—I never made much progress. Back in those days, my future seemed light-years away, and time was not of the essence. Up until now, that is.

Over the years, thoughts burst in my mind, and burst is literally the best way to describe it. I would be sitting around minding my own business, and *pop!* A vision exploded into view and wouldn't cease replaying until I wrote it down. I kept promising myself, and God, that I would not hold it back any longer. Here and there, I would jot down notes and scribble drawings on napkins. These little tidbits have accumulated in a folder without any organization, a cornucopia of puzzle pieces waiting to be formed for readers' enjoyment.

Would it surprise you that it has been over twenty years since that Sunday church service? My life has taken twists and turns since then. I'm married now, have a few kids, own a business, and pay a mortgage. I've seen a few things, felt hurt and love, lost friends and family, experienced fear anxiety and hope all in the matter of a moment. In other words, I think the sum of my experiences and knowledge may just finally be able to handle the explanation and depth of the story which was gifted so many years back.

Some may say the way I have decided to approach this is not normal. My inner dialogue or my desire to have a conversation with you, the reader. To them, I say, "So be it."

Job said, "Naked I came into the world, naked I'm gonna leave."

Well, this is how God gave me the story, so I'm gonna share it with you just the same. All right, deep breath; let's begin, and bear with me as I set this up. It'll be worth it!

1

Who here remembers the elation of the last day of school? Well, it was no different for a little boy in small bustling suburb of Dallas, Texas, named Noah. Today was his last day of fifth grade, the last day of elementary school, the last day of being considered a little kid. Next year was middle school and the approaching teenage years, but before all that madness, summer.

Summertime! Man, there's no better time for a kid. Swimming pools, ball games, late nights, sleeping in, video games, sleepovers, and junk food. This is what life is about. The best years. The golden years.

Noah ran out of school like an unleashed puppy at a dog park. His emotions bursting forth, the restraints of formal education loosed, relief filled the air. All the children were smiling and laughing. Many spoke of plans of upcoming vacations. Noah's buddies were already planning a sleepover and when to meet at the neighborhood pool. "Who is gonna bring what?" and "Don't forget to ask your mom!" and "Gosh, I hope we can order pizza."

As much as Noah wanted to jump in, he couldn't. Sure, summer was here, and yeah, he was happy school was out. But his summer was already booked, planned, sealed, and spoken for. No, it wasn't with camps or beach vacays and slumber parties. His was a summer all to himself…and his father. A summer in another world: Israel.

After the goodbyes and high-fives, Noah jumped on his bike and pedaled home. For those five minutes, his mind emptied, and he took a few big breaths. Peace overcame him, and relaxation poured in.

The feeling, however, melted fairly quickly when he arrived home. *Upheaval* is probably the best term for his home. The last few weeks were spent packing and repacking. Spending a summer in Israel requires planning, and their house was the staging ground. Noah's home was located twenty miles north of Dallas in a middle-class neighborhood of Frisco, Texas, one of the fastest-growing cities in the US.

His father, a short and stocky man forty years young, as he would say, was a teacher in Dallas at the theological seminary. His skin was olive in color, and his green eyes stood out in a crowd. Solomon's hair started to fall out in his late twenties, and what was left wasn't even worth visiting a barber to care for. He kept his hair short so he wouldn't have to waste time fixing it in the morning. Most of the time, he donned a worn-out Pine Cove Camp hat. His face stayed covered with a five o'clock shadow no matter how often he shaved.

Solomon didn't so much care for the hustle and bustle of the city, so when Noah was a baby, he moved the family to the suburbs and a quieter life. Sure, his commute was long into Dallas for classes, but it wasn't a daily burden. Classes were only on Tuesday and Thursdays.

It had always been Noah and his father since Noah could remember. His mother passed on at an early age after cancer took over her body. Neither ever really brought her up in conversations those days. On special occasions, there was an acknowledgment between the two, but the lingering pain kept it from much more than that.

Noah loved his home. The mood of a house is just as important as the structure. You ever think about how you feel when you walk into your house? Is there comfort, dread, angst, maybe a twinge of anger or worry? Is it filled with love and acceptance, peace and hopefulness?

For Noah, his home was calm, contented, and breathable. He could be himself, relax, and spread out. He was safe, and his heart knew it. As for the actual home, well, it was too big for the two of them yet not big enough. LOL. The space was there for sure. I mean, why would two people need four bedrooms and three bathrooms?

His parents purchased the home with plans of growth and the future large family dream. God had other plans.

As for the street he lived on, it just worked. Neighbors who converse with one another is about all one can ask for, and boy, did his like to talk! Noah loved to listen to the adults complain about the goings on in the area. Lots of them had kids as well, so he had ready-made playmates close by. All the yards on his street were groomed weekly, and each household maintained a quaint garden. The people were so friendly; each concerned with the other's well-being.

At Noah's home, one of the spare bedrooms was used as an office and for his father's many collectibles. The other room was used as a guest bedroom, although they had not entertained a guest in years. The décor obviously lacked a female touch. Each room was sparse, the walls blank. Everything to his father was frivolous.

"If you don't use it regularly, then don't buy it," his dad would say.

Little tapes like that would play in Noah's head. Everything his father did and said was a lesson for the future. Sometimes it was okay, but lately, Noah was becoming annoyed. Listening to his father made him miss the idea of his mother more sometimes. Noah knew his life was going to change now that elementary was over and puberty was right around the corner. Maybe his dad thought the same. He was losing hold of his boy, and his one-liners were nothing more than the desperation he felt in the loss of his baby. *That's probably what this trip is about*, Noah thought.

"Dad?" Noah called out.

"Yes," he replied.

"Can I use your grey bag as a carry-on?" he asked.

"I suppose."

"Where is it? I can't find it anywhere."

"Check downstairs in my closet, toward the back behind my boots."

Jeremiah and Isaiah are so lucky, Noah thought. *They get to spend their summer away from their parents at camp. I, on the other hand, have to endure both my dad and the summer heat in another country,*

13

digging up needless relics. Sometimes I wish I had a normal family like my friends.

It was Christmas break when Noah's father dropped the bomb. Instead of enjoying the summer playing baseball, video games, and sleepovers with his buddies, Noah was going to travel with his father. Of course, Solomon had spoken many times over the years about how much he wanted Noah to join him on one of his expeditions. And Noah actually did want to see it, just not yet. He wanted his summer, and come to think of it, even though the thought of the trip was great, Noah never believed he would ever do it. It was a "Daddy pipe dream."

Needless to say, Noah was crushed when his father unloaded the news, and his resentment grew daily at the idea. The rest of the school year in his mind was wasted in preparation and mournful expectation. Learning about the country more so than his father normally would share, packing for the few months they would be away, coordinating with relatives to care for their home when they were gone, going to the doctor to get inoculated for the journey, and best of all, waiting in line to apply for a passport, which was way more complicated and slow than it should be in the twenty-first century.

Rummaging through his father's closet, Noah yelled out, "I still can't find it!"

"C'mon, bud, I'm trying to get packed here as well. Do you have to use that bag? It's so old."

From the time Noah could remember, his father owned that bag. Worn with use from his many excursions, the bag weathered quite impressively over the years. Being a biblical archeologist, Solomon needed a pack that could go wherever the journey took him. Functionally, it was a bag before its time. With enough pockets and zippers to divide all that Solomon would need on any journey, Noah knew it would fit his plans well enough. Obviously, technology had changed in the last ten years, so some of the original use the bag allowed for wasn't needed, but Noah still wanted it.

"Found it!" Noah yelled out more enthusiastically than he planned. Now it was just a matter of organizing his possessions into it.

2

Over the last five years, Solomon's project entailed retracing the steps of the past kings of Israel and Judah. He and his team, which assembled in Israel each summer, worked through the year in their various universities and seminaries trying to uncover the hidden secrets the Bible did not explain. While most people are satisfied with what they read in the biblical books of Kings, Chronicles, and Samuel, Solomon wanted more.

"Noah, we really need to get going to the airport, we have a long trip ahead of us. You almost ready?" he asked.

"Yeah, Dad, just finishing up. Gimme five minutes." Noah was in a blur. He just walked out of fifth grade and elementary school for the last time, and here he was, about to leave the country. He hadn't even caught his breath.

Noah prayed and spoke to himself, "Just keep going. I'll be fine once we load up. Stay focused. God help me. Breathe, Noah." Noah did this type of inward speak often. You ever find yourself doing that? His father explained to him years back that most people look at prayer as something formal. It's not just about the act or the posture.

"You don't have to clasp your hands together. Close your eyes and bow your head," he would explain. "Prayer is a conversation between you and your Creator. All God wants is a relationship. Call on Him whenever life seems to overwhelm you. It'll help you calm down and fill you with contentment."

Traveling to another country was not an easy affair anymore. Solomon and Noah had to be at the airport three hours ahead of time, and Noah's father was not one to be late. *Three hours, and for what? To stand in a line for two hours*, Noah thought.

Going through customs is a horrific time, especially when you are traveling to one of the most dangerous areas on Earth, Israel. For years, there had been unrest in the Holy Land, the three largest religions fighting over who had the right to claim the land as their own. Solomon explained the problems many times to Noah, but this time, he was going to see it firsthand, and if Noah was honest to his father, he was far more excited than he let on. Muslims, Jews, and even Christians all praying and worshipping in the same place—it was always a wonderful image that Noah wished to see. It also made him question why there was fighting between the people if they all taught peace and love.

"Okay, I got the passports. We're loaded up, you got everything?" Solomon called out.

"Yeah, Dad," Noah answered, "for the twelfth time." He muttered under his breath, "Why does he always treat me like I'm still a kid?" Two months alone in the desert with his dad was not going to be easy, he thought.

Solomon was not big on impressions, obviously noted at the "piece of junk" car they drove. A beat-up minivan, six years out of its prime, but his dad always said, "If it runs, it's worth driving." The windows did not roll down, one of the back doors could not be opened, and the windshield wipers scraped more than wiped; it was always so embarrassing for Noah to be seen in it. Neither had much to say on the drive. Noah pondered the beginning and end of summer. His friends, no doubt, were already swimming and laughing or grinding a new level on the most recent video game while he faced an entirely different reality.

"Well, you ready for this?" Solomon asked as he pulled out of the neighborhood, making small talk to fill the silence more so than igniting a conversation.

"I guess," Noah sullenly replied, looking back one last time. Reality hit him like a ton of bricks.

"It won't be a bad as you think, ya know. Besides, you can finally see your old man at work. I think you may just enjoy yourself, Noah," Solomon said empathetically, "if you give it a chance."

"We'll see," Noah responded in a sarcastic friendly way. He shrugged his shoulders and stared out the window.

They were flying out of DFW, the third largest airport in the nation. Even though this was not going to be Noah's first time on an airplane, it was his first international flight. A whole twenty hours in the air and multiple hours on the ground waiting for the next flight, and at each stop going through customs again. To think his father did this regularly impressed him.

Noah never really understood his father's passion for his job. Sure, there were some cool aspects. Solomon actually got to put boots on the ground in the areas others heard about during Sunday school. And then after his expeditions, Solomon would return and teach seminars to scholars and students alike about his findings. Noah remembered the many times his dad left him with a babysitter or a relative to go to some far-off country he could barely pronounce, let alone spell.

That issue was quickly remedied, however. Noah's father made it a point to teach him the basics of all the languages he used on his excursions. He always hated it too. Instead of speaking English with his father when he got home from school, Solomon would question him in Aramaic, Greek, and even Hebrew. At this point, Noah reconciled that it was a way for his dad to prepare himself more for his next trip, rather than for his own education. As Noah grew older, it seemed more so that his father yearned for him to follow in his footsteps and become an archeologist. This summer, Noah was going to receive firsthand experience in using his teachings in a real-world environment.

After thirty minutes of listening to quiet music and each passenger contemplating the road ahead, Noah turned to his dad and asked, "So how long exactly till we get to Israel?"

"Well, let's see here. We leave DFW for Chicago. There is about a five-hour layover, and then we depart for Zurich. From there, after an hour or so, we head to Tel Aviv, barring no weather problems, maybe tomorrow dinnertime," he answered simply.

"So, all in all, how long is this trip going to take?" Noah asked confusingly.

"Around twenty-three hours, I think. Or sorry, a day to be fair," he answered.

"Twenty-four hours on a plane! What are we going to do that whole time? I'll run out of battery in my phone less than halfway through. There has to be a faster way! Why can't we take a direct flight to Israel?"

Solomon laughed, "You can charge your phone on the plane, bud."

"But still—"

"Well," Solomon replied, "we could fly direct, but with all of our luggage and the price per ticket, it just was not reasonable. Besides, we're going to be there a long time as it is, so what's the rush?"

There it is, Noah thought. *The penny pincher shows his face. If my dad would only fork over a little more money, we could spend more time on the ground than in the air. What's another thousand bucks, ya know?*

Pulling into the airport parking garage, Solomon said, "All right, let's do this. Wait by the car, and I'll go and get a luggage cart, okay?"

"Sure, I'm not going anywhere" Noah mumbled.

"What's that?"

"Nothing."

A little while later, his father was back with the cart. It only took a few minutes to stack the luggage together, and with one last look at their ugly van, they were off. Upon entering the airport, Solomon told Noah to wait with the luggage while he went to check-in at one of the terminal booths.

Airports had always fascinated Noah. Not the planes, per se, but the many different people. All types roamed the terminals. People from his town, other cities, other states, even other countries. People of all nationalities and cultures, short people, tall people, fat and skinny people, young and old, white, black, Asian, Hispanic, and on and on and on. Everyone's clothes were different, the way they talked and walked, the music they listened to, what they read from magazines to newspapers to novels. Some carried Bibles while others carried iPods and cell phones.

Even where he lived, it seemed like the people who were not from his city lived in another world. The small differences stood out greatly in his mind. When he would go and watch the junior high football team play a neighboring city's team, the people in the other crowd acted and talked with a little something else in their voice. He wondered if anyone else could hear it. *How odd it will be in Israel,* he thought.

After about an hour's wait, Solomon interrupted Noah playing on his phone. They pushed their cart of luggage over to a baggage checker and watched him tear through their belongings. While he rummaged through their things, he asked questions but did not seem to care what the answers were. "Have you left any of your bags unattended?"

Noah's father replied, "No, sir."

"Do you have any lighters, firearms, or paraphernalia?" the checker asked.

"No, sir," Solomon replied.

Noah thought to himself, *Who would say yes? I have a loaded pistol in that bag over there, you just happened to miss it, but I was not going to say anything unless you asked.*

The checker was particularly interested in Solomon's archeological tools. He had three large metallic trunks. They looked like the cases in the movies the terrorists would use to transport a nuclear weapon. The baggage guy—by this time, they noticed his nametag read Marvin—took everything out of the cases. He seemed determined that he would find something that shouldn't go aboard the plane. A look of disappointment quickly washed over his face, however, when his search for the missing weapons came up empty.

In a nonchalant tone, Marvin said, "Okay, we're all done here. You may proceed. I'll put everything back in your bags. Have a good trip, and thank you for flying with us today."

"Thank you, Marvin," Solomon responded, "but I'll wait until everything is placed back into my bags."

Per airport normality, the line for the metal detectors was long. After fifteen minutes, Noah and his father snaked their way through the crowd where they were met by a boarding pass checker, a short black woman who seemed more interested in moving the people in the line fast than the actual information she reviewed. They gave her a picture ID and their boarding pass; she scribbled something on the pass and directed them on their way.

They were met by yet another man assisting the flyers in advancing past the metal detectors. "No liquids over three ounces, and that includes water bottles. If you have a laptop, I need you to take it out of your bag and place it in a crate. If you are wearing a belt or have a cell phone on you, please do the same. To speed up the process, please remove your shoes and place them on the conveyor belt as well. Any assistance needed, let us know," he said.

In Noah's eyes, this was the worst part of flying. Not often did Noah feel like a cow being herded. That was one great thing about Texas, space for all to roam around. But one man messed it up for all of them. Just because he had a bomb in his shoes, they all had to suffer. Noah thought his father was right when he told him, "One person can ruin it for everyone."

Now through the detectors, bags in hand and shoes on feet, Solomon and Noah made their way to the gate. Since they were flying to Chicago first, they did not have to go through the international terminal yet.

"C'mon, Noah, we need to move fast," he said as his pace quickened. DFW was a large airport, so the distance between gates took time to overcome.

"Why? We have twenty minutes until the plane departs," Noah said, breathing heavily, trying to match his father's speed.

"Because they start to board the plane around this time," Solomon answered.

As they approached the gate, sure enough, people were already lining up. They rushed to get in line. The nice thing was they did not have to wait. The attendant, a thin blonde-haired woman in her late forties hurried them into their seats.

Solomon pulled out his cell phone and turned it off. The plane pulled away from the tarmac. One of the flight attendants stood up at the front of the plane to walk through the safety protocols for the passengers as Noah situated his father's grey bag.

"Flight attendants, prepare for departure," the captain's voice called out over the intercom.

"No turning back now," Solomon said, looking at Noah with a smile.

Noah glared back, annoyed with his dad's words.

This was Noah's favorite part of flying. Speeding down the runway, the G-force pushing him back in his seat as the plane slowly lifted off. The ascent seemed to last for ten minutes and, for some reason, relaxed Noah into a stupor. His eyes began to close slowly, and then he was out.

Fifteen minutes or so later, he heard his father say, "Noah. Hey, bud, do you want something to drink or not?"

"Just some water. Thank you," his response directed more to the flight attendant hovering over Solomon.

"Would you like some pretzels as well?" she asked.

"Sure," Noah replied. He took them from her hand.

As she walked away to take the other flyer's orders, Noah turned to his father and asked him the question that had been on his mind since he first found out he was going to Israel for the summer, "So what are we going to Israel for?" He had a general idea from previous conversations, but now the subject was consuming his thoughts. School was over, friends were left behind, no video games or swimming pools—just him, his dad, and the desert of Israel.

Solomon looked up from the paperwork he was busy perusing and smiled to himself. The opening he was waiting for reared its head.

"You remember what I've been doing the last five years, right?" he asked.

"Studying the kings of the Bible?" Noah questioned.

"That's right. I have been retracing the steps, mapping the land, studying the people, researching the culture, and more since the time of Joshua."

"Oh, that's right, Joshua. So, who are you... I mean, we going to study this time?" Noah asked.

"One of the kings of Judah, the Southern Kingdom," he answered.

The thought of Joshua alone made Noah recall some of the stories his dad shared with him over the years. There was the famous David and Goliath, then the wars between the Israelites and the Canaanites, and miracles performed by the prophets that came to mind. So many names and places were hard to keep up with, but even with his meager education in biblical history, Noah was excited. If there was anyone who could guide him, his father was the best option.

"Tell me about this king," Noah said.

"Well, before I tell you his name, why don't we start from the beginning just so you have an idea of his significance? Plus, we have a little time till we get there." A smirk appeared on Solomon's face. He continued, "You understand by now most of what we do in life is because of our past. Well, the Bible, in particular the Old Testament, is a prime example." He waited for Noah to comply with his thinking and continued.

"Let's see here... Okay, so after Moses led God's people out of Egypt, the Israelites sinned against God in the desert. Their punishment was severe. They would be forced to wander in the desert for forty years until everyone over the age of twenty-one died, except for two men, Joshua and Caleb. Once that disobedient generation died off for their rebellion against God, Joshua was chosen to lead the new people into the promised land. The twelve tribes of Israel under the leadership of Joshua won every battle, save one, that they fought to gain the land. Once the Israelites had a firm foot in the land, Joshua, under God's guidance, divided the land between the twelve tribes, and he died. Over the coming years, the tribes met with conflict arising from their sin and disobedient hearts toward God. So in response, God sent judges to lead.

"Judges is one of my favorite books in the Bible. Time and again, the Israelites would rebel against God. Their penalty for rebellion was being subjected to slavery by an outside nation. The people in their distress would recognize the reason for their subjection was a result of disobedience to God. The people would cry out to God for rescue, and He would send a judge to rescue them. The people would then turn back to God for a generation until the coming generation would rebel, and the cycle would continue anew. Eventually, the people were tired of not having a king. So they approached Samuel with the request."

Solomon paused to catch his breath.

"Samuel at first did not want to comply with the request. God instructed him to tell the people it was not a wise decision, but the people persisted, and God gave them over to their demands. Thus, introducing the time of the kings, the first of which was Saul, followed by David, of course, and then to Solomon, my namesake."

"Wait, wait, wait…why are we going to study a king in Judah then? I thought you studied Israel," Noah interrupted.

"I'm getting to that," he answered and proceeded where he left off. "Soon the kingdom divided into the north and the south after Solomon. The Northern Kingdom retained the name Israel and consisted of ten tribes while the Southern realm of two tribes acquired Judah as its name."

As Solomon finished his explanation, the flight attendant arrived with their drinks. "Here is a glass of water for you, young man, and a Coke for your dad. Do you need anything else?" she asked.

"No thanks, looks like we're good here," Solomon replied. As she went on to the next aisle, he took a drink.

Noah stared out the airplane window. Thick white clouds floating over multicolored blue sky littered the view. They seemed to go on forever. He often wondered how anyone alive could not believe in God after looking at creation. Noah knew from a young age that God was there, and he was lucky to have someone like his father to nurture his beliefs.

Noah peered back toward his father and asked, "Well, what happened to make the kingdom of Israel divide into the north and the south?"

Solomon sat his drink down, reached into his carry-on bag, and pulled out a blank sheet of paper. With the pen in his shirt pocket, he drew an outline of Israel's boundaries. He then drew a line dividing it into the northern and southern territories.

Pointing to the picture, he answered, "It all happened during the reign of King Solomon, son of David. Solomon, the wisest man who ever lived, sinned against God by marrying women who practiced idolatry. God warned him not to do this, but Solomon ignored Him. And not just once, but twice…guess we all learn the hard way. Then God came to him and said he would be punished for his disobedience. The punishment, however, would not come until his death. When Solomon died, there was a rebellion. The kingdom was split between Jeroboam, the leader of the slaves who took ten of the twelve tribes and retained the name Israel in the north, and Rehoboam, Solomon's son who, after following horrible advice from his friends, received the southern portion and named it Judah."

Solomon took another drink of his Coke and let the words sit a moment.

Noah sat in silence, exhausted. He let the story linger in his thoughts, savoring the image like a perfect bite of pizza. *What were they really like?* Noah pondered. *Scholars know so little about these men of old. Thousands of years of history summarized into forty pages of text just is not enough. Sure, we can learn a lot through the broad strokes of human history, but it's the small things that make us who we are.* Noah drifted into a daze, his eyes heavy from the rush of the day and on into slumber. Sleep crept on him quickly, and now dreams filled his mind. The day was young still, though. The sun shone bright in the sky, but Noah's energy was drained by the long day.

And what felt like minutes later, his dreams were cut short by the captain. The pilot's voice came over the intercom and announced, "Ladies and gentlemen, please bring you seats and tray tables into their upright and locked position and prepare for landing. The weather in Chicago is sunny…"

3

The flight from DFW was quick. Noah gathered his belongings along with his father as the captain taxied the airplane to the tarmac. Still waking up from the rather abrupt intercom harassment, visions of what Solomon told him were playing out in his mind like a motion picture movie. Flashes of Moses leading the Jewish people out of Egypt, the dividing of the sea, the massive wars carried out in the times of David—questions were brewing in Noah's mind that he wanted to ask once they got to a stopping point.

"What do you have a taste for?" Solomon asked as they were leaving the tarmac and entering the terminal of Chicago O'Hare Airport. O'Hare was nowhere near as nice and clean as DFW.

"A sandwich is fine," Noah replied as he tried to keep up with is father's long strides.

"Sounds good to me."

Noah followed his father through the crowd of people waiting to board the plane they just departed from. *People can be so rude and impatient*, Noah thought as he looked on. *Children in elementary school have more control than adults in the airport.* Noah laughed to himself about the ones who lined up before instructed. *If you watch someone long enough, they'll show you who they are*, he supposed. And this lot of people were impatient with a capital I!

"How 'bout this place?" Solomon proposed, pointing ahead at a small restaurant off the main walkway.

Noah gazed up and read the sign: Mike's Deli & Bar. "All right," he replied.

They entered through a cafeteria-style line to order their food. Only a few people were ahead of them because it was between lunch and dinner hours. Since this was going to be their last meal in America, Noah wanted to taste one of everything. *I mean, who knows what the food is going to be like over there.* Solomon, on the other hand, kept it light. Flying never agreed with his stomach.

Noah grabbed a bag of chips, a chocolate chip cookie, fruit cup, slice of pie, and ordered a club sandwich with extra meat! "You sure you're going to eat all of that?" Solomon questioned, looking down at Noah's tray in amazement.

"Yep. I'm a growing boy," Noah answered with a smirk.

Noah left the line while his father stopped to pay and found a table away from the other people so they could spread out. Sitting next to strangers on a plane for hours on end annoyed him so much he did not want to sit in earshot of another conversation. After stuffing his mouth for ten minutes or so in silence, Noah asked a question to break the mood. "You never told me who you… I mean we, are going to study in Israel?"

Solomon finished chewing the food in his mouth, wiped his lips, and answered, "Well, I'll give you a hint. You're named after him."

"Josiah?" Noah remarked, knowing that it wasn't his first name.

"That's right," Solomon replied.

"I always wondered why you gave me that name," Noah said, thinking about how he loved the way his name sounded: Noah Josiah Williams.

"It's funny you say that," Solomon said. "Your mother and I had a time agreeing on your middle name. Noah, on the other hand, we both loved."

"Who wanted my middle name to be Josiah?" Noah asked.

"Your mother, of course," he said in a matter-of-fact tone.

"Figures? What did you want it to be?" Noah asked taking another bite of pie.

Solomon looked off at some people walking by. A lady grabbed her lingering child by the hand, noticeably in a rush. He answered, "I always preferred the name Job. But now, seeing how you turned out, I think your mother made the right choice." He looked at his son.

"Why did you like the name Job?" thinking how ridiculous that would have sounded, thankful his mother won the debate. His friends would have never let him live that name down.

"Well, your mother and I both believe that a name is important to a child. Like in the past, in biblical times, names defined who a child would grow up to be. Selfishly, I was partial to the name Job because his story meant more to me than others."

Noah couldn't recall the story of Job. Only snippets came to mind, so he asked, "Why Job's story?"

"I think it was the character of Job that made me love his name for you. This guy lost everything he held dear to his heart, and yet he loved God, and because of his love, God rewarded him with twice what he lost," Solomon answered.

"Oh yeah...that's the guy that lost his kids and all his stuff in one day, right?" Noah discussed.

"The story goes like this: Job was the epitome of a good, nearly perfect man. In everything he did, he honored and feared God, and God blessed him for it. Makes sense, right? He was wealthy, probably had a beautiful wife, a bunch of healthy kids, and when he spoke, people listened—basically what all men want still today. One day, and we don't know why, God said to Satan, 'Have you seen my man, Job? That guy is something else.' Satan sneered and said, 'The only reason Job is like that is because you spoil him with all his heart's desires. Let me take his family and possessions away from him and see if he still honors you.' So God, wanting to make a point, allowed Satan to have at 'em."

Noah interrupted, "Wait, wait, wait...you're telling me God *allowed* Satan to hurt Job for no reason? Now that's just mean!"

"Uh-huh, I know it is difficult to understand. But God allows evil, bud. He let the devil do this to test Job so as to be an example to us all. Think about it like this: if God is sovereign or in control and he blesses us with good, why not also with evil? I mean, evil is just another tool that God can use to teach us, mold us, build our character."

"God lets evil happen to us? That doesn't make any sense, Dad," Noah interceded. "God is good, God is love. Satan is the bad one. That's what they teach us in Sunday school."

"Well, let's look at Job after he lost everything," he answered. "God says to Satan, 'Look, even after you have taken away his family and his land, Job still honors me.' Satan snickered back, 'The only reason he still worships You is because he has his health.' Wanting to prove another point, God allowed Satan to hurt Job but not kill him. Satan does so, and Job is covered in painful sores, but yet he stills worships God."

"What did Satan do to his body?" Noah asked, his interest growing with each answer.

"From the descriptions of the illness, many scholars believe he was infected with leukemia of the skin, which is disgustingly awful." Solomon continued, "But that's not even the whole story, bud. After all this awful stuff happened, Job's friends—you know, the ones who are supposed to care the most—well, they came to him, even his wife for that matter, and they had the nerve to confront him that he must have done something wrong against God to bring this on himself."

Noah was shocked as he imagined this great man sitting on the street with nothing, alone, mourning his loss, and having to listen to ridicule and judgment that wasn't even deserved. *People love to kick each other when they're down*, he thought. *It's easier seeing others struggle than succeed. The struggle of another makes you feel better about your own life while other people's successes can make you feel less than.*

Solomon continued, "Job in his pain declares he did nothing wrong and tried to convince his friends to stop. His three friends tell him to renounce his sin and ask God for forgiveness, as does his wife! But Job persists."

"Sounds like he had a great wife," Noah said sarcastically.

"Don't forget, Noah, she lost everything too—" He paused. "You know, one thing I've learned in my limited days, everyone has their breaking point. There comes a time when everyone will question God's existence. I've had mine, and you'll have yours soon enough. This was Job's, and everything and everyone he loved was taken away from him or turned their backs on him. Through it all, though, Job continued to love and fear God."

"But he lost everything," Noah said, bewildered by the idea of Job's struggle.

"Gotta tell ya, nothing else matters in the end. Life is simple that way. I know being young, it's a bit confusing, but all this meaningless stuff people clamor for—their cars, houses, fancy clothes, electronics—it's all pointless. Suffering can be a blessing to us, a way of checking our priorities when we stray from God. Like a wake-up call. And just like Job, if we can persevere and keep our eyes on God, He'll reward us for it," Solomon added.

Solomon paused in the conversation to take another bite of his sandwich. Meanwhile, Noah tried to wrap his head around the story. A group walked by the deli near where they were sitting. He looked back to his dad. "I don't think I could live up to that name."

Solomon gazed back at Noah and smiled, seeing the discomfort in his eyes. "You will become the man God wants you to be, bud. You're young now, but soon you will realize that deep inside of you is something special. I already see it."

A pause in the conversation ensued. Noah finished eating his lunch while Solomon made a few notes in his journal. To change the subject, Noah said, "You still never told me why you and Mom decided on Josiah for my middle name." Noah enjoyed an opportunity to hear his father speak about his mother. It was rare chance and becoming less frequent the last few years.

Solomon finished writing and paused to gather himself. Emotions moving within, he adjusted his position in his chair and leaned forward. "When your mother was pregnant with you, she had an idea of who she wanted you to become, who she thought you would be. Even before the doctors announced we were going to have a boy, she knew. The name, I suppose, just solidified it. Goodness, she loved you, Noah. All those sleepless nights we would sit and wonder about our future with you." Solomon's gaze fixed on his son. Their eyes locked.

Noah could feel an emptiness swelling inside. His stomach swirled about, and tears began to form in his eyes. Noah could smell his mother in the air and hear her humming voice drift around him. Not wanting to cry in public, he quickly changed the subject, "So tell me about Josiah." He cleared his throat.

Solomon could tell his boy was struggling, so he played along, "Well, unlike King David and King Solomon, not much is known about him, except for what we have in the Bible. We do know he was one of the few good kings."

Noah interrupted, "Good kings? How's that?"

"That's what we call 'em. After the division of the kingdom I explained to you earlier, many kings lived and died. The Northern Kingdom was evil to the core and forsook the teachings of God. As a punishment for the people, every king that came to rule was evil, and the people suffered. The few good kings in that time were from the Southern Kingdom of Judah. And when I say few, I mean few."

"Why only from Judah?" Noah wondered.

"Well, they were the rightful heirs to the throne. Remember on the plane? Solomon's lineage passed through his son, Rehoboam, who was given the southern land of Judah after the rebellion."

"So like in the movies, the division was pretty much between the good and the bad," Noah remarked confidently.

"Aw, sorta, but there were bad kings in the Southern Kingdom as well. In fact, the majority of the kings were evil there too," Solomon added.

"Josiah wasn't, though," Noah declared with confidence. "Is that why Mom wanted that name for me?" he asked, composing himself from earlier.

"I'm sure it was," Solomon discussed. "Josiah was different than those who came before him. He is the only king in the Bible that no sin is attributed to. Not only that, but he was given the Kingdom of Judah at an early age."

"How old was he?" Noah questioned.

"By our accounts, around eight years of age?"

"What? How in the world could a child inherit a kingdom at the age of eight? There is no way I would take orders from a kid, and I'm almost twelve," Noah proposed.

NOAH AND THE HOLY SCEPTER

Solomon chuckled. "Confusing, isn't it? Back then, when children inherited a kingdom, much like in medieval times, regents were setup to assist in the rule. A regent is like a counselor. We know of two people who most likely aided Josiah early on. The first was his mother, the second was a priest named Hilkiah, who we will be studying in the days ahead as well," Solomon replied.

"So how old was Josiah when he actually gained control of the kingdom by himself?" Noah was getting interested, and Solomon could see it.

"Our best guess is around sixteen to eighteen years of age. Although there is no way to determine this. At least there isn't yet." He winked.

Noah took one last bite of pie. Any more than that, and his stomach would've burst. Growing boy or not, he had overeaten lunch, and his brain was begging him to stop. His heart, however, had a question. "What about him made Mom want me to have his name?" Noah questioned.

"The way he lived, I'm sure," Solomon answered. "I tell you what, why don't we make our way to the gate for our next flight and pick up from there? I'd rather find a spot closer in case there are any announcements."

4

Noah and his father cleaned up their trash and discarded it in the receptacle. They gathered up their carry-on baggage. The gate they departed from was not far from where they ate lunch. As they approached, Noah could see people congregating, even though the flight was still two hours away. Noah and his father found a place to sit and relax away from the others.

"Do you still wish you were going away with your friends to camp?" Solomon asked after a few minutes had passed. As a father, he knew Noah just wanted to be a boy.

Noah looked over at his dad. He paused to choose his words carefully. "Don't get me wrong, I'm looking forward to seeing Israel with you, but yeah, I would have liked to go with them." Noah hoped that he didn't hurt his father's feelings. He didn't want to lie to his dad either, but he also wanted him to know where he stood.

Solomon folded his arms across his chest and responded, "Noah, the reason I wanted you to come with me is because I feel this may be one of our last times together uninterrupted. You're going into junior high next year. Juggling sports, classes, and girls—oh boy—will overwhelm our schedule. It's not a bad thing, though. They are going to be some of your best years. I guess I'm just not ready to give you up yet."

"I'm not going anywhere, Dad," Noah said, leaning back in his chair.

Solomon put his arm around his boy. "You're about to go through some changes in your life and face issues I can't even begin to put into words. How about we both just make the most of *this* summer?" Solomon replied.

Noah got goosebumps on his arms. His father had a way with words. "I'll do my best," Noah answered, "but I know all about peer pressure, Dad, we had a speaker talk about it this year at an assembly. You don't have to worry, old man, I'll be fine."

"If that was enough to prepare you, I'd be the happiest man in the world," Solomon said definitively. "I know you think you're ready, but you haven't experienced it yet. Words and actions are two different things." Solomon paused for effect. "Let me put it another way. You're about to become a man. I just want to ensure you have one last look at what a man should be, and there are few better examples than those we are going to study together this summer."

"Like Josiah?" Noah responded, turning his head back toward his father.

"Yes, like Josiah." Solomon removed his arm from Noah's back.

"All right, so tell me about him already," Noah replied, wanting to change the mood from being so mushy-mushy, touchy-feely.

Solomon leaned over and picked up his carry-on bag, a brown leather backpack worn down from constant use. One of the straps was missing. Solomon unlatched the flap covering the top and pulled out his journal. Solomon always had some sort of writing pad to keep his thoughts straight.

"Here ya go," Solomon said to Noah as he handed him a notebook. "I know, I know, you don't want to record your thoughts, but on this trip, let's try something different. You and I are going to discuss a lot of stuff, and most of it you are gonna forget. I'd like you to at least try to keep some notes for when you get older."

"Uhh, okay," Noah replied, taking the journal from his father's hand reluctantly. He wasn't exactly excited about journaling. *School just ended, for goodness sake!* The time now was meant for distraction, not learning. Noah knew it was important to his father, though, so he didn't argue.

"I will tell you anything you wish to know, but I will only explain it once. After that, you're on your own. That journal could be your saving grace for this trip."

Noah opened up the journal and perused the pages. *Stay positive. Its only for a couple months. What could it hurt? Take a few notes, scribble here and there, maybe even learn a few things.*

"So, Josiah," Solomon said, handing Noah a pen from his shirt pocket, "what would you like to know?"

"Start from the beginning like you always do. Tell me about his father." Noah brought his feet up on the chair, knees high, leaned the journal against his thighs, and prepared to write.

"The true influence on Josiah's life really came from two men. His father, Amon, of course, but also his grandfather Manasseh. Neither of these kings were good. In fact, Manasseh is considered to be Judah's worst king of all, the complete opposite of the great King David. He's even mentioned in the book of Jeremiah as the cause for Israel's ultimate demise."

"Seriously? So what did he do?" Noah asked as he struggled to spell Manasseh in his journal.

Solomon cleared his throat and continued, "So this Manasseh went against everything Moses, Joshua, David, and Solomon ever stood for. I mean, this guy went his own way. Like a misbehaving deviant who just wants to break every rule put out, he lived above the law, above God's law. He set up idol worship inside the temple built for God, he murdered his own children, and it is even speculated that he killed the Prophet Isaiah."

"He killed a prophet! Did God punish him?" Noah asked, astonished by what he was hearing.

"That's not even the most shocking part, Noah. Not to get to sidetracked, but Manasseh's father, Hezekiah, is looked upon as one of the best kings. Hezekiah depended on God wholeheartedly and because of his dependence, the Kingdom of Judah flourished. When Manasseh was young, maybe twelve, Hezekiah allowed him to be vice-regent. Ya know, learn the ropes with his old man. But for some reason, after Hezekiah passed on, Manasseh turned evil, evil to the core."

"Are you serious? That doesn't make any sense, Dad," Noah declared.

"Just because the father is good doesn't mean the kids will be."
Solomon nudged Noah. "Besides, most of us learn the hard way,"
Solomon answered rhetorically. "I've told you before and I will say it
again: you, Noah, are responsible for your own life. I can teach you,
show you, and explain things, but in the end, you have to choose,
bud."

Noah paused to consider Solomon's statement and asked, "I'm
curious, how did God end up punishing Manasseh?"

Solomon laughed. "That's the interesting part. Many of the evil
kings only ruled for short periods of time. Like Amon, Josiah's father,
his reign lasted just two years. God, on the other hand, allowed
Manasseh to rule for fifty-five years!" Solomon exclaimed clearly as
excited about the history as Noah was in learning of it for the first
time.

"This sounds like a messed-up movie. No way!" Noah asked,
bewildered.

"Crazy thing was in his old age, Manasseh came to understand
what he did during his reign was wrong, and he actually repented
and sought forgiveness. Sometimes," Solomon paused, "sometimes,
people do bad things, but God does not give up on them. Just like
a patient father who loves his kid no matter what, God will wait
for us... He'll wait for you." Solomon pressed his finger lightly into
Noah's shoulder.

Noah did his best to outline what his father explained. All
the while, he thought about how God could allow so much evil.
Every time Noah activated his cell phone, he saw stories about people shooting each other, viruses, stories of children being harmed
by their parents, looters and rioters, robberies, deadly storms, and
more—all these horrific things happening to innocent people.

Noah stopped writing and scanned what he wrote. He came
across what his father said about Amon reigning for only two years
and asked, "So Amon, Manasseh's son, I'm guessing he did not follow
in his father's path of being good?"

"Well, he followed the beginning of Manasseh's reign for sure.
He rebelled against God completely, which provoked some of his
officials to assassinate him. Probably out of frustration and worry

that Amon would take them right back to where Manasseh had them for fifty years or so."

"And that's when Josiah took over, I suppose?" Noah said.

"That's right." Solomon waited for Noah to write down his thoughts and then continued, "But like I told you earlier, he had help from regents until he came of age to handle the kingdom on his own."

Solomon took a moment and leaned down to pull his Bible from his carry-on bag. He turned to the back of the leather-bound book. Once he found the page he was looking for, he turned the Bible toward Noah. "This is a map of what the world looked like in the times of Josiah's reign." He pointed at the map. "The world power at the time that Josiah's reign began was Assyria. However, Ninevah, the capital of Assyria, had just fallen to the up and coming power, Babylon. And if history teaches us anything, when the capital falls, so eventually does the entire empire. Judah, under Josiah's leadership, was able to stay out of conflict for the time being."

"Was Josiah in complete control of the kingdom when Assyria fell?" Noah asked.

"Not in complete control, no," Solomon answered. "Babylon continued to grow in power, but Judah wasn't a threat to them. But Josiah is not known for his great battles like other kings, bud. Instead, he is remembered for his reforms."

Solomon took the Bible back from Noah and turned to the Second Book of Kings. Using the chapter as an outline, he explained the story of Josiah, "During his reign, Hilkiah, the head Levitical priest, found a copy of Israel's Covenant Constitution. The fact that this is even noted in scripture leads scholars to surmise the laws were lost during the times of Manasseh and Amon. It's quite possible in Manasseh's rebellion he did not want a reminder left in the kingdom of his deviancy, so he had all the copies destroyed. Someone must have hidden this one."

"How could they destroy the copies of the constitution? I mean they're kings," Noah asked.

"They were evil men. Back then, copies of manuscripts were rare. It's not like today where everyone can go to the local library and look up the United States Constitution or log onto the Internet."

"Can't believe this is in the Bible. How have I never heard of this?" Noah said with a hint of a smile.

"All right, when Josiah was told about the newfound laws, he quickly implemented them in all the lands. Josiah was a humble man who feared the Word of the Lord. With God's law in hand, he made monotheism, the belief in one God, the official theology again. Remember, his grandfather had set up idol worship, so this was a big change for everyone."

"Did the people follow him in his reformation?" Noah questioned.

"It is hard to say how many of them abandoned their gods. The prophets who lived during this time spoke about the people's lack of true godliness. Josiah was nevertheless undeterred. He went throughout Judah and destroyed the idol temples built by Manasseh and Amon. He even entered the Northern Kingdom of Israel to dismantle their temples. No fear at all."

"And the people of Israel let him?" Noah questioned again, imagining the conquest of destruction.

"The Northern Kingdom was weak by then. They had fallen into captivity a couple hundred years earlier to Assyria," Solomon answered. He tried to continue but was interrupted by the ringing of his cell phone. He glanced down at the caller ID. "Great," Solomon said sarcastically, "Noah, I really need to take this."

"Gotcha," Noah said. He knew the drill.

"It may take a while. Just hang out, I'll be right over there." Solomon pointed to a vacant corner near the windows overlooking the runway.

"Go ahead, I'll be fine."

Solomon picked up his black organizer and walked away where there were no people around to keep his conversation private. Unlike others, Solomon was discreet while in public on his cell. Some people talked louder on their phone purposely to get attention, annoying Noah to no end.

While his father was away, Noah opened up his journal and perused the pages he wrote. He thought about the stories of the kings. *Manasseh, Amon, and Josiah—what were they like? Maybe they lived like the movies depict, in lavish surroundings, wearing elaborate jewelry and elegant robes. They were probably larger than life. They got whatever they wanted and no one could tell them otherwise. And with God by their side in war, who stood a chance?*

Noah looked over and saw that his father left his journal behind on the chair. He glanced over to where Solomon was talking. He was now sitting alone on a bench with his head down, writing something, the phone attached to his ear. Noah reached out his arm to pick up his father's journal. "He won't care," he muttered to himself.

This was Solomon's fourth journal. It took years for him to fill the pages. The journal was bound in tan leather, worn at the seams; loose papers littered out of the sides. Noah opened the notebook in the middle and examined the contents. Random notes spilled over the margins. Tiny drawings of objects Noah never saw before were scattered about in no perceivable order.

Tabs sticking out from the side categorized the notes Solomon collected. Noah read the tabs. One stuck out to him. He thumbed his finger over the yellow plastic marker that read, "The Boy King." He lifted the tab over to find a collage of information. Miscellaneous pictures and artist's renderings, an illustration of Josiah's appearance based upon archeologists understanding on the people of that time. A normal fellow with a beard, of course, his body was wrapped in a long robe. "Why do they always have to have a beard?" Noah whispered to himself.

Unlike the rest of the chapters in the journal, information on Josiah was sparse. His dad was right when he said not much was known about him. Copies of the biblical text in Second Kings were pasted on the pages. Noah read the words. The meaning was hard to comprehend because it was written in Old English. The writer used words like *hath, thus,* and *wilt thy.*

Noah was enamored. As he was reading the journal, he felt the hair on the back of his neck rise. A full body tremor shook him from the inside out. This was not the first time he felt like this. Anytime he was captured in the Word of God or was caught up in worship at church, the tingle wrapped his skin. Solomon described what he was feeling many years ago. He said, "The Holy Spirit is moving inside you." Whatever it was, it made Noah feel good.

Thirty minutes passed while Noah examined his father's notes. Everything around him, the ambient noises, disintegrated into silence. A familiar voice from behind him called out, "Find anything useful?"

Noah jumped. The sound of his father's voice was startling.

Noah turned around to see Solomon smiling back. His father sat back down in his chair and said, "It's okay, bud. I'm glad you're interested."

"It was just lying there. I didn't think you'd mind." Noah paused to catch his breath then resumed, "You weren't kidding when you said there is not much known about Josiah."

Noah handed the journal back to Solomon. "And that's why we're going to Israel." Solomon smiled back at his son.

Just then, a voice rang out over the speakers. Noah looked over to the ticket counter in front of the gate and saw attendants gathering. A petite Hispanic woman took hold of the intercom. "We are going to begin boarding in a few minutes. Keep your boarding pass out and hand it to the attendant. Please wait until your boarding group is called before getting in line. Thank you."

"Do you have your ticket?" Solomon asked.

"Yeah. Looks like we're in the A group."

"C'mon, we'll go ahead and get in line."

5

Noah's patience was wearing thin. The first flight from DFW to Chicago went by without a hitch. Even going through customs and waiting at the gates wasn't so bad. But this stretch of travel from Chicago to Switzerland was more than his energy-filled body could handle. Noah was already on his third inflight movie, and every other one available to watch he had already seen. Plus, trying to watch a feature film with airplane issued headphones just did not sound right. The roar of the engines drowned out the audio. Most of the dialogue turned into mumbling.

To make matters worse, his seat would not recline. He didn't notice the issue until the plane took off. Try as he could, no matter how hard he pressed the button on the armrest and pushed with his legs, that seat wasn't going anywhere. The plane was full, so changing seats wasn't an option either. He thought how crazy it was reclining a few inches could be the difference between comfort and agony. Or maybe his sleep deprivation was causing him to turn a simple annoyance into a major grievance.

He glanced over at his father snoring away, oblivious to his surroundings. A few times, Noah was tempted to jab him in the side "accidentally," of course, so he too could feel his discomfort. Inside, he wanted to scream. Most people on the plane were sleeping or struggling to get there. Noah envied them. Each time he started drifting into slumber, there was a jolt of turbulence or some commotion from someone walking down the aisle to reach the restroom.

Noah and Solomon were a few hours outside of Zurich now. Upon arrival, after an hour or so layover, they would be on their way to Tel Aviv, the final stretch. The anticipation of feeling ground beneath his feet was his hope. *Just keep busy. Watch the movie. Who cares if I can't hear it? Relax, man. Just get lost in the story, and before long, we'll land.* He tried to motivate himself to hang in there.

Solomon slept deeply while Noah suffered quietly. Flying to Israel was nothing new to him. Solomon fell asleep an hour into the flight and had not aroused since, not even to relieve himself. Noah's irritation with the audio coming from the headphones boiled over. He gave up. Removing the headphones, he looked around at his options to keep his mind off the flight. He saw his father's journal peeking out of the leather bag beneath Solomon's feet and reached for it.

Noah glanced one more time at his father, ensuring he didn't wake him in the process. He took his time thumbing through the endless pages of drawings and scribbles. Solomon's journal was like a comic book jigsaw puzzle. Noah slowly perused each page, savoring it as he would a work of art. Short notes were strewn about the margins. He made sure to scan each and try to decipher their meanings. Arrows pointed to passages and then onto paragraphs like a spider's web stretching from front to back. Artistic renderings of buildings, hieroglyphic type writings, and maps littered the pages. Some pages folded out into larger illustrations. Noah lost track of time, processing the content.

He found himself once again in the section about Josiah, the Boy King. He decided to take the time and read the inserted pieces his father pasted from the Bible. As he read, he conjured up visions of what it must have been like in those days. He imagined the clothes the people wore, the food they ate, animals they raised, and the land. Noah could hear the sounds play in his mind of the livestock and the clamoring of people in the villages. He pictured soldiers tearing down the idol temples and Asherah poles under Josiah's orders and the people rebelling against his zealous mission. *How could this one man change so much? How amazing it would be to be remembered as Josiah was!*

While he studied the pages, the pilot's voice came over the intercom, "Ladies and gentlemen, this is the captain speaking. We are putting the 'Fasten Seatbelt' sign on again. There is some turbulence up ahead. Please remain seated until we are through it. Thank you." The interruption ended with an awful screech as the captain disconnected the mic. Those awake on the plane cringed at the sound.

"Wha...what was that?" Solomon drearily asked, startled by the awful noise.

"Nothing. Captain just said we're heading into some turbulence," Noah answered pushing on his ears as he moved his jaw in a circular motion to stop the ringing.

"How long have I been out?" Solomon questioned, rising in his chair stretching his arms high, yawning deeply.

"Couple hours, I think," Noah answered, closing his father's journal, excited at the chance to speak again.

Solomon breathed deep and stretched from side to side to loosen himself. "Did you get any sleep?"

"I tried to but just couldn't get comfortable," Noah answered. "Every time I started to dose off, the turbulence hit." Noah did his best to mask his irritable feelings.

Solomon brought his seat to its upright position. He stared off down the aisle, gaining his composure. "Whatcha been doin' this whole time?"

"Watchin' a few movies and looking at this," Noah answered, holding up his father's journal.

"Aw, find anything interesting?" Solomon asked as Noah turned the pages.

"Yeah. What's this? I've seen it throughout the pages." He pointed at a drawing.

Solomon reached into his shirt pocket and pulled out his reading glasses. He started wearing them a year or so back. Noah would sometimes give his old man a time joking about his aging. "Let me see that." Noah handed the journal to his father, careful not to change the page. "Oh, the Ark of the Covenant," he answered in a matter-of-fact tone.

The illustration on the page looked like some sort of ancient chest the size of a casket. Noah assumed it maybe to be a resting place for a pharaoh or possibly a king of Israel. By the scale of the rendering, the trunk was about eight feet by three feet and two and a half feet tall. The box itself was handcrafted from wood and was then overlaid within and without by gold. A gold crown encircled the rim of the chest. At the four corners, golden rings had been cast; through them passed bars of wood overlaid with gold to carry the chest, bars long enough for four men to shoulder the load contained within.

In all the depictions of the Ark, the two bars remained within the rings regardless of it being carried by men. On top of the chest, two cherubim (angels) of beaten gold were placed looking toward each other, spreading their wings over the trunk.

"The what?" Noah questioned, eyes focused on the illustration.

"The Ark of the Covenant. I'm sure I've mentioned it before to you." Solomon looked over at his boy.

"Not that I can remember," Noah replied. More than likely, his dad did bring it up in the past, but like usual, Noah was probably playing a game or on his phone or both. He probably even asked questions of his dad about it without really listening to what was being said.

"Let me show you a better picture of it," Solomon said, turning to the front of the journal. He came to a two-page spread. The depiction of the Ark covered both sheets. Notes were scribbled all around the illustration.

"What was it used for?" Noah asked as he scanned the gold-colored rendering of this ancient relic.

"Well, it's written that the Ark contained the stone tablets given to Moses by God. The Ten Commandments," Solomon answered. "You remember learning about the Israelites leaving Egypt after the plagues? You know, 'Let my people go,'" Solomon said, raising his arm clenching his fist for effect. "Moses and the Jewish people crossed the Red Sea on dry ground to get away from Pharaoh and began their journey to Mount Sinai. Once they got there, God told Moses to ascend the mountain. Moses did, and God gave him the law to lead the people. And that law changed everything."

Noah listened to his dad, recollecting some of what he explained. He interrupted, "I remember that story, but why do you have this here in this journal? I thought we were studying the kings of Israel. That part happened way before this."

"Confusing, right? Well, in the times of Joshua, before the age of the kings, the Ark was carried before the people for protection. But…let me just say here that this wasn't some talisman or good luck charm. You know how some superstitious people say 'Knock on wood' or they carry a rabbit's foot? This was so much more. This was a gift from God."

"Was it a weapon then?" Noah was intrigued at the idea.

Solomon took a drink of water parched from his high-altitude nap. "The Ark was the very presence of God among the Israelites. When the men of Israel carried it before them into battle, success was guaranteed. When the leaders refused to carry it, defeat soon followed."

"Sounds like a good luck charm to me," Noah interjected sarcastically.

"Hard to argue that when you see it as a mere object. Let me try again… Oh, all right, how about you look at it more like an obedient child? Suppose a father tells his kid to do something, and if he does it, he'll be rewarded. If his kid listens, *bam!* Good stuff happens. However, if his child disobeys, the situation turns bad." Solomon let the thought sit with Noah.

Noah shrugged, "I guess so." He answered flippantly, not wanting to argue.

Solomon continued, "There are so many good examples of the Ark being used, like the battle of Jericho, for instance. You remember that one? The Ark was carried in front of the soldiers as they encircled the city walls per God's instruction. And on the seventh day, the walls fell and the war was won."

Noah somewhat remembered the story of Jericho. "Is that when the men were told to march around the city for a week and on the last day to shout?"

"That's right. And when they shouted, some of the priests blew trumpets. The crescendo of noise reverberated through the city, and the walls collapsed, catching the enemy soldiers off guard. Game over." Solomon was pleased at the culmination.

"Oh yeah, I remember that from Sunday school." He paused then asked, "So, where is the Ark now anyways?"

"You and every government in the world would like to know." Solomon chuckled then continued, "Imagine a weapon so powerful it could wipe out an army by simply lifting the lid off the chest. When the Israelites constructed the Ark, God had them follow a very specific outline. Upon completion, God gave them detailed rules or routines on the handling of the chest to avoid catastrophe. If the Israelites failed in the slightest way, death was immediate."

Noah objected, "Wait, you said it wasn't a weapon. If it worked like that, why didn't the Israelites just take the Ark, put it in front of the enemy, open the lid, and run?" It seemed obvious to a twelve-year-old video game playing kid from north Texas. Why not these people from a few thousand years ago?

"Because it violated the rules set forth by God. There is a story in the Bible when the Philistines, Israel's enemy, captured the Ark from Israel. They viewed it a victory for their gods. The Philistine men carried it into their encampment and presented it to their king. A great celebration took place. Over the next couple of days, however, a plague, similar to the bubonic plague, swept through their land, killing thousands of men, women, and children. It didn't take a genius to figure out why this tragic death toll occurred. The Philistines quickly returned the Ark to Israel."

Noah aggressively interrupted his father, "Well, that makes my point then! Why not just throw the Ark into the enemy camp, like an Old Testament nuke. Seems easy enough." His patience from the long day of travel was wearing on him.

Solomon gave his boy one of those "Careful now" looks.

"Sorry, Dad." Noah knew he overstepped.

"Why does everything have to be a weapon?" Solomon shifted in his seat. "Men always take something that was meant for good and turn it evil. The Ark was supposed to be a reminder of God's presence. To give confidence and hope to a chosen people, not another tool to harm others. And that's why God took it away ultimately."

"So where do you think it is now? Destroyed, I'm guessing."

"Well, now, that's the ultimate question in archeology. Some theologians believe King Solomon hid the Ark so it wouldn't fall into the wrong hands again. Others surmise the Babylonians carried it away after their conquest of Israel, stored it away in one of their treasure troves, never to be seen again. Truth is, bud, no one knows. But that hasn't stopped men from searching it out for the last few centuries." Solomon closed the journal.

"You ever tried to find it?" Noah questioned, knowing his father probably had. "I mean, you've obviously studied it."

"Of course, I've studied the Ark because of its significance in wars during the time of the kings." Solomon paused a moment. "What's the point? If God wants it to be found, then He will reveal its location. I'm sure we'll see it again one day."

"Or who knows? Maybe we'll find it this summer!" Noah chuckled. He then questioned, "Where in the Bible did you say the Ark was used?"

"Look at the story of Jericho in the book of Joshua. It's near the beginning." Changing the subject, Solomon asked, "Did you by chance read about Josiah while I was sleeping?"

"I glanced at the story you pasted from the Bible," Noah answered. "One area confused me, though. I read that because Josiah followed the Word of God, he was given a peaceful death. But then it said he was killed in battle? What gives?"

Solomon replied, "Josiah was a good king. When he received word that Pharaoh Neco II of Egypt was advancing north to ally with Assyria and battle with Babylon, he tried to thwart their plans. We don't yet know fully why, but for some reason, Josiah preferred the Babylonians to the Egyptians. Maybe it was because of trade or a promise from the Babylonians or maybe he knew that Babylon was going to win no matter what. Whatever it was, there was a battle at Megiddo, and during the onslaught, Josiah was killed."

Solomon continued, "As for the use of the word *peaceful*, it may have been used to show he died while Judah retained controlled of their land. That he didn't suffer torture from an enemy king or get assassinated like his father. Soon after his death, though, Judah fell to Babylon, and it's people were carried away into captivity."

"Doesn't sound like a peaceful death to me," Noah replied with a confused look on his face.

Solomon put away his journal. Noah looked out the window and yawned. When they departed Chicago, it was still light outside, but now Noah could see nothing from his window seat in the blackness of the sky.

"Why don't you try to get some sleep, bud?" Solomon suggested, seeing the dreariness in Noah's eyes.

"I can't. My seat won't lay back." Noah pressed the button and jostled back and forth to show his dad the frustration he'd been dealing with.

Solomon smiled and tried not to laugh at the suffering of his kid. "Goodness gracious," he chuckled. "Well, switch with me then," Solomon said, standing up in the aisle.

Annoyed at the laugh but not willing to give up the opportunity for a little more comfort, Noah moved to his father's place. His body was weary from the flight. When they arrived in Israel, it would be early morning. He needed some rest because they were going straight to the excavation site. Solomon did not like to waste time.

"I'll wake you up in a few hours when we get close to Zurich," Solomon said as Noah shut his eyes.

Noah thought about Josiah as he drifted off. The picture of the Ark flashed in his mind as well. Visions of men carrying the vessel into battle, he saw the great towering walls of Jericho and the men of Israel marching around the outside in battle formation. How magnificent it must have been to witness. Noah hoped he would have an opportunity to see the original site before going home; little did he know he was in for the adventure of his life.

6

Noah slept hard through the remainder of the flight in the comfort of his newfound chair. Solomon worked while Noah slept, perusing pages of documents and correcting papers of his graduate students. Even when Solomon excused himself to the lavatory, Noah didn't stir. A few hours passed for him in deep slumber until the jostling of the plane jockeying through turbulence startled him. The noise created by its descent from the sky was loud. The landing gear was dropping underneath. "Flight attendants, prepare for landing," was heard over the intercom

His eyes opened wearily. "Are we already here?" Noah said, confused. His short-lived sleep ended sooner than his body desired.

"Yep, were goin' down," Solomon answered. "You were snoring like a baby." He smirked.

Noah was not interested in banter and simply shook his head. He brought the chair back to its upright position and gathered his composure for landing. His father handed him a stick of gum to chew on as the air pressure pushed against his eardrums.

Five minutes later, they were on the ground in Switzerland. The layover in Zurich was nothing compared to Chicago. As soon as they departed the plane, Noah and his father hurriedly made their way to the next gate. They had no time to shop or even grab a bite to eat. Still in a daze, Noah did his best to keep up with his father. Food was the last thing on his mind anyhow. He followed closely behind his father who made a path through the crowd.

After stopping at the restroom, they sat silently for twenty minutes or so at the gate before the boarding commenced. Each spread out as far as they could to relax their cramping muscles. One more hour, and the two of them would be in Israel. Butterflies started to fill Noah's stomach in nervous expectation. Their journey was nearly complete. All the years of listening to his dad talk about Israel, and it was time to see it for himself.

Buckling his seat belt, Solomon turned to Noah. "Hey, bud, when we get to Israel, stay close to me. It can be a little crazy at Ben Gurion International. Arham will be at the gate waiting for us. He'll drive us to the dig site." Arham was Solomon's right-hand man stationed in Israel. He visited their home a few times when he lectured with Solomon at Dallas Theological Seminary. Noah enjoyed him like an awesome uncle from afar.

The liftoff was swift and the flight quick. It took only fifteen minutes for them to reach their cruising altitude. Noah's exhaustion lingered still. He wanted to sleep, but his anxious mind would not allow him. He closed his eyes anyway. Solomon, on the other hand, was busy studying a map of the dig site and notes in his journal. Noah could see his father had switched into work mode already. He had a single-minded approach to his work. It's what made him great in his field. After ten minutes at the cruising altitude, the plane's nose dropped for their descent.

Much like Solomon described, the Israeli airport was a madhouse. There were thousands of people hurrying to different destinations bumping into Solomon and Noah at every turn. Arham was there as promised, standing tall amongst the crowd. He looked just as Noah remembered. His skin was a cool hazel brown from working in the sun on a regular basis. A small cap covered his short black curly hair, which burst out on the sides over his ears. A thin beard wrapped his face but could not hide his huge smile. Arham's deep-brown eyes peered out over his sharp protruding nose. He wore a white thin robe and a pair of mud-stained mountain boots.

"Shalom!" Arham shouted above the clamoring people waving vigorously. "So good to see you." He walked over and embraced Solomon. Looking back toward Noah, "And how are you, young master?" taking the bag from Noah's hand. Noah loved to hear the way Arham's accent pronounced the English language.

Noah smiled at Arham, but before he could speak, Arham interrupted, "Come, come. We have much to do. Long ride ahead of us. Come, come." Together, the three hurried along through the ruckus. On the way out of the airport, they grabbed their luggage. Solomon loaded everything into Arham's van, and away they went.

Arham's van was an old model from the early eighties. Clearly out of its prime, the lime green paint was hidden underneath a layer of rust that formed over years of hard use. Piles of tools, junk, and miscellaneous clutter littered the back. Noah was forced to sit on top of his luggage because Arham had removed the seats to store more essential items. He sat directly behind his father in the front passenger seat. The air conditioner stopped working years earlier, so his only hope for circulation was by Solomon's window.

The salty cool Mediterranean breeze blew through the window and into Noah's face. The feel of the wind against his closed eyelids was the relief he needed. Noah breathed deep through his nostrils, taking in the air. He opened his eyes and looked out the front of the van at the city.

Arham spoke with Solomon in Hebrew while they drove. Noah was able to decipher some of their conversation; most of it concerned the dig site. He was more interested in the view outside. Israel looked just like the pictures. Rolling hills and mountains of desert surrounded him with palm trees scattered sporadically about. Small neighborhoods of crowded, colorful cinder block homes lined the streets. Israeli soldiers could be seen patrolling about protecting the people. In the distance, Noah could see the waters of the Mediterranean Sea. So many places to visit and enjoy, Noah hoped he would get to see them all. A sign was posted up ahead: Bethlehem 16 Km. *The actual birthplace of Jesus! Amazing!* He was less than ten miles from where Jesus walked.

"What do ya think, bud?" Solomon said to Noah, noticing his obvious excitement from the rearview mirror. "We will stop by Bethlehem later."

Noah was speechless, the feeling inside of him indescribable. All the places he learned about over the years from his father and the stories from the Bible were right in front of his eyes. He quickly moved to the back of the van to grab a fleeting glance of the area as they drove on to Beersheba. The dig site was outside the city limits there. Another sign came into view that caught Noah's eye: Jericho 48 Km.

"Dad? Is that the actual place with the wall?" Noah asked in unbelief.

"That's it," he answered.

"Can we go there as well?"

"Already planned, bud."

"This is nuts!" Noah said, his eyes opened wide, his mouth left open as the sign passed on the left side of the van.

Arham jumped in the conversation, "I wish I still got that excited." He smiled toward Solomon.

"We gotta get to the camp first. Arham and I need to assemble the team and set up for the next couple of weeks here. But I promise, we are going to visit every place you want." Solomon looked back at Noah square in the eyes to convey his word.

"You better," Noah responded in a playful but serious tone.

"Solomon, the team is already at the site," Arham interceded.

"Already?" Solomon was shocked. "That's great. Why don't we just head there first then? We can unload later." The original plan was to go to the campsite, discard their luggage, and then drive over to the dig about two kilometers away.

Arham drove to the excavation per instruction. The dig site was out in the middle of nowhere. It reminded Noah of the movie *Holes* where the boys were made to dig random holes in the never-ending desert. Civilization was absent from view; they were the only people for miles it seemed. Upon arrival, Noah and Solomon were greeted by all. Noah could see the men were excited to see his father. One of the men spoke with Arham, then quickly got into his van and drove off. He was to deliver Noah and Solomon's luggage to the others who were busy constructing the living arrangements. Noah was reminded by his father to grab his carry-on bag from the van before the man drove away.

Introductions and salutations began. There were twenty-eight men in all on the search team, each of different ages and backgrounds. Some were from Egypt, Lebanon, even as far away as Turkey. But all came together for a common goal under Solomon. Some had been with his father since the beginning, yet for others, this would be their first adventure into the past. Solomon and Arham excused themselves from the group to discuss plans and survey maps. The rest of the team went back to their individual duties. Noah lingered near his father.

It did not take Noah long to get tired of waiting. He longed for an air-conditioned hotel room, a cold shower, and a soft bed. The stifling desert breeze blew against his travel-weary body. The flight had taken a lot out of him, so his patience with the waiting game waned quickly. Solomon had much to do in preparation, and Noah felt like he was in the way. He trailed Solomon like a puppy dog for an hour or so. *Does he even want me here?* Noah thought.

"Dad?" Noah eventually interrupted. "Is it okay if I walk around while you do this?"

Solomon looked up from the map he was studying with Arham, noticing Noah's frustration, "Well… I guess. Do you have water?"

"I can grab some," Noah replied.

"Take your bag with you. And don't go too far. I want to be able to see you."

"I'll be fine. How long until we leave?" Noah questioned, gathering his bag.

Solomon looked at his watch. "Maybe an hour or so, so don't wander too far."

Noah walked back over to the area they exited from the van and grabbed a bottle of water from the Yeti cooler nestled under a large tent. He threw his bag over his shoulder and off he went. It was hot; too hot. The sun felt like a heating lamp on his face. Without the occasional sea breeze, the heat would be unbearable. Sand blew up around his body, striking his skin and collecting in his hair. Noah wiped the sweat from his forehead and placed his baseball hat firmly back in place. He saw a hill not far off in the distance, maybe a few hundred yards, and decided that would be a good place to head. The excavation team was busy in their chores and hardly noticed his departure.

It took him fifteen minutes to reach the base of the incline. He climbed up the face of the hill. Upon reaching the summit, Noah turned back. He had an eagle's-eye view of his father and the search team diligently at work. *So this is it? This is what I am going to be doing for the next couple of months?* He scoffed at the idea and shook his head.

He wanted to go and explore other regions like a tourist. Bethlehem, Jericho, even Tel Aviv, not sit in the open desert while his father dug holes in the Earth. It was only the first day, and he was already bored, and the heat—oh the never-ceasing overbearing heat. *What could they possibly be looking for out here anyway?* Noah turned his back on the excavation site and continued down the opposite side of the hill, even though his father asked him not to leave his sight. "Nothing over here either," he muttered under his breath.

He wandered on. Putting his hands in his pockets, he kicked a stone lying on the ground. The rock skipped off fifteen feet ahead of him. Noah surveyed the vastly barren landscape for a minute and then turned, deciding it best to head back to the dig site. The heat was stifling, he was parched, and shade was nowhere to be found. As he shifted his body weight, he felt the ground quake underneath his feet. The shaking Earth growled below.

A loud rumble echoed around Noah. He twisted his body to the left to see the rock he kicked just moments ago disappear into the Earth below. The ground was caving in! Noah spun back toward the hill he had just descended and ran as quick as he could in desperation. His heart was pounding, his legs moving feverishly ahead. The dirt was loosening below him! "Oh no!" he screamed.

He took one more stride and leapt as far as his body could muster. But it was too late. The desert swallowed him in an instant. He fell suddenly into a shallow cavern a few feet below the surface. The hot sand broke his fall. A few moments passed before Noah woke from the shock of what just transpired. He stood up and wiped the sand off his shorts and shook out his hat. Noah looked up to where he fell from. The hole was shallow enough for him to climb out, and that was his first thought. But before he did, Noah hunched down and peered into the now uncovered dark ominous cavern. He could see the remnants of a path leading into the abyss ahead. It was much too dark for the naked eye. Noah removed his satchel and opened it up. Reaching into the sand-covered bag, he pulled out a blue metallic flashlight.

Now the moment of truth. Noah pondered his options. First, the obvious—he could simply stand up, grab the side of the hole, work his way out, and head back to the camp to tell the others what happened. That was the smart play. Or for the bravehearted, he could he gather his courage and walk the path ahead before his father and the others arrived. He grabbed the water from his bag and took a long massive gulp. He weighed his options. There was only one choice here, and he knew it. The noise must have been heard by the camp. The team was probably headed his way already.

Noah chose his fate and began the descent into the unknown. The hole was tight about him, the air stale. The light from the flashlight was powerful enough to illuminate the darkness. The glow shone on creepy-crawly things, worms, spiders—he even thought he saw a snake. His curiosity drove him farther into the tunnel. Every step was easier than the last. His courage grew. Noah slowly navigated the now rocky terrain. The tunnel made a slight decline into the bowels of the earth. With every step, he shone the flashlight here and there as not to fall into a trap like in the movies he had seen time and again.

The air around him was moist now, almost cool. Ahead, he could hear water cascading down the walls. His steps echoed through the corridor as pebbles skipped in front of him. The path made a tube around him, maybe five feet tall and just as wide. Up ahead, the hall ended, and he entered a room.

Noah reached the entrance and paused to survey his surroundings. He found himself at the doorway of some type of chamber. Five stairs were carved into the rock below him, descending from the doorway into the room. He scanned the room with the flashlight. Ancient drawings were carved in the walls. Hieroglyphics of some kind; he recalled similar pictures scribbled in his father's journal. The ceiling of the chamber was probably ten feet off the floor, the size of the room no bigger than a school classroom.

In the middle of the room built from the very same stone the chamber was made from was an altar. A small stream of water wrapped around the base of the altar like a moat around a castle and traveled out the far end of the chamber underneath the wall. On top of the stone pedestal was an object wrapped in some kind of brown burlap cloth.

Noah hesitated a moment, shining the flashlight on top of the altar. The object which stood before him was old, no doubt. Sand and dirt covered the cloth. Hundreds if not thousands of years must have past untouched. "I didn't come this far for nothing." He walked toward the altar. "What is this?" he whispered to himself.

Noah quickly surveyed the object and altar. He so wanted to grab the artifact, but he had to make sure it was safe. He took a deep breath and blew lightly to clear some of the dust that had accumulated over the years. Building up his courage and not wanting to see any danger, Noah took another breath and blew even harder. Satisfied by the view, he made his mind up.

Behind him, in the distance, Noah heard the search team calling for him as they approached. "They're coming!" he said to himself. Throwing his personal safety out the window, Noah reached out with both hands and carefully clutched the object. He did not have time to examine his find. That would have to wait. The relic was heavier than it looked. Noah dropped to his knees, holding the relic in one hand. He removed his backpack. The men were getting closer. He could hear their voices growing as they neared. Time was of the essence. Noah moved his stuff around in the satchel to make room for the object. He stuffed it as far down in the bag as possible, burlap wrap and all.

He stood up, ready to make his way back to the tunnel. Then it struck him. The team would know something was here. The altar had a void where the relic once stood. Noah thought for a moment. *What do I do? He'll know...* He looked at the stream of water moving slowly by his feet. "That's it!" He reached down, put his palms together, and took a large scoop and began sloshing the water over himself and the altar. *They'll think I got thirsty,* he thought, hoping it would hide any trace hidden in the dust outline of where the piece once laid.

By now, the men were almost upon the entrance of the cave. Noah could hear their footsteps as they ran. He called out, "I'm down here!"

"Noah, Noah, are you all right?" Arham exclaimed. "Are you hurt?" he got down on his knees and leaned into the hole as he exclaimed.

"I'm fine, Arham! I don't know what happened. I was just walking around, and the ground caved in," Noah answered back, making his way up the tunnel to the hole.

"Come, please. Let us get you out of there," Arham shouted, relieved at the sound of Noah's reply.

The men reached down and grabbed Noah's arms. With one swift pull, he was out. Arham dusted him off and rubbed the sand out of his hair. "We heard the rumble. What happened?" Arham asked, bending down to meet his eyes and placing his hands on Noah's shoulders.

Noah gathered himself and calmly replied, "I was just walking around and out of nowhere, the ground, it just… I don't know, it just opened up!" He paused. By now the search team was examining the cave entrance, clearly preparing to enter where Noah just came. "You may want to go down there, Arham. There is a room with funny drawings on the wall." Noah did his best not to reveal what he knew.

"We got you." Noah was relieved to hear the strong voice of his father from behind him. He felt his father's arm wrap around his shoulders and embrace him. "Stay here, bud." Solomon sidestepped Arham and Noah and approached the team.

"Arham, I need you," Solomon said, bending over to climb down the hole. Arham quickly followed. Noah watched as the two of them disappeared into the darkness. A few minutes later, they returned. Noah could see in their eyes the excitement from the enchanted chamber. Solomon instructed the men to cordon off the area and move the dig site to this new location.

Two of the members from the search team were left behind to guard the entrance until Solomon and his team could return the next day. The sun was setting fast, the men were hungry, and they had to make it back to camp while there was still light. A ration of food, plenty of water, and two sleeping bags were left for the two men until they returned.

The rest of the search team headed back to the original excavation site to gather their equipment. After the men packed up the dig site, they made a line by the vans and waited. Noah was confused by what was happening, but being a school-aged child, he followed suit and lined up as well. He watched as one by one, each man approached Arham who stood by the vans and held their hands out in a "T" pose. One of Arham's responsibilities was to search each man. Theft of ancient artifacts was a common problem at archeological digs as relics could fetch into the millions of dollars to the right bidder. The men were apparently used to the custom as each posed without hesitation when it was their turn. Noah, on the other hand, had no idea he was going to be searched. His heart began to race...

No use in hiding his find. Should he relinquish it before Arham found it or try to slip it past him? His anxiety grew as each man took his place, moving Noah closer in line. There were no options. The closer he moved toward Arham, the louder his heart pounded. *What am I going to do? God, help me...*

Arham smiled at Noah when he saw him next in line. A look of intrigue was on his face. "What are you doing, young master?" he asked.

"Waiting my turn?" Noah questioned, surprised by Arham's tone.

"Ha-ha!" Arham laughed loudly. "Not you, little master." He threw his arm around Noah's shoulders. "Come, my friend, let us be on our way." Together, the two boarded the van and away they drove. Relief swept over Noah, removing his anxious heart. *Thank you, God.*

Noah closed his eyes and took a deep breath. What a day this turned out to be. He was exhausted from travel, hungry, and filled with anticipation. Maybe his discovery was meant to be a secret. He could not wait to be alone so he could examine it.

"So what was that place?" Noah asked Arham. "You know, the hole..."

Solomon overheard the question and joined the conversation. He turned around from the front seat and answered, "Below us, ancient cities lie hidden, waiting to be discovered. Centuries of wars and destruction, people abandoning their homes, and sandstorms have swallowed these cities whole. Occasionally, if we're lucky, the ground weakens at just the right time, leaving us an opening into the past."

Arham added, "What happened to you was not the first time. Some of our most important discoveries happen by accident." He winked at Noah.

"As for what that place was," Solomon continued, "we will find out soon enough."

7

Noah took a moment to gather himself on the short drive back to camp, his clothes still covered with sand. He clutched his backpack close to his chest, trying not to draw attention to his secret. He could feel the outline of his find beneath the leather backpack. The men in the van were speaking in their native tongues, enjoying pleasantries and small talk. Solomon and Arham were busy discussing the possibilities of the cave Noah fell into. Excitement was buzzing amongst them all. Noah only had one thing teasing his thoughts: the relic.

What was it that he found? Did it have any value? Should he, could he tell his father at this point? He didn't feel guilt necessarily over his secret, but he did have a little anxiety about it. *This thing, whatever it is, could be something hugely important to Dad's study. A find that could make his career flourish. What if the artifact was the very thing Dad was there to locate in the first place?* He needed to get a hold of his father's journal. He did not recall seeing anything about it on the plane, but then again, he was too focused on the Ark and Josiah.

These questions bombarded Noah until they reached the campsite. The men quickly exited the van once Arham pulled in and parked. It had been a long day for all of them, and food was the focus now. Noah thought briefly about home, wishing to lay in his bed for respite. Then a whiff of dinner hit his nostrils, reminding his stomach how hungry he was. Whatever was cooking smelled amazing!

His father took him by the shoulder and pointed him to their temporary sleeping quarters. *The day isn't a complete loss,* he thought as he clutched his backpack closer to his body. Noah looked around as they walked. His legs were aching from the long day of travel.

He was pleasantly surprised at the makeshift village propped up in the middle of the desert. The men in charge of constructing their shelter did an amazing job. Each tent was placed equidistance from each other wrapping around a middle meeting area, creating an almost perfect square. The tents faced inward. The middle tent was much larger than the rest. This particular tent was used as both a cafeteria and meeting room for announcements and daily planning.

The personal tents were designed for one to two adults, depending on the need. For this expedition, each man was given their own quarters. Inside each tent was a cot and a chest to store belongings. The chest came with a combination lock so each man could secure their personal effects. In between each tent were placed solar-powered lights to illuminate the area and keep critters away. Near the main tent, chairs were set up around six oblong tables as a place for the men to eat and converse. A large fire pit was constructed near the center as well to keep warm at night and prepare meals.

"So do I get a tent?" Noah asked his father, hoping he got to stay alone for obvious reasons.

"Yes, sir, right over there," he replied, pointing off to the left of the main entrance.

"Can I go check it out?" Noah questioned.

"Yeah, take your time. Think dinner will be ready in fifteen."

Noah left the group and ventured over to his tent to put his things down. *This may be the best thing so far on this trip,* he thought. *Privacy.* The tent measured ten by eight feet, the opening on the eight-foot side. Next to the entrance of the tent was a folding chair and a personal table. Atop the table sat a battery-powered lamp. Noah grabbed the lamp and approached the entrance of his new home. He reached up and took hold of the zipper in the upper right corner of the opening, slid it to the left, then down the side of the tent, and back to the right. He took hold of the loose end and pushed it inside.

With the lantern in one hand, Noah entered inside. The light of the lamp illuminated his personal hideout. The first thing that caught his eye was the metal pylon situated in the center of the tent to keep the ceiling from sagging down. A circular red thin rug spread over the floor around the pylon. In the far-left corner of the tent was a cot with bedding for a single person. Beside the cot was another small end table. It reminded Noah of a TV tray because of its ability to fold up and create more space inside if needed.

On the right side opposite the cot toward the front of the tent was a small bench. Beside the bench was a chest with a digital combination lock. And situated neatly atop the chest was Noah's luggage. Noah walked over to the bench and sat down to survey his surroundings. "This isn't so bad," he muttered to himself.

"So what do you think?" Solomon announced, standing outside the opening of the tent.

"What the? Geez, you scared me!" Noah exclaimed.

"Ha-ha! Well, you ready to eat?" Solomon smiled at his reaction.

"Depends," Noah replied, forcing himself up on his weary feet again, "what's for dinner?"

"C'mon, think you'll like it," Solomon said, putting his arm around Noah. His father's happiness being in Israel with his son was clear to see.

Noah was surprised when he saw the men had prepared some good ole barbeque in honor of their Texas guests. The feast consisted of a slow-smoked brisket with a nice dry rub, maple flavored baked beans, creamy potato salad paired with fresh warm bread. And what Texas-sized BBQ would be complete without a glass of iced tea? Noah was pleased with the meal, even though it failed in comparison to the original. He sat and listened to the men talk to his father while he ate. Most of them could speak some English, broken though it may be. When the conversation really got going, the men couldn't help mixing in some Hebrew. The remainder of dinner was filled with laughs and fellowship. It was perfect. Everyone was just happy to be there.

After dinner, the men moved the tables to the side and carried their chairs closer to the fire to continue the festivities. A few men went into the large tent where the food was prepared and came out with hot tea and dessert for all. Arham, excused himself and went into his tent. Within a few minutes, he appeared, carrying a contraption of sorts.

"What is that?" Noah asked his father, pointing at Arham.

"A hookah," Solomon answered, excited to see his friend carrying the piece.

Noah stared at this odd-looking device. The main body of the hookah was a pipe that extended from the top where a clay bowl attached to a glass base. Surrounding the pipe was decorative metal with shapes formed all around. There were four holes on the outside of the hookah leading into the glass base. Along with the hookah, Arham carried four hoses. Each hose was open on one end; the other had what looked like a mouthpiece.

"An uhka?" Noah asked. "What does it do?"

"People around here use it for smoking tobacco."

"What in the world?" Noah laughed. "This is nuts! How does it work?"

"Why don't you go ask Arham?" Solomon suggested, pointing to his partner.

Noah anxiously stood up and walked over to Arham who was situating the hookah on a small table in the middle of men. The fire cracked and popped nearby. Noah could feel the heat.

"Hey, Arham, what's going on?" Noah asked.

"Oh, Noah!" He chuckled. "Pull up chair, I show you." Noah looked around and grabbed the first chair he could find. He slid it up close to the table and took a seat.

"This is *hooquah*," he replied, much thicker with his accent this time.

Pointing at the top to the clay bowl, Arham explained, "Da tobacco placed here and heated with coal. Unlike you American's pipe, we de not burn da tobacco." Arham attached the hoses one by one to the holes and continued, "We put water here," he said, pointing at the glass base. "You breathe deep in hose, and da tobacco go ov'r da coals and heat up. Smoke comes down da hose to me. You watch, little master." And with that, he showed Noah a proper use of a hookah. Arham took a deep breath, the hookah made a gurgling sound, and Arham exhaled a large clear puff of smoke.

"Now…you try." Arham handed the hose to Noah.

Noah was shocked by the offer. He glanced back at his father, thinking there was no way he would allow this, but before he could ask, Solomon called out, "Give it a try!" And he winked at Noah!

What in the world is going on? he thought. *My normal dad would never let me get away with this!*

Noah gently grabbed hold of the hose. He brought the mouthpiece up to his lips. It was similar to the mouthing part of the recorder in music class he played in school. He sucked in deep like he would an Icy through a straw from the movie theatre. A rush of light smoke filled his lungs. He must have breathed in too much. He lurched forward and forced out a loud cough. He exhaled, nearly vomiting out the smoke in disgust.

"Oh! No… Ugh, kuh, kuh!" Noah struggled. "This is…awful!"

The men could not help but laugh at the scene. Embarrassed though he was, Noah smiled at himself still coughing the junk out of his body. Even Solomon had a belly laugh at his son's expense. The men were poking and pushing on Noah in a playful way. Arham took the hose away from Noah and handed him a cup of tea.

"Well done, lil' master," Arham said. "You did better than your father's first time." He smiled big at the little boy still struggling for air.

Noah, his father, and the men sat around and joked into the night. Stories were told of past digs and recent travels. Arham asked Solomon how his current lecture tour was going. An occasional question was asked of Noah about home. But eventually, the long day of travel caught up with Noah, and he was ready to turn in. He made a face at his dad to let him know it was time, plus there was an added bonus waiting for him in his backpack. Solomon, seeing his son's exhaustion, stood up and thanked the men for everything they had accomplished. He took hold of Noah, said goodnight, and together they walked to their tents.

"Are you as tired as me?" Solomon whispered as they strolled together.

"I can't believe I can walk," he answered.

"What do ya think so far…of Israel?"

"It's hot!" Noah smiled at his dad, giving him a hard time.

"Hot? It's not much hotter than it is in Texas this time of year. You'll get used to it anyway. All right, I'm gonna get some sleep, gotta be up early tomorrow. Do you need anything else?" he asked.

"No, I'm good, I think," Noah said, turning toward his tent.

"Okay, I'll be next door if you need me. It can be a little awkward sleeping out here, so don't be embarrassed if you need something. I mean it, bud."

Noah called out, "Okay, okay. Goodnight, Dad." He walked away.

"Love you."

"Love you too."

Noah was excited and relieved to finally be alone. The thought of his secret was on his mind through dinner and dessert. He wanted to exit earlier for his tent but could not find an opening that would not arouse suspicion from his father. A part of him felt guilty still for not spilling the truth to his dad, but another side of him wanted to do this on his own. And besides, he would tell his father eventually.

He zipped up the tent from the inside and grabbed his backpack. He unzipped the pack and carefully removed the object. Thank goodness his dad reminded him to grab his carry-on earlier before the van left; otherwise, he would not have been able to sneak it passed Arham. He placed the object gently on the ground and slowly unraveled the relic from its burlap covering. Years of sand fell from the artifact onto the rug. The piece was cold to the touch like metal or iron.

Now completely out of the wrapping, Noah lifted the relic up to the light and glided his hands over it. There were no noticeable nicks or blemishes of any type. The artifact was one piece, hollow in the middle by the sound of it. The bottom was rounded off like the bottom of a baseball bat, and a hand grip was engraved into the metal. The shaft was perfectly cylindrical and led to the crown, which was about two inches wider in diameter.

Removed entirely from the wrapping, Noah thought it looked like a rod or staff of some sort, maybe a weapon, something you may see in medieval times. It must have weighed ten pounds and stretched at least two and a half to three feet long. Studying the size and weight of the object made him realize how lucky it was to sneak it past the watchful eyes of others. At the top of the crown of the staff, there were six indentions. Each engraving was similar in shape to the other. Apparently, something used to sit inside the holes, maybe jewels or stones of some sort. At the top, there were four prongs sticking up. It reminded Noah of his mother's wedding ring where the three platinum fingers held the diamond stone in place.

A noise nearby interrupted his observation. Startled, Noah froze to listen closely. He looked around to prepare and hide the rod. He could hear the men laughing outside. He waited a few seconds to make sure he was safe and relaxed. The staff, or whatever it was, was like nothing he had ever seen. His father never mentioned anything about this. No Bible story ever spoke of it. Maybe it was nothing. Who even knew how old it was? *But it must be old*, he thought. *It was in that cave, wrapped up, hidden from the world. And those engravings on the wall in the cave, they have to mean something.*

Noah thought for a moment and decided to go to his only research tool available. He reached into his backpack once again and pulled out a copy of the Study Bible Solomon made him bring on the trip. It was a heavy book too, no less. Not exactly something you want to lug around. *Two thousand pages...where to begin?* He paused, then remembered how his father would sometimes flip to the back and find commonly used words throughout the book to help people locate verses.

He flipped to the back. There were maps, tons and tons of maps. Then came the "Topical Discussion Section." Nothing there. And finally, the Concordance, an alphabetical reference for common words found throughout the Bible. It was a pretty thick section. Noah looked down at the relic and thought about what this thing could be called. *A stick, maybe. Could be a rod, maybe some type of weapon*. He started scanning the pages. He read through tons of odd names and places. Occasionally, he found a word he actually knew.

He first came across *Bar*, but there were just four verses mentioned none of which made sense. Nothing under *Bat*. He laughed to himself. *Beam maybe? Nope*. In the C's, he saw the word *Chaff* which reminded him of Moses' staff, so he turned to the S section to speed the search up. The verses mentioning *Staff* didn't fit though, mainly because it was made of wood. He started to flip backward to the beginning. "Sickle…no, that won't work." Then he saw another possibility, a word that was rarely used but may fit this particular piece: *Scepter*.

Noah read the description beside the word *Scepter* in the Concordance: "Symbol of authority." Noah immediately thought authority meant supreme or important. *Like a leader or a king! That could be it!* He recalled pictures from the middle ages at school in art class. His teacher ran slide shows showing the kids how art has changed over the years. There were pictures of kings in their crazy colorful gowns with opulent crowns on their heads. In their hands, they usually held something. Sometimes it was a sword, but in many of the depictions, it was a rod or a scepter like the one lying on the ground in front of him.

Noah looked at the verses listed below the word *Scepter* in the Concordance. The first reference was located in the book of Genesis, chapter 49, verse 10. Noah quickly turned to the front of the Bible and found the chapter of Genesis. Beside the number forty-nine, in large bold letters, it read, "Jacob's Blessing of His Sons." *What on Earth could that mean?* Noah skimmed quickly through the words, verse by verse. In summary, Jacob was an old man dying, and he was passing his final words to his boys. First came Reuben, then Simeon, and Levi was mentioned. In verse 8, it was Judah. "Judah!" Noah spoke out loud. He knew that name from the plane ride over with his father and his journal. *The kingdom split. The north was called Israel, the south, Judah, with the good kings.*

He read verse 8:

> Judah, your brothers shall praise you; Your hand shall be on the neck of your enemies; Your father's sons shall bow down to you.

Noah thought about the verse and lined it up to his earlier conversation with his father. Made complete sense to him. Judah was the rightful kingdom. He continued reading verse 9:

Judah is a lion's whelp.

"What in the world is a whelp?" Noah giggled aloud to himself. "Maybe it's another word for roar or growl…who knows?" He continued reading.

From the prey, my son, you have gone up.
He crouches, he lies down as a lion, And as a lion,
who dares rouse him up?

Now this was getting good. *No one messes with Judah or they get the teeth.* Noah remembered how his father always spoke about a lion representing a king, royalty, a monarch—something to be feared. Judah was a warrior, no doubt.

Verse 10:

The *scepter* shall not depart from Judah.

Oh my gosh, there it is. The scepter! That must be it! Jacob was talking to his son Judah about becoming a king. *He was the king, so he gets to carry the scepter.* Noah looked down…could it really be? *I mean, in the Bible, Jacob was just talking. Does it say anything else?* He continued reading.

The *scepter* shall not depart from Judah,
Nor the ruler's staff from between his feet, Until
Shiloh comes, And to him shall be the obedience
of the people.

What in the world does that mean? Shiloh? Who is Shiloh? Noah looked down at the bottom of the page to the notes section in the study Bible. There was a section specifically written out about the verses pertaining to Judah. "Thank goodness my dad bought me a Study Bible," Noah muttered to himself. He had already forgot how tired he was!

The study notes first indicated that Judah meant "Praise." Also, that this section foretold how Judah would become the leader amongst his brothers who represent the twelve tribes of Israel. Strong as a young lion that eats his prey and also secure as a mature lion that no one would dare challenge. The notes went on to explain that this blessing or prophecy was fulfilled 640 years later when King David took the throne. "King David!" Noah got excited to see a familiar name.

Noah continued reading the notes. "'Shiloh comes' more than likely meant 'the one who brings peace.' Many believe that this refers to the coming Messiah that he would be from the Tribe of Judah. 'Until Shiloh comes' as in the second coming of Christ?" Noah stopped, shocked at what he was reading. He laid the Bible carefully on the ground in front of him and stared down at the scepter below. He reached out and slowly gripped the metal rod with both hand and whispered, "The Scepter of Judah."

8

Suddenly, he felt something move inside of him. The lamp beside him flickered in excitement. A wind blew into his tent, even though the opening was closed tight. The light went out, completely leaving him in pitch black solitude, no longer able to hear anything. The hair on the back of his neck started to rise. Noah gazed down at his hands in the darkness. Something was happening to the scepter. A glow broke through cracks on the shell of the object as it transformed from the dirty aged iron color into a brilliant pure gold.

"Wha-what's happening?" Noah called out, fear filling his inmost being.

The staff continued to glow brighter and brighter. The brilliance so powerful, Noah was blinded to his surroundings. It was as if the sun rose inside his tent, feet away from where he sat, beaming at such an intensity human eyes could not focus. So bright, so utterly blinding, the light made a buzzing sound. Another gust of wind swirled into his tent and up all around Noah. He felt himself rise from the ground. He was hovering, even though he could not see it, he felt nothing solid below him. *Don't let go, Noah.* That single thought repeated over and over. *Whatever happens...don't let go!* Was that him speaking, though? The voice sounded different, but it was in his head.

"Oh my God! I'm...uh...what do I do...wha—" Noah exclaimed. "Dad, help! Dad! Somebody!"

Noah reached out one hand while he grasped the scepter with the other. He desperately tried to find something in his tent to grab onto, but to his dismay, he could find nothing. Surely there should be something to grab—the cot, the chest, the pillar in the middle of the tent. That's when Noah realized he was no longer inside of his tent. He felt himself rising higher and higher into the night sky. *Someone must see this below!* Noah screamed out again for aid, "Help me! Help…someone!"

Rising…rising…the world shrinking away…until…nothingness.

Suddenly, as quick as the event started, the light from the staff faded away rather abruptly, but the gold exterior remained on the scepter. It was cold to the touch now. Noah refused to let go his grasp. He had no idea where he was except that he was no longer in his tent. The smell of the air around him was pure and clean. There was no breeze. It was eerily silent. There was no noise coming from the other men. His surroundings…they were gone. And not just gone as in somewhere else, but gone like disappeared. He sat on nothing surrounded by nothing, under nothing. No walls, no ceiling, and no floor. The stars in the sky were all around him, the campsite completely forgotten. Yet, even though there was no floor, he sat nonetheless without movement.

Noah slowly lifted his head to peer out. "Where am I?" he whispered to himself. He sat for a moment, gaining what little bit of courage remained and spoke louder, "Hello? Anyone?" he called out.

Noah looked all around him in fear. There was nothing—nothing except the thick night sky full of stars shining all around him. He looked down and became queasy. Nothing—no land, no water, no Earth…just nothing. Discouragement crept into his heart. He tried to comfort himself. "Surely someone must have seen me. There is no way no one saw that light!" *But how would they find me, wherever I am? Is this outer space? I'd be dead if it was.*

The light from the scepter had completely faded, and along with that, Noah's hopes. He meekly crouched down, pulled his knees to his chest, and began to sob. "I should have told my dad. What was I thinking? How could I be so stupid!" He beat himself up for the situation he was in. "So stupid."

Noah clutched his knees close to his chest. Peeking through the crevice of his thighs, he saw light bursting forth again. He opened up his position and looked down to see the scepter start to glow. But this time was different. The light emanated like a flashlight or a spotlight, actually, pointing off in the distance. Noah picked up the scepter to try and control the beam of light, but however he tried, the light was transfixed on a position in the distance.

"What in the world is going on?" he questioned aloud.

Noah stared off in the distance where the light was shining. Something caught his eye. Movement! An ominous figure was approaching. It looked like the silhouette of a man walking toward him. Noah froze in fear. His mouth turned dry and his voice locked up. His adrenaline was drained from the initial scepter experience.

"Who's there?" he forced out in a soft, choked up tone. There was no response.

The figure continued to gain ground. Noah's heart was beating through his chest. This was it. This is where it all ended for him. Noah forced himself to yell, "Who's there? What do you want with me?"

A reply came forth. The voice was deep like an aged man large in stature. It reverberated across the dark sky. Clear and crisp, echoing through the expanse, the voice sounded as if the figure was already next to him, "Silence!"

That is not my father, Noah thought, fear's grip tightening. The figure continued his approach. Noah could now see the silhouette coming into the light. It was definitely a man. He wore thin tan leather sandals similar to ones Noah saw depicted on the people of old. A thick purple robe stitched and outlined in a red twine wrapped around the man covering nearly his entire lower body as he strolled toward Noah. His gait was hypnotizing, demanding attention from onlookers. He was confident, his shoulders upright, his arms held with strength at his sides. The robe cascaded over his shoulders and wrapped his arms, his hands entering into the light. He was almost upon Noah now.

"Noah," the voice commanded, "stand up."

"How...how do you...know my name?" Noah stuttered, reluctantly rising to his feet. "Who...who are you?"

The stranger towered over the boy casting a long shadow. He stared forcefully at Noah, his eyes penetrating into his very soul. He stood well over six feet. His long black wavy hair fell to the top of his shoulders. A thick beard wrapped his tan sun-beaten face and flowed neatly into his hair. Noah could tell he was older by the defined wrinkles around his brown piercing eyes. His sharp nose sat above his thin lips.

In an unexpected move, the man knelt on one knee, bringing himself face-to-face with Noah and answered, "Noah, I have known you since you were born." He paused, the silence deafening around them. "My name is Josiah, King of Judah."

Noah took a moment to gather himself a look of shock covered his face. "Josiah? What?" Noah asked confusingly. "Aren't…but you're dead!"

Josiah's appearance was calm and spoke with comfort, "In your understanding of death, yes. You, however, know that a person's soul never dies."

"Is this heaven?" Noah asked.

"No," Josiah answered, shaking his head as he rose to his feet again.

"Where are we?"

"Let us call this a meeting ground," he replied, "a place where people who have yet to experience death can interact with others who have passed on."

"This is crazy! I have to be dreaming! I am in my tent right now passed out on the floor, dreaming about this, right?" He waited for Josiah to answer, but there was no response; just a stare from this regal man before him. "Has anyone else traveled here before?" Noah asked.

"You are not the first," Josiah replied. "You will not be the last."

"Why me? Why am I here?"

"Because of what you hold in your hand, my son," Josiah said pointing at the scepter.

Noah gripped the scepter tighter as he looked down at the relic. "What is this thing?" he asked.

"You hold the Scepter of Judah in your hand. A symbol of the promise to the people of Jacob's son's tribe." He paused and then continued, "For many years, the scepter has lay hidden from the Sons of Man. It was waiting for you, Noah. And now that you hold it, the scepter will reveal its wonders to you and you alone."

"This is too much! You're saying that this was planned? That you were waiting on me to fall in that hole and find this thing? No way!" Noah was not convinced.

Unmoved, Josiah explained, "Many years ago, God chose a man named Jacob. He told him that all of God's chosen people would come from his seed. He was given twelve sons to carry on his people. On his deathbed, he blessed each one of his sons, which would become the twelve tribes of Israel. The blessing of Judah announced that the scepter would not depart from Judah nor the ruler's staff from between his feet until He comes to whom it belongs. To Him will the obedience of the people be."

"I read all of that, but what does it have to do with me? I am not from Judah," Noah inquired.

"The scepter does not decide who wields it. God does."

Noah stiffened at the thought that an infinite, all-powerful God would even bother with an average boy from a no-name city out of billions of people. He asked, "So what now?"

"You have an opportunity to join the few who came before you on a journey of immeasurable adventure. This journey will challenge you in ways you cannot fathom. Persevere, and greatness will be yours. Fail, and this life will be but a dream. The choice is yours, my son." Josiah looked upon Noah. "Come with me."

9

The ancient king turned his back on Noah and walked into the darkness. Noah gathered his composure and followed meekly behind. *Where are we going? There's nothing even out here.* And then…something changed. Suddenly, the darkness wasn't so dark. Shapes and colors appeared slowly out of nothingness. First a staircase; a different but familiar structure came into view, appearing a few feet in front of Josiah as he walked ahead of Noah. The staircase was just there, firmly situated but planted on nothing but space and air. It seemed to float in the night sky, each moment transforming into a more solid shape losing its transparent appearance.

Noah raised his left foot onto the first stair, following Josiah. Just as his foot reached the step, the stair suddenly changed into a rich color of gold. As he planted his foot on the stair, the gold rippled like liquid and then solidified underneath his weight. Noah raised his eyes and watched in amazement as the entire staircase formed in front of him in moments. The empty darkness which had engulfed him minutes ago was disappearing rapidly. A new world formed steadily. It was as if he was in this place the whole time but was not allowed to see it yet.

At the top of the stairs, a building took shape. Marble walls rose around him. The rapid building echoed like thunder in a storm as its structure formed before him. Noah turned his head to look back down the stairs to see thick green grass sprout out of the invisible ground. Vibrant flowers blossomed, all types of shapes and sizes spewing forth the most amazing colors. Great trees, oaks, redwoods, weeping willows, trees of profound stature and grace took root. The sound of birds caught Noah's attention. He looked up to catch a glimpse of a creature he had never seen before. The bird's colors made it almost difficult to gaze upon. The glow like that of the sun, it flew in front of Josiah and landed on his shoulder.

Josiah reached his hand up and brushed lightly on its beak, and the creature took flight again. The awesome sight left Noah in shock, his mouthing gaping open at the view.

Noah watched as a stream formed below the first step, rippling here and there in a symphony of sounds, water so pure he could see the scales on the fish floating by, fish so beautiful they looked like jewels. Some were gold, others silver, another bronze; one of the creature's scales look like diamonds. He followed the stream with his eyes tried to see its beginning and its end, but like everything, it just was. It came from nothingness and disappeared in nothingness.

Fountains sprouted like flowers around the building, pushing water up into the air in ballet-like rhythms. The water even acted differently; it hovered in the air longer than normal gravity would allow before cascading in perfect form back to whence it came, causing minimal splash. The aroma that rose about Noah was indescribable. The best word was *pure*—pure beauty, pure calmness, pure and clean, pure and full of life. A moist breeze encircled his body, cooling his skin. Noah's senses fired like never before, overwhelmed by this perfect place. "This must be heaven," he whispered.

"Noah," Josiah called down from the top of the stairs.

Noah turned to look back up the staircase to see Josiah holding his hand out. He approached Josiah and grabbed his hand.

"This place is amazing," Noah whispered.

"Stand here," Josiah said. He walked forward toward a substantial white marble wall. Josiah planted his feet within reaching distance of the impenetrable structure. He raised his hands to the heavens and shouted, "Amen!"

A rumble arose from behind the wall. Dust fell from the top of the structure, covering the view. When the commotion had ceased, an ornately decorated carve out remained, large enough to drive a semi-truck through. Noah looked at the ground, expecting to be covered by debris, but none could be seen. It was as if the doorway had been there all along.

Josiah turned back toward Noah. "Come, my son." And he turned to enter the newly created doorway. Noah followed, staring in awe at the doorway. A thick gold vine wrapped beautifully up and around the opening, leaves protruding sporadically about. There were large flowers overlaid with gold coated in jewels and carvings of animals sitting on the vine. Noah let his hand touch the structure as he slid over the smooth golden exterior. There were no blemishes, no scratches, no smudges, just perfection.

Now inside the doorway, Noah stood in a massive hall the size of a football field. The view was breathtaking. Noah bent his head back to take in the massive room. The ceiling was at least eight stories tall. The walls were covered in murals of all types. Pictures of animals, depictions of nature, the deep blue sky, men and women splashed the scenery. Everywhere he looked, gold bordered it all. Precious jewels sparkled throughout magnifying its beauty. Even the floor was impressive. One never-ending piece of white marble as smooth as glass. Noah looked down at his feet, his reflection perfectly bounced back in the floor. He slowly walked ahead, following Josiah's path each step echoing in the gigantic hall.

Josiah kept a steady pace across the expanse. Positioned in the middle of the room, like an island floating in the ocean, was a throne. Surrounded on all sides by stairs, the throne demanded attention from all directions. The shear magnificence was too much to describe. Sturdy, powerful, regal, golden, yet inviting and respectful, this seat was meant for someone very important. Noah's eyes were transfixed on the chair.

"Have a seat," Josiah said as he climbed the stairs to the throne. Noah looked around for a chair. He could see none. Then, in front of him, like a hallucination, a chair appeared. He examined the seat to make sure he was not dreaming it and sat down.

Looking down from the throne, Josiah said, "I am sure you are wondering where you are—"

"Uh-huh," Noah muttered, still in disbelief.

"When I was young, younger than you are now, my father died, passing his kingdom onto me."

"You were eight, right?" Noah asked.

"Very good. Many people in my father's kingdom tried to teach me what I was to become. While they did their best to guide me, something was lacking."

"My dad told me about you," Noah responded. "Your mother and some priest helped you."

"Your father is a wise man, Noah," he answered and continued with his story. "On a summer day many years ago, I went on a journey with my mother to see the land which I was to rule, the Kingdom of Judah. On our expedition, we happened upon a cave. For some reason, the men who traveled with me, even my mother, could not see this cave. I memorized the surroundings so I could return later on alone. That night, I waited until my mother was asleep and ventured back to this cave. I was an adventurous child, just like you, Noah."

"Was this the same cave I found today?" Noah interceded.

"Yes," Josiah answered. "Inside, I too found the scepter you hold now." He looked down at the object situated comfortably in Noah's lap.

"So, like me, you were brought to this place?" Noah asked as he scanned the large hall.

"Yes, my son. I was met by another king who lived many years before me, King David. I am sure you are familiar with him."

Noah nodded his head.

"He took his seat on this very throne and I on the chair you find yourself upon, and he explained to me what I am going to tell you."

Noah sat upright in his chair and leaned forward, awaiting the fate God had chosen for him. He took a deep breath.

—⋅⟡⋅ 10 ⋅⟡⋅—

Noah sat motionless inside the great hall, still bewildered by his situation. He gazed up at King Josiah, hanging on his every word. The sound of an unseen harp played softly in the background, filling the room with melodic tones. Up above the throne, high in the rafters, white doves flew here and there, cooing with sounds of joy.

Behind him, Noah heard the faint sound of something approach. The tapping was not like the trounce of human steps but the soft whisper of an animal. It reminded Noah of his friend Isaiah's dog, Rooster, when she walked over the ceramic tile in his kitchen. Rooster's claws would lightly scrape the tile in a slight ticking noise. Noah turned his head around and was immediately overwhelmed by what he saw.

A magnificent lion was within a few feet of his chair. His stealthy, nearly silent approach surprised Noah. The animal stood four and a half feet off the ground, its sheer size engulfing the boy. The animal's body stretched out like a mid-sized car. The beast's head was as big as Noah. The lion opened its mouth to yawn, showing the talons for teeth, a grumble bellowed forth rattling the boy. His great mane wrapped around his head like the tire of a large truck wrapping around its wheel. Course beige hair covered the animal from head to tail.

The lion casually strolled past Noah, swinging its tail to and fro. Its muscles flexed in the light, showing the massive strength and power of the intimidating predator. Easily maneuvering up the stairs with grace, the lion perched itself beside Josiah and faced Noah. It sat with its head beside Josiah's left hand eagerly awaiting a petting. Josiah rolled his hand over the beast like a musician would a guitar. The lion was enamored. It closed his eyes in approval.

Noah sat in disbelief. Sure, he had seen a lion before, many times, in fact. He saw them at the zoo behind massive barriers. He watched documentaries on TV and CGI captures of the beast in movies. But never like this, never this close, never this real!

Throwing caution to the wind, Noah asked, "May I?" and pointed to approach.

"By all means," Josiah agreed, inviting him up.

Noah stood, cautious not to startle the massive animal. He slowly climbed the stairs and approached the lion head-on. The magnificent cat did not flinch. Its eyes locked on Noah without blinking. The beast's presence ignited fear, but its face was inviting. Such majesty and power it possessed. Noah reached out his hand slowly. The lion closed its eyes and gently bowed his gigantic head in approval.

The mane of the animal was soft to the touch. Noah's fingers were enthralled by the experience, his heart beating rapidly. He rubbed his other hand over the snout of the lion, stopping to scratch the beast around the ears. Slowly, his hands descended down to the cat's massive chest. The lion's heart was pounding like a bass drum. The thud of each beat pushed against the boy's hand. With each breath, the lion's chest swelled, pushing Noah away and then back again.

"He is an amazing creature," Josiah interrupted Noah's out of body experience. "Shall we continue?"

"Yes, sir!" Noah replied. He sat down next to the beast, unable to release his touch on the animal.

Josiah rose from the throne and walked over to the opposite side of Noah and took a seat next to the boy. "I remember when I first came here. This place still amazes me. King David was very kind. He showed great patience because he too came here at an early age and met with another. This hall has started the beginning of many great stories throughout history. Every good king, every key leader, was brought here to learn what you have an opportunity to experience."

"But I am not a king," Noah interrupted. "My father is just a teacher."

"I understand you doubt. Confused you may be. You *are* the sole possessor of the scepter of Judah. If God did not want you to take this journey, He would not have allowed you to find the scepter in the first place," Josiah responded.

"But why me?" Noah questioned. "There are so many others to choose from. To be honest, I barely even know the Bible. I live in a small town. I have a handful of friends. I play video games and eat junk food. I've got nothing to offer."

Josiah smiled as he watched the boy react. "Do you know the story of Moses?"

"Well, sure. Of course, I'm not *that* dumb! Most kids do where I come from. You know, like the ten plagues, and 'Let my people go.' Yeah, I've seen the movie and heard the story a hundred times."

"Did you know, Noah, Moses questioned why God wanted him as well? He even had a choice to ignore his calling, just like you." Josiah paused. "Moses grew up in Egypt as an adopted son of Pharaoh. He was known by the people. Wealthy, respected, and proud—he was somebody. After Moses was forced to leave Egypt for killing an Egyptian soldier, he wandered in the desert for forty years. He eventually married, fathered a few children, and lived an unknown life as a shepherd. One day, he was tending his father in law's flock in the shadow of the mountain and saw something amazing. Do you remember what it was?"

"No...sorry, I don't."

"The burning bush, Noah. Moses saw a bush on fire, yet it was not consumed. Here was Moses' opportunity. He could simply ignore the bush and continue on in his unknown life or he could approach. In the Bible, it is written that Moses 'turned aside.' He chose to approach."

"So are you saying that I have a choice like Moses?" Noah asked.

"The Scepter of Judah is your burning bush, Noah."

Noah looked down at the scepter. He could see his reflection in the gold staring back at him. So many questions raced in his thoughts. "I don't know what to say—"

"Say nothing, my son. Words are not required. Faith is all that is needed. Moses had faith. Do you?" Josiah locked eyes with Noah.

His mind flashed with visions of his father, home, the cave, Arham, the great hall, Josiah, the beast. There was only one answer. "Yes," he whispered.

"Wonderful!" Josiah wrapped his arm around the boy and shook the nerves out of him. "Have you ever wondered why you were given the name Noah?"

Noah was confused by the sudden change in conversation. "My dad told me why. He said he liked the way it sounded and thought it would be a good name for me to live up to."

"Do you know what your name means?" Josiah asked.

"No, I never asked. I just know the story about the ark and the flood and the animals being saved."

"Names have great meaning. A name is not merely chosen by your parents but gifted by God. Would you like to know the meaning of yours?" Josiah questioned.

"All right," Noah complied.

"In Hebrew, if you reverse the N and H in Noah, you would spell out the word *Hoan*. The word *Hoan* means grace. For it is by God's grace that we escape his judgment, much like the flood that Noah and his family survived."

"Okay, but I don't follow," Noah interceded.

"Noah, your namesake, was belittled for his faith. Imagine living in a land that had never seen rain and trying to warn people of an impending storm that would flood the world. You see, sometimes you have to stand alone and trust God to do something amazing and rely on His grace. Or similar to Moses, God takes somebody who thinks they're nobody to do something amazing. And now it is your turn to stand alone, my son."

Josiah stood and walked down the stairs, peering back up at Noah who remained seated next to the magnificent beast. "This path you have been selected for is meant only for a few men whom God chose because of their hearts. This path he chose for you, Noah."

"What is this path? Is it safe?" Noah asked as he rose to his feet.

"It is a journey to understanding. A path that gifts leadership and character to the brave one who walks it. It is an instrument to mold men into disciples. I now offer you this choice to continue on an adventure of unspeakable happenings that transcends anything you once knew."

"So you're not gonna tell me where this path goes, are you?" Noah interjected.

"That is correct." Josiah smiled at Noah.

"Will I be alone?" Noah asked.

"Not exactly." Josiah turned and walked around behind the throne. Noah turned and watched Josiah approach a door in between two large granite pillars on the back wall of the great hall. Josiah opened the ornate golden doors and disappeared inside. Noah watched, eagerly waiting for whatever other amazing thing was going to captivate him.

11

A few moments passed until Josiah returned, but he was not alone. A companion was at the king's side, a mere child. This threw Noah for a loop. A child was the last thing he expected to see wherever this place was. The boy, however, had a huge smile on his face, and his excitement at seeing Noah was not held a secret. He rushed forward around Josiah and came face-to-face with Noah.

"Hello!" the child shouted at Noah. "I am so happy to finally meet you!" His joyful expression made Noah grin.

"Hi," Noah shyly answered. He was immediately drawn to this boy's enthusiasm. Something about him was inviting and comforting. "I'm Noah...but I guess you already knew that."

Noah turned his attention to Josiah as he neared the two boys. "Noah, I would like to introduce someone to you."

Noah turned his attention back to this new stranger staring at him in arms reach. It was astonishing how much the boy's appearance matched Noah's. He had the same build, height and weight, the same dirty brown hair, even the same green eyes—a true doppelganger. The boy had an honest face too. His skin was a little darker, clearly a tone derived from the Middle East. He wore a robe and sandals, both of which were worn from use. "Noah, this is Thios Lypri," Josiah announced.

"But you can call me Thio. It may be easier for you to remember." The boy's added excitement bubbling up, his speech coming out so fast sounded mumbled. "Are you as excited as me? I have been back in that room forever, you know. I mean, could you two hurry

89

this up? Lots to do, ya know, lots to do. Have you told him where to first, King? This is gonna be awesome!" Thios barely took a breath as he spoke.

"It's nice to meet you, Thio," Noah answered, overwhelmed by the conversation. "But who exactly are you again?"

"I am going to be your guide. That's right. You and me, partners for life. We are gonna be best buds."

"My guide for this path Josiah keeps telling me about?" Noah questioned, nodding his head toward Josiah.

"Ohhhh, so he does not know yet?" Thios questioned Josiah. "You are too slow, old man. Go on, tell him…go on."

"We were just getting to that, Thio. Why don't we all sit down for a moment. It is time you learned what the scepter does." Josiah climbed the stairs back to his throne.

Noah sat down on the chair from before, still clutching the scepter. And Thio…well, Thio decided to do his own thing. He ran up the stairs, making a beeline for the magnificent lion perched near the throne.

"Hey kitty-kitty!" he blurted out, leaping onto the gigantic cat's back. "Giddy-up, Boy!" he screamed out.

The Lion was more than obliged to appease the boy. The graceful beast leapt from the top of the stairs, clearing each step below and sprinted around the room, Thios laughing uncontrollably as he went.

Josiah smiled. Noah was in shock and a little jealous he hadn't considered the same earlier.

The entire scene was better than any dream Noah had ever envisioned or movie he'd seen, for that matter. This overwhelming place, the amazing hall, sitting in front of this regal man—no one would ever believe what he was experiencing. Noah wished his dad could see it all. His thoughts turned to home. *I wonder if he misses me? I bet they are searching for me right now.* Sadness crept into Noah's heart at the thought of the pain he was causing his father back at camp. He should have told him about the scepter. Why did he keep it a secret?

"Your father is fine, Noah," Josiah interrupted.

"What? How did you…you can read my mind?" Noah exclaimed.

"Don't worry, my son. I thought the same thing as well when I came here for the first time. I worried for my mother just as you are for your father. I imagined her sending the king's guard out, scouring the land for me. But King David put my heart at peace. You see, while you are here with me, time as you know it back home stops. So breathe deep."

"Oh yeah, you bet!" Thios interrupted. "We will getcha back sooner or later." Still laughing, joyfully riding around on the back of the lion.

"On to more important matters," Josiah continued, ignoring Thios, "let's talk about the scepter. Have you a had a chance to study it?"

"A little bit," Noah answered, looking down at the piece in his lap. The last time he took any real notice of the scepter, it transported him into another realm.

"Did you notice the holes carved at the top of the scepter? There are six of them."

"These indentions here?" Noah asked, pointing at the holes in the side of the scepter. "Yes, I saw them in my tent back at camp." Noah rubbed his fingers inside the markings.

"As you probably concluded on your own, something was meant to sit in each of the crevices. This is where you come in, Noah. God desires the scepter be whole again. Your mission is to locate the jewels needed to complete the scepter of Judah."

"Like a scavenger hunt…but how do I find these jewels?" Noah asked.

"I can help you with that!" Thios jumped in enthusiastically. "You have to kinda, sorta earn them. And don't worry, together, you and I will complete the tasks at hand."

"Okay, wait now. What kind of *tasks* are we talking about here? What am I, Hercules about to complete feats of strength or something?" Noah interjected sarcastically.

"I knew you'd be funny!" Thios belted out. "Feats of strength… hah! This kid is great!"

"Not quite," Josiah answered. "We are simply going to send you out to find them, like a detective in your picture shows."

"You mean like back home at the campsite with my dad's crew? My dad is the archeologist, not me. I don't know the first thing about digging up relics in the desert. And there is no way I can just wander off again after what happened today in the hole."

"Noah, you misunderstand. We are going to send you back in time," Josiah explained. With the words spoken by the ancient king, time stopped. He no longer heard the lion bounding around the room or Thios laughing, no cooing doves. He felt gut-punched.

"Time travel," Noah whispered.

"You see, my son, the jewels are hidden within the ancient stories of the Bible. There is an order that must be closely followed and completed within a fixed time to accomplish your mission."

Noah froze. His mind reeled at what he just heard. *Could this be real? Time travel?* He supposed it was possible. It had to be plausible in the very least. He was sitting across from a king who had been dead for thousands of years. He was catapulted into the heavens by a glowing piece of metal, for goodness sakes. And now he found himself sitting in front of a throne with a lion prowling around in a building that appeared from nothingness thirty minutes ago. *Time travel through the Bible. Yeah, it's probably a thing here.*

"Noah…did you hear me?" Josiah coaxed the boy to respond.

"So let me get this straight." Noah giggled a little bit by what was coming out of his mouth. "I am going to travel back. Or better yet, you are going to send me back in time on a scavenger hunt to find some jewels for a scepter I found in a cave?"

"Exactly!" Thios declared, throwing his hands in the air. "I knew you got this!"

Noah laughed at the silliness of Thios. "And how do you suppose I'm gonna to find these jewels? They just gonna be sitting on the ground or something?"

Josiah motioned to Thios. "What? Oh yeah… I almost forgot. Here, this will help." Thios reached into his pocket and pulled something out. He handed it to Noah.

"What is this?" Noah questioned. He observed a unique necklace nestled in the palm of his hand. It looked much heavier than it felt. It was a medallion; an amazing work of art. Noah had never seen anything like it. The craftsmanship was outstanding. The medallion was circular, divided into four equal sections by an orange cross carved in the middle. In the upper left-hand quadrant, a red flame. In the upper right, a wing of some type etched in green. Below the wing in the lower right area was what looked like a stick painted white. Beside the stick on the opposite side was a sword shaded in light blue. As Noah studied the piece, the cross in the middle began to glow orange, causing the medallion to pulsate like a heartbeat.

Thios explained, "This will be your compass and swiss army knife all in one, Noah. I will only be able to take you so far, being a kid and all. When you get in trouble or lose your way, the medallion will bring you back to where you need to be. Just be careful not to lose it or uh-oh...ya know?"

"How does it work?" Noah wondered as he placed the necklace around his head, holding the medallion in his hand for a closer look.

"You will find out soon enough, my son. Just know that if you are ever in need, simply grab the medallion and call out to God," Josiah answered.

"Wait...these symbols," Noah wondered aloud, "I think I remember seeing these somewhere. That's right... I saw these in the cave! They were carved on the walls near the altar. I thought they were hieroglyphs, but I was wrong."

"Well, where else would you see them? Duh!" Thios laughed.

Noah was mesmerized by the jewelry. He could feel the power from within like the piece was alive. Each section twinkled in his hand, flashing like Christmas lights. He could feel the warmth from the red flame and a gust of wind blow at his face from the green wing. As Noah eyed the sword, the medallion felt like a weapon in his palm. He glanced at the stick which wasn't a stick but more like a staff now that he reexamined it. The necklace now felt like a compass urging him forward in a particular direction. The whole scene felt like an out-of-body experience. He was hypnotized.

"Noah. Noah," Josiah called to the boy. "Focus, Noah..."

The medallion suddenly stopped whatever craziness it was exuding and once again lay in his hand like a normal piece of jewelry. "What was that? I never felt anything like that. It was wonderful!"

"This necklace is everything you will need to complete the path ahead," Josiah answered. "The journey is going to ask more of you than you can imagine, my son. You are going to need all the help you can get. There is one more important issue we need to discuss before you begin."

Noah listened close to Josiah as he spoke. "There are some who do not want you to be successful on this journey. Some will take the form of friends, others you will know immediately to avoid. The objective of this sinister group is your failure. You see, Noah, God has chosen you. You are precious to Him. And when you become precious to God, you become just as important to Satan."

A shiver ran up the spine of Noah. The hair on the back of his neck rose, and an uneasy feeling flittered in his stomach. A frog clogged his throat, making it difficult for him to respond. "Can he hurt me?"

"Not if I can help it," Thios declared. He winked at Noah. "Stick with me, I got your back!"

"God would not have chosen you if He didn't think you could handle this, Noah. All it requires is faith. Faith like that of Moses. Faith to build an ark when it had never rained. Faith to rule a kingdom at the age of eight. Faith to walk into a dark cave alone."

Reality finally struck home with Noah. This fairy-tale setting that he found himself in wasn't just for fun. The mood shifted in the great hall. This was serious. This was going to be his story. This was going to be his path. His journey into the wardrobe, his Fellowship of the Ring, his Hogwarts. Every great hero in every movie or book he had ever experienced was challenged. They battled and struggled. They went through suffering and loss. Sure, he had never experienced much in his sheltered life before coming to Israel with his father. But if God thought enough of him to place him in that cave to find the Scepter of Judah, then why not? Why not take the first step to greatness and see what other amazing gifts were in store?

Noah took a deep breath. "Let's do it."

12

Thios leapt toward Noah, placing his hands on his shoulders. "That's the spirit! We got this!"

Josiah smiled at the reaction of the boys. "Follow me, you two." Josiah stepped down from the throne and headed off to a new area of the great hall.

Noah asked a question of Josiah while they walked. "If I am going back in time to find these jewels…how am I supposed to blend in? I mean, look at me. I don't look like someone you'd find in walking around with Moses."

"Anything else?" Josiah asked, staring straight ahead, unmoved by the boy's hesitation.

"Yeah, what about talking with these people. My Hebrew isn't exactly the best either." Noah's worry was apparent.

"You got that right," Thios mused.

"I'm gonna stick out like a sore thumb! And these people who are trying to stop me will see me coming a mile away," Noah continued. "Is this necklace gonna blind them or something?"

Josiah motioned to Thios. The boy moved quickly ahead of Josiah to a table along the wall. On top of the table was a package wrapped carefully by a piece of rope. Thios picked up the package and brought it to Noah.

"Here. Open it."

Noah unwrapped the rope and removed the top of the box. Inside was a robe and a pair of beaten leather sandals. The outfit was worn from use and discolored by sand and weather.

"This will help you fit in," Thios added as Noah observed the outfit. "Don't forget the rope. You may need it."

"And as for speaking, Noah," Josiah commented as Noah turned away to change, "you have been taught well by your father through the years. You may not think you can communicate effectively, but I assure you, you can speak better than you know. And if you find yourself in a situation you cannot talk yourself out of, just be still and know that He is God." Josiah pointed his finger to the heavens.

Noah shook the robe out before trying it on. It was an earthy tone of brown made from what felt like cotton. The design was simple, the stitching elementary. "Your clothes will be here when you return," Thios called out to Noah. The robe was simple to slide on. It was the sandals that gave him a fit. They weren't like slide-on Birkenstocks or Adidas flip-flops. He had to wrap the sandals up his calf to hold them in place. Once they were situated, they actually felt pretty good. As for the rope, Thios was right. He tightened it around his waist to make the robe more snug. Noah took the medallion and carefully placed it under the robe, out of view of any onlookers.

"Now what?" Noah asked, walking back to the others, carrying the scepter. He was surprised at how roomy the robe was and how it allowed him to move much more easily. But he did have to admit he felt a little awkward like he was wearing a girl's dress.

Josiah walked over to him and placed his hands on Noah's shoulders. "One last thing. Close your eyes." Josiah placed his hands over Noah's face, covering it completely. He felt the warmth from the King's hands. A few seconds later, he removed them.

"What was that for?" Noah asked, confused by his actions. "Did I have something on my face?"

"That's terrific! Take a gander." Thios handed Noah a mirror. "I like the new look."

What Noah saw in the mirror overwhelmed him. "Wow!" Somehow, Josiah was able to alter Noah's appearance. His skin was a few shades darker. He looked like any other Middle Eastern child, but it was still him. His bone structure, hairstyle, everything was the same, just colored different. "How did you do that?" he asked, but

Josiah did not answer. *Skin color is just that—color,* Noah thought. *Everything else is the same underneath.*

"Shall we?" Josiah said, walking back to his throne. He ascended the steps, the lion now lying next to the throne keeping an eye on the king as he approached. Noah, however, didn't move. He was frozen in place by his altered appearance staring at the reflection. "Noah, come," he commanded. Noah quickly followed.

Josiah once again took a seat on the throne and peered down at Noah. Thios was by his side. The two boys were ready. They looked at each other. Thios smiled which gave Noah some added courage to begin. Josiah spoke.

"Noah, raise the scepter of Judah high in the air."

Noah did as he was instructed. He clutched the scepter by the grip with one hand like a baseball player calling his shot and hoisted it in the air. Noah watched as the ceiling above the throne opened, allowing a radiant beam of sunlight to shine down onto the golden rod. The scepter glowed ever brighter as the light penetrated it's exterior. Noah squinted, trying to keep his eyes on the relic. A single ray of light shot off from the scepter to the left of Noah onto a nearby wall. He turned to see the laser beam of light pierce the solid marble structure. Noah watched, speechless at the power of the light as it melted the stone.

"Let go of the scepter, Noah," Josiah instructed.

"I can't," Noah answered, not wanting to release his grip.

"Noah," Josiah compassionately said, "do as I say, my son."

Noah gently released his hold on the scepter. The golden rod hovered in midair, its brilliance cascading throughout the hall. The laser-like beam continued to disintegrate the marble wall to his left. A loud cracking noise arose from within the light covered wall. The beam of the light grew ever larger in diameter, consuming more and more of the marble. The light shone brighter and brighter.

Noah closed his eyes. It was too much. Suddenly, the light stopped. The ceiling closed. Noah, now sensing it was safe to open his eyes, took a look at the scepter. It was still hovering in the air where he last saw it.

Noah peered over at the wall. What he saw made him shake his head in shock. There standing where the impenetrable marble wall once stood was an altar. An altar that looked eerily identical to one Noah found himself at earlier in the cave. This altar, however, was pristine and clean, made of one solid piece of gold ornately decorated all around with carvings of a vine with leaves. Atop the altar was a resting place designed specifically for the Scepter of Judah.

"You may now take hold of the scepter, Noah," Josiah instructed.

Noah complied. Reaching out, he grabbed the levitating piece. "If you please," Josiah motioned for Noah to rest the scepter in its rightful place. He moved past Thios and walked slowly toward the altar. He allowed himself one last look at the relic and rested the golden scepter atop the altar.

As soon as Noah laid the piece down, a noise emanated from within the altar. It sounded like the inner workings of a large clock, gears shifting and releasing. Thios approached Noah and put his arm around his shoulder. "You ready?" he asked.

"No," Noah laughed. "Just kiddin'." He smiled at Thios.

Noah turned around to see Josiah standing nearby. Something was different now. The floor below him, the crystal clear, smooth as glass floor he just walked across to place the scepter was changed. It must have shifted as soon as he placed the scepter. He found himself standing with Thios and Josiah atop a perfect replica of the medallion. The colors were the same except jewels were used instead of paint. The red flame was created using the deepest red rubies. The wing was filled in with the most hypnotizing emeralds. The staff was created with diamonds, some the size of baseballs. And the sword was designed with royal blue sapphires. Dividing the illustrations was a moat of moving orange lava taking the place of the cross.

Josiah held out his hands, one toward Noah and the other to Thios. Noah took hold of Josiah's hand. At the same time, Thios grabbed Noah's other hand. The three made a circle as they stood within the medallion outlined on the floor. Josiah bowed his head. The boys followed suit.

"Heavenly Father, Creator of heaven and earth, provider of all. We thank you for this day. We ask, Lord, that Your strength would fill Noah and Your hand would guide his path. You have chosen this boy to undertake the journey a select few before him have walked. We ask, Lord, for Your sovereign protection and grace as he travels this road. May Your will be done. We ask this in Your awesome and holy name. Amen."

Noah opened his eyes and looked over to Thios whose head was still bowed low. He glanced at Josiah as well, his position the same. "Amen," Noah whispered under his breath.

As soon as the words left his mouth, the medallion outline the three were standing on came to life. The colors glowed bright. Josiah released his hold on Noah's hand and stepped away outside the medallion outline. Noah looked over at the king. He smiled and nodded ever so slightly in Noah's direction, then turned and walked away.

Noah quickly lost sight of him. The light and rushing wind coming from below his feet overwhelmed him. He looked over to his right for Thios, but he too was out of sight. A new voice, deep like a man but not Josiah's shouted from behind Noah, "Be strong and courageous, Noah."

"Who is—" Noah was not able to finish his question. The floor shook violently underneath. Light enveloped him on all sides. The wind grew more and more severe like a geyser spewing forth with such force, lifting him off the ground. He was at the mercy of the medallion. Noah closed his eyes and prayed, "Lord, help me."

"Noah, grab hold of the medallion!" Thios shouted.

Noah reached down and took the necklace into his hands. The necklace pulsated just as it had earlier. "Be strong and courageous, Noah," the unknown voice called out again.

"Hold on tight, Noah!" Thios yelled.

The once solid ground beneath Noah's feet started to move. At first the floor descended slowly like an elevator, but as the distance increased, so did the speed of the descent. The free-falling sensation made Noah nauseous. His stomach felt like it was in his throat. At least now Noah could see Thios beside him, and he, of course, was calm as could be. This wasn't his first rodeo. Radiant beams of light in all colors filled the environment around them. The falling persisted for only a few moments. As fast as the ride began, it ceased, leaving the two boys hovering over the abyss. The rainbow ride was finished, and silence echoed around them.

"Is that it?" Noah asked.

"Not quite." Thios smiled at Noah.

Noah heard a rip, like the tearing of corduroy jeans behind him, and before he could turn around, he felt himself being sucked away. The powerful G-force moved his body like a leaf in a hurricane. Noah caught one last sight of the medallion floor as it rose back to hall in the distance. He clutched the necklace as tight as could, fearful he would lose it in the wind tunnel.

The speed was too much for Noah. He couldn't feel his body anymore. He was about to pass out. "*Thio!*" Noah screamed out. "*Thio!*" again he yelled, but there was no response. Twisting and turning, up and down, firing like a bullet from a pistol, he moved down the wormhole. His hair was pulled straight back from the shear velocity. "Thio, where are you?" he called out again in desperation.

In the distance, once again, Noah heard an unknown voice utter the words, "Be strong and courageous, Noah!"

Faster and faster he moved, like a roller coaster flipping this way and that. At times, he felt like he was on a slide, other times like he was flying up in the sky. Wind was gushing so hard he could hardly catch his breath. "I can't take much more of this!" he called out, desperately hoping for a response from his companion.

There was no answer. He was alone. Somewhere in the labyrinth of tunnels and wormholes, the two were separated. *What have I gotten myself into?* Noah thought to himself. The speed of the tunnel was overwhelming his little body. His stomach was doing flips from his throat to his knees. The intensity was more than he could bear. Noah let go of the necklace as he tried to balance himself in the turbulence. As soon as he did, the medallion around his neck began to float up in the air, threatening to break loose. In desperation, Noah tried to reach it. He mustered what little strength remained and raised his hand to grab the necklace. He knew without the medallion, he would have no protection.

As Noah stretched out, he lost whatever control he had in this never-ending free fall. His body went into a vicious death roll. Flip-flopping along, Noah concentrated on the task at hand, getting that medallion before it was too late. The speed and velocity of the roll increased. Noah was losing sight on the medallion. Noah lunged toward the medallion with the last bit of his strength he had and snagged the piece tightly in his palm. As soon as his hands clasped the necklace, everything stopped. No more rolling, no more suction, no more light, no more sound—the sudden halt was enough to make him throw up. The orange glow from the medallion ceased.

Noah breathed deep, trying to calm his anxiety and catch his breath at the same time. He turned his head here and there, looking for a point of reference. "Where...where am I? Thio, can you hear me?" Noah shouted, his breath laborious to the task. Noah realized quickly that he was still in the tunnel, even though he couldn't see it. He reached out his hand and touched the invisible wall of the tunnel. He rose to his feet, trying to gain back some of his equilibrium.

As time passed, his composure returned, and the spinning sensation subsided. "Where am I?" he whispered. "And why have I stopped? Hey, *Thio!*" he called out, looking every which way, hoping for some type of reply. Noah sat down, exhausted. "What a day." He shook his head and bowed his eyes. The long day's travel by plane, lack of sleep, weariness from standing out in the desert, being transported by the scepter, and now the wormhole—Noah was running on fumes.

He sat alone against the transparent wall, motionless, trying not to doze off into slumber. Visions of Josiah, Thios, and the great hall played out in his mind. *When did this path Josiah mentioned begin? He said I was going back in time...where back in time?* Noah looked down at the medallion still tightly gripped in his hand. The orange glow was returning. "Oh boy." Noah rose to his feet. "Here we go again." Noah readied himself.

There was no rushing wind this time and no flashing lights. He heard no rip in the space-time continuum or felt a geyser begin to blow against his body. No rocketlike G-force shot at him like a bullet. It was just the floor this time. It simply opened wide beneath him, and the boy fell like a rock off a cliff. Noah didn't scream, though, didn't flail about in fear. He simply closed his eyes, gripped the medallion as tight as he could, and waited for whatever God had in store for him. His path was about to begin, and he knew it. Whether or not Thios was there, Noah had the medallion and was ready.

Eyes still closed, Noah suddenly felt warmth wrap around his body like a blanket. Then light, not flashing, multicolor light—just the steady comfort surrounding his body from the sun. Fresh crisp air circled his frame as he gently fell from the sky. He slowly opened his eyes to focus and waited as they adjusted to the new environment. He looked below to see his rapid descent to the Earth. "This is gonna hurt!" he screamed. And with a loud thud, he landed.

13

Noah slowly regained his composure from the fall. His head was still spinning from the wormhole. He felt like he had just been in a car accident. His neck and back were throbbing, and his fingers tingled as he lay there in a daze. The impact of the fall had knocked the breath out of him as well. With what little strength remained, Noah tried to sit up.

His eyes slowly adjusted to his new environment. *Where am I?* He could feel dirt and grass beneath his hands. He felt the warmth from the sun on his skin. Everything was a blur. Maybe it was from exhaustion or the time travel or it could be that he was suddenly dying of thirst, possibly even a concussion; Noah's body was not responding. He felt the ground vibrate underneath. It was not the same sensation as the time-travel escapade nor was it as strong as an earthquake. The rumble felt more like a marching band shaking the Earth as they moved in unison. His eyes still straining to focus, he noticed a large black object bearing down on him. The size of the dark silhouette was massive, the ground thumping as it moved toward Noah. The mysterious beast let out an intimidating bellow in warning.

"Is that a cow?" Noah squinted. Whatever it was, it was humungous and closing in. Noah tried to shift his body out of the way, the menacing animal ever lumbering toward him. Noah's body would not respond. His legs were cramped beneath him, his shoulders burning. He had exhausted all the energy his body had to offer. "Argghhh!" Noah screamed, trying to force his body to wake up. "Come on, Noah!" He tried to lift himself by his arms alone. He was stuck.

His eyes finally focused in on the foreboding object. Bearing down on him was a massive two-thousand-pound hunk of flesh. An ox covered with think black fur approached. With each step toward Noah, its gigantic hoofs planted into the Earth, kicking dust in the air. The ox's horns shot forth from its massive skull like swords threatening anyone who dared aggravate the behemoth. Again, Noah tried to move out of the way, but nothing, no response. The beast snorted, firing mucus onto the ground. Its eyes locked onto Noah ever approaching. The monstrous animal let out another bellow, announcing his disapproval of the boy blocking his path. The ox's pace quickened, taking Noah's presence as an insult.

Noah bowed his head, knowing he was at the mercy of the beast. "This is it," he whispered as he closed his eyes. "God, help me."

Noah laid back against the Earth in utter exhaustion. In a few seconds, the behemoth would trample him, and there was nothing he could do. Then a sound rang in Noah's ears. It wasn't a sound that an ox could possibly make. It was the sound of a wheel grinding as it turned, treading against the mud and grass. In Noah's fatigued state, he hadn't noticed the ox was pulling something. He lifted his body up to see what it was. Noah heard voices as well. "Help! Help me!" he yelled as loud as he could, but there was no response. The sound of the cart and the ox drowned out his feeble voice. Again, he screamed, "Someone please…help…please, help." The boy was drained. Not only could he not physically move his body out of danger, he was too tired to scream at this point. Unable to fight any longer, Noah slumped back to the ground, letting out one last desperate plea, "Help!"

Sleep. That is all his body desired. His eyelids were heavy. He had no choice but to accept his fate. Noah drifted away into slumber. He felt the vibration of the ox beneath his body. The beast was nearly upon him now. He could feel the warmth from its breath on his legs. Just as Noah was about to lose consciousness, he heard the voice of a man. "*Halt!*" The force of the command froze the ox in place instantaneously. The last thing Noah heard was a shriek from a woman and the pattering of feet beside his body.

His eyes shut tight before he could see who stopped the beast. The excitement from the day's events zapped his last ounce of energy. He was safe. That's all that mattered. He drifted away without a care in the world. He dreamed deep and long; visions of flight filled his imagination followed by the sensation of being on a train.

*****

When he finally came to, the first thing he felt was the soft ground under his body like a bed of pillows. The last he remembered, he was lying in an open field with dirt and grass beneath him. A light breeze blew gently around his body, cooling off the summer warmth.

A woman's voice whispered softly nearby, "Wake up, child." She repeated, "Wake up."

Noah opened his eyes. He slowly lifted his weary body from his resting place. He was inside a tent of some sort. His head was throbbing and his stomach yearning for sustenance. "Well, hello. It's nice to finally meet you," the woman announced. "And how are you feeling today?" she asked, approaching Noah.

It took Noah a few seconds to gather his wits. He rubbed his eyes to better focus on his surroundings. In front of him stood an elderly woman. She was short, not much more than five feet tall, but what she lacked in height, she made up in weight. Her plump body was wrapped in a light-blue robe. Her hair was covered with a wrap. Her eyes were inviting and comforting. Her smile lit up her face. She reminded Noah of his grandmother. He instinctively felt comfortable around her.

"Where…where am I?" Noah questioned.

"What did you say?" She looked confusingly toward Noah.

Noah forgot about the language barrier. An interesting predicament because he understood every word she said perfectly. Noah's mind just needed a jolt to get him going. He thought for a moment. This time he questioned in Hebrew, "Where am I?" He hoped his words hadn't startled the woman.

"Oh goodness…thought you were one of them for a moment," she said.

"One of who?" Noah asked.

"Oh, never mind that now, child." She approached him with a moist cloth and wiped his face clean. Noah rather enjoyed being cared for. Her eyes sparkled up close. They were so kind. Her rosy cheeks perked up when she smiled. *There is something special about this woman,* Noah thought. God sent him here, to be with this woman for a reason. *Is this part of the path?*

"You gave us quite a scare yesterday on the road," she said.

"It's been a whole day?" Noah answered, bewildered.

"Oh, yes. You had quite a fall. What were you doing in the middle of the road anyways?" she asked accusingly as she rose to her feet to wet the cloth again.

"I... I don't remember." Noah did his best to answer her question, not wanting to give away why he truly was in the middle of the road. "Was that your animal? the big black thing?"

"Ole Bethem? Yes, he's been with us for quite some time now. Had lots of travel time with him over the years. Blessed my husband saw you before Bethem got to you. He would have crushed you underfoot," she replied.

"Thank you, ma'am," Noah offered his appreciation.

"Ma'am?" she looked at Noah awkwardly. "What is this Ma'am?"

Noah hesitated, "Sorry, it's what I call my grandmother." He hoped the explanation would be enough.

She smiled in approval. "Now you wait here." She called out as she left the tent. Noah didn't know how long he had till she returned. He removed the blanket and rose to his feet. Thankfully, his robe was still attached to his body. He rubbed his hands over his chest, anxious to feel the necklace from Thios. He took a deep breath once he felt the outline of the medallion. Everything was good. He was alive and dressed. He had the necklace in case he got lost. Now he needed to figure just where he was or better yet, "when" he was in time.

Noah took the free time to examine his surroundings. The bed he slept in was made from straw and covered by a thin piece of cloth. There were two more such sleeping areas on the ground nearby. The tent was large enough for three or four adults with openings cut to allow for circulation. The corners were held up by sturdy pieces of timber and connected from above by more pliable beams of the same material. The tent was fastened to the beams for extra support. A rug covered the floor. There wasn't much to the structure. It was clear to Noah that the tent was designed for travel at a moment's notice.

From outside, he could hear many voices and the clamoring of people. He wanted to go and explore what the ruckus was all about but decided to follow the instruction his caretaker had given. She was kind enough to take him in and care for him. The least he could do was respect her request. *Be patient, Noah.*

From inside, Noah watched as two silhouettes approached through the cloth walls. One of them was obviously the woman, but she was flanked by a tall skinny figure. She entered the tent first, followed by her companion. "Well, hello!" the man called out joyously at the sight of Noah. "I am happy to see you are sitting up." He walked over and bent down to eye level to speak with Noah, resting his hands on the boy's shoulders. He was lanky, built like a basketball player. His arms hung far down his side, reaching halfway from his hips to his knees. His demeanor reminded him of Arham. A much older version of Arham, apparently the same age as the woman whom Noah inferred was his wife. The man was just as inviting and friendly as her. "And what shall we call you?"

"My name is Noah," he answered.

The man motioned for Noah to sit on the bed. He quickly joined Noah. Noah was surprised to see a man his age move with such ease. He even sat cross-legged. Most men in his time couldn't move like that.

"Shalom, Noah! This is Hani, my bride," he related, pointing at the caretaker. "My name is Mathius." He paused to let Noah add the names to his memory and then asked, "And who is your father?" The man wasted no time in his friendly interrogation.

Noah hoped that his body did not express his anxiousness the way it poured through his mind. He quickly ran through how to answer his host. The couple was so nice to take him in and care for him while he recuperated. The last thing he wanted to do was lie. "My father's name is Solomon," he answered.

"Noah, son of Solomon. I like the sound of that." Mathius looked over in Hani's direction. "Well, I am blessed to have you in my home, Noah."

"Thank you, sir. I really appreciate you both watching over me," Noah said looking at both Hani and Mathius. "I hope it wasn't too much trouble—"

"Nonsense, my child. It makes us happy to help," Mathius replied. "Please tell us," he continued, "where can I find your father? What tribe are you from?"

How am I supposed to answer this? Noah thought. *Tribe? Oh my, he must mean the twelve tribes of Israel.* "I was separated from my father a few days ago by accident," Noah answered, hoping that would quell the need for information. "I don't want to be any trouble to you sir. I can leave if you like."

"Don't be foolish. You will remain with us until God shows us otherwise," Hani interjected. "I am sure Mathius will locate him. He is probably with the other men preparing," she added, looking directly at Mathius. "Why don't I go and get you something to eat? I am sure you are famished."

Noah wasn't going to argue with that. He couldn't remember the last time he ate. Hani departed quickly.

Mathius arose from the floor and approached the opening to the tent. He pulled back the covering, letting the fresh air and sunlight burst inside. "Imagine you would like to stretch your legs." He motioned toward Noah. Noah picked himself up from the bed and walked toward Mathius. As he neared the doorway, Mathius stepped aside, allowing Noah full view of his surroundings. The warmth of the afternoon sun felt intoxicating on his body.

Once Noah's eyes adjusted to the sunlight, he was overwhelmed by what he saw. Mathius and Hani's tent was perched atop a hill overlooking an endless horizon of people, livestock, tents, and more. Noah turned all around, taking in the scene. The entire valley was covered. There had to be thousands, tens of thousands, possibly hundreds of thousands of people. "Look at all the people," Noah muttered under his breath. "How many are there?"

Mathius calmly answered, "Last count, we have 603,000 men over twenty years of age. I would put the entire camp at over two million." Noah was speechless at Mathius's blunt answer.

The nation of Israel was on full display before Noah. A fledging nation on a journey. A nation looking for a place to call home. The people below had similar tents to Mathius and Hani. As Noah watched on, it seemed as though the people were preparing for movement soon. He watched as some gathered animals. Others were preparing carts. Some were bundling possessions. People were laughing and conversing about the day's affairs. Each clearly had a purpose and duty. The scene was staggering to behold.

"How did you get this spot up here?" Noah said to Mathius.

"Usually happens that way," he answered nonchalantly. "What does your father do for trade, Noah?" he asked. Yet another question for Noah to carefully answer.

I cannot tell him he is an archeologist. That will just confuse him. They probably don't even know what that is. These are the people that archeologist's study, he thought. "He is a teacher." It was Noah's best reply. "What is your trade?" Noah switched the line of questioning.

"I am a Levite," Mathius responded. "I am responsible for specific duties in the Tabernacle. I also sit as Judge over the people in settling matters of dispute. Some would even call me an elder."

Noah vaguely remembered his father speaking about the Tabernacle. That word always sounded funny to Noah like a board game. *Hey, you wanna come over and play Tabernacle with my family?* But what was it? Maybe he could get Mathius to explain.

"You must be good at your job." Noah shook his head in disbelief with his location. Mathius glanced at the boy, interested in his comment.

"Have you visited the Tabernacle with your father?" Mathius questioned Noah.

Noah remembered the tribe of Levi was the chosen tribe for priests. The men were responsible for the temple and the sacrifices for the Jewish people. Again, Noah found himself with a difficult question. "No, sir, I have not."

"You must not be of age. Soon, though, I'm sure." Mathius motioned for Noah to follow him. "Why don't we go for a walk while Hani prepares the meal? I have someplace I need to be. Would you mind accompanying me?"

Noah nodded and followed close to his guide.

14

They made their way down the hill to the multitude of people below. Noah stayed close by Mathius's side in the crowd. The people all gave notice to their approach, their eyes fixed on Mathius. The respect for Noah's caretaker was obvious. Mathius took his time to acknowledge each person as they strolled through the camp, shaking hands with the men and patiently stopping to pay attention to the children running about. He was like a great uncle or grandfather to the people.

"Where are we?" Noah asked, trying to gather information on where he was sent by the Scepter of Judah.

"We are close to the Jordan," Mathius answered. *The Jordan?* Noah thought. *He must mean the Jordan River.*

"It looks like the people are preparing to move. Do you know where?" Noah continued his questioning.

"I do not choose the time or place for our encampments, Noah. I merely follow the commands given to me. I may be able to shed some light on that shortly," Mathius replied. The two of them continued walking further into the camp, stopping here and there to greet the people. Noah could tell they were headed for something other than a mere stroll. The two neared a large tent, the largest amongst any Noah had seen on their walk. He could see this was an important place. Soldiers were situated around the outside. Older men, the same age as Mathius, were entering the tent, leaving their attendants to wait outside.

Mathius stopped and turned to his companion. "Noah, you cannot join me inside, my son. This meeting is for tribal elders only.

I ask you to wait here until I return," Mathius said of Noah in his absence.

Noah nodded in agreement and watched as Mathius entered into the tent. He walked around to the side of the opening so as not to get trampled by the others entering. He stared at the people around him, bustling here and there in anticipation for the results of the meeting. The nation of Israel clamored in excitement by the day's events, eager for direction. The people were smiling and hugging. It reminded him of the mood before a big sporting event back home in Texas. Fans would ramp up their enthusiasm as hopes of victory, and prestige filled the air. The whole scene was hypnotizing to watch, so much so Noah nearly missed the invitation at the side of the tent he was standing by. A small obscure opening perfectly situated for a boy his size to see inside the tent.

Noah glanced around to make sure he was not being watched by any of the soldiers. Convinced that he was safe to proceed, he peered inside. It took a few moments for his eyes to assimilate to the darkness. Torches had been placed around the interior of the tent to give light to the meeting space inside. It wasn't difficult for Noah to locate Mathius amongst the group for he stood nearly a foot taller than the rest. There were around twenty or so men standing in a circle, listening intently to their speaker. Most of the men looked to be the same age as Mathius, dressed in similar robes. However, there were two men who were clearly older than the rest, and one of them was leading the group.

The speaker was in his eighties by appearance. His muscular stature and bold voice demanded attention. It was clear to Noah that he had some type of military training by the way he spoke and instructed the others. His skin was tan, his gray beard trimmed closer to his face than the others. He did not wear a crown, but Noah surmised if Israel had a king, this man would be it. The speaker wore a light-brown robe and held a staff in his right hand. The staff stood a few feet taller than the man.

The timbre in his voice carried around the interior of the tent. The elders hung on his every word like students to a teacher. Noah tried to make out what he was saying but could not succeed. The noise from the crowd outside was drowning out the speaker's words. As the leader spoke, he locked eyes with each elder encircling him. There was more going on in this meeting than a mere lecture. He was instructing the men about something important.

Suddenly, the speaker glanced in Noah's direction and locked eyes with the boy. Noah froze. *Can he see me?* The speaker did not hesitate as he turned his attention back to the meeting and continued teaching the elders.

Noah watched on. Again, the speaker turned his attention toward Noah. This time, he slightly bowed his head, acknowledging the boy's presence. *He must see me!* Noah continued to watch as the speaker became more animated in his explanation to the elders, raising his arms in the air. At one point, he raised both his arms in the air and made a Y-shape, like he was opening something quite large. The elders listened intently. Noah wished he could hear the subject matter of the conversation.

Minutes later, the group disbanded, joining the crowd outside who cheered in excitement. Noah hurried away from the hole back to the opening to find Mathius. Mathius exited with another man in tow. The two elders mingled for a bit and then departed ways. "Hani should have supper ready by now. Shall we?" Mathius motioned for Noah to follow as he made a path through the crowd. Noah had so many questions to ask but did not want to insult his host by telling him of his eavesdropping. Besides, the noise from the people was too much for small talk.

The two of them slowly traversed their way back to Mathius's tent. Noah watched as people did as people do, although maybe slightly differently here. There was a mother hanging damp clothes on a line to dry them out. Another woman was busy preparing dinner for her family. In the distance, Noah saw children playing in a field. They ran to and fro with their arms behind their backs, kicking around what looked like a ball. Men were busy corralling animals into pens. Others were sharpening tools or weapons. Noah couldn't tell.

Noah continued to follow Mathius. It was refreshing watching the people living in such close proximity to one another, working together, the way it should be. Back home, living was more spread out and independent of one another, only coming together when needed; otherwise, people kept to themselves.

"Did you see anyone you know while you waited?" Mathius asked as they neared the hill.

"No, sir," Noah answered. "I am sorry if I am a burden."

"On the contrary. It is a pleasure to share my home with you, Noah." Mathius smiled.

"What was that meeting all about?" Noah questioned. "Looked pretty important."

"All in due time, my son."

Up ahead, they heard Hani, "There you two are! I was getting worried." She was waiting at the tent opening. "Come on, come on. The food is ready." They all entered the tent. "And how was the meeting, husband?" she asked.

"Good, good. Just as expected. Let us sit, and we can talk," Mathius replied.

Noah was starving to say the least. Time may have stopped back home, but his stomach did not. He was famished; not only had he spent all that time with Thios and Josiah in the great hall along with traversing the wormhole, but he was also bedridden for a day. Add that with waiting for Mathius to wrap up the elder meeting, it must have been almost two days since Noah tasted food!

In their absence, Hani had reorganized the tent. On the floor was a mat laid out with their meal. Surrounding the rug was an assortment of pillows for the three to lounge on. There was a bowl of water that Mathius and Hani used to wash their hands after which they passed to Noah. He did his best to mimic their behavior so as not to draw attention. After washing, they each took a seat. Hani took the liberty of serving the men first. Mathius waited as did Noah until she had completed. He then reached out his hands, one to her, the other to Noah. He bowed his head, and together, they gave thanks for their food.

The meal was mouthwatering. On each place setting, Hani placed a handful of luscious grapes. Along with that were a few freshly picked green olives. Each person received a piece of bread shaped like a tortilla, yet thicker. Noah took a bite and was elated at the sweetness. It was like sugary cereal formed and baked slowly over an oven. Noah savored each bite as he ate. The food was so fresh.

"We are nearing the final day," Mathius interrupted the silence. "Soon, the manna stops."

Hani froze at his statement. "Blessed be. Are the people aware?"

"We have been instructed to warn the people, yes," Mathius continued. "The journey to the river begins in the morning. Joshua explained to us all what he was instructed. Noah, you will accompany us to the river. Once we cross, I'll locate your father, Solomon."

"Joshua!" Noah blurted out, maybe more excited than he should have. "I'm sorry. I didn't mean to interrupt. But you said Joshua. Was that who you were listening to in the tent?"

"You seem to know a great deal more than I thought." Mathius smiled at Noah. "Do tell."

"I apologize, sir. I know it was wrong of me to look inside. My curiosity got the better of me. My dad's always getting on to me about that," Noah continued. "What was the meeting about? It looked pretty important. All the people were huddled around, waiting outside. And you didn't say anything on the walk back."

"Much on my mind, my son. Tomorrow is a big day for our people. We have been waiting forty years for a place to call home. God has been so good to us. He has provided food for our table when we had no lands to farm." Mathius held up the bread. "The manna ceases to fall soon. We will cross the Jordan into the land promised to our fathers many years ago. A land flowing with milk and honey." Mathius smiled at Hani, tears filling his eyes.

15

Noah's mind was spinning. He knew where he was...this was it! He was with the Israelites in the desert. These people camped with Hani and Mathius were the ones who escaped Pharaoh under Moses. Now Joshua was leading them. Tomorrow, the nation was going to break camp and head to the Jordan river for crossing and then to war! Kingdom by kingdom, city by city, village by village, these people would conquer the land. And Noah was going to witness the beginning of the conquest. But where to first?

Noah pondered the thought until Mathius broke the silence. "Where did you get the necklace you wear? It is unlike anything I have seen."

Noah hesitated a moment. He thought the medallion was unknown to them, "A friend gave it to me, sir."

"It is quite beautiful," Hani added.

"May I?" Mathius outstretched his hand, gesturing for a chance to hold the medallion.

Noah hesitated for a moment if there would be any consequences but decided to allow Mathius his request. He removed the medallion and handed it to his host.

The old man carefully studied the necklace. His long fingers traced over the symbols. First the flame, then the sword—he was transfixed. He balanced it in his hands. The craftsmanship was something to behold. Even Noah couldn't stop looking at it. He handed the necklace to Hani who was just as interested to study the piece.

"What do the engravings mean?" he questioned.

"I don't know. But once I find my friend, Thios, I will ask," Noah answered simply.

"Thios? Interesting name," Mathius interjected.

"Why do you say that?" Noah questioned.

"Thios means God."

"Huh." Noah was caught off-guard by the insight. "I didn't… I guess…how did I miss that?" Noah was speaking more to himself than to Mathius.

"It's a lot heavier than it looks," Hani interrupted, handing the necklace back to Noah. Noah slipped the medallion back over his head. She turned her attention to Mathius, "The river is high this time of year. How are we to cross?" she anxiously proposed. "The animals and children are not strong enough."

"God will provide a way as He has before," Mathius answered calmly. He turned to Noah, "It may be a few days before I can locate your father, Noah. You will stay by my side until then, understood?"

"Thank you, sir," Noah accepted. "You are both too kind."

"You are most welcome, Noah," Hani replied. "I need to introduce you to my brother."

"Funny you say that. He asked to meet the boy earlier today," Mathius added.

"Who is your brother?" Noah questioned.

Hani smiled. "Why, Joshua, of course." Her eyes twinkled.

Noah was dumbfounded by her answer. He wiped the grape juice from his lips. His mind was racing. This was no accident, him falling from the sky landing in front of Bethem, their ox. "I… I… would be honored, ma'am," Noah stuttered.

Mathius made a face. "Ma'am?"

Hani answered, "That's what he calls his grandmother." She smiled at her husband.

"Well, it's settled then. Tomorrow we travel to the river together, and you will meet Joshua." Mathius was pleased with his plan. Hani rose to clean up the meal. Mathius stood to his feet and walked to the tent opening, motioning for Noah to follow. The two sat on the ground atop the hill, overlooking the people below.

Noah found the courage to ask Mathius, "Can you tell me your story?"

"What would you like to know, Noah, son of Solomon?"

"How long have you been traveling? How did you meet Hani? And Joshua? You know, the important stuff." Noah answered.

"Stuff? What is this stuff?" Mathius was confused.

"Oh, sorry. It's what my friends and I say. Just about the important parts or the highlights?"

"Very well," Mathius agreed. He took a moment to stare up at the stars, allowing his thoughts to align. "We were both very young when we left Egypt, younger than you even. I remember my father and mother telling me and my siblings one night that we were going on a journey. We were to stay dressed that evening and wait for the Lord. It was the sounds of screams that I recall of that night. Many Egyptian families lost loved ones that day.

"Then we marched out of Egypt. Our people were happy and scared at the same time. All we had ever known was life in Egypt under Pharaoh. But God was calling us out of the land to a place He promised our fathers Abraham, Isaac, and Jacob. We journeyed a few days, Moses urging us forward. Our spirits were high, my son. We sang and laughed. It was perfect. Everyone was sharing what they had in hopes of where God would lead. When we came to the sea, everything changed. My father instructed us to be patient. He kept reminding the family of the goodness of God."

Hani interrupted from behind, "I remember men screaming at each other the longer we waited, saying, 'Why would God have taken us out of Egypt just to kill us in the desert? It would have been better if we stayed.' I was a terrified little girl."

Mathius continued, "Then the worst thing happened. From behind us, Pharaoh approached with his iron chariots. I can still see the sun reflecting off their weapons and armor. They blocked the only exit, our backs to the sea. We were trapped, Noah. Suddenly, like rain...fire fell from the sky, creating a barrier between Pharaoh's army and our people. We all rushed to the water, but Moses commanded us to stop.

He waded into the water and raised his hands. And my boy, we all witnessed the power of Yahweh that day. The sea stood up on both sides. A wall of water the size of a mountain. And the noise… Noah, the noise was deafening."

Hani interjected, "My mother gripped my hand so tightly. I think it was Aaron who entered first, wasn't it?"

"Correct, wife," Mathius answered. "Once the men saw it was safe, we all moved forward. No one rushed. We all calmly, together as one people, marched ahead. The ground was dry, Noah!" Mathius's eyes lit up. "You would think the mud would slow us down, but it was dry, dry as the desert. Our animals, our carts, the children, even the elderly—there was no problem walking through. God must have held that wall of water for hours as we crossed.

Once the final man had reached the other side, the wall of fire falling from heaven, the barrier God used to hold Pharaoh back, it disappeared into the clouds. What happened next still is spoken about amongst the people. Pharaoh commanded the army to give chase. And chase they did, my boy, headlong into the sea. There was an insatiable bloodlust driving them on!"

Hani broke in, "The sound…that awful clanging sound. Those Egyptian soldiers were so angry. They were screaming. I ran with my mother and brothers, but we had nowhere to go."

Mathius nodded his head. "Moses, he turned and approached the water once more. He raised his hands yet again. As soon as he did… God let go! That water crashed down like an avalanche. The Egyptian army was gone in a breath."

"My dad has told me that story many times," Noah said. "You went to the mountain next."

"Correct. And there, our people began a pattern of disobedience that God would not long stand for. Time and again, our fathers rejected the Lord's commands until His patience ran out. For the last forty years, we have wandered in this desolate wasteland until each one of our parents passed on. Noah, tomorrow, our wandering reaches an end. God once again commands us forward into the promised land. This is what Joshua's meeting was about."

Noah let the story sit for a moment and then asked, "So how did you two meet?"

Hani smiled. "Joshua invited Mathius to eat with us one night. After that evening, you couldn't separate us if you tried."

Mathius looked at Hani with love. "What can I say, Noah, she stole my heart that night. Soon we were married. Joshua conducted the ceremony, of course."

"And children?" Noah questioned.

The mood shifted. Hani bowed her head and turned to head back into the tent. "Excuse me."

Mathius waited for her departure. "The Lord gives and the Lord takes away, Noah. Though we prayed night and day, God did not see fit to bless us with children. I now know He had other plans. Noah, we all are given a path to walk. Sometimes the path is straight and good, other times there are difficulties and obstacles. We must learn to accept what God has given. This is the only difference between each of us. Those who choose to obey and accept the Creator and those who deny and fight against Him."

Noah could see that Mathius had struggled along with Hani for many years with this. Many take for granted the gift of children. "I am sorry. I did not mean—"

"Nonsense, Noah, you could not have known," Mathius interrupted. "All is well."

"You said Joshua wants to meet me?" Noah changed the conversation.

"It is not like him to ask such a thing, Noah. He pulled me aside after the meeting while the others were departing. He informed me that you and I are to accompany him to the river. From there, Joshua will explain the rest." Mathius stared off in the distance.

Noah's head was full of questions. *How does Joshua know me? How does he know I am with Mathius? Why does he want us at the river? This is no coincidence.*

The two sat awhile longer outside the tent, giving Hani some space with her thoughts. The stars lit up the sky, more stars than Noah had ever seen. "Come, Noah," Mathius interrupted, "we must prepare."

16

Noah assisted Hani and Mathius as they packed their belongings for the morning. Together they stacked everything neatly by the tent opening before lying down for the night. Hani and Mathius were asleep as soon as their heads hit the pillows. Hani made a sweet wheezing noise as she slept whereas Mathius released an occasional snore that rattled the room. Noah, on the other hand, couldn't relax. His mind raced with visions about what tomorrow would be like.

He thought about his father for a moment. He knew that he took for granted how blessed he was to have a man like that raise him. His father cared enough to bring him to Israel, to teach him the language, to love him unconditionally. He thought about the mother he never really got to know as a child, how she must have been like Hani and how amazing it would be to have her with him. He thought about Josiah and the great hall. And finally, he thought about how everything in his young life was designed and planned to get him to the Scepter of Judah.

Noah was soon startled by the sound of a twig snapping close by the tent. Someone was approaching. Noah held his breath so he could hear better. Hani wheezed and Mathius snored, but Noah was on high alert. He saw the silhouette of a stranger walking slowly around the outside of the tent where he was lying. The figure stopped near where Noah was situated.

"Noah?" the voice whispered. "Noah, are you awake?"

It was a familiar voice to Noah. "Thio? Thio...is that you?" Noah whispered back.

"Yes, yes! Come, Noah, we must talk," Thios returned. "Quietly, if you will."

Noah rose carefully from his bed so as not to disturb Hani and Mathius. He was already dressed for the journey in the morning, so he did not have to fiddle finding his clothes in the dark. He gingerly tiptoed around the couple and out the tent opening. Hani continued to wheeze, and Mathius released another snore. Thios did all he could to not laugh at the sound the old man made.

"Where have you been?" Noah questioned Thios, frustrated and happy at the same time. "I didn't know what to do, so I stayed with these people."

"I have been near you the whole time, Noah," Thios explained, trying not to laugh out loud. "I had to wait for the right moment. Do you like Hani and Matty? They are sweet people, are they not? I thought you may fit well with them."

"What? How do you...you know them?" Noah stammered. "Why did you not come sooner?"

"Of course I know Matty and Hani. You are funny, Noah." Thios smiled. "I had to make sure it was safe before I approached. No call for needless questions. Follow me, please." Not waiting for compliance from Noah, Thios turned and strolled away.

"Wait, wait, wait, how exactly do you know them?" Noah followed close by coaxing for a reply.

"Never mind that now. Keep your voice down. We can talk once we are out of camp."

Noah followed Thios as the two made their way through the endless sea of people. It was quiet now. Besides the soldiers on duty posted around camp for protection, there were a few Israelites still preparing for the morning travels. A few gave notice to the boys, but most kept to themselves. Thios moved with purpose. Noah stayed as close as he could.

The camp was situated in a valley surrounded by thick forest. As they neared the edge of camp, it was clear to Noah that Thios was taking him into the wilderness. They walked into the darkness of night keeping quiet. Noah had so many questions he wanted to ask but stayed silent until Thios instructed him it was safe to converse again. About a hundred yards into the forest, Noah noticed a small clearing in the woods. As they neared the opening, Thios's pace slowed, and he turned to Noah.

"All right, this should do." He took a moment to catch his breath.

"Please, Thio, tell me what's going on," Noah eagerly asked, breathing heavy from the hike.

"Oh no…you first. What have you figured out so far? Then… maybe I will answer your questions," Thios proposed as he sat down on a log, motioning for Noah to do the same. The light from the moon lit up the forest floor. The clearing in the woods was breathtakingly beautiful. There was a light easterly breeze softly blowing around them.

"Well, I know I'm not in Texas anymore, that's for sure." Noah giggled sarcastically shaking his head. He gathered his composure.

"Ha-ha… Funny," Thios laughed. "Continue, please."

"Well, Mathius said that we are moving to the Jordan River tomorrow. He and Hani have been wandering with the people for forty years, waiting. Did you know they were actually there when Pharaoh let the Israelites go? It's absolutely crazy to even think. But Joshua is in charge now not Moses, and he just so happens to be Hani's brother! But you probably already knew that! And Mathius is some kind of important person here. All the people look up to him. I'm going to meet Joshua tomorrow as well. Did I say that already? Mathius thinks he is going to find my dad once we cross the river too. I don't know what I'm gonna do about that one." Noah was spewing out any and every thought that came to mind.

Thios just listened patiently, letting Noah release everything he had to say.

"Oh, and good news, I still have the necklace you gave me." Noah pulled the medallion out to show Thios. "Mathius and Hani took a liking to it as well." The moonlight hit the medallion, causing the amber glow of orange to begin again, the same orange hue that pulsed as before. The necklace trembled softly in Noah's hand. And then it stopped.

Noah jumped. "What was that?" he said aloud. He looked over to where Thios was sitting. He was gone! It was like he vanished into thin air. "Thio!" Noah looked around this way and that. "Thio! Seriously, Thio, this isn't funny!" Noah was nervous, scared, and angry all at the same time. Frustrated to be alone again, frustrated by the unanswered questions clouding his thoughts, and annoyed by the unknown, Noah screamed, "Goodness gracious! Could I get a little help here?"

As soon as the words left his mouth, the medallion glowed even brighter, but this time was different. Instead of the cross dividing the engravings shining orange, it was the emblem of the wing that glowed. The glow from the necklace turned a rich shade of green. The light steadily rose in magnificence. The medallion's shine illuminated the entire forest around him. Noah worried that someone may see the light and be found out. He tried to cover the necklace with his hands, but it was no use.

In all the excitement, Noah nearly missed the silhouette of a person coming toward him from the opposite side of the clearing. The figure made no noise and seemed to float rather than walk. As the stranger neared, the light from the medallion calmed down. Noah stood, speechless. He glanced down once more at the necklace to see nothing more than the wing pulsating green.

"Noah, do not be afraid," the voice of a man announced, echoing around him.

Everything in Noah wanted to bow to his knees in response to the stranger's presence. He started to drop, but the voice interrupted, "I am not God, Noah. Stand to your feet."

"Who...who are you?" Noah stammered.

"I am Gabriel, Archangel to the one true God. I have been sent by God to explain your path, Noah." Gabriel came near the boy. He looked like a man and he didn't at the same time. His skin glistened in the night sky, glowing like fire. His crystal-clear blue eyes were piercing. His hair was perfect blonde, waves cascading across his forehead. Gabriel's body was wrapped in white linen. His voice was without imperfection.

"Noah, be strong and courageous. Your path is ordained by our heavenly Father. Before God formed you in the womb, He knew you. Before you were born, God consecrated you. Have no fear."

Noah didn't move. He was frozen like a deer in headlights. His eyes could not blink, and his mouth would not close.

"Tomorrow, you will meet with Joshua. He has been given instruction pertaining you. Obey his commands. You will cross the Jordan River with him soon. Stay near to him, Noah."

"Where am I going?" Noah asked.

"Your path begins in Jericho. There you will need to locate the first jewel for the Scepter of Judah."

"How will I do that?" Noah questioned. "What does the jewel look like?"

"The first jewel is green, the size of a walnut. You will have seven days from when the Israelites march on Jericho to locate the jewel. If you fail to find and take hold of the jewel, your path will end, and you will be unable to return home."

"What?" Noah was confused. "King Josiah didn't say anything about this. What do you mean I can't go home? That was never the agreement!" Noah's blood was hot. Fear rose in his gut, sweat gathering on his forehead from the anxiety.

"If you fail, the path will be forfeit. All the secrets to be uncovered by you will be hidden forever. Do your best, Noah. Be smart and cunning. Listen to your guide. Ask for help when needed. Do not be proud. The necklace you received is for your aid. But be on your guard. There are those who aim to thwart the plans of God. They too know you are here. They seek you out, Noah. Therefore, be strong and courageous."

"You can't leave me here like this! This is crazy. What does this necklace do anyway?" Noah asked, holding the medallion out toward Gabriel.

Gabriel ignored the question and peered intently at the boy. Again, Noah begged, "Please. Please tell me what to do! I can't stay here! I must get back to my dad. Gabriel, please help me." Still no response from the angel.

Gabriel stoically turned his back on Noah. Noah nearly lost control until he looked upon the departing angel. He blinked furiously, his eyes astonished by the amazingly beautiful wings folded gracefully across Gabriel's back. He ceased his ramblings and watched as Gabriel neared the edge of the clearing, almost out of view. Noah heard one last piece of advice speak from God's angel. "Call out to God, Noah." And he was gone.

The forest grew darker without Gabriel's presence. For the first time since finding the scepter, Noah was fearful. *How could Josiah not tell me there was a chance I would not make it? Why would God put me in this situation? God knows everything, He had to know that I would feel this way. If He knew, then He must have a plan. Take a breath, Noah, calm down.*

A chill ran up his back, causing him to shake a little, that same feeling he had in the airport.

"You ready to head back?" The voice of Thios almost gave Noah a heart attack.

"Where in the world did you go?" Noah was relieved to see a familiar face. He rushed to Thios and hugged him, more so to comfort himself.

"Thought I'd give you some alone time with Gabe. He is so serious. Do this… Do that… Careful with these…. da di da di do. Nice enough fellow, though," Thios answered.

"How come y'all didn't tell me about what would happen if I failed? Ya know…how I may be stuck here?"

"Would you have come if we had?" Thios stared right into Noah's eyes, freezing him in place. Noah had never seen Thios act so serious. He said nothing in response. Thios continued, "You will be fine. The Scepter of Judah does not make mistakes. Just keep reminding yourself that you were chosen. There are many who desire to be amongst those called by God. Some even try to force their way into His blessing."

"Anyone I would know?" Noah questioned flippantly.

"Come to think of it, there is one who recently, at least in the time we find ourselves now, tried that very thing. His name is Balak, King of Moab, the land where the Israelites currently camp. He along with all the surrounding kingdoms around here have grown fearful of the Hebrew presence in the land, a promise God gave Moses to keep the people safe while they travel. Balak saw the sea of people camping near his land and wanted to rid himself of his fear. Well, Mr. Balak thought he could buy God's blessing by getting a prophet for hire named Balaam to turn God's favor upon him."

Listening to the story and how ridiculous it sounded, Noah chimed in, "Are you serious? He actually thought he could buy God's loyalty? Not exactly the sharpest tool in the shed."

"You know, Noah, seeing what I have seen from man, nothing surprises me anymore. Well, Balaam sought God, and God warned him not to even ask for Balak what he desired. So the prophet told the king it's gonna be a no go, adios, and good luck. But Balak wasn't having it. Oh no, he was not. So the king, in all his wisdom, sent his men to get Balaam and force him to come to Moab and curse the Israelites! Three times he asked Balaam to curse the Hebrews, and all three times, Balaam blessed the Israelites per God's instruction."

"I bet Balak was spitting mad at that!" Noah laughed.

"Oh, you should have seen his face, Noah. He was so mad he had tears welling up in his eyes. He was screaming at Balaam, stomping around like a child, but the prophet knew better than to go against God. There was an interesting piece to the final blessing Balaam gave on the third attempt by Balak. Listen." Thios repeated a portion of the blessing of Balaam.

> The oracle of him who hears the words of God,
> And knows the knowledge of the Most High,
> Who sees the vision of the Almighty,
> Falling down, yet having his eyes uncovered.
> I see him, but not now;
> I behold him, but not near;
> A star shall come forth from Jacob,
> A *scepter* shall rise from Israel,
> And crush the forehead of Moab.

Noah perked up when he heard the word *scepter*. "As in the Scepter of Judah?"

"What do you think?" Thios smiled. "It's getting late, we need to head back."

"Hey, Thio, don't leave me again," Noah begged his friend. "I don't want to do this alone."

Thios nodded his head. "I need to get you back to Hani and Matty before they realize you're gone. Come, come…morning approaches."

The two boys departed the opening in the woods and headed back through the wilderness. The moon was high in the sky illuminating their path. Thios moved swiftly now. Noah stayed close, much more confident in the direction they moved. Back in camp, fewer people were awake than when they left. Those who were still roaming about must not have seen the light in the forest because none were seeking an answer. Once they reached the hill where Mathius and Hani slept, Thios stopped and turned to Noah.

"This is where I leave you."

"What? Not again, Thio, you said—"

Thios interrupted, "Yes, Noah, I know what I said. Go with Mathius in the morning. Meet with Joshua like Gabriel instructed. Stay close to him. When the time is right, I will come to you again. Sleep well, Noah." With that, Thios turned and walked away into the camp. Noah watched on for a moment. He was tired. Sleep was the medicine he needed. He crept up the hill and into bed. Hani was still wheezing, and Mathius continued to rattle the room with a snore.

17

Morning came faster than Noah desired. He felt as if he just laid down before he heard Hani humming away preparing a morning snack. Noah drearily watched the elderly woman as she used a tool to mash something in a bowl, adding a little water periodically. She removed the mushy ball and formed it into flat cakes and laid them over a small fire on a dish. As soon as the fluffy tortilla looking morsels hit the flame, a sweet smell filled the room. *This must be the manna.*

"Well, good morning, Noah." Hani noticed the boy watching on. "I will have breakfast ready shortly. Go ahead and get cleaned up."

Hani went back to the meal while Noah roused himself out of bed. He was fully dressed from the night before. He splashed some water on his face, straightened what he could on his hair, and gave one quick check that the medallion was still by his chest. She handed him a small piece of warm manna bread and a few grapes. Noah took a drink of water out of the jug close to his bed. The first bite of the bread was sweet and sumptuous. The flavor was like a Frosted Flake pancake dipped in honey with a shot full of vitamins and nutrients. "Mathius is outside preparing. He is waiting for you."

"Do you need my help with anything?" he asked, politely hoping to get another piece of bread.

"No, child, I can handle the rest. You two need to get moving. I will see you later this afternoon." She came close to him and gave him a big hug. Not just a friend hug either but a full heart-filled hug of a mother. It was enough to charge his spirits as much as the meal. "Be strong and courageous, Noah." She smiled at him, placing her hands on his shoulders tightly.

Noah shook his head. "What? Why did you say that?" Noah could not believe the words Hani used.

"Oh," she laughed. "Sorry. It's what Joshua always says. Be strong and courageous, Hani. When Moses passed on, God chose my brother to lead the people. God spoke to Joshua and said to be strong and courageous three times. He has told me that story more times than I can stand. In fact, I suppose he has told us all about it." She paused in thought. "He is a good man, Noah. We could have no better leader, in my opinion, and God's as well. Even Caleb knew he was the man for the job. Oh, look at me rambling on. Go, child, go… Mathius awaits." She brushed Noah along who was still speechless by her words.

The morning sun felt good against his tired body. His stomach was pleasantly full from the small meal. A strong cool breeze hit his face, causing Noah to shut his eyes and let it blow over him. "There you are," he heard Mathius call out. "Here, take this." He handed Noah a satchel. "Did Hani fill your belly?" He winked at Noah just like Arham would.

"Yes, sir," Noah answered.

"Well, let us be on our way. Joshua and the elders await." Mathius moved passed Noah to his wife. They embraced sweetly, and he gave her a loving kiss. The day they had prayed many years for was upon them. The people were all excited as well, and so was Noah. It was time for him to walk the path God ordained. "Come, Noah." Mathius moved ahead down the hill.

The nation of Israel was on full alert this morning. Each family, clan, and tribe were prepared for movement. They were veterans by now in packing up their supplies. Emotions were high. The end of wandering for their disobedience was upon them. Noah stayed close to Mathius. Walking through the people was different than yesterday. The Israelites were much too focused on their personal affairs to acknowledge Mathius. And the elderly man was not bothered in the least by it. He moved with purpose.

"It is a great day, Noah," Mathius called back over his shoulder to his companion. "The people are ready and excited…as am I!" Noah listened and watched as they traversed the camp back to the main area where he witnessed the meeting of the elders. Upon their arrival, the soldiers moved aside allowing Mathius and Noah quick entry. Noah's stomach moved with butterflies in anticipation of the meeting.

Noah studied the tent as they entered. At the far end, he could see Joshua conversing with a few others. He was flanked on either side by soldiers in full military garb. Mathius remained off to the side, Noah attached, until motioned to approach. Noah watched Joshua in amazement. *I wish my dad could be here. All the questions he would ask. All the answers to mysteries he searched out. He probably would notice so much more than me.*

The two young men Joshua was speaking to excused themselves and exited the tent. Mathius awaited permission patiently. Noah's heart beat hard and fast. Joshua jotted notes on a scroll before looking over in Mathius' direction. He quickly looked down to Noah, locking eyes with the boy. A soft smile appeared on the old man's face. He motioned for them to approach. Joshua's soldiers eyed the two as they moved forward.

"Blessed day." Joshua smiled. "My name is Joshua, brother to Hani." He reached out his hand to Noah.

Noah was stunned that he was going to shake the hand of Joshua, one of the greatest leaders in the history of the world. He swallowed hard, his mouth dry. He reached his hand out and clutched the course weathered palm of the leader of Israel. "Noah…my name is Noah, sir."

"I am thankful to meet you, Noah." Joshua turned his attention to Mathius. "Will you find Enud and Eliab for me? I need to speak with them about what we discussed yesterday. Meet me near the overwatch."

"Right away." Mathius nodded his head to Joshua and looked at Noah as if to say stay here. He exited the tent in the rear, leaving the boy with Joshua.

Joshua turned to the bodyguards behind him and gave a motion with his head, excusing the men from the vicinity. They walked farther to the rear of the room out of earshot, but not out of sight. Joshua returned his attention back to Noah. "That is better."

Noah said nothing.

"Would it surprise you that I was told of your arrival?"

Noah shook his head, indicating a no.

"I did not expect it would," Joshua said in a matter-of-fact tone. "Not long ago, I received a visitor in the night. An angel of the Lord by the name of Gabriel came to me. He told me that a child, taken in by my sister, would arrive in camp soon. He commanded me that I was to find you." Joshua waited to see if Noah wanted to speak, but the boy remained quiet.

"He spoke to me about the Jordan River. He told me of the City of Jericho. His instructions were clear. I am to send spies into the city in advance of our crossing. These selected men are to survey the land and collect information on the people." Noah nodded his head in remembrance of the childhood stories ringing in this head.

"Noah, Gabriel told me you are to go with these men." He paused.

Noah's countenance changed. Fear seized his heart. It was one thing to be amongst the nation of people protected by soldiers with Mathius and Hani watching over him. But to go out in the wilderness as spies to infiltrate a target of conquest? "I thought... I was told I was to stay with you. Gabriel said that I would cross the Jordan with you. He was very specific about that."

"And that you will, Noah. It will take our people a few days march to reach the river before crossing. By then, you will be back with Enud and Eliab." Those were the names of the two men Noah overheard Mathius was sent to locate.

"Did Gabriel say anything else?" Noah questioned.

"Come with me, Noah, we can talk on the way." Joshua motioned to the soldiers. One of them left the room and entered again rather quickly this time with a platoon of men. Noah followed close by Joshua's side as the group left the tent. The people outside cheered at the sight of Joshua. He waved to the nation and turned down a path. The people parted ways, allowing Joshua to pass easily. They all knew where he was headed.

Noah followed as the group of men walked up the side of the largest hill in the area. Atop the hill was an overwatch where an armed cohort was stationed. Once atop the hill, Joshua motioned two men dressed in linen robes. Noah assumed they were Levites because of their attire. The two men grabbed two rather large silver trumpets. At Joshua's behest, the men blew long and hard. The blast of the trumpets echoed around the valley below. The people froze in place and looked up at Joshua. In unison, they cheered loudly. The anticipation of God's promise was upon them.

"It is time." Joshua said to Noah. "The Tribe of Judah will lead the way." Joshua pointed. Noah watched as the people on the edge of camp began bustling forward. "Next, the Tribes of Isaachar and Zebulun will follow them. These three tribes are the point of our spear when we journey." Noah watched on, listening to every word Joshua spoke. Joshua could see how enamored the boy was. What a spectacle it was to witness.

"I can still remember standing alongside Moses the first time we set out into the wilderness. What a day, Noah, what a day."

Noah turned to listen closer. Joshua stared on at the people below as he spoke. "It was the first time we moved the Tabernacle of the Lord. Look there." Joshua pointed. A group of men wearing similar outfits as the two men who blew the trumpets were beginning their march. "Those are the sons of Gershon and Merari. Those two families are in charge of the Tabernacle when we break camp." Noah observed below carts being pulled by large oxen.

Joshua yelled out from the heights to the people below, "Rise up, O' Lord. And let Your enemies be scattered. And let those who hate You flee before You!" He turned to Noah. "Those are the very words Moses shouted the first time and every time the camp moved ahead."

Noah listened like a schoolboy stunned by the historical sight happening before his very eyes.

"Look, Noah, the Tribes of Reuben, Simeon, and Gad. The Levites are not warriors, Noah. They must be protected. Moses was very smart to organize us as he did. There are many nations that do not want us to succeed. They would love nothing more than to see to our demise."

"And what about those people? Are they not Levites as well?" Noah noticed another group of men dressed like the Levites carrying the Tabernacle.

"Yes, they are the Kohathites, another family of the Levites. They are responsible for all the holy objects inside the Tabernacle. They carry the Tables, Candles, the Ark."

Noah immediately perked up at the mention of the Ark.

"Our goal when we camp is that the Gershonites and Merarites will finish construction of the Tabernacle before the Kohathites enter the new encampment. This way, there is no delay in our continued worship of the Lord." Joshua watched with Noah. "Oh, and here now the Tribes of Ephraim, Manasseh, and Benjamin are to advance, flanking the Kohathite family."

Noah was shocked at what he was witnessing. As the boy watched the people move like waves in the ocean, Joshua changed the subject along with his mood.

"I can see that you are not one of my people."

Noah stared into the expanse of people, not daring to make eye contact with Joshua. He said nothing in reply.

"But I can also see that God has chosen you. Noah, look at me," Joshua urged the boy to turn.

"Yes," Noah responded.

"I know what you are feeling, my child. I too have faced similar circumstances. My brief time on the Earth has taught me that even though you have a path you desire to travel, God ultimately determines your life." Joshua paused. "You are undecided on joining with the spies…are you not?"

Noah took a deep breath. "I don't think I would have come here had I known what I have to do. I am just a dumb kid from Texas. I don't know the first thing about infiltrating an enemy land. I have no training on how to defend myself. I just don't get it."

"What is Teshus? I do not know this place." Joshua gave a funny look to Noah.

"It is where I live. It is very far away from here." Noah tried not to reveal too much.

Joshua smiled. "Would you mind if I told you a story?"

Noah nodded his head in agreement.

"When we left Mount Sinai on our journey to the promised land, our hopes were high, much like this day. We traveled for a while, working together as a fledgling nation. Tribes each had their duties. Moses led the way with great wisdom and humility. When an issue arose, Moses would speak to God for guidance, and we would follow his instruction. God is so good to us. Every morning, He sent manna from heaven to feed the people. Otherwise, we would have starved in the wilderness. We had no lands, Noah, no crops, no produce, very little livestock. Without His provision, we would have perished many years ago."

"Sounds amazing," Noah interrupted.

"It was…it is. But you know what never ceases to amaze me, child? The ungratefulness of man. Even though we had food to eat each day, food that required no money, no effort, no work, the people began to grumble against God and complain that they were tired of His manna. How could one get tired of food falling from heaven? To this day, Noah, my heart hurts at the stubbornness of my brothers and sisters. These ungrateful men cried out to Moses, complaining about how unacceptable the manna was. They wanted meat, fish, they wanted variety. God was not enough for them, you see."

"That's ridiculous!" Noah said.

"I do not know this ridiculous, what do you mean?"

"Sorry. I mean to say that it makes no sense."

"But God is good, Noah. He heard the grumblings of the people and spoke to Moses. He told Moses to have the people prepare, for He would give this obstinate people what they wanted. God caused a wind to blow, and blow it did. He sent quail upon the camp, so thick that men could swing a club and easily knock a few birds out of the air with little to no effort. For days and days, quail is what the people ate. The manna, it ceased to fall from heaven. Quail was our food for weeks. By the end of the second week, the mere smell of roasting fowl made me nauseous. And you know what the people did next?"

"Let me guess. They complained?" Noah answered sarcastically.

"Amen!" Joshua exclaimed. "They came crawling back to Moses, begging him to beseech God on their behalf. Give us back His manna, Moses! Please tell God no more quail. His manna is enough." Joshua paused momentarily for a guard who approached. Joshua nodded his head and returned to Noah. "Mathius is on his way up."

"Why tell me this story?"

"Simple. Because God's plan is always better."

"I know that. My father has explained it many times."

"Oh, I see…but explaining a story and having to live through the consequences are two different things, Noah. It is always easier to hear how someone else accomplished something amazing for God. It is entirely different when God calls you to be the one. I can still see in your heart that you are unsure about what lies ahead. The path is scary, I am sure of this. But the path was chosen for you by God. The very same God who not only provided manna from heaven to feed His people for forty years but also knew that manna would satisfy far more for far longer than quail."

Noah bowed his head, taking in the wisdom of Joshua. He knew what he said was true. Deep down, he knew he had the ability to go with the spies. He just needed a push. Before he could say anything in response, Joshua bowed to one knee beside the boy, put his hand upon Noah's shoulder, and softly said, "Be strong and courageous. God spoke those words to me many years ago. When Moses died and leadership fell to me, God told me time and again to, be strong and courageous. Noah, it is your turn now." The two locked eyes momentarily before being interrupted by Mathius and two younger men.

"Enud, Eliab…this is Noah, son of Solomon. He will be traveling with you today."

Without argument, the two men bowed in subjection to Joshua's command. Joshua did not seem like a man one would argue with. "You are to keep him safe at any cost. He is to you as I. Guard him with your life. You have three days until we cross over. By then, I expect you back with what I desire. Understood?"

"Yes, my lord," the men replied.

"Noah, this is where I leave you. I am blessed to have met you, my child. Your father must be proud to have you as his own. Be safe." With that, Joshua excused himself and pulled Enud and Eliab aside. Mathius approached.

"I did not know you were to go with them, Noah. I would have—"

"Neither did I," Noah interrupted.

"Is there something I need to know?" Mathius questioned.

"Just that I am thankful to have met you and Hani. You have been so kind to me."

"It has been my pleasure, Noah. You are welcome in my home anytime, my son."

Enud and Eliab returned. Enud spoke to Noah, "Are you ready, Noah?"

Before Noah could reply, Joshua returned and called Noah over to himself just out of earshot of the others. He bent down and spoke softly to Noah. "I nearly forgot. Gabriel said that what you seek is inside the city walls. I do not know what this means, but I assume you do." And with that, Joshua stood and left the boy with the others.

Enud and Eliab began to walk down the hill. They turned to motion Noah along. He took a deep breath, waved to Mathius, and ran to catch up.

18

Noah followed closely behind the two men assigned by Joshua to spy out Jericho. As they moved through the Israelite camp, each kept quiet so as not to draw attention from the people. Their journey was secret, their time limited. Every now and then, Enud would glance over his shoulder to make sure Noah was keeping pace and make a motion, acknowledging the boy's presence. Enud reminded Noah of a younger version of his dad. If he lived in his time back in Texas, he would have been a football player. He was stocky, his shoulders stretched wide across his back, his legs like pillars of muscle flexing as he walked. Eliab, on the other hand, was more graceful in his movement, fleet of foot, and quick.

Nearing the edge of the caravan, Eliab turned to speak with Noah. "The journey ahead is not long. We are closer to Jericho than you think. We will cross the river upstream where it is not as deep. Do you understand the water?"

Noah took that to mean if he knew how to swim. "Yes, I have been trained by my father."

"Very good. I am sorry for not speaking until now. I am honored to have you on this mission."

"As am I," Enud interjected.

Eliab continued, "We have undertaken many such missions from Joshua over the years. You are in good hands, Noah. I will say this is the first time Joshua instructed us to bring a child."

"I am just as confused as you," Noah answered back.

"Do not worry," Eliab said confidently. "Joshua has never commanded us to complete a task that failed. He does what he is commanded by God, so we shall do the same by him."

The terrain was easy enough to traverse. Just like when Noah's father would take him hunting in West Texas. The ground was rocky. The three climbed and hiked over boulders, nooks, and crags. The men stayed close to the Jordan as they made their way upstream. The breeze coming off the water cooled Noah's body, and the fresh air was intoxicating. Noah decided Eliab was probably in his thirties. He was a handsome man. His hair was shorter than Enud's, and he had a groomed beard similar to Joshua. He was muscular as well, like a soldier. He confidently moved up and down the embankment.

The two men marched in tandem. Their trust was apparent. Enud and Eliab must have been a team for years. They did not speak. They just knew what each other was going to do and adjusted accordingly.

Noah noticed early on as they were leaving the camp that each man had a sword at their side under their robes. He also saw a dagger strapped to Enud's right leg. *Must be a lefty,* he thought. Noah surmised they were something of a special force unit created by Joshua for delicate missions. Their mission now the City of Jericho.

Jericho. How many times had Noah heard that name since he was a child? The great walls of Jericho. Of course, at Sunday school, Jericho was always pictured in a cartoon illustration with silly characters behind the walls. He remembered a game when he was young where he along with his classmates walked in a circle around some blocks to the beat of a song, and then the teacher knocked them over, and everyone laughed. His father spoke often of Jericho as well. He would describe to Noah what the attack was like and the fire that followed.

Eliab made a motion to the others. Up ahead, the Jordan was calm in the fork. "We cross here." He glanced up and down the stream to confirm they were not being monitored and entered the water. With his long legs and strength, he made it to the other side with no issue, the water only hitting him up to his waist.

Enud was next. He charged into the water like a bull splitting through brush. He bounded out the opposite side like nothing. "Now you," he called to Noah.

Noah looked at the slow-moving river water. He took a deep breath and plunged in. The coolness of the river shocked his skin for a moment. The current was not as strong as he imagined. He pushed hard against the water. Suddenly, he felt his body start to give way underneath, but Enud reached out and grabbed him by the arm. He plucked the boy with one motion out of the water and onto dry ground like he weighed nothing.

"You good?" Enud asked.

Noah nodded in approval thankful for the man's help.

"Noah, before we go farther, I must explain a few things to you," Eliab spoke. He reached in his satchel and pulled out a few pieces of manna bread for the three. "The people of Jericho know of our presence on the opposite side of the river. They do not know that we plan to enter their land as of yet. I imagine they will be on alert for this. Whether or not they recognize us as Hebrew is up to God. We shall act and dress like them to enter the city. They will have soldiers looking for men like us, so be on your guard."

"What is the plan once we get inside?" Noah questioned. "Are we looking for something?"

Enud answered, "Weakness. How the people are acting, what preparations have they made to fortify their position, are the gates open? Will they let foreigners enter still? These are important for a plan of attack."

Noah listened intently.

"Our mission is to gather as much information as we can and relay it to Joshua. What he does with the information is between him and God." Eliab paused. "Now as to why you are here, Noah—" Eliab stopped talking, hoping to coax an answer from the boy.

"Oh...uh... I had no idea I was coming with you until this morning. I am just as bewildered as you. Joshua said to me go with Eliab and Enud, and he does not seem like a man you say no to. So here I am," Noah stammered forth.

Enud smiled and put his arm on the boy's shoulder. "Do not worry, little master. You will be safe with us."

"I imagine God has told Joshua that you are important to this mission. I have learned one thing over the years, whatever our leader asks us to do is the only thing we should do. No matter how difficult or confusing it is, things turn out well for our people," Eliab replied.

The three rested for a few more minutes, eating their snacks before heading off again. They climbed a small hill and traversed more rocky ground. Noah estimated they had hiked around three to four miles from camp. There was a cliff that blocked their path ahead. It wasn't too steep but required a bit of teamwork to climb. It was nothing too difficult for the two experienced men.

Once atop, they caught their breath and continued on their way. They scaled a hill on the other side of the cliff, and when they reached the precipice, the view was more fulfilling than Noah ever imagined.

There, situated in what seemed like a never-ending valley below, was the City of Jericho. The city was surrounded by thousands of palm trees and farmland to provide food for the citizens. It was like nothing Noah had imagined. A manmade fortress with walls wrapping the exterior on all sides, like a gigantic football stadium on steroids. Surrounding the city were small villages, home to the people charged with caring for the land. There was a caravan of villagers entering and exiting the City of Jericho on the south side.

All his life, Noah had pictured the walls of Jericho as one gigantic wall wrapping around the city, but it was nothing of the sort. There were actually two massive walls of rock and dirt bricks surrounding the city. At the bottom of the outside wall was an embankment with a stone retaining wall at its base. The retaining wall rose about fifteen feet high. On top of the outside retaining wall was a mudbrick barrier at least six feet thick and another twenty or so feet tall.

From the view where Noah and the spies watched, Noah could see that the people had constructed a ramp in between the outside and interior wall, which rose higher and higher. The interior wall was another fifteen feet tall.

In between the outer and inner walls, the people of the city had constructed living quarters and marketplaces for their daily needs. It was evident by the dilapidated buildings and filthy structures that those in poverty lived in between the walls while the upper echelon (nobles) ruled from the top portion of the city. Noah spoke, "I can see why Joshua sent us. The walls are like nothing I have ever seen."

"It is a sight for sure," Eliab answered. "But with God, all things are possible, Noah."

The spies noticed that the villagers were carrying newly harvested crops into the city. "They must be preparing for a siege, look." Enud pointed. "With the food from the surrounding land, they could lock down in the city for months. We may run out of supplies before we can successfully breach the outer walls."

The impenetrable city walls stretched menacingly in the valley. The outside loop around the city was more compact and had less room for people to live, but the interior of the city was open. Handmade rock-and-mud brick buildings rose even higher above the city walls. The people had constructed overwatch towers every hundred or so feet for an advantage in battle.

"We must enter the city today," Eliab spoke. "We need to see their water source and what preparations they have made militarily. Noah, I suggest you say nothing unless absolutely necessary once we enter the walls. The people know where our camp is located. They may not yet know that we are on the move, but once they find out, the soldiers in the city will seek to expel any foreigner from Jericho."

"Very well, but once we are inside, where will we go?" Noah questioned.

Enud smiled. "The best place to gather information, of course…a glass of wine at the dirtiest inn."

The men adjusted their garments to match the people of the land, discarded what was unnecessary, and descended the hill into the valley of palms. The villagers were busy harvesting the crops and hardly noticed the three amongst the many others headed to the city. There was a heavily traveled road worn in the land to and from the city gate. The spies walked closely behind a group of farmers with their families. Enud approached an elderly man who was struggling to carry his portion of crops and motioned to offer assistance. The man obliged the offer. Enud grabbed the crops and slung it over his shoulders. Eliab immediately followed and took hold another portion on his back. Noah stayed close by their sides.

As the three neared the city, the true magnificence of the wall came into perspective. Noah reared his head back to take in the view. He saw a group of birds perched atop the wall suddenly take flight and coast down the sides. It reminded Noah of downtown Dallas, standing next to the skyscrapers and looking straight up into the sky. In his day, these walls would do little to stop a tank, helicopter, or fighter jet. But in ancient Jericho, the loss of life from trying to breach these walls would be astronomical. *Joshua would know this already,* Noah thought.

There were soldiers posted at the gate. Their faces were covered by veils hiding their expressions. Noah watched their eyes scanning the people entering the city. The soldiers glanced in their direction but hardly took notice. Enud and Eliab easily blended in, carrying the crops. Noah did his best not to make eye contact. The three entered through the main gate unimpeded. The elderly man whose crops they carried motioned for Enud and Eliab to follow him through the crowded corridor. They walked in between the massive interior and exterior walls to the depot, astounded by the sheer size of the barrier. Once inside the depot, the three witnessed the massive store of provisions the villagers had been busy gathering for months in preparations for the approaching invasion.

The elderly man pointed to a place in the depot to drop the provisions and gave a nod in appreciation for their help. Enud made a motion with his hand to the man as if asking for food. The elderly man pointed down a walkway into the city center to locate it. Eliab shook the man's hand, and the three departed quietly into the bowels of the city blending in as they went. From the smell emanating from the area, it was evident that this was not going to be pleasant.

— ⟡ 19 ⟡ —

The quality of life in the city would not even qualify as Third World. The stench was almost unbearable. Dogs with matted hair roamed the streets. Flies swarmed rotting food left on the ground. The waste of humans and animals filled stagnant water forming a murky stream down the city walkway. The smell of sewage under Noah's sandals made him nauseous. What an experience for a small-town Texas boy, in the seedy underbelly of a pagan society. Idols were set up with burning candles and bones of small animals scattered about.

Drunkards lay motionless on the filthy ground. Children played in the streets, unfazed by the living conditions. They were desensitized to their surroundings. This was their life; this was their home. Noah observed awful sores on the people's skin from bad hygiene. Roaches climbed the walls, and maggots descended upon the rotting carcasses of animals left on the road. There were markings of different colors written upon the walls of the houses. Many of the people were covered by scars and tattoos.

As the three descended farther into the city, they entered the marketplace. The shopkeepers took little care with their food. Animal carcasses hung by ropes in the open air like a Chinese wet market. The poor circulation from the swelling population of the city made the rotting flesh putrid. For Noah, all he could think of was this must be what hell was like.

Noah heard screams mixed with laughter from the citizens. A few men up ahead were arguing, and it quickly turned into a fistfight. In the throes of the tussle, the two men fell to the ground and continued hitting and biting one another, blood spilling out everywhere. A group of soldiers approached the ruckus and parted the two men aggressively. One of the fighting men did not care to be manhandled and tried to fight against the soldier's commands. He was quickly dealt with. The head of the guard reared back and threw a vicious right cross into the obstinate man's face, sending a few teeth flying. The discarded chompers landed at Noah's feet. He was without words.

The head of the guard commanded the other soldiers to take the defiant man away. A scantily clad woman dressed in torn clothes covered in mud begged the soldiers to stop, but they ignored her. Apparently his wife, she pleaded for the prisoner. The frustrated soldiers threw her to the ground and escorted the man away. She collapsed, sobbing on the road alone.

The people of the city watched without emotion. None came to console her. None cared. There was no love in this place. Evil was the law of this dog eat dog world. The ruthless reigned here, ill-repute was king; there was nothing else.

Enud grabbed Noah by the shoulder. "Stay close." He, unlike the boy, was unfazed by the scene. It was, in fact, a great diversion for the three as they journeyed deeper into the city unnoticed. They wove in and out through houses and filth, doing their best to avoid the soldiers, monitoring the crowds. People impatiently bumped into them, annoyed at their presence. Random dogs were roaming around, scavenging for leftovers on the road.

The three made their way into the crowded northern marketplace of the city, a place home to the lowest of low in Jericho. This was where the worst of worst operated, the seedy underbelly of this ancient pagan stronghold.

Hanging from a pole near the edge of the square was a sign posted outside a small dilapidated building. It was made from scraps of wood and leftover materials that Noah could not read but the spies could. Eliab motioned for the others to follow. They cautiously entered the dark establishment. Wooden tables constructed from garbage, leftover material, and scraps discarded around the city littered the room. Wicked men were seated throughout, eating on day-old bread.

Enud spotted an isolated table, and the three sat down, careful not to make eye contact nor draw attention to themselves. A barely covered woman approached.

"What do you want?" she asked abruptly. Her accent was strong.

"Food for me and my companions," Eliab answered, looking directly at her. "And some drink."

She made a suspicious face at him. She glanced quickly around the room to check and see if anyone else had noticed the three enter. Once satisfied, she leaned over close to Eliab and whispered, "Follow me." She turned and walked to the end of the room to a curtain-covered opening. The men slowly rose to their feet and followed, careful not to draw attention.

Inside the new room, the woman closed the curtain behind them. She peeked outside once more to check if the coast was clear and then motioned for the three to sit. "My name is Rahab. I am owner of this place. You are from them, are you not? The people beyond the river." She was an attractive woman for her age, maybe in her late thirties, early forties. She had thick straight black hair tied back with a red ribbon to keep it from her face. Her body was tan and weathered. She had clearly been mistreated, scars on her arms and shoulders. Noah could see she struggled greatly in the city. Her confidence was gone, even though she acted tough. But she had the most beautiful inviting hazel brown eyes. She was dressed in less clothes than the other women Noah recalled on the walk through the city.

"We are." Eliab nodded his head. "Will you help us?"

"I knew this day would come. My people are with fear and dread because of you. We know of what your God has done. We prepare as a city now."

"What have you heard of our people?" Enud questioned abruptly.

"I have heard it said that your God destroyed Egypt. That He guides you on your journey even now. I overhear men speak of the Amorite kings and the wars. Your people destroyed Sihon, king of

Heshbon, and all of his people. You take the cities as your own and dwell in them. You killed Og, the giant king of Bashan, and took his land as well. And the sea divides before you." Rahab was hesitant as she spoke.

"What you have been told is true. We were slaves to Pharaoh in Egypt. The iron furnace was our home for four hundred years. The Lord brought us from Egypt with a mighty hand. The Lord showed great and distressing signs and wonders before our eyes against Egypt, Pharaoh, and his household. He brought us out from there in order to bring us in, to give us this land which He swore to our fathers, Abraham, Isaac, and Jacob. We will be upon the city soon. If you help us, we promise to watch over you and your family. We will keep them safe. You have my pledge," Eliab confidently answered.

The woman fell to her knees, tears filling her eyes. She grabbed the hands of Eliab and clutched them close. "Thank you, my lord. How is it that you would be so kind to someone like me? The people spit at me. They insult me. My son is mistreated because of me. I am but nothing in Jericho."

"God has smiled upon you, child," Enud whispered compassionately. "You were created for this very day."

"Who is in command of the city?" Eliab asked, wasting no time.

Rahab regained her composure. "An evil man. He tortures the people. There is no pleasing this man. He does not fear you. These walls are his strength, his fortress. Once they shut the gate, you must know there is no getting inside."

"What is this man's name?" Eliab insisted. He grew angry hearing Rahab describe what she thought was an insurmountable opponent.

"Natsa. He is governor of Jericho and leader of the city guard. He rules the people with an iron fist. His family assumed leadership over the city many years ago, and he will never relinquish control. You must know, he has lived here all his life. He knows every brick in these walls. You cannot scale the walls, my lord. Your men will be slaughtered." She clutched Eliab's hands tighter, indicating her concern over the loss of life.

"I assume he lives higher up?" Eliab questioned, pointing to the second level of the city.

"That is where they position the high citizens and soldiers." Rahab pointed to her place. "Here, they store the provisions and workers. The city swells at your approach. The villagers are pouring into the city now. They know that Natsa is closing the gate soon. Once shut, there is no entering or exiting the city. The people who did not arrive in time will be cast out."

"What will you do for water? We saw the food depot at the entrance of the city, but you cannot survive without water," Eliab questioned.

"There is a spring, but it is heavily guarded. Its only access is here inside the city. It is plentiful," Rahab answered.

"How long can you withstand a siege?" Enud questioned.

"Many years ago, our people survived a siege for two years from a rival kingdom until we defeated the attacking army who ran out of provisions. Most who threaten to attack Jericho fail and return home once they experience our defenses. All the people are trained to defend the walls, my lord. I wish I had better news. I am afraid your numbers are no match for the walls." Rahab was downcast in her answer.

"Our God will decide that," Enud boldly pronounced.

"Calm, Enud," Eliab motioned. "Rahab, will you escort me around the city so I can get a better look?"

"I can and will, but you must understand, I have a low reputation. My past is not easily forgotten or forgiven. I was a woman of the night and am treated as one still today. My family is mistreated because of me. I must live with the regret of my past. Just speaking to me is bad for you." She could not look Eliab in the eye when she answered. Her shame overcame her demeanor.

"Your past is not my issue. Your assistance is all I desire. Our God is a great God. With Him is forgiveness of sins. How awesome it is for your transgressions to be remembered no more?" Eliab comforted Rahab.

"You have an amazing God. May He smile on me as He has on your people." Rahab's eyes filled with tears once again.

"He already has." Enud placed his hand on her shoulder.

"What about the boy?" Rahab asked, regaining her composure looking in Noah's direction. "He cannot come with us. Go to my son. Tell him I sent you. Go now. His name is Ashem." She pointed to a door leading outside.

Rahab rose to her feet and excused herself to check on the inn. She closed the curtain behind her, leaving the spies and Noah together in the room. Enud and Eliab spoke quickly with Noah. "Our time is limited here. We have the remainder of today and tomorrow to gather as much information as we can. I will go with Rahab. Enud, walk the city perimeter. Look for weaknesses and soldier movements as well as location of lookout posts."

"What should I do?" Noah questioned.

"Go to her son. Speak with him and see if he can offer anything that may be of use to us. Keep low and out of sight. Do not draw unnecessary attention to yourself. The enemy is on alert." The words Eliab spoke resonated with Noah, reminding him of what Gabriel said in the wilderness about those who want nothing more than to see him fail.

Rahab returned and motioned for Eliab to join her. She wrapped a dark maroon shawl around her head. Enud departed close behind. Rahab pointed again as she exited to indicate to Noah where he would find her son. He watched them exit the room.

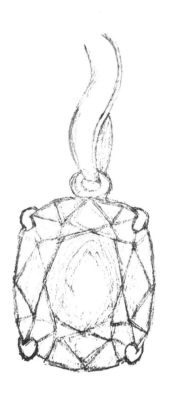

20

Now alone, Noah mustered the courage and walked out the back of the inn down a dark corridor that led to the rear of the building. Fear gripped every inch of his body as the scenes of the city played fresh in his mind. Entering the alley, he noticed a boy close to his age cleaning up refuse and discarding trash. Rats scurried beneath him, unfazed by his presence.

The boy was about Noah's height. His clothes were but rags covered in filth and holes. He wore no sandals. His dark brown hair was disheveled from manual labor. The boy heard Noah coming and turned quickly, defensive at the interruption. Noah realized too late he should have announced his approach.

"Who are you?" he quipped.

"My name is Noah. Your mother told me to find you."

"Well…you found me. What is it that you want?" The boy was defensive still.

"I am to stay with you until my friends return. Rahab escorted them into the city."

"I see." The boy's demeanor slowly shifted. He became softer and kinder. "My name is Ashem. I am sorry if I was mean to you. Most children want nothing to do with me. My family is not welcomed by any."

"Can I help you?" Noah offered.

"Oh, you do not want anything to do with this job. It will destroy your pretty clothes," Ashem jokingly answered, pointing at the pristine robe Noah wore. "Why do you come here, Noah? Are you fleeing the Hebrews like everyone else?"

151

Since Eliab chose to trust Rahab, he decided it equally necessary to trust Ashem. "You should know," Noah offered, "I am with those people."

Ashem froze at the answer. "I do not understand. Why are you here then? Does my mother know?"

"Your mother is helping us," Noah calmly replied.

"I see." Ashem paused. "Then I shall help you as well." He smiled.

The boys made a quick connection. In any other circumstance, Noah imagined the two would have been friends. Ashem had a gentle spirit much like him. He was a kind boy trapped in a vicious pagan world. He was cast out of society along with his mother and family, but he had inner strength. His quiet confidence calmed Noah's fear of being alone without Enud and Eliab. Noah nobly assisted Ashem in his duties and shared his repulsion the same.

"Hey, trash boy!" the voice of another boy echoed down the alleyway from the opposite end interrupting the small talk between Noah and Ashem.

Noah turned to see the silhouettes of two unknown figures approaching. One of the kids was scrawny and tall. The other was short and fat. By their clothes, Noah could see they did not live in this area of the city. They were from a wealthy family, and from the way they spoke, they understood their position. The looks on their faces seethed with evil. Beady black eyes and pointy noses made them look like trolls in boy's clothes.

"Who is that?" Noah whispered to Ashem as the boys neared.

"Oh no...their names are Laba and Nomed. They are not friendly, Noah. They think they run this city because their dad is governor. Just keep quiet, and I will talk to them."

Noah stood still. Ashem rose from the ground with his shoulders back, preparing for an onslaught he was all too accustomed to receiving.

"Arghhh...what is that smell? Is that the trash or you, maggot?" Laba joked, and Nomed laughed.

"I think it's his breath!" Nomed offered in reply.

"Who's your friend, trash boy?" Laba questioned Ashem.

"None of your concern." Ashem declared.

"What did you say? Not my concern?" Laba was angered by Ashem's insurrection. "How dare you speak to me like that! Know your place, maggot!"

"We should have you beaten for that!" Nomed screamed. "*Guards!*" The cry from the spoiled brat echoed down the alley. Noah looked behind the boys to see a cohort of ten soldiers sprint around the corner into the alley. This was the boy's personal bodyguard as they roamed the city. Not only did they have the opportunity and permission to bully anyone, there was no one to report the behavior to. The soldiers flanked the boys, awaiting orders.

"Let's try this again. Who is your friend, Ashem?" Laba asked aggressively, his confidence increased by the soldiers' presence.

Ashem reluctantly answered, "His name is Noah. He was hired by my mother to help me in my chores."

Nomed looked Noah up and down. "He does not look like he belongs here."

"Where are you from?" Laba questioned Noah.

Noah looked them in the eyes as he quickly thought of an answer. "I came with the villagers. I am here for protection from the Israelites."

"You picked the wrong family to associate with. Don't waste your time with this filth!" Laba picked up a piece of a rotting animal carcass and threw it on the ground near Ashem's feet. "Pick it up, trash boy!"

Ashem didn't move in defiance of the command.

"Pick it up…*now!*" Nomed screamed.

Ashem stared defiantly at the two evil brothers. Their tempers flared up by this poor kid living in the bottom rungs of society. He refused to be treated like the trash he was charged with picking up. Shocked by his disobedience, Laba picked up the piece of flesh and threw it once more at Ashem, hitting him in the face. The spoiled juice from the carcass oozed down his cheek. Yet Ashem stood firm, refusing to comply.

"Do what I say, maggot! Pick it up!" Laba demanded obedience. "Or you will be punished severely!" The boy's face contorted as he spoke, his countenance seethed with evil.

Nomed bent down and picked up a long stick lying in the gutter. He took a few steps toward Ashem and prepared to hit the boy. As he neared striking distance, Noah moved directly in his path, blocking him from swinging on Ashem.

"How dare you approach me!" Nomed shouted.

Laba was just as shocked at the defiance. "Guards, remove him!"

The soldiers advanced swiftly around the brothers and flanked Noah and Ashem on both sides. *So much for blending in,* Noah thought. There was no exit. One of the soldiers stood directly behind Noah and grabbed him firmly by his arms near the elbows.

"Now, let's try this again." Laba menacingly approached Ashem. "Pick…it…up!" Toying with this helpless boy was the entertainment the brothers were looking for. The more Noah and Ashem struggled, the more the boys seemed to enjoy themselves. It was hopeless to protest.

Ashem glanced at Noah, defeated. Not wanting his newfound companion to suffer on his behalf, he bent down and grabbed the carcass with his bare hands. He rose to his feet and looked at Laba. "Now eat it!" Laba commanded with an evil smirk across his face.

Without hesitation, Ashem raised the animal to his face. He closed his eyes and opened his mouth. Noah could not believe what he was witnessing. *Who do these kids think they are? What gives them the right to treat someone like this?* Noah wrestled one of his arms away from the soldier holding him captive and swatted at the dead animal, knocking it out of Ashem's hands and into the chest of Nomed.

The action enraged the governor's son. The soldier repositioned his grasp on Noah, Nomed rushed straight at him, reared back, and punched Noah squarely in the nose. The searing pain sent a shockwave through his body. Tears filled his eyes and blood rushed from his nose. The soldier let go of his hold on Noah, sending his body collapsing to the ground. Seeing an opportunity to release his frustration, Laba ran up and kicked Noah in the stomach for good measure. The brothers laughed at his agony.

"That'll teach you! Don't you ever get in our way again." The brothers stood over Noah, taunting him and spitting on him. The guards did nothing to stop them. As Noah lay helpless on the ground, the medallion fell out from under his robe, catching Laba's eye. He was like a moth drawn to the flame. Before he could inspect the necklace, the voice of man called out from behind the guards, "What is going on here?"

The brothers knew the voice and responded in kind, "Just taking out the trash, Father."

"Quit wasting your time with that boy. Time for your lessons. Return to the palace at once," the governor commanded.

Laba could not take his eyes off the medallion glistening in the light. He ignored his father's wishes. Instead, he started to walk toward Noah still lying in the fetal position in agony on the ground. "*Now!*" Natsa screamed at his boys. Laba looked at his father defiantly but was not stupid enough to ignore the command. He turned to look at Noah once more.

"If I see you again, I promise it will be your end," Laba hissed. Noah saw Laba glance at his medallion. He quickly moved his arm to cover the piece so no one else could see it. The evil look in Laba's eyes and the tone in which he spoke made him sound and look more like a demon than a human.

The brothers turned in obedience to their father. The boy's soldiers followed them as they exited. Natsa stood tall as the group departed the alleyway. Natsa was a large man. He stood over six feet tall. He had broad shoulders. His body was covered with golden armor. On his head, he wore a crown of beaten gold with a few multicolored jewels added for decoration. His skin was dark from the sun. He wore a large sword at his side, the handle made of gold. A few bracelets dangled from his wrists along with a handful of necklaces about his neck. Noah thought it unusual for a man to wear so much jewelry. The governor locked eyes with Ashem. "Where is your mother, boy?"

Ashem replied, "I do not know, my lord."

"Tell her it has been too long. Send her to me." Natsa looked down at Noah. "Who are you? Your face is unfamiliar to me." The gold covering the governor reflected the sun right into Noah's eyes, making it difficult for him to focus on the man.

Aching from Laba's kick, warm blood still dripping from his nose, Noah struggled an answer. "I am here with my friends. We came with the villagers."

"Too many unknown people in the city," Natsa whispered to himself. He stared at Noah. Something bothered him by the boy's presence. He squinted his eyes in disapproval. Noah could see the governor deciding what to do with the boy. Time seemed to slow down. The words of Gabriel repeated in Noah's mind. *Does he know?*

From behind the governor, a messenger approached and whispered something in his ear. Whatever it was changed the countenance on Natsa's face. The content of the message spread worry across his face. The governor immediately turned and called his guard to him. "Shut the gate!" he declared. "Shut the gate now!'

"My lord, the villagers are still entering. There is much crop to bring in," one of the soldiers offered.

Natsa, clearly uninterested in other opinions and annoyed by the interruption, turned his attention to the soldier. The soldier bowed his head, knowing the mistake he made. "Sorry, my lord, I did not mean to question your authority." Without saying a word, Natsa took a step toward the soldier and stared him in the eyes. In one deft move, Natsa pulled his golden sword from its sheath and thrust it without hesitation into the soldier's belly. The soldier choked from the loss of breath. He fell to his knees, blood pouring from his wound. Natsa put his foot on the soldier's shoulder for leverage as he forcefully removed the blade, wiping the bloodstained sword on the fallen soldier's clothes. He stared at the man as he lay dying in the alley. He glanced up at the remaining soldiers around him and repeated quietly, "Close the gates...or would anyone else care to disagree?"

None of the men dared argue with the governor. The soldiers quickly departed, Natsa turned to look back at Noah and Ashem, but something caught Noah's eye. In all the commotion, one of the necklaces that Natsa wore had fallen out from beneath his armor. There, hanging around Natsa's neck, fastened to a thick golden chain, was a green emerald the size of a golf ball encased in a gold amulet. The emerald jewel was breathtaking.

The governor, noticing the piece had fallen out, grabbed the necklace and returned it underneath his armor. Natsa slowly stared at Noah; Noah looked at the necklace, then at the governor. Natsa recognized the clear interest Noah had for the necklace. The governor looked down at his chest of armor and then back at the bleeding boy staring at him from the ground. An evil smile appeared on his face. He knew!

The governor, however, had more pressing matters to attend to at the moment. It was obvious that the message he received was about the Israelites breaking camp and heading toward the river based on the commotion in Jericho. The governor nodded his head at Noah and departed as quickly as he arrived. As he walked away, Noah saw Natsa turn once again to get a good look at him. Noah knew this was all for his benefit. The bloody nose, the kick to the gut, the sudden message, the objecting soldier—all so he could locate the jewel for the scepter. A jewel that was clearly out of reach but one that he must devise a plan to lay hands on.

Ashem and Noah were alone again in the alley. Ashem rushed to his side. "I am so sorry, Noah. You did not have to stand up for me. I am used to being treated this way."

"No one should be treated like that, Ashem." It hurt Noah to even speak still laying in the alley.

"I am thankful to know you, Noah. I have never had a friend. I know I have one now."

"Yes...yes, you do. Will you help me?"

"I will help you, Noah. What is it that you need?" Ashem asked.

"Where do Laba and Nomed live?"

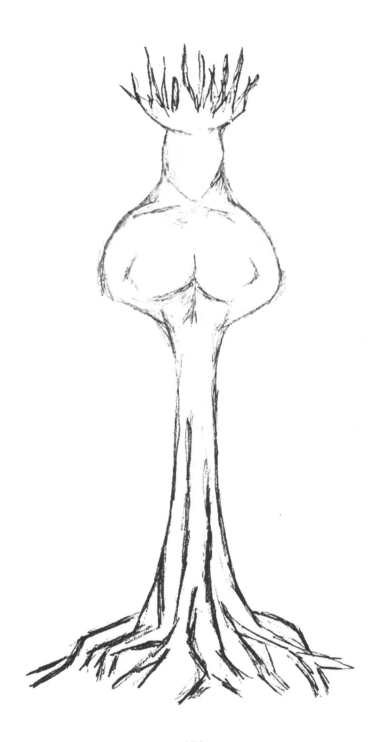

21

When Noah awoke, it was already the next day. His head pounded in pain, and his stomach ached from the vicious kick by Laba. He could hardly remember what transpired after Natsa left them in the alley. He found himself on the floor in small room. He was lying on a heap of hay covered by torn rags. Even though the walls were dirty and worn down, the room was well taken care of.

Ashem entered to check on his friend. "Good day, Noah."

"Ashem," Noah answered groggily. "How did I get here?"

"It was no easy for sure. We made our way down the alley, but your body gave out. Your friend, Enud I think is his name, he came and carried you the rest of way." Ashem approached Noah's side with a small brown cup of water.

"Where are my friends now?" Noah asked as he rose slowly from the ground, propping himself up on his elbows.

"My mother takes them once more around the city. They said you are to rest."

"Ashem, you must show me Nomed and Laba's home. You gave me your word." Noah knew his time was limited. He had already lost one night.

"This you ask of me is not possible. People like me must be given permission to enter the top of the city. There is another way, but it is not easy to travel, Noah. Are you sure you are well enough?" The concern on Ashem's face reminded Noah that he had a friend in Jericho.

"I must go, I have… I have no choice." Noah gingerly rose to his feet and stood for a moment, allowing his equilibrium to restore. He adjusted his robe and double-checked the medallion under his garment. The pain was throbbing throughout his entire body. Everything in him wanted to lay back down to recuperate, but this was his only opportunity to investigate the city.

"You are a very stubborn person." Ashem smiled. "I like you, Noah."

"And I you." Noah reached out and grabbed onto Ashem's shoulder to steady himself. "I am ready. How far is this place?"

"Come with me." Ashem turned and exited the room.

Noah took a deep breath, straightened his body, shot up a quick prayer of hope, and followed his friend.

Day two in the city was well underway, the sun was high in the sky. Once the Israelites cross the Jordan, Noah's seven-day clock explained by Gabriel began to count down. If he could not access the jewel by then, he was doomed to remain in this time for the rest of his days. Entering the alley behind the inn, the first thing to hit Noah was the smell. There was just no way to escape it—raw sewage mixed with rotting food, animals roaming the street soaked with grotesque liquids other than water. It was shocking to Noah how people could get used to living in such squalor.

Ashem glanced back at Noah to make sure he was following. Noah anticipated Ashem would lead him into the marketplace to the right, to some hidden passage. However, Ashem walked deeper into the recesses of Jericho, turning to the left and into the abyss. Noah hesitated. There were no people down here for obvious reasons. The smell was unbearable. Even the ground was repulsive. Every disgusting thing you could imagine littered the floor beneath. Like the bottom of a dumpster outside a New York Chinese restaurant that was left untouched in the hot summer sun for too long was the best description Noah had for the area.

Feeling as though he was about to vomit, Noah grabbed his robe and pulled it up over his face. "Where are you taking me?" he called out as loud as he could so Ashem could hear.

Ashem turned around unfazed by the surroundings. He smirked at his friend's struggle. "I warned you, this is no easy way to go. This place is the bowels of Jericho. All the sewer drain here along with trash from above. People like me are charged with cleaning the area. Not many can do this duty. We can turn back if you need, Noah." Ashem stood for a moment, waiting for a reply.

Noah shook his head. His eyes were watering from the urge to hurl. He squeezed the robe tighter around his face. He pointed ahead of Ashem, indicating his approval to continue and said but one word, "Hurry!"

Ashem turned and picked up the pace. He no longer checked his back to ensure Noah was close behind. He traversed the alley, quickly dodging the worst areas, hoping Noah would follow his steps. Noah did his utmost to ignore the surroundings. He visualized the end. Fresh, clean air was up ahead, and he knew it. Time was limited. Eliab and Enud would return with Rahab soon. Noah knew it was no coincidence that Nomed and Laba happened upon him when he met Ashem. And then the escapade with Natsa… God was at work; the path was prepared. All he had to do now was locate Natsa's home and the jewel.

Up ahead, the alleyway came to a dead end into a small cylindrical room the size of a large tree trunk. Ashem glanced at Noah and pointed up. He then entered a doorway to the room and grabbed onto a ladder hidden underneath the filth against the wall. Ashem quickly climbed the slimy structure about twenty feet up. Next was Noah's turn. He hesitated, then wrapped his robe around his face as tight as he could, freeing his hands for the climb. He grabbed the first rung and felt his hands slip a little over the slimy residue. The sensation nearly caused him to vomit. He mustered his courage, ignoring his inclination to walk away, and climbed the obstacle.

The repulsiveness of the climb helped Noah make swift work of the obstacle. Ashem stood at the top to aid his friend from the hole. Once out, a light breeze lifted the horrific aroma from Noah's nostrils, momentarily giving respite from the disgusting place he exited. Ashem returned the grate. "We are here," Ashem whispered. "We must wash ourselves or the people will know of our trespassing.

Come." Ashem moved to his right down a narrow cobblestone walkway. The farther they walked away from the manhole, the crisper and cleaner the air became. Now with the robe removed from his face, Noah could breathe normal once again. "Over here," Ashem called out.

Noah saw an isolated hand-chiseled fountain situated in an atrium surrounded by buildings. Water was trickling out of a pipe flowing into a large hand beaten copper basin. The overflow from the basin fell into a man-made trough carved into the street running the length of the road. The designers of the city had created a freshwater spring for the people to use that lived on that particular street. It was marvelous for Noah to see how they innovated their own plumbing system.

Ashem neared the corner of two buildings near the fountain. He removed a loose piece of wood and pulled out a linen bag. Inside the satchel was a few changes of clothes. "I leave these here so I can blend in more." The outfits are still but rags, but at least they don't smell like they were soaked in raw sewage. The boys quickly washed the filth from their limbs and changed their outer garments before being spotted by a citizen. When Noah removed his robe, the medallion caught the light of the sun, reflecting its colors around the atrium.

Ashem was mesmerized. "I have never seen anything like that."

Noah slid the clean robe over his shoulders, quickly covering the piece. "A friend gave it to me."

"Must be an amazing friend." Ashem smiled. "Ready?"

"I am." Noah nodded in approval.

"There are slaves up here who take care of the chores. People like my family," Ashem explained. "You must act like them. No eye contact. Stay out of the master's way. You walk on the sides, not the center of road. That is reserved for the masters. Agreed?"

"Understood." Noah nodded. He could see in Ashem's eyes the seriousness of his words. He followed closely behind Ashem as they made their way up the cobblestone street between the buildings. On his left and right, the apartments were built side by side. Space was limited. The area reminded Noah of the pictures his father showed him of Rome, each building attached the next to the next and so on.

As they exited the corridor, another rush of air hit Noah. He leaned his head back and took in a huge gulp of it and exhaled. How often he took for granted the little things in life! He could not remember a sweeter aroma.

He stood motionless in the hot afternoon sun as it warmed his still wet body and invigorated him with the energy he needed to keep going. If it wasn't for the sudden pull on his arm by Ashem, Noah would have stayed in that daydream for a while. "Come now, Noah, you cannot stand here."

Ashem kept his head down and moved quickly and quietly among the people like a little mouse trying not to draw attention to himself. The difference between the slums of Jericho and this area was staggering, far more spacious and clean. There were no animal carcasses on the road, no mangy dogs roaming the streets, no drunkards lying about or people screaming and laughing. The roads were clean and free from debris. The only animals Noah saw were well-groomed and obedient to their masters. The people were well-clothed and adorned with jewelry. The children played with proper toys.

Noah followed Ashem along the side of the road as it veered to the right and into a large open forum. Hundreds of people were crowding into the area, transfixed by someone or something. Noah moved farther into the square along the sides away from the masters, doing his best to stay close to Ashem but also trying to see what was drawing everyone's attention. Then, as he passed a short elderly woman, he saw it.

Towering ten feet in the air was a hand-carved wooden pole. The sight of it made Noah's skin crawl. The bottom of the statue looked like roots of a tree spreading into the cobblestone street in all directions. From the roots up the pole was carved like the bottle-shaped body of a woman, her hips, and her bosom. The arms of the woman were pulled behind her back like a queen showing her stature amongst the commoners as she strolled along. A thin neck led to a vacant face, no eyes, no nose, no mouth, just a smooth oval like a mannequin in the stores at the mall. Atop the head, a wooden crown burst forth in all directions like horns. It was like nothing Noah had ever seen.

On the ground, the pole was surrounded by an assortment of colorful flowers and burning candles. People were clamoring and jostling for position around the statue. Some stood and looked up at the object in reverence. Others bowed their heads, muttering words as if praying to the pole. Some were on their knees while a few lay prostrate on the road. The crowd was swaying and moving, chanting and mumbling—it was controlled chaos.

Noah watched as a well-dressed, middle-aged woman approached the pole and lovingly kissed the wooden structure, tears running down her cheeks. The crowded mass parted ways, suddenly opening a path. Noah watched as an elderly man dressed in opulence approached the pole, holding a live animal in his hands. The people hummed a melancholy chord as he neared the statue.

He removed a gold-plated knife from beneath his robe. The people watching on held their breath in anticipation as he raised the dagger in the air. The priest lifted the animal up to the pole and, in one deft move, stabbed the creature. He pressed the animal against the pole, allowing the blood to run down the idol as life left its body. The elderly man began to chant some words in a language Noah had never heard. The people around joined the priest, repeating the chant and swaying to and fro in place. The more they moved, the louder they chanted until the entire group was convulsing in worship of this pagan idol.

Noah stiffened as he watched the ritual. Part of him wanted to scream in disgust, another to run; all he could do was stare in bewilderment.

Ashem, noticing his friend was no longer following, turned to see Noah transfixed. He rushed to him and clutched his arm tightly. He leaned in close and whispered, "No... Noah, you move now! It is not safe here." He pulled Noah from his stupor.

"Ashem," Noah whispered. "Ashem."

"Not now, Noah, just move."

22

The swooning mass didn't notice the boys exit, their chanting slowly fading in the distance. The smell of fresh-baked bread now filled the air. Noah was still overwhelmed at how far superior this part of Jericho was compared to where Rahab's inn was—cleaner air, no stagnant water, swept streets, and well-dressed along with well-mannered people. *What a difference!* Noah thought.

Ashem was not impressed. He had been here many times, no doubt on disgusting missions and horrible duties to fulfill. He glanced back over his shoulder to make sure Noah was still following. He motioned his head as if to say, "Follow me down this way."

The two boys turned off the main thoroughfare and again into an alley between two rather large buildings. Once they were far enough into the alleyway and out of sight of onlookers, Ashem turned to speak with Noah. "The king's palace is up ahead. The soldier's barracks are near as well. We cannot venture too close or trouble will come. You must stay in the alley, Noah."

Noah, still shocked by where they just were, said, "What was that place back there…with the pole?"

"It is the goddess of this people. It is their Asherim," Ashem answered without concern.

"I don't understand," Noah questioned.

"The high citizens call it Morgotha. It has been here since before my family. Only those who dwell on the top level may worship at this Asherim. You and I are unworthy to even look upon her. This is why I pulled you away. The penalty for our presence is torture and death."

"What was that man doing? The one with the animal?" Noah asked

"He was sacrificing to Morgotha for victory in battle. They have been doing this more since your people near our city."

Noah thought for a moment while they waited and then asked one more question of his new friend, "Do you believe in Morgotha?"

Ashem locked eyes with Noah. "No, I have not seen Morgotha do anything but be Morgotha pole. She does not talk, does not move, does not cause anything to happen. Morgotha pole is just a pole. The people all scream and dance and act like Morgotha is god, but a god it is not." Ashem smirked.

"What do you believe?" Noah asked.

"I do not know. Your people seem to have the answer. I have heard the men in my mother's inn speak of your God. The stories of 'blood water' and locusts and the destruction of Egypt. My mother also told me of the war with Bashan and the Amorites."

"What war?" Noah questioned.

"I was hoping you would tell me." Ashem smiled. "My family have told the stories of Og, king of Bashan. We had a treaty with his nation for trade. My mother told me that he was the largest man she had ever seen, as tall as two men put together. They called him the giant king. Your people fought against Bashan. They killed his entire army and not one of your soldiers died! How can that be?"

"Amazing," Noah whispered as he listened.

"Morgotha cannot do this...no, she cannot. But your God, the God of the Sons of Israel can. That is a God I can follow!"

The two were interrupted by a loud rumbling noise coming from the end of the alley. The boys made haste and squeezed into a small crevice to hide themselves. Ashem peeked out, checking the direction from whence the noise came. Up ahead, he caught sight of a platoon of soldiers in full military garb marching forth. Once the noise disseminated, the two broke cover.

"Come...we move closer, but we can only stay for a moment. We must return before nightfall."

Noah nodded. "Understood."

They quietly walked down the alley to an opening. As they neared the exit, they stopped short of the shadows to keep hidden. Before them was the most amazing building Noah had ever laid eyes on. Like a majestic palace from the Roman Empire Noah had seen in history books, it was a man-made structure out of chiseled stones and magnificent rocks. Carved atop the rocks were ornate renderings of nature and man. White rock towers built at the corners of the palace lingered high above the city. Jewels of all colors lined the outside walls, reflecting the sunlight onto the ground below in rainbow hues. The palace was surrounded by guards like a fortress. At the precipice of the palace, a large balcony protruded forth, allowing for a view of all the city and the lands outside the walls of Jericho.

"That is Natsa's chambers." Ashem pointed to the main building balcony. "He speaks to the high citizens from there each week."

Noah scanned the palace grounds for a way inside. The area in front of the palace gates was large, about the size of half an American football field. Soldiers marched here and there under command from their leaders patrolling the area. Other soldiers stood guard at important positions in the square with weapons ready at their sides. The high citizens along with military personnel walked to and fro, discussing the affairs of the city. The only children Noah saw were young servants standing close to the sides of their masters. They kept their heads low and stayed quiet.

Noah again focused high up on the balcony extending from Natsa's home. He questioned Ashem, "Is there any way up there?"

"Up where?" Ashem looked at Noah and then followed his gaze up to the top of the palace. "Why would you dare risk your life to get up there? Are you a fool?"

"There is something I need to find," Noah calmly answered.

"Noah, this thing you ask is not possible. You cannot simply approach the palace, let alone walk across the forum without permission from a high citizen or a soldier escort. I am afraid there is nothing I can do." The concern on Ashem's face left little doubt that he was speaking the truth.

Noah continued to survey the area. "Besides the front gate of the palace, is there any other way inside?" Ashem gave Noah a confused look. "Like the hidden path we took to get here…there must be another entrance."

Ashem could see that there was more to Noah wanting to find Laba and Nomed's home than he revealed. "I must know, why have you asked me to lead you here? Did your leader give you orders different from your guides?"

Noah thought about it for a moment. *Could he trust Ashem not to say anything to his mother about the jewel?* Believing that God had led him specifically to this boy, Noah threw caution to the wind and offered, "The green jewel Natsa wears around his neck… I must find it and take it." Noah paused and waited for a response.

His newfound friend's expression said it all. A look of confusion and shock all rolled into one spread across his dirt-covered face as he twisted his head side to side in disagreement. "You are a fool for sure!" Ashem announced loudly. "The jewel is everything to my people. The man who wears the necklace controls the city! It is the signet of power for Jericho, the prized possession of Natsa and his family. He will do anything to protect it. He cares more for the jewel than he does his sons."

"I did not know," Noah somberly spoke, a hopeless feeling rising in his stomach.

"Is this what your king told you to come for?" Ashem accused.

Noah did not answer. He turned his back on the palace and moved away from Ashem into the shadowy alleyway. He glanced back again at the palace and turned around once more. So many thoughts and questions raced in his mind. *Gabriel made it sound so simple: find a jewel and take it… Do I just make a break for the gate and hope for the best? Maybe I hide until nightfall and sneak in… This is ridiculous! I'm a kid! I cannot tell Enud and Eliab about this. What do they care of a necklace? If only Thios were here.*

Ashem spoke, "Noah? Noah, it is time to go. We cannot stay here. Night is approaching—"

But Noah needed more time to decide on a plan. He began thinking about everything that had taken place over the last few days since his discovery of the Scepter of Judah. Suddenly, Noah realized he had what he needed the whole time. He looked at Ashem and slowly reached his hand inside his robe and pulled out the medallion Thios had given him. He scanned the colorful piece lying in the palm of his hand.

Ashem said nothing and moved closer to Noah in awe of the artifact.

"How does this thing work?" Noah mumbled to himself.

"What do you mean?" Ashem asked with his eyes transfixed on the necklace.

"Think, Noah, think. It did its own thing when I was with Josiah. But when I was in the wilderness, I think I activated it." Noah turned in place. He thought better when he was moving.

"Activ...what is this meaning?" Ashem was trying to follow Noah's trail of logic.

"What did Gabriel say? Call out to God." Noah looked at Ashem who stared back like an animal caught in a spotlight. "Here goes nothing."

23

Noah tightly gripped the medallion in his hands. He bowed his head and closed his eyes. After one deep breath, Noah spoke, "God, I need you…. help me."

The necklace immediately began to pulsate in his palm like the beat of a heart. Ashem, not understanding what his friend was doing, moved closer to Noah. Noah opened his eyes and looked down at his clasped hands. A pure yellow light was glowing from within. Noah's surroundings froze. Everything locked in place, the trickling water on the road, the dog scratching a flea, the marching soldiers and talking high citizens—even Ashem froze mid-sentence. Noah stood motionless in deafening silence.

Darkness, like an overwhelming shadow, covered the forum reminding Noah of the place he found himself before he met Josiah. He was isolated but not alone. Noah looked up to see the silhouette of a man approaching from across the courtyard opposite the palace. He was a tall elderly man by the way he walked. He wore a thick brown robe that skimmed along the ground. His face, what a face it was, shone like lightning in the bleak environment. He had a long thin gray beard hanging down to his chest. In his left hand was a staff to assist him as he moved. Noah squinted from the glow of the man's face.

It wasn't the same glow as from the angel Gabriel in the woods, however. Clearly, this was a man because he did not move with as much grace as Gabriel hovering above the ground. As the man neared Noah, the glow from his face subsided enough for him to look the visitor in the eyes. He was very old, much older than anyone he had met since leaving his father. Older, in fact, than any man Noah had ever laid eyes on before. The stranger stood for a moment, looking the boy up and down. He cleared his throat and spoke softly, "I am Moses." The man placed his hand over his heart and slightly bowed toward Noah humbly. "How may I be of help?"

Noah's mouth dropped open. He couldn't speak. He could barely blink. He was more shocked at the guest than the fact that all life had frozen around him. Here before him was the man who spoke with God, the Ten Commandments guy, the "Let my people go" dude from the stories. *This is Moses!* Noah was overwhelmed.

"How...or where...wait...you're really Moses?" Noah stammered forth.

"As far as I know, I am." The old man smiled at the boy's genuine shock. "I am but a man, my boy. I do not get to return here often. But God has deemed my service necessary. Therefore, here I am." He spoke slowly and softly, carefully choosing his words.

"What is it that you can do? I mean, I met Gabriel, and his color is green. He speaks the messages of God. What is it that you can do?" Noah did not know how to formulate the question in such a way not to offend the great man who stood before him.

"Show you the way, of course." Moses cocked his head. "May I?"

Noah agreed by shaking his head up and down vigorously. The old man winked as he raised his hands into the air. He held the staff with both hands and called out, "May that which is hidden be revealed." Suddenly, all remaining light disappeared. Fading into darkness, light from the sun, candles, reflections—everything. Noah and Moses were still in the same area, but darkness overtook the land. Then, appearing like an eraser of darkness, a glow began to stretch forth from where the two stood. Moses turned around to face the now hidden palace. Noah stood by his side. A path the size of a sidewalk of goldish hue started to push away from Moses on the ground like a vine.

The golden path smoothly crossed the courtyard nearing the gate of the palace. Before reaching the doorway, the walkway made a sharp turn to the right and led around the front face of the palace through multiple soldier positions; Noah could see the guards still frozen in time. Weaving in and out, the golden road wrapped around to the far side of the great palace. Noah moved with Moses along the path as it was heading out of view. Moses said nothing as the boy followed. They walked around to the side of the palace to find a narrow corridor that only a small child could fit through.

Moses nodded to Noah, inviting him to follow the path as he waited at the entrance. Noah squeezed through the opening, careful to keep his eyes on the golden ground. He shimmied his way through the crawlspace until he found himself in a small hidden room. The enclosure was some kind of storage area with miscellaneous containers stacked in one corner, a few dead plants still in their pots, and a couple other random decorations. There was a small door allowing entrance into the palace which Noah could clearly see, but the golden path did not travel to it. Instead, it approached the wall of the palace, illuminating something else. Noah moved closer to the wall and spotted a well-hidden series of rungs like a ladder carefully carved into the rocks.

Noah surmised whomever constructed the palace must have designed this area specifically for escape whether from an invading army or a fire. Whatever it was designed for didn't concern him now. Noah had his way inside. The boy stood and peered up the towering side of the palace. From this angle, he could climb and not been seen by anyone below. It was brilliant! The golden path began to fade away before his eyes. His route was set, the path defined, but the time was not right. He turned around and squeezed his way back through the corridor to join Moses. Upon exiting the crawlspace, time remained frozen, but his companion was nowhere to be found. Noah quickly retraced his steps back from the starting position, figuring Moses would be there waiting.

Without hesitation, he made his way along the face of the palace, across the forum, and into the shadow-covered alley where Ashem remained a living statue. Moses wasn't there. As he neared his friend, color returned to the environment along with sound and then life.

Ashem made a face at Noah. "Where's the medallion? You just had it in your hands."

Noah looked at Ashem, realizing that his position had changed from whence time stopped. "Oh…uh… I put it away." Ashem made a funny face. "I am ready to return," Noah continued, changing the subject.

"Very good. For a moment there, I thought you may try to make a run for it." Ashem laughed at the thought.

"We should hurry. Enud and Eliab will be back soon with your mother. Thank you for bringing me here, Ashem."

Before the boys left, Noah paused to memorize the forum and palace one last time and set the golden path to memory. In his mind, he retraced the steps highlighted by Moses. Ashem continued his lookout duties, patiently waiting on his friend. *But how will I cross the square? There are so many soldiers! Will there be this many when the Israelites are upon the city?* Just then, the people around Noah stopped moving and talking. The sudden silence caused an eerie feeling to overcome his body.

Ashem grabbed his arm. "Noah, come now. Hurry!" he whispered. The urgency in his voice was enough for Noah to immediately comply to the request. The two turned and raced down the alley, retracing the steps from whence they came.

"What is going on?" Noah whispered ahead to his friend.

"Did you not hear the bell?" Ashem was shocked.

When Noah was memorizing the palace grounds, he guessed he missed it. "No, sorry."

"They know that there are spies in the city." Noah's heart sank at the words. He had to make it back to Enud and Eliab.

They arrived back to the grate unnoticed. The boys made quick work of changing their robes and climbing back down into the depths of the city. The smell was still awful, but the fear of being caught far outweighed the uncomfortable environment. Now back into the alley behind Rahab's inn, the boys picked up their pace. At the far end of the alley, Noah saw a group of soldiers jogging in the marketplace. "Hurry, Noah!" Ashem blurted out as they ran.

The two hurriedly entered the back door of the inn, Ashem commanded Noah to sit and wait while he checked the main lobby. Ashem opened the curtain, and right as he did, Enud, Eliab, and Rahab came bursting inside. "Quickly, Ashem, to the roof!" Rahab commanded.

Ashem motioned for Noah and his friends to follow. He must have been trained to know what the plan was. The spies, still wondering why Noah and his guide smelled so awful, rushed up the stairs to the roof of the structure. Rahab remained behind on the first floor, diligently preparing the inn for a visit from the palace guard. Ashem led the three outside onto the roof. Rahab had covered the rooftop with stalks of flax earlier that day. The sections of flax were still damp, drying in the hot sun. The pieces of flax looked like wheat bundled together three to four feet in length, layered like shingles across the structure. "Under now." Ashem raised a portion of flax that was not attached, and the spies along with Noah slid underneath.

The damp pieces scrapped and poked the three. The wetness of the flax created a humidity bubble, causing the temperature to increase and making it more difficult for the three to catch their breath. Blood ran from superficial cuts on their arms and legs, but the pain was nothing compared to the torture they would experience if they were caught by Natsa's men. "Stay and be silent," Ashem whispered. "I will return soon." The boy quickly moved back down the stairs and out of sight.

The hot sun continued to beat down on the three hidden infiltrators. The air was thick, and there was little breeze on the roof to give relief from the sticky, hot environment. The pain from the cuts and scrapes along with the inability to reach the wounds was torturous. The three kept as still and silent as possible, even controlling how deep they drew breath. From below, they heard the commotion from the soldiers entering the inn.

"Where are they?" a man's voice screamed.

"I do not understand," Rahab answered.

"Don't toy with me, insolent women! I will throw you in the streets like the dog you are!" Noah heard furniture being hurled about. "Where are the spies of Israel?"

"Two men came to me, but I did not know where they were from. The men left already. Night is coming. They went out the gate before it was shut. Pursue them quickly, for you will overtake them," Rahab spoke confidently.

174

Unconvinced by Rahab's steadfast denial of the Israeli men's presence, the head guard shouted, "Search the place!"

"But my lord," Rahab protested.

"Silence!" The voice of Natsa entered the inn. "You four over there. You two back there. Go now."

From the roof, the three spies could hear the cohort of soldiers tearing apart the inn. Furniture shattered against the walls. Dishware broke on the ground. These men cared nothing for this woman's place of business. But in all the ruckus, Noah heard no protest from Rahab or her family. There was no indication that she planned on violating her promise to the Israelite spies. Her hope was planted in the promise that a great God and his people would remove her and those she loved from this pagan city.

Soon the commotion subsided and the men calmed. Natsa spoke again, "Rahab, it has been too long." The smugness of his tone made Noah's skin crawl. He could see him in his mind standing pompously over Rahab.

"My king," Rahab acknowledged her superior. Enud nudged Eliab at the remark. Eliab shook his head, knowing that they were heavily outnumbered and there was nothing they could do, even though the commander of the city was right below them within striking distance. "My king, I know not of what your soldiers seek here. The foreign men have already left. As I said, if you hurry, you can and will overtake them on the road."

Natsa spoke, "There are those who want nothing more than to see the fall of this great city. The Sons of Israel are on the move, Rahab! Citizens mentioned seeing two men and a boy enter the city yesterday and make their way to this area. Yet you do nothing to notify my soldiers of their presence." He paused to let Rahab speak to her looming sentence.

"I thought nothing of it...so many new faces have entered the inn, lord. I have not seen them since they departed, my king," Rahab resolutely answered. The sound of footsteps could be heard below and then a vicious slap. A body collapsed to the ground. Natsa had struck Rahab.

"Do not lie to me, vile woman!" His venomous tone echoed inside the inn. "I saw the boy yesterday! Where have they gone?"

Rahab answered quietly, "I know nothing more, my king. Please…"

"Where is your filthy son?" Natsa questioned. There was no response from Rahab. "Find him." Natsa commanded his men to search once more.

Noah and the spies lay motionless, unable to help their hostess below. Noah sensed the frustration of Enud like a caged animal beside him yearning with everything to leap from his hiding place and rush the unsuspecting enemy. Ashem must have abandoned the area. Maybe he put two and two together, knowing that yesterday's episode with Laba and Nomed would bring suspicion. For the next few minutes, Noah listened as the soldiers tore apart the inn once more. "Sir, there is no sign of the boy."

For a moment, Noah thought it was over then. "Check the roof," Natsa ordered the men.

The words caused Noah's heart to begin beating vigorously, and his breathing quickened. The only thing that calmed him was the grasp on his wrist by Eliab next to him. "Peace. God is for us," Eliab silently whispered. The footsteps of the soldiers approached quickly. There must have been five or six of them. They walked across every inch of the roof, stabbing the flax with their swords, missing the three each time. However, the pressure of their weight from above was crushing on Noah's chest. It took all his strength to hold back his instinct to gasp for air.

They returned below to their captain. "No sign, sir."

Natsa, unsatisfied by the unsuccessful search, huffed and puffed, then spoke again to Rahab, "I miss our little meetings, Rahab. We must speak more often." There was a moment of silence, and then Natsa ordered, "Position men around the marketplace. If you see the boy, bring him to me immediately. Prepare a unit, and send them on the road. Run the Hebrew infiltrators down. Dead or alive, it matters not. The rest of you, with me." As quickly as the commotion began, it was over. There was no movement below. Just silence.

·:·24·:·

Noah and the spies remained silent in their hiding place. They had no eyes on the area, so their trust was entirely on the goodwill of the woman and her family below. The heat from the afternoon sun relentlessly beat down on the roof. The weight from the thatch stifled the air. Noah could not take much more. It seemed like hours passed as the three remained motionless, their very lives depending on their ability to withstand the pain. Finally, the sun slowly began to set behind the city walls. Fewer people bustled below on the street.

Noah heard footsteps climbing the stairs toward them. It was Ashem. He lifted the portion of the thatched roof from earlier. "Quietly now. Follow me." The spies and Noah stealthily crawled out. The four made their way downstairs. Ashem led them back to his room where Noah found himself earlier that morning. "Stay here," Ashem ordered and left the room.

All three were drenched with sweat, blood dripping from their limbs from superficial scrapes. Eliab and Enud were calm and remained silent, not knowing if anyone was close enough to hear them speak. Ashem soon returned with a jug of water and a few pieces of bread. The three ate and drank to regain their energy. "A little longer, and we will get you out of the city," Ashem spoke softly.

"Where is your mother?" Eliab questioned. "Is she all right?"

"She finishes her work. Few soldiers remain close by. They must depart, then she will come to you. You stay." Eliab nodded his head in agreement. "Noah, come with me," Ashem motioned. Noah looked at Eliab for permission. Eliab nodded in approval, and Noah followed the boy.

The two exited the room from the rear. Ashem headed out to the alley where Noah and he had begun their journey earlier in the day. "You remember the way to the palace?" Ashem questioned.

"Yes, of course…why?" Noah wondered.

"Come," Ashem told Noah to follow him back to the disgusting sewer.

"Oh no, not again," Noah exhaustingly complained to his new friend.

"Please, Noah, there is something I must show you," Ashem protested, and Noah followed. The sun was nearly set. Ashem lit a small candle to illumine their surroundings. Once they reached the tunnel, Ashem turned to Noah and pointed down a hidden corridor. "Here, this shaft leads out of the city. It drains the waste under the walls when it rains. Very few know of this place. Noah, this is the only way into Jericho now that the gates are shut. You and your friends will leave tonight. If you want back inside for the jewel, you must enter through here."

"Where does it come out?" Noah questioned, only able to see the entrance from Ashem's view.

"My mother plans to lower you all from the wall when it is dark. The entrance is nearby on the northside of the city. It is not hard to find. Just follow the smell and look for standing water." Ashem smiled, knowing Noah's feelings about the horrific aroma. "Be careful on days of rain, for the water moves quickly. If you decide to return, come to my room and wait. I will look for you." At that, Ashem led Noah back inside the inn. The two boys found Enud, Eliab, and Rahab already discussing their escape.

"How did they know?" Enud questioned Rahab accusingly as he paced the room.

"The boy yesterday." Rahab looked up at Noah. "Natsa's sons knew he looked out of place. Once your presence was confirmed by the old man, the palace guard knew right where to come. You must leave the city tonight. The soldiers will return."

"Very well," Eliab spoke. "How will you get us out undetected?"

"There is a way, follow me." Rahab looked at Ashem. "Get the rope." The boy left the room quickly. The spies and Noah followed Rahab out of the main area of the inn, back through a hallway and into her living quarters. She approached the wall at the rear of the room, pulled back a curtain, uncovering a window. Noah moved toward the wall and peeked his head out. He had no idea her home was nestled against the outer wall. The view was spectacular. The window was at least twenty feet from the ground.

"What a view," Noah whispered.

"It is the best part of my home," Rahab replied. "This is where you exit," she said to the spies. "Before I help you leave, you must promise me my family will be spared. I have dealt kindly with you, risking my life and my family's well-being. Will you also deal kindly with my father's household?"

Enud reached for a red piece of cloth lying on a bench at the far end of the room. He approached Rahab and spoke. "We are thankful for your assistance. We will keep your family safe." He handed her the red piece of cloth. "This will be our pledge of truth. Tie it to a string and hang it from your window. This is to be a signal to our men to spare your family."

Eliab interrupted, "Our lives for yours if you do not tell our business to anyone. When we enter the city, tie another red piece of cloth to the front door but not until we enter. Your family must remain inside this place." He looked at Ashem and continued, "If they leave the inn, we are not responsible for their welfare. We will come for you, Rahab, you have my word."

"I will do as you say, my lord." Rahab bowed her head.

"You have done far more than we could ask. May God bless you and your family until that day," Eliab said.

Ashem attached the rope to a secure area on the wall and lowered it down. Enud boldly went first. It was a tight squeeze for him out of the window, but once he was free, he scaled the wall easily with his strong shoulders, barely making a sound. Eliab was next. He moved even faster. Finally, it was Noah's turn. Before he left, Ashem approached. "I am most thankful for your friendship, Noah. I hope we meet again."

"As am I, Ashem." Noah hugged his friend. When he was close, he whispered to Ashem, "I will see you soon." Noah stepped back, and Ashem smiled. Noah turned and made his way carefully to the edge of the window. Never too fond of heights, Noah took a deep breath, swallowed hard, held on to the rope with all his strength, and began the descent. He kept his eyes forward toward the wall and slowly slid down the rope to his friends below.

Once down, Enud shook the rope to motion Ashem that it was okay to raise it back. The boy quickly recoiled the rope and shut the curtain. Darkness spread over the land. "Ready?" Eliab whispered to Noah.

He nodded. And with that, the three headed back. Noah took note of the area, memorizing the landmarks. This was it, the doorway into the city, the path that was created for him to reach the jewel. He would be back.

25

The three journeyed through the night. Every so often, they would stop and hide in a bush or behind large rocks and wait to make sure they weren't followed by Natsa's men. Eliab instructed Noah not to speak unless absolutely necessary. It wasn't long until they found themselves back at the hill they traversed near the Jordan. Together, they climbed the side, each exhausted, each relying on the other to pull them through. Once they reached the precipice, they could see the morning sun cresting on the horizon behind the mountains. Noah looked upon the waters of the Jordan once again and at the multitude of Israel downstream preparing to cross. Just the sight of the nation of Israel gave them an extra burst of energy to finish the journey.

The three hastily crossed the Jordan upstream to avoid being noticed by the people. Once across, Eliab moved stealthily along the river's edge to the caravan, Enud and Noah in tow.

The mood of the people was one of elation. Kids were playing, women laughing, the men handled the animals. All waited patiently for their marching orders. Eliab, Enud, and Noah strolled virtually unnoticed to Joshua's Tent of Meeting. At the bottom of the hill where the tent was located, Eliab stopped to speak with a commander who answered directly to Joshua. He turned and walked up the hill. Eliab motioned for his companions to follow. Noah's legs ached at the climb. Exhaustion was creeping in from the midnight trek. His adrenaline was wearing off.

Atop the hill, the three found Joshua conversing with the elders once more. Noah listened in. "The Lord said you shall command the priests who are to carry the Ark of the Covenant, saying, 'When you come to the edge of the waters of the Jordan, you shall stand still in the Jordan.' Behold the Ark of the Covenant is crossing over ahead of you into the Jordan. Now, then, take for yourselves twelve men from the tribes of Israel, one man for each tribe. It shall come about when the soles of the feet of the priests who carry the Ark of the Lord, the Lord of all the earth, rest in the waters of the Jordan, the waters of the Jordan will be cut off and the waters which are flowing down from above will stand in one heap. The twelve men shall—" Then silence.

Joshua, noticing the arrival of Noah and the spies, cut short his speech, quickly disbanded the meeting, and had the room cleared for the report from Eliab. The elders quickly exited, understanding that the interruption and their leader's reaction deemed the intrusion understandable. The two men spoke quietly to the side while Enud and Noah stood by patiently. Eliab was quick in his reconnaissance, knowing that time was limited.

On their walk back that evening, Noah overheard Eliab and Enud discussing the most pressing information to present to Joshua in order of importance. From Jericho's stores of provisions, water supply source, military movements, lookout positions, and the land surrounding the city. They discussed what Rahab had said about the failed siege, the governor of the city Natsa, and the pledge they made to the woman for her assistance. Noah decided it best not to speak of the underground entrance his friend showed him before their exit, believing that the information shared by Ashem was for his benefit alone.

Eliab ended the conversation, "Surely the Lord has given all the land into our hands. The inhabitants of the land have melted away before us. Fear has gripped them Joshua. We could see it in their eyes, my lord. They have heard the stories of our people."

Joshua listened intently to the report. He only interrupted a few times for additional details from his confidant. Once Eliab was finished, Joshua waved Enud and Noah over. "I am aware of the great risk you three took on behalf of our people. For this, I am eternally grateful. The information you gathered will be more useful than you can imagine. The rest is up to God. Eliab and Enud, go to your tribe and prepare to cross. Speak nothing of this to anyone."

The two men bowed in reverence to their commander.

Before they departed, each exchanged goodbyes with Noah. "You are a brave boy, Noah," Enud spoke. "It is my honor to know you." He gave Noah a great bear hug.

"I will second that." Eliab embraced Noah as well. "Be strong and courageous, my friend," he whispered with a smile. And with that, the two men exited, leaving Noah alone with Joshua.

Noah turned back to Joshua who was staring at him. Joshua waited a minute before speaking, measuring the boy's attitude. Noah could hardly look him in the eyes. "Is there anything you would like to add?" Joshua questioned. His tone inviting, understanding, like a father speaking to his son, Noah was disarmed.

"What do you mean?" Noah replied.

"I am first commanded by God to have you, a mere child, enter Jericho with my most trusted warriors. Then you return to me clearly beaten and bruised in the process. I knew what to expect from Eliab and Enud. I have known them since they were children. You, however, are a mystery to me." Joshua paused, making sure he had the boy's full attention. "Noah, I can only help as much as you allow me. Have I not shown myself trustworthy?"

Noah threw caution to the wind and spoke, "I befriended a boy in the city. He is the son of Rahab, the one whom Eliab spoke of. His name is Ashem. I have seen far more of the city than I let on. More than Eliab and Enud. I know where the king sleeps." Noah stopped.

Joshua nodded his head as he processed the revelation. "What else must I know?" Joshua questioned.

"There is another way into the city besides the main gate." Noah had to trust Joshua. Why else would God have put him there? "Ashem showed it to me last night before we left."—Noah moved toward Joshua—"I believe the way is meant for me alone. I must go back. There is something I must do."

"And what is this task God has for you?" Joshua rubbed his hand over his beard.

"Natsa, the king of Jericho, wears a necklace. Attached to the necklace is a green jewel. Ashem explained to me the possessor of the jewel controls Jericho. I must find it and take it." Noah waited for Joshua's response. The head of the Israelite people turned his back on the boy and paced the room a moment.

"Is this your desire? To rule the city of Jericho?" Joshua was confused.

"No, not at all. God has commanded me to take this jewel. What He wants me to do after that is up to Him."

Joshua looked deeply into Noah's eyes, searching for any hint of dishonesty. He approached Noah and dropped to one knee, putting himself near eye level and said, "Then the jewel you must have, Noah, son of Solomon. Come with me."

Noah followed Joshua outside the tent, joining once again with the elders and the Levitical priests. Joshua motioned for Noah to stay put. He walked ahead and spoke to a priest. The priest was nearly the same age as Mathius. He was not quite as tall as Joshua. His beard was long, colored a mixture of brown and gray. He had friendly blue eyes. His presence was inviting. His robe was bright white, made from linen and more opulent than the others, clearly the head of the group. Joshua turned to introduce Noah. "Noah, may I introduce Eleazer, High Priest of Israel."

Noah bowed to honor the man he had read about in the Bible, the very son of Aaron, Moses's brother.

Eleazar spoke, "Joshua mentioned you yesterday. It is my pleasure to make your acquaintance. Perhaps we may speak again once the day's excitement is over."

His voice reminded him of Gandalf from the *Lord of the Rings* played by Ian McKellen. Noah was in awe. "I would be honored, sir." He shook Eleazer's hand.

Joshua interrupted, "Excuse me." He walked ahead to the precipice of the hill and looked out over the nation of Israel. He waited a moment as the people quieted down. The Sons of Israel looked up and listened intently to the words that were about to be spoken. Joshua raised his hands above his head and leaned his head back to give thanks to God. The people below fell to their knees in reverence.

"Heavenly Father," Joshua began. Noah bowed low as well beside Eleazer. His father would be overwhelmed by what he was witnessing—the nation of Israel on the edge of the promised land. He was listening to Joshua pray while kneeling beside the High Priest of Israel! *This is crazy!*

Joshua continued, "Oh Lord, my God! Has any people heard the voice of God speaking in the midst of the fire as we have heard it and survived? Or has a god tried to take for himself a nation from within another nation by trials, by signs and wonders and by war and by a mighty hand and by an outstretched arm and by great terrors as the Lord your God did for you in Egypt before our eyes? To you it was shown that you might know that the Lord, He is God." Joshua addressed the people while pointing to the heavens.

"There is no other besides Him. Out of the heavens, He let you hear His voice to disciple you. And on earth, He let you see His great fire, and you heard His words from the midst of fire. Because He loved your fathers, therefore He chose their descendants after them." The people cheered at the words of Joshua, words spoken to them before by Moses, words to rally and remind the people to continue their pursuit of God their father.

"And He personally brought you from Egypt by His great power, driving out from before you nations greater and mightier than you, to bring you in and to give you their land for an inheritance as it is today. Know, therefore, today and take it to your heart that the Lord, He is God in heaven above and on the earth below. There is no other." And all the people along the Jordan River and on the hills and in the valley in unison announced, "Amen!"

"My people, I beseech you to keep His statutes and commandments which we were given many years ago that it may go well with you and your children after you and that you may live long on the land which the Lord your God is giving us this day and for all time. Each of you must decide." The words of Joshua riled something from within Noah that he never felt before—the Word of God coming alive right before his eyes. All the truth, all the lessons, the stories from his father, here it was before him, standing with the fledgling nation who had wandered in the desert for forty years, patiently waiting on God to open the way. A people fed by manna from heaven, whose clothes did not wear out, whose shoes never broke under travel. A people blessed. A people chosen.

Joshua continued, "Today, you will once again witness the power of our God. Remember what He has done for you. Remember His great strength. Remember His patience. My people, be strong and courageous." With that, Joshua ceased speaking, and the people cheered enthusiastically. The roar was deafening. Without any doubt, the thunderous echo from the nation of Israel was heard for miles, striking fear into the hearts of the Canaanites.

—·✧· 26 ·✧·—

"Would you be so kind as to escort an old man to the water?" from behind Noah, Eleazer calmly asked.

"Yes, it would be my honor." Noah could not believe how close he was going to be to witness the miracle. He walked beside the High Priest, allowing him to brace his weight for balance as they slowly descended the hill. There, waiting below, was a group of Levites. Eleazar moved ahead of Noah and spoke to the group. Four of the priests exited to the side to a wagon parked nearby. There was a stretch of thick red cloth covering the wagon. Two of the men threw back the cover revealing the most amazing object Noah had ever laid eyes on. "The Ark!" he exclaimed.

Covered from top to bottom by gold, the Ark sparkled in the morning sun. Two hand-beaten angels perched atop the golden box, wings spread across like eagle's wings covering her chicks in shadow. It was just like the drawings from his father's journal. Each of the four men took their positions at the corners, allowing the golden cast poles to rest on their shoulders. In one deft movement, the Ark was up, and the men were walking.

They waited for the High Priest. Eleazar pointed upstream away from the camp. The men carrying the Ark made their way along the bank of the Jordan. The people situated near the river bowed in reverence of the object as the men journeyed farther and farther up the river. Once they were a good distance away—about a half a mile in Noah's estimation—the priests stopped and looked back to Eleazar and Joshua. Eleazar glanced over to Joshua who nodded his head.

Eleazar then raised a hand high. The men carrying the Ark slowly entered the moving river.

"My boy," Eleazar whispered, "behold…the power of God."

Noah stood motionless, expectant of a miracle. He held his breath and planted his feet firmly on the grassy embankment in anticipation with the rest of the Israel. Noah overheard Eleazar quietly praying to himself.

What happened next was beyond anything Noah could have ever imagined. Keep in mind, this was a boy who grinded fantasy-infused video games with his buddies on the weekends. A small-town boy who watched action-packed superhero movies in gigantic movie theaters. He also read hundreds of comic books and novels about made up faraway lands. With all that background, nothing compared to the sight taking form right in front of his eyes.

As the four priests entered deeper into the river, the water reaching each of their knees, an abnormal breeze began to blow from the south. It started light and then picked up in intensity. However, the stream of air was only blowing within the banks of the Jordan. The people standing on land away from the river's edge could only see the water ripple from the wind, unable to feel the gust.

The water beneath the men holding the Ark began to recede back from whence it came upstream. Like a reverse mud slide or avalanche, the water stacked on top of itself as it moved farther and farther upstream, creating a gigantic moving wall. Noah watched in amazement as this impossible act of nature occurred before him. It was like a backward tsunami. *Water isn't supposed to be able to do this! It's not rocks or dirt! One cannot simply stack water on top of water!* This was a violation of nature's law! And the sound, the rushing wind, was like a train. The water sloshed against itself as it moved farther away and stacked higher and higher.

The Sons of Israel fell to their knees and bowed their heads, honoring the power of God. This was not the first time they witnessed the work of God, and they knew who should be praised. Overwhelmed, Noah dropped to the ground as well.

"How can it be, Lord?" Noah prayed quietly to himself. "Why would you bless me like this? I am not worthy to witness this. Thank you, God. Thank you for loving me and choosing me. Thank you for all You do. My life is Yours, Lord." Tears filled his eyes. He gathered himself, wiped away the tears, and as he rose to his feet, everything around him was changed. The gust of wind that powerfully pulled the water upstream was gone and with it every drop of water. It was as if there was never a river to begin with! There was a riverbed but no mud, no flailing fish, no algae-covered rocks. The ground on which the men with the Ark stood was dry. Dry as the sand in the Sahara Desert. All the people of Israel stood motionless and quietly awaited the command.

Joshua was the first to move. He walked out upon the dry riverbed and gave thanks once more to God. He motioned to his men, and with that, the people began to cross. First came Eleazar and the Levites. Following close to them, the elders. Once the people saw the leaders crossing, their confidence grew, and one by one, ten by ten, hundred by hundred, they entered the waterless riverbed.

Noah started his entrance. He was shocked at how dry the bottom was. No mud, no slush, not even a puddle. Halfway into the river floor, he felt a tug on his robe. He turned to see who it was. "Good day, Noah," Thios announced.

A huge smile appeared on Noah's face. He embraced his friend, happy to see someone familiar. "Thio!"

"Special day this is." Thios pulled Noah aside. The two boys stood where just moments ago, a powerful river flowed. The Israelites were walking around them in droves. Like an obstacle, the people parted around the boys as they stood there. It was as if the people could not see them but knew they had to go around.

Noah looked at the people passing by. Their faces were happy and confident. They assisted each other as they crossed the dry riverbed. Nearby, Joshua barked orders to his men to help where it was needed. Eleazar and the elders encouraged the people. The stronger younger men took hold of their elders as they traversed the uneven ground. Women carried young children. All the while, Noah and Thios stood in their midst. Then it struck Noah no one was looking at him. Not in a self-centered or self-conscious way, but literally no one took notice of him or Thios. No one bumped into them. No one smiled at him. The people parted ways around the two like water around a rock. "Something isn't right," Noah muttered.

"They can't see you, Noah," Thios replied.

"But I was just here. I am here. I was just speaking with Eleazar, and he is right there."

"I know." Thio was calm in his reply. Suddenly, the noise around them quieted like someone pushed the *mute* button on the world. The people kept walking, but the only noise Noah could hear was his own breathing and the voice of his friend. "Noah, look at me."

Noah focused in on his friend. If this was the first unusual happening he'd experienced, it would not have been as easy a task. From where he was what seemed like a week ago to now, anything was possible. Everything around him became blurry. He was still in the riverbed, but the only person in focus was Thios.

Thios spoke, "Once all the Israelites complete their crossing, they will camp up ahead in a nearby village named Gilgal. Israel will then celebrate Passover. The Lord will visit with Joshua thereafter and give him the battle plans for Jericho. When Joshua initiates the plan of attack, your clock will begin. Rahab's son showed you the way inside Jericho. I compel you to get back there as soon as you can. And remember the path Moses showed you."

"Wait, are you not coming with?" Noah anxiously questioned.

"This path is yours, Noah. Look at how far you have come. You stared down death, befriended an elder of Israel, spoke with Joshua, infiltrated Jericho with two spies, and escaped Natsa's soldiers. Noah, you can do this!"

"I was afraid you would say something like that." Noah took a deep breath and paced for a moment. "I just…well… I can't decide if I should be excited or scared. I want to cry and scream and laugh at the same time. My gosh, I just met Eleazar, for goodness sakes. Joshua knows my name. Moses came to me yesterday. I got to meet Rahab." Tears were filling his eyes—good tears, overwhelmed tears.

Thios walked over and put his arm around Noah. He continued, "And now I am literally standing inside the Jordan River while Israel crosses into the promised land. Why, Thio? I just can't take it. Why me?" The last three days inside Jericho the close calls to the escape in the night—his emotions were spilling out. "I just don't know if I can do this—"

"I believe you can," Thios reassured his friend. "Stand up, Noah, shoulders back. Wipe your face. Everything you need for success is inside you. The story is written. Have faith to follow what you know. Look over there." Thios pointed to Joshua. "Go to him."

Noah wiped the tears from his face and straightened his body. He pushed his shoulders back and focused on Joshua standing resolute in the riverbed, urging the people forward. The people around Noah came back into focus. The noise from the environment rose once again. Suddenly, he was back. "Excuse me," a lady spoke as she walked by. "Pardon me," another man said. Then a young boy bumped into Noah.

He glanced over his shoulder to where Thios was just a moment before, and once again, he was nowhere to be found. Noah spun in place as he looked for his friend, but he knew it was of no use. Within the ruckus, Noah heard his name called out. "Noah! Come here!" It was the voice of Joshua. Noah looked upon the leader of Israel as he stood stoically on the dry riverbed. Noah pushed politely though the sea of people and made it alongside their leader.

Joshua winked at Noah and returned to commanding his men. Noah took a breath. He was where he needed to be. He decided to wait patiently for whatever was next.

27

"Eleazar, it is nearly time," Joshua commanded. In Noah's absence, while he spoke with Thios, the majority of the Israelites had crossed the river. The sun would be setting soon. Joshua had stood alongside the elders the entire time the people passed through the dry riverbed.

Eleazar motioned to a soldier beside him and said, "Gather the twelve chosen men."

Noah looked at Joshua and questioned, "What is going on?"

"The Lord commanded me to have one man from each tribe take a stone from within the dry riverbed. They are to take the stones over to the shore and with them erect an altar of remembrance for our people."

Noah watched as the twelve men, aged somewhere between their twenties or thirties, the cream of the crop, the future leaders of their respective tribes, entered the riverbed. Each one searched the ground for the perfect stone to represent their tribe. As they searched, Joshua spoke to Noah, "A magnificent day, wouldn't you say? I was there to see the sea divide with Moses as we escaped the Egyptians. I never thought I would witness God divide the waters again. It is truly something to behold!"

"Yes, it is," Noah agreed as he turned north to see the waters continue to rise on top of itself.

"This is what my people need. To witness the hand of God so powerful amongst them, how He cares for us. He fills us with hope and courage to take the next step. Everything my people have experienced over these many years waiting in the wilderness, and to part the Jordan during harvest season while the waters burst forth at flood stage, what a miracle it is! Without God's help, it would have taken us weeks to move across the river. Weeks! We would have been exhausted, and who knows how many we may have lost."

Noah listened to Joshua as he watched the twelve men carrying the stones to the opposite shore. The last of the Israelites finally crossed the river. Once they did, Joshua and the elders crossed over as well. The sun was nearly set by now. Eleazar walked to the river's edge and motioned to the priests upstream holding the Ark still. The four men moved to their side of the river, and as soon as they did, whatever invisible barrier that was holding back the river let loose. The waters came roaring downstream back to its rightful place. The gushing flow quickly settled. The current began to push as it would normally. Nature resumed its course as if nothing abnormal had taken place.

Joshua moved ahead of the elders to the place where the twelve men had situated the stones. He took a moment to silently give thanks, then erected the stones, one atop the other, creating a tower. He took a few steps back and raised his hands. The people around him took notice and fell to their knees. As they did, like dominoes across the countryside, the other Israelites fell to their knees, and silence swept over the land.

Joshua spoke aloud and gave thanks. He then announced, "Let this altar be a memorial to all of Israel. When your sons ask you why these stones sit atop one another, tell them of the power of God. Remind yourselves of how He brought you up out of Egypt. Remember how He protected and provided for us in our wanderings. And recall this day, the day He made a way for us into the land He promised our fathers."

In unison once again, the Sons of Israel replied, "Amen." The people marched a little over a mile to the nearby city named Gilgal. A feast was prepared in celebration of the crossing, and it was declared that the men need once again institute the practice of circumcision. Joshua explained to the people that God had come to him and commanded, "Make flint knives and circumcise again the Sons of Israel the second time." A practice that was abandoned in their wanderings.

*****

The next morning, Joshua and the elders led the men to Gibeath-haaraloth, a small village nearby. Along the way, he explained to Noah the reason for the men to be circumcised. "The men who came out of Egypt under Moses, all the males, the men of war, they died in the wilderness on our journey. All of them were circumcised in Egypt. But all the people who were born in the wilderness, the men who you see marching now, they have not been circumcised. We have not performed this rite because we have been under God's judgment. Now, before we take possession of the land, it is necessary for all men to be reminded of the covenant God made with our fathers."

Noah's father had explained circumcision, the removal of the foreskin from the male genitalia, many years back. In fact, Noah was already circumcised at birth. He informed Joshua that the procedure would not be necessary on him. Joshua looked at him and smiled. "I am not surprised."

He stayed at Joshua's side as the men marched to the camp. Noah was concerned by Joshua's announcement to reinstitute circumcision and questioned him as they walked. "Joshua, we are now in enemy territory. Why would you leave your army so vulnerable to attack? All the men will be in pain for days. Won't the people be at risk?"

Joshua stopped marching and turned to Noah. "You believe God would dry up the river for our crossing just to send calamity upon us? Besides, there is no better time to remind the men that God is the decider of wars. We live and die by His will, not our own. In the end, victory is more about obedience to the God of heaven and earth than tactics. When you get older, you will understand."

"Understand what?" Noah asked.

"That life is far more simple than we men make it out to be. I believe all of life can be summed up in one decision. Do you live for God or do you live for yourself? In my limited years, watching the hand of God work amongst my people, witnessing the miracles the Lord performed through Moses, the provision of bread from heaven these last forty years, all of it points to our Creator. Yet, as many who choose to believe, there is an equal amount who deny. Noah, son of Solomon, which will you be?" Joshua winked and began marching with his men once more.

Noah was left speechless.

The men remained in Gibeath-haaraloth for three days. After the procedure of removing the foreskin, a fever set in for a few days. Noah did his best to assist the men while they lay incapacitated, carrying water and food. Joshua and Caleb worked alongside the priests who performed the procedure. With the men of Israel bed-ridden and nothing to occupy their minds, their two leaders, Joshua and Caleb, spoke to them of faith and obedience. The pain was a reminder of the sacrifice God made and the covenant he declared for Abraham's descendants. The land they had entered was the very land God promised Abraham hundreds of years ago, a land that no doubt their fathers and grandfathers had told them stories about, the land that Moses declared, the land that each male who lay prostrate had waited their entire lives for.

28

On the third day, the men returned to Gilgal. Joshua told the people that God had come to him the previous night and said, "Today, I have rolled away the reproach of Egypt from you." It so happened that on the day they arrived, the fourteenth day of the month, on the desert plains of Jericho, was Passover. A very special day indeed for the people. While the men were away completing their rite, the women were busy preparing the meal.

"I would be honored if you would join my family this evening for the Passover meal," Joshua asked of Noah. "Mathius and Hani will accompany us, of course."

Noah was elated at the idea. "Really?"

Joshua smiled.

Nighttime fell on the community. The people gathered by tribe and family. The atmosphere was full of love and memories. Grandfathers, grandmothers, fathers, mothers, husbands and wives, children giggling, hugs and kisses—a sense of community lifted the area. God was working in each and every one of their lives. Hope caressed their souls, and comradery glued them together. Fires were lit throughout the camp. Joshua was diligent to post soldiers around the caravan for protection, but he explained to Noah that each soldier would celebrate at scheduled intervals for this day of special remembrance.

Upon entering the tent, Noah was immediately bear-hugged by Mathius. "Noah! I am so blessed to have you once more supper with us. I wondered when we might meet again. I want—"

"There he is! My turn." Hani pushed Mathius out of the way and embraced the boy. Her arms felt good around his body. So much had transpired since he left the loving elderly couple. "You look like you've had a couple rough days." She licked her hand and brushed Noah's rowdy hair to the side.

"Hope you two don't mind, but I invited a few others," Joshua interrupted. He embraced Mathius as brother and kissed his sister on the cheek.

Just then, two men entered the tent to Noah's approval. "Enud! Eliab!" Noah moved quickly and hugged the two soldiers of Joshua. "What are you doing here?"

"Shalom, Noah!" Enud embraced him first. "Thought we may find you here."

"Good to see you again, Noah." Eliab hugged Noah as well. "Joshua has watched over us since we were young. After our fathers passed, he brought us into his family."

After the quick greetings, Hani interrupted the group and instructed the men to sit while she served the food. "Joshua," she proposed, "would you do us the honor."

"Of course, sister." Joshua rose to his feet while the others lounged at the table. "Tonight is a special night. A night of remembrance for some and a reminder to those who are yet to come. It seems like yesterday, doesn't it?" He looked over at Mathius and Hani. Each shook their heads in disbelief at the thought.

Joshua continued, "I can vividly recall my father, Nun, speaking to us that night about what Moses had commanded of the people. After all the plagues that God had punished the Egyptians with, Pharaoh would not release us to go and worship Him in the desert. Moses had warned him one last time, but nothing—" Joshua paused a moment, staring off into space. The images in his mind were playing like a motion picture.

Noah sat quietly, listening to this hero of the faith describe the tenth plague. The story was not new to him. Countless times he listened to sermons and his father speak of Passover. But this time was clearly different. This time, he was going to hear a firsthand account of the day.

Mathius spoke, "Go on, Joshua."

Joshua smiled at his friend and continued, "Father told us not to undress. Keep your clothes on and your sandals tied. Hani, you remember? It made no sense to us at the time."

She smiled, "I said, 'Mommy, I'm going to get my bed dirty if I don't change.'" Hani giggled. The men smiled.

"Father took the lamb that had slept with us that week. He said a prayer and then sacrificed the animal, careful to collect its blood in a bowl. I thought he was just trying to be clean. Then he called me over and said for me to hold the bowl and follow him outside our door. He took a dried palm branch, dipped it in the bowl, and wiped the crimson blood along the doorposts and lintel of our house. Once it was thoroughly covered, he shut us in. The door, as well as the windows, and our mother took the lamb and roasted it over the fire. We ate in silence. Who could speak?"

The spies and Noah sat silently. Mathius rose to his feet and stood by Hani. He placed his arm across her shoulders. The fire crackled. She smiled at her groom, then went to the fire and picked up a pot. She went around the room, serving a piece of lamb to each man. Joshua continued, "Father spoke of the plagues. He spoke of Pharaoh's hardened heart and unwillingness to let the Hebrew people leave to worship God. After all Egypt had been through, the suffering, the frogs, and gnats, the death of their livestock, even the Nile turning to blood." Joshua shook his head. "He then told us of what Moses had explained. That this night, the Angel of the Lord would visit the land of Egypt. This would be the last judgment finally breaking Pharaoh's will."

Joshua turned and moved toward the entrance of the tent. "I recall sitting near the door, wanting to look out and maybe catch a glimpse of the angel, but father scolded me. He said, 'Inside we are safe. The blood of the lamb protects! When the angel of the Lord sees the blood, he shall pass over our house and continue on. Anyone who does not have the shed blood covering their house shall be punished at the cost of their firstborn.'"

Every time Noah heard this story, he always got goosebumps. *The angel passed over.* His dad spoke of this story often, especially around Easter, "Noah, this is why Jesus is called the Passover Lamb. Death will not conquer you because Jesus has conquered death, and His blood covers you like the lamb for the tenth plague."

"There was a wind. Do you remember?" Joshua looked at Mathius.

"It shook the very walls of our home," Mathius answered, "like a powerful sandstorm sweeping through Egypt."

"The wind blew swift. In and out, up and down the streets. Our family held their breaths. Other than the quick rush, you couldn't hear a sound. As soon as it came, it went." Joshua stood silently for a moment, allowing the men to understand how quiet the country-side was. "It wasn't long after till we heard the first screams. Then like a cascade of whelps, the entire land of Egypt was gripped in mourning. There was not a family amongst the Egyptians that went untouched. Each and every one lost their firstborn that night... including Pharaoh.

"The command came quickly to Moses, 'Leave now and never return.' The call went out to the Hebrew nation, and within the hour, we were marching in silence through the streets. Once the thought of our exodus finally became a realization, the women began to sing until all of our people joined in!" Joshua started to hum and smile.

"What a night it was! The beginning of all this." He put his arms out wide. "God was taking us out and up to the land He promised Abraham many years ago, the promised land. The very land we find ourselves this evening, enjoying the Passover and reliving the grace of our heavenly father. I am so thankful to be here with each and every one of you." Joshua's eyes filled with tears of relief and hope. They celebrated into the night, laughing and talking.

—✦· 29 ·✦—

Noah awoke, ready to start the day, refreshed and excited. The night's meal prepared by Hani was amazing as expected. Spending time with friends and laughing into the night brought back memories of home. Joshua and Mathius were already up and out of the tent. Eliab and Enud were away on duty preparing the men per Joshua's orders. Hani, of course, was fixing breakfast.

Noah gathered himself, adjusted his robe, grabbed a piece of bread, and went outside to find Joshua. The sun was rising, and the people were stirring below. Something was different. Noah sensed a bit a confusion amongst the people. He approached Joshua and Mathius who were looking down at the Sons of Israel.

"What's going on?" Noah asked.

"The manna has not fallen this morning. Forty years, God has provided food from heaven on our journey. Forty years without missing a single day," Mathius answered.

Joshua interrupted, "He brought us to the promised land. The land shall provide our sustenance now." He turned to Mathius. "Shall we begin? Tell the elders to gather." Mathius nodded and moved ahead down the hill.

"So what's next?" Noah wondered.

"I was hoping you could tell me that," Joshua laughed. Noah smiled back. "Come with me." Joshua walked around the far side of the hill from whence Mathius left. From the height, Noah could see the valley of Jericho and the city stretching out over the land. "It's not a large city, but it is impressive to look upon. No doubt many kings have thought the same thing over the years." Joshua pondered.

"Many men will fall trying to climb those walls. Our numbers are great, it is obvious, though I am not willing to sacrifice one, let alone many."

Noah was listening to Joshua speak as he looked down upon the valley at the city, thinking of his friend, Ashem. *How scared and full of fear the city must be in!* When he turned back to Joshua, Noah noticed a foreign soldier with sword drawn standing behind him about fifteen feet away. "Joshua!" Noah yelled.

Joshua swiftly turned to the stranger and reached for the hilt of his sword, drawing it from its sheath. "Who are you?" Joshua commanded. The soldier did not respond nor tremble. The stranger stood in stoic magnificence against the backdrop of the valley of Jericho. Joshua and Noah were alone. Joshua had dismissed his bodyguard for preparations. The unknown soldier was well-built, his body covered head to toe in thick golden armor. His skin was unblemished, brown hair waving in the wind. He had calming blue eyes and olive skin. The soldier's body was wrapped in pure white linen, his gold armor atop the cloth.

"Again, I command, who are you? Are you for us or for our adversaries?" The timbre in Joshua's voice gave Noah assurance that he was prepared for battle. Joshua was no slouch in fighting. He had led numerous battle formations to victory over the years, training thousands in the art of hand-to-hand combat.

The mysterious soldier in full military garb took a few steps toward Joshua and Noah, his armor glistening in the morning sun. Joshua stepped in front of the boy, prepared to protect Noah with his life. Fear gripped Noah. He could not form words.

"No," the voice of the soldier echoed around the hill. "Rather, I indeed come now as captain of the host of the Lord."

Joshua froze and said nothing. He immediately fell to his knees, dropping his sword in the process, and bowed his head. Noah, still stunned by what was happening, copied his companion and fell, keeping his eyes low.

Joshua, overwhelmed at the heavenly presence, whispered, "What has my Lord to say to his servant?"

The captain came near Joshua and Noah, his shadow covering the two as they knelt with heads down. "Remove your sandals from your feet, for the place where you are standing is holy." Tears filled their eyes as they each removed their sandals. Noah peeked up and locked eyes with the captain. Something about his presence sent a tingle up and down his back. Not knowing why or what had come over him, Noah stood up and lunged at the captain, wrapping his arms around the soldier's waist, embracing him. Overwhelmed with emotion, Noah sobbed uncontrollably. He was drawn to this man like a baby to his mother's bosom, like metal to a magnet. An unexplainable feeling of elation and relief filled Noah's entire body.

The captain wrapped his arms around the boy and softly said, "Peace be upon you, Noah, son of Solomon."

Behind the tears, Noah whispered, "You know my name?"

Before the soldier could respond, Noah felt the hand of Joshua on his shoulder. He tugged the boy away from the captain. "My Lord, what would you have me do?"

The captain stood resolute on the mountain. His face shone like the sun. His aura was tender and fierce simultaneously. He turned and glanced over to Jericho and then back to Joshua. "Jericho is tightly shut, no one comes in and no one comes out. Fear has gripped the kings of the land before you. The city, its king, and its soldiers I have given them into your hand." His words lingered in the air.

Joshua listened to the plan of the Lord. "I have chosen you to lead my people. Moses followed me. Abraham followed me. Now you will follow me. Only be strong and courageous. Take hold of the land promised to your father, Abraham."

"I will, my Lord." Joshua bowed his head once again. Noah stood beside and behind Joshua in shock of what he was witnessing—the Bible unfolding before his eyes.

"You shall march around the city, all the men of war circling the city once. You shall command them to do this for six days. Also, seven priests shall carry seven trumpets of ram horns before the Ark as the men march. On the seventh day, you shall march around the city seven times, and the priests shall blow the trumpets. It shall be that when they make a long blast with the ram's horn, and when you hear the sound of the trumpet, all the people shall shout with a great shout, and the wall of the city will fall down flat, and the people will go up every man straight ahead."

Joshua listened until the captain was done speaking. "My Lord, will my men not be vulnerable to attack from the wall as we march around the city?"

The captain patiently replied, "I will hold Jericho's hand."

"The loss of life on those walls—" Joshua paused; he was concerned for his men.

"Be strong and courageous, Joshua. Let your men be silent as they march for six days. Your heart is not the only one that needs to be prepared for the way ahead. This test of faith is for all the Sons of Israel, not just you. Your people are but one part of the war. Be still and know that I Am."

Joshua bowed low again. "Everything I am is Yours, Lord. I will do all that You have asked of me."

"Now go and tell the elders what I have commanded. Prepare the Sons of Israel," the captain ordered. "You march today."

Joshua rose to his feet to leave and motioned for Noah to follow. The captain interceded, "The boy stays with me."

Joshua nodded and walked away, leaving Noah with the magnificent presence of the captain on the hill overlooking the valley.

The captain smiled at Noah. "What about your path?"

Noah stared.

"You have seen the way. Now you must return to the city."

Noah's heart was racing at the thought of entering once again into Jericho. There was a war coming, he knew it. He read the words and heard the stories. Was he really going to enter the lion's den again? Laba and Nomed would be waiting for him. What if he couldn't get to Ashem or find the entrance under the wall? But all he could respond with was, "When?"

"March with the men today and observe. On the second day, enter the city, and follow the path laid out before you. You have seven days, Noah."

Noah stood on that hill contemplating all that had brought him to this point. The blessing of all he had witnessed washed over him.

Here he was, a small-town Texas boy, standing on a mountainside overlooking Jericho days before war began between the Israelite and Canaanite peoples. There was one thing that he yearned to know, a question that was brewing in his gut and racing in his mind. He turned to the captain and asked, "Are you—"

The captain interrupted, "I AM." The words lingered in the air.

All time seemed to stop around Noah. He was speechless. He stared at the man before him, his soft eyes and inviting presence. He was handsome, no doubt, his trimmed beard wrapping around his unblemished skin. Tears filled Noah's eyes again. Tears of thankfulness. Tears of happiness. His knees grew weak. He dropped to the ground, overwhelmed again by the captain's presence. The man moved closer to Noah and dropped to one knee, placing his hand on Noah's shoulder.

"The people of Israel call me Adonai. You may do the same." His voice was tender and strong.

"Why me, Lord? Why choose me for all of this? You could have taken so many others. My father even. Wouldn't he have been a better choice?" Noah sobbed uncontrollably.

Adonai smiled. "Before I formed you in the womb, I knew you, and before you were born, I consecrated you. I search to and fro throughout the earth, looking for a man whose heart is fully committed unto Me that I may strengthen and uphold. I choose you, Noah. The Scepter of Judah, the medallion, Josiah, Thios, all of it—it was all for you. I love you, Noah."

— ✧ 30 ✧ —

Noah kept his head down. The tears stopped flowing. He wiped his eyes and cleared his throat. He raised his head. As he opened his eyes, he found himself alone on the hill. He turned all around. The captain was gone. He sat for a few minutes, allowing himself to ponder the words of Adonai.

Once again, he stared down into the valley at the pagan city of Jericho. Smoke rose from the fires lit throughout the city. He could see the soldiers standing on the walls in preparation. The gates were shut, the land was clear. A feeling of strength filled his body, and he rose to his feet. He announced, "Be strong and courageous, Noah." He turned and walked down the hill to find Joshua.

When he reached the bottom of the hill, he found Joshua already in discussion with the elders about the plan of attack. Noah could see on their faces, a look of unbelief. No siege towers were to be constructed. No spears to launch over the walls. Just marching. And not a rallying march, but a march in silent unison around the walls for days on end. Noah believed in the plan. He knew the story and its finality, but trying to convince the elders was another objective all its own.

One of the elders, a short man named Jehoida, raised his concern, "Our men will be in full view for attack as they march! The loss of life will be debilitating before we even strike."

"The Lord will hold back the enemy's hand. Fear has gripped the land, Jehoida," Joshua confidently responded.

Another elder, Hunamai, asked, "In silence they march? I don't understand."

Joshua looked at Hunamai patiently and then scanned the remaining group of elders, making sure he had eye contact with each, and then announced, "If there is nothing else, prepare the men immediately. We march within the hour. The tribe of Judah shall lead." Joshua dismissed the elders. He watched on as the elderly men hesitantly went their ways. Joshua was confident in his command, for he knew who gave him the battle plans.

Noah moved closer once they were alone. "Joshua?"

"Yes, Noah." He turned to look at the boy. "What is it?"

"I am to march with your men," he hesitantly spoke.

"Why am I not surprised?" Joshua smiled wide. He motioned for one of his soldiers, "Bring me Eliab."

"Yes, my Lord." The soldier departed.

Joshua winked at Noah. The two moved up the hill for a better vantage point of the valley and Jericho once again. The sun was rising still, warming the land. The walls of Jericho stood magnificent over the countryside. Smoke continued to rise throughout the city, no doubt in preparation for the oncoming approach of Israel. Noah could hear the faint yells of enemy commanders moving their men around inside the city. Outside the walls, in the valley all the land, was a ghost town. Tools, barns, wagons all abandoned in fear of invasion.

"Master," Eliab announced from behind Joshua.

"Noah marches with you today. Keep to the rear behind the Levites."

"My lord." Eliab bowed in obedience and waited for Noah to follow.

Joshua took Noah by the shoulders. "You saw what I saw and heard what I heard. I trust you will be safe. Stay close to Eliab and Enud. Whatever you need, I am yours." He embraced the boy and dismissed them both.

Eliab walked quickly ahead and down the hill. The entire military force of Israel was assembling in the valley, tribe by tribe, family by family. The organization of the men was impressive. There were commanders of tens, hundreds, and thousands shouting orders. Each tribe dressed slightly different from the next in order to keep some type of understanding of who went where. Most of the men carried a sword shaped like a sickle sheathed at their side. The sword was three feet long and made a half-moon shape at the top. The soldiers lined up ten across by tribe. Their commanders marched on the inside.

Noah followed Eliab to the rear, behind the Levites with the trumpets and the men carrying the ark. There they joined Enud.

Noah's heart was racing from moving so fast. The morning was far more eventful than he'd expected. The army of Israel stretched out for miles across the horizon like a snake ready to strike. The men stood in unison and awaited the command to move. Joshua observed from above resolutely. It took no more than thirty minutes for all of Israel to come into formation. Joshua strolled down the hill to speak with the elders once more.

"Remind the men no one unsheathes their sword. No words are to be spoken. March around the city once and return. Understood?" The elders bowed in obedience to their leader and passed the message on to the commanders.

Like a well-oiled machine, the army set out at Joshua's signal, the tribe of Judah leading the way. The sound of their footsteps shook the earth below. Other than the initial order by Joshua to move, no words were spoken, nothing from the captains, sergeants, lieutenants—just silence. The men followed each other, one after the next, eyes straight ahead. Into the valley they marched. The scene was something to behold.

Being in the rear allowed Noah an awesome view of the spectacle. As Judah neared the walls of Jericho, Noah could see the enemy soldiers atop Jericho brace for battle. The city's general raised his hand to begin their defense, all of Jericho waiting on bated breath. But nothing. The army of Israel turned east and moved along the exterior of the city in utter silence. Marching in unison, their steps pounded the sand, vibrating the valley.

The people of Jericho remained frozen in fear, staring at the oncoming mass of military might. The soldiers on the wall gripped their weapons tight. The general of Jericho held their attack, not given permission to let loose by Natsa. All the while, the Israeli soldiers made no noise other than the reverberating beat of footsteps striking the earth. The rear guard started their descent into the valley.

It was time for Noah to march. Enud and Eliab flanked him. The soldiers of Israel wrapped the city of Jericho like a boa constrictor squeezing the life out of its prey.

Noah and the rear guard were close now to the behemoth walls. The front lines of Judah had already made their path around the city and were returning to camp on their left. Noah glanced up at the people of the city peering over. Fear warped their faces along with confusion. A military force far outnumbering their own stood ready for assault, and nothing; no swords raised, no spears thrown, no words spoken—just a morning stroll. Noah heard an occasional command shouted from atop the walls, "Hold! Hold!"

The citizens of Jericho clamored to see the object being carried by the Levites. Noah imagined many had heard stories of the Ark. Noah looked up to see men and women pointing. Screams were released. He saw a woman spit over the wall, hoping to hit the object. Children's heads bobbed up and down as they tried to get a look. The soldiers moved the people back so as not to start a war because one of them hit a soldier of Israel. The Levites carrying the trumpets and the others shouldering the weight of the Ark stared straight ahead and walked, unfazed by the commotion.

As the rear guard neared the northern section of the city walls, a few familiar landmarks reminded Noah of where they were. He looked up high on the walls and located a red piece of cloth hanging from a window blowing in the wind. To most, the article of clothing wouldn't draw a second look, but Noah knew its significance and who lived behind that window. He hoped that his friend, Ashem, was safe. Enud and Eliab saw the red sash as well. What Rahab did for them was not lost. The covenant between Israel and Rahab's household held fast. As they marched a little farther, the stench of sewage and rotting garbage filled the air. Noah knew he was close to the entrance his friend had told him about. He made a nonchalant move to get closer to the wall on the inside. Enud made a move to stop him, but Noah was too quick. Eliab motioned, and Enud followed close by to ensure his safety.

The wall of Jericho was horribly discolored in this area. For years, the citizens of the city heaved their refuse and excrement over the walls, the remnants staining the exterior and pooling below. A swamp of stagnant water settled against the structure and poured out into the valley. The circumference of the area was not much larger than an Olympic-sized swimming pool. Flies swarmed around the small trees and bushes growing within the nasty liquid. Junk littered the banks of the water, other articles of waste protruding from within the filth. Garbage was thrown about the area as well.

Behold the dump of Jericho. Noah scanned every inch he could as the men marched in tandem around the water. He looked high on the walls. There were fewer soldiers in this area for obvious reasons. The murky water would slow any advancement to attack here, and the smell alone would drive the enemy away.

Surrounding the germ-infested pool were large boulders left over from the original construction of the city walls. The army of Israel marched close to a few of these large stones, so near in fact Noah could simply step out of line and out of sight if he desired. Noah quickly scanned each boulder to find the perfect one to fit his body in shadow. As he scanned the stones, something caught his eye. Where the water met the walls of Jericho, a piece of iron reflected ever so slightly a ray of sunlight, and it flashed in Noah's eye. There it was! The way Ashem spoke of: the entrance into the heavily fortified city. For anyone small enough and willing to push through the disgusting mess, the way inside could be theirs.

Noah moved over to his original place in line as the men continued their silent march. Enud followed close, not pleased by the disobedience of the boy. The rear guard completed their circuit around Jericho. From beginning to end, the march lasted no more than thirty minutes. As Noah and the soldiers turned their backs on the city and headed to Gilgal, there was an audible sigh of relief and cheer from within Jericho. The people of Jericho could see they were heavily outnumbered by the invading force. No doubt their confidence grew with Israel's lack of attempt at a siege.

The rear guard neared the encampment to join the rest of the army already disarming and discussing the escapade. Joshua was there, encouraging the men, watching and saluting as each group reentered camp. "You did well. Breathe easy, for tomorrow we march again." When Joshua spotted Noah, Enud, and Eliab, he moved close and pulled the three to the side, out of earshot of the other men. Joshua's bodyguard made sure no one interrupted while he heard their account of the day's affairs. "Tell me what you saw." He was very calm and expectant.

Eliab was first to answer, "The soldiers on the wall did nothing but watch as we marched. We could hear commands from within the city, ordering the men to stand down, even though it was clear they desired to strike. They wait for our advance, Joshua."

"And the walls?" Joshua questioned. "Tell me of them."

Enud took this question. "They are solid all the way around the city. I did not see a weakness. Construction of a proper siege ramp would take weeks in order to reach the top."

Joshua pondered a moment and looked at Noah. "Noah?" He waited for the boy to answer.

Noah looked at both the spies and then to Joshua, knowing what he must do, "There is a way inside." The very words caught himself off guard.

Eliab turned in shock. "What did you say?"

Noah ignored Eliab and continued, "The way that Ashem, Rahab's son, told me the night we escaped. He said to the north of the city, where Rahab lowered us from her window, is an area where the waste of Jericho is discarded. Underneath the swampy water is a small entrance into the city."

Enud nodded his head and smiled. "This is why you broke rank and moved when we neared the boulders."

Noah nodded his head and continued, "Joshua, tomorrow... I must reenter the city."

Eliab interrupted, "This you cannot do. It is surely a death sentence! Natsa and his son's men look for you, and that is if you can even make it inside! It is suicide!" He was not happy about being left in the dark. He paced around. He cared for his child companion which showed in his aggressive disagreement.

"Calm yourself, Eliab," Joshua sternly ordered. "Please continue, Noah."

"My time is limited here. The captain"—Noah looked at Joshua in the eyes—"He ordered me to enter the city on the second day."

"Captain?" Enud interrupted "Who is this captain you speak of?"

Joshua ignored his trusted warrior. "Let the boy continue."

Noah, filled with confidence, stood tall amongst the three. "Tomorrow, when we near the boulders, I will slip away and wait until cover of darkness to enter the city." Noah took his time to look each man in the eyes. "Will you help me?"

The three men towered over the boy in silence. A boy who they met just days before. A boy who clearly did not belong to their people yet understood them better than any stranger could. Joshua spoke for them all, "We are yours, Noah. Whatever you need." Eliab and Enud bowed in unison at their leader's answer.

·❖·31·❖·

After the meeting, the group disbanded, each to their own duties. Joshua met with the elders once more while Enud and Eliab joined their tribes. The rest of the day seemed to pass faster than normal. Noah stayed to himself, replaying his visit with Adonai and reminiscing on the march around the city walls. He did his utmost to recall the large boulders and which one would suit his body the best. He imagined what it would be like tomorrow to wade through the swamp and find his way to Ashem. Danger was looming in his future, so he didn't much feel like conversing with anyone. Before his departure earlier, Joshua had mentioned in Noah's hearing that he wanted more weapons constructed. Noah thought it may be something interesting to check out, so he decided on an evening stroll through camp.

The Israelites gathered together again as they had all the nights previous since Noah's arrival. Huddled together, they laughed and conversed, fires burning as they broke bread. Noah listened as the men spoke of the silent march. Children wrestled with each other and played war with sticks for swords. The animals were bedding down for the night.

There was a soft green light coloring the horizon close to the Jordan River from whence the Israelites crossed a few days back. Noah decided a closer look was in order, so he headed in that direction. As he neared the area, he found multiple groups of men in organized chaos working diligently. The scene was truly something to behold. Like an assembly line in the middle of the desert, these craftsmen were creating weapons of war for their upcoming battles.

There was a large group of at least a hundred men lined along the bank of the Jordan. They were placing small stones atop larger boulders and pulverizing them to dust with iron hammers. After smashing the smaller stones down to manageable pebbles, the men carefully separated the pieces they wanted and dropped them into a wicker basket. Once the basket was full of the desired material, a runner carried the container to other groups of workers huddled around small-looking pyramids constructed across the countryside. The runner gave to each group the amount of material they desired and moved on to the next.

Then, the groups of men huddled around the little pyramid furnaces placed a small crucible filled with pebbles inside the oven and began pushing air into the pyramid with a bellow. As the heat increased inside the furnace, the material within the crucible gave off a mesmerizing green light. Once the men were satisfied with the melting of this precious ore mined near the river, they removed the crucible and added another ingredient, tin, in order to create bronze. The tin strengthened the metal and improved its fluidity for casting it into a weapon.

Finally, once the ore was smelted with the tin, another soldier using a pair of rustic tongs reached into the furnace, grabbing the crucible. He carried the crucible to a blacksmith and poured the mixture into molds made of clay. There were multiple molds, some for swords, others for spears. The weapon factory commissioned by Joshua was churning out hundreds of swords and spears by the hour. The Israelite army under the tutelage of Joshua had become masters in weapon creation. Furnaces now littered the countryside of Gilgal casting a green light resonating on the horizon for miles.

Noah listened to the clanking of the metal. The sound hypnotized him. After a few minutes of rest, a metal worker lifted the cooling bronze sword from its mold and set it in troughs of water to cool quickly. After a few more seconds, the man lifted the sword out of the water, still sizzling from heat, and began to hammer it into shape. Back in the water and back out again, *bang-bang!* He formed the piece. Fires burned, men huddled working in unison, green light filling the night sky, banging of tools, the sizzling water—Noah was transfixed. That's probably why he did not notice a stranger behind him approach nor did he acknowledge when that same stranger stood beside him.

A familiar voice interrupted, "An exciting time, is it not?"

Noah spun quickly to his left, startled not only by the interruption but the sound of the voice. He focused in on the man dressed as a common soldier, "King Josiah? Is that really you?"

The regal man smirked at Noah. "How do you find yourself this evening, Noah?"

"What are you doing here?" Noah was shocked at his presence. "You are the last person I thought I'd run into. And how are you here? I mean, I didn't know you were allowed to visit this…this time."

"Oh, my boy! I have visited this place many times." Josiah took a deep breath, filling his lungs with the smells of the land. "You see, the battle of Jericho is just the beginning for our people. These men's trust in God's plan and preparations made now drive our victory and conquest of the promised land. If you would allow me the time, maybe I could teach a few things." Josiah began to walk ahead. Noah followed.

After a moment of silence and watching the weapon builders at work, Josiah continued, "Joshua spoke of Pharaoh, I am sure, during Passover?"

Noah acknowledged the question.

"How he released the Israelites to leave after the tenth plague, and the people moved on to Mount Sinai and stayed for two years? During that time, Moses commissioned Joshua to build and train up an army. Not just a group of 'lay' fighters, you know, common farmers and herders, but a legitimate military. An elite group of men. Men trained in the art of hand-to-hand combat. The task was substantial but necessary. War, you see, was inevitable, so preparation for the journey and skirmishes ahead was key. That is why God had gifted Joshua with such a marvelous military mind. Come, let me show you what he created many years ago in the shadow of Mount Sinai."

Josiah and Noah stayed on the outskirts of camp, peering into the area where soldiers had gathered. Like two customers appreciating works of art at a museum, Josiah pointed first at a sword lying on the ground, the same sword Noah saw the soldiers march with earlier that day. "Look here. The design of this sword was Joshua's idea, some of the thought taken from the Egyptian army watching Pharaoh's soldiers."

Noah looked down at the sword. The top portion of the blade made a half-shaped moon, like a sickle. The sword was about three feet long. Josiah bent down and took the weapon in his hand, allowing the object's weight to play in his palm. "Here." He handed it to Noah.

Noah was surprised at how light the metal sword felt, no more than a few pounds. Josiah continued, "Joshua knew that speed would be his primary focus for his elite guard. The Israelite military's ability to cover a multitude of terrains quickly and adjust to an attack at a moment's notice was what led to their domination. Therefore, he ordered a weapon be created that would allow swift movement and the ability to swing hard and fast. But this alone would not be sufficient in open field battles as the people of this time were prone to use, so he added another layer of attack later on. Look over here." Josiah pointed to a spear.

"The second group of the military formation in the Israelite army is the heavy infantry. This group of men are trained in the use of spears. The Romans would later adapt some of what Joshua came up within their battalions."

Noah looked at the long stick weapon. At the tip was a metal head sharpened to pierce a man. The bottom of the rod was another point allowing a soldier to plant the weapon into the ground for leverage against an oncoming assault. Next to the spear, leaning up against a tree trunk, was a large shield.

Josiah continued, "The heavy infantry unit marches in unison, some carrying shields and others spears, commanders shouting orders from behind to keep the men operating as needed, moving here and there. During a skirmish, the men with the shields will interlock creating a phalanx or barrier. The soldiers with spears would stand behind the shield bearers, placing the spears between each shield to overhand thrust. If unsuccessful, the soldiers may even resort to the underthrust to hit their opponents in the legs."

Noah was shocked by what he heard. The movies he had seen through his life could never capture the horror of such close quarters combat.

"Behind the heavy infantry, Joshua trained an additional group of light infantry soldiers armed with the same bronze swords the elite guard carried. These men could support the flanks quickly unimpeded by large shields or spears." Josiah continued his walk farther into the camp.

"You have heard the story of David and Goliath?"

Noah nodded his head in agreement.

"Look over here." Josiah bent down. He picked up a strap of worn leather draped over a fence. The stretch of material unfolded to around five feet in length. In the center of the leather strap, a large glove-like piece of leather was sewn in, big enough to fit a baseball. "This is a sling, the same type David will use to defeat the giant many years from now. I remember my instructor teaching me how to use it. Children are trained early on to see if they have a propensity with it. Those that show promise are designated for advancement. The Benjamite tribe have excelled with this weapon. The amazing thing about their tribe is their uncanny ability to use both hands in war."

"What about a bow and arrow?" Noah looked around unable to find any. "Have they not discovered them yet?"

"Soon. Some of the kingdoms Israel will go to war against after Jericho use them in their arsenal. As of now, their use is limited. Joshua will adapt them in the future. By the time of my kingdom, we had scores of deadly accurate marksmen with the bow. Personally, I still prefer the sling. Something about hurling a rock with such velocity and the spinning leather strap that hypnotizes your adversary as well. Although, I will say the silence of the bow is its true strength."

King Josiah continued, "Yes, my boy, Jericho was just the beginning for our fledgling nation. Over the next twenty years under the leadership of Joshua, the fighting prowess of our people comes to bear. Their weapons will advance for sure, but the heart of the people is what gives me hope to this day. By my time, the sword for our military looked far different, but the basic design of our military set up by Joshua remained. It is truly amazing how God blesses one man, and if that man is fully devoted unto Him, he will make a lasting impression on all mankind." Josiah locked eyes with Noah.

"But why no horses? No chariots?" Noah questioned the king. "Pharaoh had chariots. Horses must be like the tanks of this time, right? If I was Joshua, that's what I would be focused on. Find as many horses as I could!"

Josiah laughed. "It is a fair question." Josiah stopped walking as he looked upon the vast army of Israel preparing for tomorrow. "I'll ask you something, Look around. Why has Joshua not commissioned the men to construct siege ramps or ladders to scale the walls of Jericho? Why no massive ram to hammer the front gate of the formidable city?" Josiah waited for Noah to answer, but the boy knew better.

"Perhaps God is teaching. Perhaps we must learn that He determines the outcomes of war. With horses and chariots, a king may take credit for victory or assume future success by the number of animals at his disposal." Joshua pointed at a group of soldiers nearby sitting in a circle around a campfire discussing the days march. He continued, "There is not a man in this camp who is not questioning, maybe not aloud but in his heart, why Joshua has not ordered the construction of siege works." Josiah paused. "God says march. So tomorrow, march the men will. And as each day passes, these very soldiers will continue to wrestle with Joshua's command ever more, requiring their trust to grow not only in their leader but also in God. As their skepticism increases, and impatience no doubt grips their hearts, the miracle around the corner will mean even more." Josiah cleared his throat. "This is why no horses, Noah. This is why no siege ramps. Victory is from God alone, not from military strategy. The same holds true in your time, whether your people believe it or not."

Noah nodded his head. "It's easier to say than do, I suppose."

Josiah smiled. "That is why it is called faith, Noah. Why do you think everyone you come across keeps telling you to be strong and courageous? It's not mere words, my boy. It is something to live by." He stopped walking. "I am sure your father has spoken of the great men in the Bible over the years who did amazing things for the Lord."

Noah acknowledged him. Josiah continued, "Those awesome feats were not known to the man in the story. It was his very life on the line. They each one made a choice to live in obedience to the Word of God. David stood before Goliath with a few stones, Daniel walked into the lion's den, Moses confronted Pharaoh. Each one had to choose to be strong and courageous. To believe God at His Word. It wasn't just a punchline but a promise to stand upon. It is faith, Noah."

"Why have you not told me your story?" Noah questioned. "You talk about these other men. My father thinks you are the greatest king, maybe even greater than David. When will you tell me about yourself?"

Josiah smiled and replied, "All in due time, Noah. Focus on the path ahead. Tomorrow is a big day for you."

"You ain't kiddin'" Noah muttered sarcastically under his breath.

"Still you doubt?" Josiah confronted him aggressively.

Noah was embarrassed by his words.

"After all you have seen, after the many men God has put in your path! Noah, it is time for you to choose. Will you walk the path appointed by God victoriously? Or will you fail in unbelief? But take this to heart, it will not be easy. Each one of us must be tested, for it is in the testing that God molds us into men."

Noah knew he had a choice to make. Tomorrow was going to be a defining moment in his life. Tomorrow, it was his time to believe God for himself. No more letting everyone do it for him. No more sitting on the sidelines while others fought. It was time to dress out and take the field. No more teaching. It was time to play the game.

32

The rumbling march of the Israelite army once again shook the earth surrounding the Kingdom of Jericho. Like the day before, the Hebrew men approached the city in steadfast unison, the tribe of Judah leading the way. Other than their reverberating steps, the soldiers remained silent per Joshua's command. Again, the pagan city was gripped in fear at the oncoming advance from this formidable invading army. And again, the officers inside the city barked orders, commanding the men on the walls to stand down until otherwise instructed. The people of Jericho felt unease that today was the end. Yesterday was nothing more than a sizing up of their defenses. Today, the assault against their way of life would commence.

Noah found himself in the rearguard behind the Levites and the Ark next to Enud and Eliab. He decided to pass on eating this morning's breakfast. In fact, he woke early and left before Hani and Mathius were up. Maybe it was the excitement of the day or possible anxiety of what he had to do; regardless, food was not going to sit well in his stomach, and small talk did not appeal to him. He hoped he hadn't offended the elderly couple, but that was the least of his worries now. Eliab and Enud stood on each side of him in stoic silence. Their confidence lifted his spirits. He wished in some hope beyond hope that one if not both of these elite warriors could join him in the city once more, but the path before him was his own.

Before departing, he had a brief moment with Joshua. The focus of the conversation was solely on the time frame before the boy. "Six days, Noah." Joshua was very stern on this. "You have six days...no more. The captain gave orders for us to attack on day seven. I do not know why the Lord has instructed you to reenter the city walls, but I trust all will be well."

Noah replied, "I will find Ashem. Six days should be more than enough time. I will meet you after."

"No matter what takes place in the city, you must be with Rahab and her family inside her home on that day. I cannot stress this to you enough, my child. The covenant between Eliab and Rahab will hold, you have my word on this. Her home will be the only safe place inside Jericho." Joshua paused and looked at Jericho in the distance. "I can only imagine the calamity God has in store for this kingdom. None will be spared."

"I understand, Joshua." Noah stood brave before the famous military leader of Israel.

Joshua was impressed with Noah's bravery. This boy who came into his life just days earlier, a child he was instructed to assist, and now his heart wanted to hold him fast and not allow him to experience the danger ahead, like a father protecting his young. "You are a special boy, Noah. Something tells me God has an amazing plan for your life. I hope this is not the last I see of you." Joshua embraced the boy. "I am most thankful to have met you. May God grant you strength."

"Please tell Hani and Mathius thank you for me. I did not see them this morning. I left before they woke up," Noah asked of Joshua. "And thank you for helping me." Noah joined Enud and Eliab in line. Joshua stood nearby on the outskirts of their tribe and waited for them to move forward. The order was given, and the rear guard began their approach into the valley below.

Throwing caution to the wind, Noah called out for Joshua's attention. The leader of Israel turned and made eye contact with the boy. Noah smiled and yelled, "As for me and my house," he paused, "we will serve the Lord!" Noah waved. A look of peace enveloped Joshua's face. He paused on the mountainside, pondering the words of this foreign boy. A smile crossed his face, not knowing this was the last time Noah would speak to Joshua on the fields of Jericho.

It was time to focus now, Noah knew it. All night, he struggled to fall asleep as he tried his utmost to remember the boulders near the swampy area on the northside of Jericho. There were three stones that clung to his memory, although he worried he had wrongly imagined their location. No matter what obstacle lay before him, he had to think quickly on his feet.

The rear guard was now nearing the front grates of Jericho. The tribe of Judah was passing Noah's group on the left heading back to Joshua and camp. No man spoke, no soldier laughed or sneered. The commanders of the Sons of Israel remained silent. March, march, the valley shook under the feet of four hundred thousand soldiers.

The men on the walls once again found themselves transfixed on the relic carried by the Levites in front of Noah. The sun gleamed brightly off the golden chest. The reflection bounced in all directions, lighting up the valley. The citizenry inside Jericho jockeyed for a position again to see the presentation. Again, the guards atop the wall held them back. The captains barked orders to the citizens of Jericho.

As Noah looked up at the walls, something caught his eye. At first, he second-guessed what he saw, and then he focused in again. There, between two soldiers, was a boy not much taller than Noah. "Ashem!" Noah whispered to himself.

The boy waved down to Noah. Enud nudged Noah in the side, apparently seeing the same thing that Noah saw. Noah glanced at Enud who winked at him. Noah's heart leapt inside. It was just the motivation he needed. Noah thought what to do next in order to notify his friend that today was the day. Today, he was going to traverse the disgusting sewer waters of Jericho and get back inside the city walls. Today was the day he and Ashem would begin their path to find and capture the necklace of Natsa. He had to think fast. He looked up again at the wall. Ashem was staring at him, still wondering what Noah was doing with the soldiers. Noah in a very large, obvious manner, bobbed his head up and down as if to say, "Yes!" He locked eyes with Ashem who smiled back at him. Noah cautiously pointed ahead toward the northern side of the city. Ashem quickly disappeared behind the walls.

Noah was ready now! His friend was put on notice. The boulders lay just around the bend. The soldiers atop the wall were thinning out. The smell of raw sewage lingered heavy in the warm air. His heart began to race again. Noah felt the strong arms of Enud grip his shoulders and move him to the interior of the marching formation. Noah glanced once more at his two heroic companions. Each locked eyes and gave an expression of support to their friend. He wanted to hug each one last time, knowing that there was a real chance he would never see them again, but the time had passed for that. The boulders approached!

The sun was now dominant on the horizon. With no trees to block its rays and a clear cloudless sky, the light shone directly into the eyes of the soldiers standing atop the walls. The reflection of the ark in front of Noah was blinding as well; even the reflection off the murky water caused the soldiers of Jericho to block their eyes. Noah felt a nudge from Enud as if to say now was the time.

Noah knew this was his opportunity. The boulder he had envisioned the night before was exactly where he recalled. A few steps ahead, and Noah lunged into shadow, so quick in fact that Eliab didn't see him do it. He turned to his left, and the child was gone. As the rear guard edged around the final bend in the northern section of the wall, Enud and Eliab slightly tilted their heads and glanced back, nodding in unison to the boy hidden within the shadow of a giant stone.

The final Israeli soldier disappeared behind the wall, the footsteps fading away with each passing minute. Alone in the vastness of the valley, Noah had to wait the Jericho watchmen out. No water, no food, no respite from the heat, he had to be careful. In the beginning, with his adrenaline pumping and his senses at 110 percent, it was easy for him to focus. As the minutes and hours ticked away, his energy started to wane. A few times in his daydreaming, he nearly fell out of the shadows and put his life at great risk of being seen. Occasionally, he peeked around the boulders to find no one atop the wall looking out over, but he knew Natsa had patrols walking the walls just in case another spy tried to enter the city undetected. A few hours passed, many more to go, and Noah thought about what lay ahead.

A week ago, he was in school, watching the seconds tick away on the last day of elementary. He remembered he ate pizza at lunch that day. *Oh man, how great it would be to chew on a slice of hot pepperoni pizza with melty cheese oozing off the sides, dipping the crust in Ranch dressing, like so many Texans are accustomed to.* He missed his friends more than he thought possible or at least the idea of being back home relaxing with them. He imagined them hanging out, staying up late playing video games, and sleeping in the next morning just to do it all over again. He realized the privilege of his life compared to the people he found himself with. Every day was a struggle for the ancient peoples. Each day, they gathered water and food for their families. They couldn't merely drive to the grocery store and pick out a few items, let alone store them in refrigerators.

Noah thought of his father. Assured that time had stopped as Josiah said it would, he still thought of how distressed his father would be in his absence. Noah wondered if he could explain to his father all that he had experienced over these last few days. He realized reading the Bible was going to have a whole other meaning to it now. The sun was high in the sky. It had to be nearing lunchtime for sure. He regretted skipping breakfast; hunger pangs shot inside his gut. What he wouldn't give for a tall glass of ice-cold water. He repositioned himself in the crevice of the boulder. He legs ached from the locked position he found himself in.

It was in this lonely silence that a thought crept into Noah's conscience. In all the craziness since entering and exiting the city of Jericho, meeting up with Joshua, marching and now here, Noah had not prayed. The quietness of the land stilled his heart. He closed his eyes and began to speak. "Heavenly Father, thank you, Lord, for all you have done for me. I cannot believe what my eyes have seen and the people I have met. Lord, I need you…" Just then, he felt a soft vibration under his robe. *The necklace!*

33

You know that feeling when you are so accustomed to wearing an article of clothing or an accessory that it becomes part of you, and you forget sometimes that it is there? Well that is what Noah was going through.

Huddled behind the three-thousand-pound boulder the size of a midsized car, Noah removed the medallion from beneath his sandy robe and held it in his palm. The light from the necklace once again beamed orange until it shifted to green, then blue, then yellow. This was new. Like a rainbow of pulsating lights, Noah stared at the object.

Time slowed down around him. Everything in his periphery turned into a blur. "What now?" he muttered under his breath.

Then like a flash from a camera, it was over. No more light, no more twinkling, no more fluttery vibration. Noah stared at the necklace, thinking he did something to deactivate it. He sat for a moment, shaking the medallion in his hand. "Come on…come on…work!" From a few feet away, he heard the chuckle of a friend approaching. The sound caused his heart to stop and him to jump nearly out of his skin in shock. He was no longer alone.

The belly laughs of Thios echoed in the frozen valley. "Fear not!" Thios continued to laugh aloud. "It is me, oh yes!" Noah was not amused. "I come in peace…peace, I say." Thios was on a roll.

Scared that the guards would hear Thios, Noah shushed his friend. Thios spoke, "Oh, do not mind them. They cannot hear us. Oh no, no, no! We are safe. Safe as anyone can be, I suppose." He continued to smile at Noah's reaction to his presence. "You are well, are you not? I see you found a fine shaded spot to rest. Although the smell is something else!" Thios shook his head like someone being woken by smelling salts.

Noah's throat was parched and dried out from lack of water. He struggled as he tried to respond, for he hadn't spoken in hours. "It's hot." The first thing to escape his dry lips. "I'm used to the smell."

"I don't think anyone should get used to this smell...woooh!" Thios smiled at his friend and then handed him a wineskin. "Drink," Thios commanded.

Noah grabbed the bag, removed the plug, tilted the skin back, pouring the liquid into his parched mouth. The ice-cold water shocked his senses. He gulped the crystal-clear liquid as fast as his body could handle. Thios warned Noah to slow his drinking so as not to vomit it up. The water was exactly what Noah needed. The feeling of refreshment reminded him of playing sports in the Texas heat and getting a much-needed water break.

Thios waited a moment before speaking, allowing Noah to enjoy the refreshment. No matter how much the boy drank, the skin remained full. Noah even took the liberty of pouring the ice-cold liquid on his head to cool his body. Thios looked out onto the swampy mess just feet behind them. He shook his head and looked at Noah. "I do not envy you, Noah. Nope...not one bit."

Noah made a sarcastic face at his friend as if to say, "Tell me about it!" They both giggled for a moment. "Thank you for the water. I am so happy to see you. I have not felt this alone since the night the scepter took me away and Josiah found me."

"It is good to be alone, Noah. It is good to sit in silence. Sometimes in the quiet of nature, we can hear more clearly." Thios took a drink of the water from the skin.

"What is it with this water?" Noah reached for the skin. "It is like nothing I have ever tasted. Is it different in this time?"

Thios nodded. "Water is life, Noah. Some water is disgusting and awful, smells of death, like this place." Thios pointed to the murky sewer water behind them. "Other water is good and pure, refreshing the very soul of the one who drinks it." Thios took another drink. "Maybe when you get back home, you should look in your Bible at how many times the Word speaks of water."

"If I get home," Noah mumbled to himself. He was mentally exhausted and questioning his actions. It seemed so obvious to him yesterday what he had to do. The captain told him to reenter Jericho. Joshua and the spies assisted getting him this far. But sitting in the wasteland of Jericho, waiting to sneak inside the pagan city that would fall in less than a week was filling him with doubt and fear.

"Hey, Noah." Thios nudged the boy. "You know what is best about water?"

"What's that?" Noah answered.

"It cleans everything." Thios had a smile on his face. "You clean your food in it, rinse your mouth out with it, wash your body, clothes, even dirty cars. No matter how filthy something is, add some water, and poof…clean."

"I never thought of it like that."

"It's why Jesus said drink of this water and you will thirst no more." Thios stood up and stretched his legs. He continued, "You see, Noah, He is the water that cleanses your soul."

Noah smiled at the thought. He took another long slow drink of water from the skin. The coolness wrapped his body, refreshing his core. "Any chance I can keep the water?"

"Why else would I have brought it?" Thios smiled. The two boys sat awhile, relaxing in the afternoon sun. Something about talking and spending time with Thios made Noah feel at ease. He forgot about Jericho and Natsa. He forgot about home and his father. When he was with Thios, life came into focus. His heart felt full and content.

"Well, that is all for now, I suppose, time to get going. A few more hours, and into the muck you go." Thios giggled at Noah's disgust.

"Thanks for the visit, Thio, I didn't know what I was going to do to pass the time. Say, you wouldn't happen to have a bit of bread, would ya?" Noah winked.

"Nope…but Ashem does." Thios turned to leave. "Gotta go! Hani is making her special stew tonight. I will make sure to eat a bowl for you."

"Will you tell her I am sorry for not saying goodbye this morning?"

"Of course! Be well, Noah."

"Will I see you again?"

"For sure." Thios waved. Before he was too far gone, Thios turned back to Noah and yelled, "And remember…water cleanses everything!" And once more, Noah was alone.

34

The afternoon sun was gone, now setting behind the western wall of the pagan city. The shadow from the wall darkened the entire swampy area. The time for Noah to break cover was upon him. Noah knew he couldn't wait until the pitch-black of night for it would be too dark for him to traverse the murky swamp. He peeked out from behind the large boulder, scanning the tops of the wall. He took a few minutes to observe if there was any movement from the few windows on the façade of the city. He felt sorry for the people forced to live in this section of the Jericho, like Ashem's family. No doubt the smell of the northern swamp was a part of their daily lives.

Noah shot up a quick prayer for courage and support, took a deep breath, and broke cover. It felt good to use his body again. At first his joints were stiff from sitting for hours on end. He was twenty or so feet away off the shoreline to the water. He used the many large boulders for cover as he neared the repulsive liquid. He brought the skin of water with him in case he needed revival along the way. There was a strap attached to the skin, so he wrapped it around his neck.

Now feet from the shoreline, he hid behind the final available stone, looking up one last time to the wall to see if the coast was clear. Convinced that no one was watching, he entered the cesspool.

The thickness of the water alone nearly made him vomit. Like thick warm mucus, he trudged deeper and deeper into the sludge. Now to his knees, he felt particles of filth rub against his skin. He marched forward, each step lifting the aroma of death and decay. The swamp was now to his hips. Every movement forward was more

237

difficult than the last, his sandals sticking into the wet earth below. His stomach started to cramp from the onslaught to his senses. The impulse of gagging was too much to hold back. He lunged forward, dry heaving violently. Nothing came out, but the sensation would not cease. Each step was worse than the last.

Halfway into the swamp, and he was exhausted. *What now?* He knew he couldn't turn back. Darkness was enveloping him. He was already losing sight of the grate where the liquid poured out from under the wall. He had to keep moving before he lost sight and light.

The liquid was now up to his belly button. It might as well have been at his mouth because the smell was so thick and so awful, he could virtually taste it. He lunged forward again, vomiting a yellowish liquid. He hadn't eaten all day and was thankful for it because if he had, that's what would be pouring out of him. Then it hit him. In all the trudging and struggling, he had forgotten about the bag of water around his neck. He spun the skin around, popped the cap, tilted his head back, allowing the cool refreshing water to pour out.

As soon as the liquid hit his lips, revival wrapped his body. The horrid smell around him dissipated almost immediately. The nauseous feeling plaguing his stomach abated. The ice-cold water cascaded down his face and onto his chest, pushing away the slimy sludge. Noah stopped drinking for a moment. Like wiping scales from his eyes, his vision cleared, his nostrils opened wide—he could breathe again! He looked down at his chest. To his utter surprise, the brown sludge that was covering his robe was gone! Not to be mistaken here, he was still in the swamp, but the slimy ooze was no longer clinging to him, at least where the water from the leather skin had touched. The new water did not just create a barrier, it took the bad and made it good.

Like lightning flashing in a moment of clarity, a crazy idea hit him. Noah removed the cap on the skin and poured some of the water from the bag into the murky liquid before him. As soon as the pure water hit the filthy cesspool, the liquid turned crystal clear, so clear he could see his body under the water like the beaches of Destin, Florida.

Overwhelmed, he could not believe what was happening! At this point in the journey, he knew he shouldn't be shocked. The words of Thios made since now. *"Water cleanses everything..."* He poured out a little more water and moved forward. Not only was the murk moving away from him, but traveling through the area was becoming easier. Instead of the sensation of walking through quicksand, it felt more like wading through his friend's pool back in TX. With the assistance of the never-ending leather skin of water, Noah was up against the wall of Jericho in minutes.

Still overcome by the miraculous water, Noah hadn't even wondered if he'd been spotted along the way. Now at the grate beneath the impenetrable walls of Jericho, he poured water over it as well to cleanse it from the years of caked on filth. The debris gave little resistance to the "all-cleansing" liquid. He didn't see any screws, and why would he, they hadn't been invented yet! He laughed to himself that he even attempted to look for them. He placed his hands on the bars of the grate, said another quick prayer, and pulled with all his might. To his surprise, the piece gave little resistance and weighed about ten pounds. He quietly moved the piece to the side and peered inside the tunnel it was guarding.

The tunnel was no more than three feet in diameter, so it was going to be a tight squeeze. The disgusting sewage was no longer an issue now that he knew he could use the water from the leather skin, but the darkness was another obstacle. Rather than remain out in the open, giving the enemy soldiers on the wall another opportunity to spot him, he crouched and moved inside. Once inside, he grabbed and returned the grate it to its normal position as best he could. He immediately poured water from the skin all around him and paused for a moment, letting the liquid work. Sitting in the fragmented moonlight, Noah took another drink as he gathered his wits. He squinted his eyes, doing his best to adjust to the darkness of the tunnel, trying to see what was ahead. But nothing.

What now? he thought. *I need some light.* "The medallion!" he spoke aloud to himself. He reached under his robe and pulled out the necklace Thios gave him. He whispered, "God, I remember when I was young one of my Sunday morning school teachers saying that,

'Your word is a lamp unto my feet and a light unto my path.' Well, Lord, I need some of that light right now."

A soft glow burst forth from the amulet in his hand. Taking hold of the medallion in his left hand, he pointed its rays down the tunnel. Like a halogen spotlight on a dark country road, the brightness lit a path inside, piercing the darkness. He could see everything! Noah was ready to move. In one hand he held the skin of water, in the other the "light of God." Step by step, he crawled through the tunnel.

Even though the light illuminated the darkness and the water cleansed the filth, Noah had never been too fond of tight spaces. In fact, back home, playing Hide 'n Seek was his least favorite past time. He paused a few yards into the crawl to catch his breath. He took a quick swig of the refreshing water. His heart was racing. He could not stop gasping for air. "Need oxygen…huff…huff…" Noah was struggling. He was near full-on hyperventilating. The walls felt like they were closing in. With each breath, he struggled more and more. What was he going to do?

"Breathe, Noah." Noah heard a voice coming from the far end of the tunnel. "Be calm. You are almost out."

Who could know his location? It was his friend, Ashem, waiting at the opening on the other end of the tunnel! No telling how long he had sat there since the morning march. He clearly must have understood the gesture earlier when he saw Noah marching with the Israelites and anticipated his arrival. "Come, Noah! Quickly now! The guards are sitting down for supper. You have little time before they return."

Noah calmed himself and took an easy slow breath. He closed his eyes and asked God for the strength to push ahead. He had come so far since the morning. His body was exhausted, the smell of rotting fish still surrounded him, and his stomach was rolling in hunger. He grabbed the sack of water and medallion and continued his push forward deeper into the tunnel. Not much farther, and he could see light coming from where his friend stood watch, Ashem's silhouette danced in the shadows. Noah put the medallion away, not wanting to draw attention to his location. He continued to pour the liquid all around the tunnel as he neared the exit. Ashem turned around to see his friend closing in. With one quick check of the environment, Ashem removed the grate and pulled his friend from the shaft. He quickly returned the grate.

Ashem looked at Noah, confused, "How are you not covered in filth from head to toe?" He spun Noah around, shocked at his appearance. "You barely even stink of sewage!"

Noah winked, removed the water skin from his neck, and poured it over his head, washing whatever sludge still clung to him. "Like this." Noah laughed and took a drink.

Ashem was in shock. He took the bag in his hands and observed the design. "Amazing! How did you come by this? No matter, come now, it would be a shame to be found out as soon as you arrive. This way." Ashem led Noah behind the dilapidated shacks that lined the marketplace. Hundreds of people crowded the area, the city population bursting at its seams. They were not too far from Rahab's inn. As they scurried around a bend in the corner, Ashem motioned for Noah to stop suddenly. There ahead, not more than twenty feet away, was a group of Jericho soldiers sitting around a small fire, eating supper. The boys were stuck momentarily, having to wait for an opening to pass. Ashem pushed his finger to his lips as if to say "Silence" to his friend.

35

The two sat with their backs against the wall, out of sight, and listened in on the soldiers discussing the days affairs. Noah was thankful for the rest, thankful to no longer be trapped inside that disgusting tunnel. Thankful for the cool evening breeze rushing over his skin. How he took for granted all the gifts of God back home. It was one thing for sure he would do his best to never take for granted again; that is, if he could get back home. He needed to focus now; time was running out. The first obstacle was complete. He was inside Jericho once more, and Ashem was beside him. All he needed now was a plan to capture Natsa's necklace.

A gruff voice interrupted his thoughts, "I told you the Israelites are scared." The soldier smacked his lips, mouth wide open as he spoke. "March, march, march...it's all them maggots are good for. Embarrassing the lot of 'em. Eat in peace, boys, is what I say!" The lug of a soldier gnawed on his food loudly.

"Oh, shut up, Misha!" another soldier blurted out. Clearly Misha was the punching bag of the group. "Eat your meat and keep quiet. The Hebrews made it this far, you imbecile, they did. How are you so sure they aren't just sizin' us up for attack? My guess is, boys, it'll come tomorrow in the morn. Probably just building some ladders and such to scale these 'ere walls. Got to prepare is what I says." The elder soldier continued eating.

"I dare 'em to try. I will hack 'em to pieces, I will," Misha spoke once more, standing to his feet with his sword in one hand, a chicken leg in the other. The look of him did not strike fear in the slightest.

The other men laughed at the sight of him, his robe disheveled and falling off his waist.

Misha was a small-minded comrade but necessary for the task ahead. Hardened over the years by the attempts from other peoples to scale the walls, these soldiers were no slouches went it came to defensive warfare. "I will say…dere sure are a lot of 'em," another soldier, skinnier than the other two spoke. "Like a plague of locusts, they are."

"Aye, they is…the thumping of their march shakes the city." Silence came over the group, each one imagining the numbers of Israeli soldiers camped in Gilgal. "I heard it said that not a man among them died when they battled Og, king of Bashan. No way it's true though. No way. Not the giant king."

Noah listened on as fear gripped the group of men, soldiers charged with defense of the city trying to enjoy a meal. Terror had stricken them to the bone. There was no other way to describe it. Sure, they could laugh and joke, but each one had eyes, each could feel the vibration. They didn't have enough men to hold back an advance. They could kill many in the attack, but in the end, destruction was imminent.

Noah looked at the marketplace as night fell on the citizens. The entire mood of the city had shifted from just a few nights before. Jericho's only hope was the massive walls; walls that had stood for hundreds of years protecting their way of life; walls that defined their kingdom and struck fear into those who dared challenge; walls that they believed could withhold any invading army, even a force as large as Israel.

Ignoring his fear, the fat soldier Misha spoke again, "No matter. Can't wait till they try to climb these 'ere walls. I'll knock 'em down, I will…and like an ant mound I step on…they'll run for cover back to their god in a box." Misha laughed.

The disrespect toward the Ark of God made Noah's skin boil with anger. *Do these men not know who they insult? The Creator of heaven and earth! These are His people. He goes before them! The battle is His!*

243

Misha's arrogant words roused the other soldiers around the campfire, giving a false sense of security to the ever-growing terror surrounding them. The elder soldier gruffly replied, "Agreed! They can only climb one at a time up their lil' ladders. Easy enough to strike 'em down. Their numbers are nothing as long as these 'ere walls stand. Even the women could hold 'em off!"

The soldiers laughed again but were soon interrupted by their commanding officer walking his rounds. "Enough, you three, break's over. Grab your gear and get back on the wall. Misha, clean yourself up...you look like a pig!" The officer moved on to the next group. Before he was out of earshot, he turned and said, "And keep your eye out for that boy!"

"Oh...a... Sorry, sir," Misha answered meekly. The other two laughed at him after the captain left. The soldiers kicked some dirt on the flame and hurried away.

The words of the officer sent a shiver down Noah's back, reminding him that his safety in Jericho was a not given, even with a friend by his side. Seeing their opportunity to move, Ashem nudged Noah, and the boys broke cover, scurrying through the alleyways behind the market once again.

Without any more hindrances along the way, the two boys made it to the back door of the inn in less than five minutes. The people of Jericho were too busy worrying about the Israelite army to notice them anyhow. Noah followed Ashem to his room. Now inside, they took a moment to catch their breaths. Then Ashem lunged for Noah and embraced his friend. "You are well? I am so happy you returned. The last few days have been very hard. I have been in hiding from Laba and Nomed. Natsa's soldiers bother my mother daily. And your soldiers scare all inside the city. It is all the people speak of now." Noah listened to his friend vent. "That and the golden chest carried by the men in white robes."

Ashem continued, "You...you, my friend, are a wild boy." He laughed, and Noah smiled back, still breathing heavy. Ashem moved a blanket in the corner of his room, presenting a small loaf of bread. He took the food, breaking it in half, handing the larger piece to

Noah. Noah forgot how hungry he was in all the excitement. Hiding from the soldiers had taken his mind off the pangs lurching inside.

He wanted to rush the food into his mouth like his friend. But realizing what he had been through and how miraculous the days affairs had been, Noah bowed his head and gave thanks to God for his escape. Ashem, seeing his friend hesitate, stopped chewing his food and bowed his head, yet kept his eyes on Noah. He was curious why Noah did not scarf the bread. The moment of silence struck him.

Noah prayed, "Lord, my father has taught me that with You, all things are possible. Heavenly Father, with You are escapes from death. You, oh Lord, are my salvation. Thank you for today. Thank you for safe passage. And thank you for my friend, Ashem. Watch over us tonight and tomorrow, Lord. Be with us and bless us in all we do. I ask all this in Your name, the name above all names. Amen." Noah opened his eyes and noticed that Ashem was staring at him.

"What did you say? O…man?" Ashem questioned. "What does this mean?"

Noah took a bite of bread. He enjoyed the morsel more so than any other bread he had before. He swallowed hard then answered, "Amen? It is what we say at the end of our prayer."

"What does it mean?" Ashem questioned curiously.

Noah actually had asked his father this before, so he was ready to answer. "It means so be it or let it be."

"I have never heard a prayer like this. I hear the priest at the Morgotha pole chant and dance, but not pray like this. Maybe I should do this…will it help my family?"

Noah smiled at his friend. Parched from the run, Noah remembered he had the skin of water. He removed the sack from his back, popped the cap, and took a long drink. It was still easily the most invigorating water he had ever had the luxury of consuming. Seeing Ashem in need of refreshment as well, he handed the bag to his friend. Ashem tipped it back.

As soon as the water hit his lips, a sensation of exuberance lifted him. He began chugging more and more. It was spilling down his chest and onto his lap. He took a moment to catch his breath and then back to his lips. Once he could take no more, he removed the skin and exclaimed, "What is this water? I have never tasted anything like it!"

Noah chuckled. "It is from my God." Noah smiled. "Water is life!" Noah laughed all the more.

Ashem took another drink, although not as big as the first one. He handed the bag back to Noah.

Noah pointed at Ashem's robe. Ashem looked down to see. To his surprise, wherever the water hit his clothing, the material was clean as new. Newer than new, in fact, as Ashem had never owned a new set of clothing. Everything he had was borrowed or thrown away, and his mother, Rahab, had done her best with what she found for him. Ashem rose to his feet, confused and excited at the same time.

"What is this? How is my robe clean? More than clean…better?"

Noah stood up and walked to his friend, making a motion with the skin. He slowly poured some of the liquid on a dirty portion of his robe. Ashem was in shock. "What is this magic water?" Ashem took the bag and poured it all over him, washing his body clean. Water was everywhere in his room. He was drenched!

"Where did you get this?" The boy was enthralled by the episode.

"From my God, I said. He makes all things new."

"I want to be made new! I want this water. Can I have it?" The expression on Ashem's face was priceless.

All his life, Noah had heard stories about people coming to know Christ as Lord and Savior and the Holy Spirit coming into their lives. He never believed God would use him at such an early age. He replied, "The water is free to all who believe."

"Believe what?" Ashem's heart was ready to hear the Good News.

"To all who believe in the God of the Israelites, the Creator of heaven and earth. He loves you, Ashem, He loves your mother and your family. He loves us all. All He asks is that we choose to give our lives to Him, to know that we are imperfect, but in His perfect love, He sent His own son, His perfect Son, Jesus, to die for us. If you believe that God loves you enough to do this, you will be His, and He will be with you."

That was the best Noah could sum it up. Sure, his father would have done a much better job if given the opportunity. He hoped that the words were sufficient. Noah waited for Ashem's response. "I know that you serve the one true God. I have seen with my own eyes that He is with you, Noah. If you serve Him, I will serve Him."

Just then, the sound of rushing wind filled the room. Like a strong autumn breeze on the plains of Texas, the cool rush of air enveloped the boys. A moment later, it was gone. When Noah locked eyes with Ashem, he could tell his friend was changed. "What now?" Ashem questioned, invigorated with new life.

"Now we plan." It is all Noah could think about. "Tell me, what is it like here when the Israelites march in the morning?"

36

A shem was excited to share with Noah. "Every morning, as sun rises, the tower guards sound the march. Soldiers run to the walls. People follow. Me too. The closer the army gets to the city, the quieter the people are. We hold our breaths, Noah. Will today be the day? The officers scream at the people to stay away. All of our men want to attack, but the officers say no."

"What about Natsa?" Noah asked. "Where is he during all of this?"

"He marches around with his strong men. He has no fear, Noah. He tells the people that they are safe, the walls are too much for your Hebrew people."

Noah thought for a moment. "So with all the soldiers on the walls and Natsa walking around, it will not be difficult for us to get back up top and into the palace—"

"*No!* Noah, not again! We cannot do this. The city is on high alert, especially the palace. If you are found, Noah, you will be punished. The soldiers still search for me. Every day, they enter my mother's inn and punish her for not revealing my location." Ashem was noticeably shaken at the thought.

"I know the risk, Ashem, but it is why I have returned. My time here is running out."

"What do you mean? Do you know when the army is going to attack?"

Noah hesitated. He did not want to give Ashem the information in case he was tortured for it, so he decided not to answer his question. "All I know is I have to get that necklace from Natsa soon. Will you help me, Ashem?"

Ashem thought for a moment while Noah ate another bite of bread. "We should have no problem making it up top once your soldiers begin to march like before. There are few guards scattered around the city, most stand on the wall. Getting away from the palace before the march is complete is the real danger. As soon your army leaves the valley, the soldiers take shifts on the wall while the others station themselves to control our people. The city is very crowded now. There is little room to travel freely. Soldiers are not letting my people into the upper level. We are meant to take the first hit when the Hebrews attack.

"My life is already in peril just being here. If I do not try to find a way, then I have risked for nothing. Tomorrow morning, we will watch and make a plan to get up to the palace and back unnoticed."

Ashem did not respond. He was worried. Just then, Rahab burst into the room. She was surprised to find her son and even more in shock to see Noah sitting beside him. "You again? I did not expect to find you here! How did you get back into the city anyhow? Are the other two with you?" She seemed annoyed and scared. "And why is the floor covered with water?"

Noah, too afraid to answer, sat silent. "I helped him," Ashem interrupted. "He is alone."

"Your very life is in jeopardy! And you help the Hebrew spies yet again? You have a good heart, Ashem, but you are a stupid boy. If Natsa's men find him here, we all will be put to death!" She threw her arms in the air and collapsed onto Ashem's bed. "Army outside, Natsa inside…where will our protection come from? We are as nothing, less than dogs. No one cares for us! I am scared, Ashem…even our family avoids me." Rahab was exhausted with anxiety.

The mood of elation shifted quickly with Rahab's presence. The excitement of returning to the city and finding Ashem, making it inside the inn safely, the scene of Ashem accepting God into his heart, and now this brokenhearted woman in desperation mourning her lot in life. Noah felt the Spirit move within him and quietly whispered, "Our protection comes from the Lord."

Rahab looked up, tears filling her eyes and pouring down her cheeks. The stress of the last few days had brought this strong independent woman to her knees. Noah continued, "Be strong and courageous, Rahab. The promise from Eliab and Enud holds. The leader of the Israelites, his name is Joshua, and the entire army knows of your covenant. Just make sure you and your family remain inside the inn when the war begins. You will be safe. I know it. Have faith." Noah's words comforted Rahab.

"What is faith?" Ashem questioned, Rahab staring at Noah, wanting to know the same.

"Faith is—" Noah paused. "Faith is believing something will be, even though you cannot see it. Faith is knowing that God has your back when everything is falling apart. Faith is risking your life to follow His path." Noah pointed to the heavens as he spoke. The very words lifted his heart as well.

"Then faith we shall have." Rahab stood up. "Now, you two keep quiet. Ashem, if you hear me scream, you know what to do. Hide yourself. There is a chance the soldiers come again tonight." Rahab hugged her son, then left the room. Before she closed the curtain to Ashem's room, she turned back and looked at Noah. "I am thankful to have met you, Noah. You are welcome here as long as you need. Watch over my son." And she was gone.

The two boys talked into the night. If Ashem lived in Texas, Noah was sure they would have been fast friends. Their hearts and personalities were so similar, almost as if they were related. They giggled incessantly as Noah described to Ashem the disgusting water he waded through. Ashem asked many more questions about the never-emptying water skin. As they spoke, each swallowed their fair share of the refreshing liquid. Thankfully, the soldiers of Jericho had more pressing matters than a ten-year-old boy in hiding. No men of Natsa's came again that evening to bother Rahab. Maybe it was God's way of giving Rahab a much-needed rest, or at the very least a chance for Ashem and Noah to get reacquainted, Noah thought. Tomorrow was to be an important day. The plan to enter the palace would be decided. The City of Jericho fell silent and along with them, Noah and Ashem slept.

37

On a normal morning in Jericho, the sound of the people preparing for the day would waken most of the lazier citizens. If it was not the bustling noise of the shopkeepers, then surely it would be the smells of morning breakfast wafting in the air. For Noah, however, it was neither. For him, morning began not by sound or smell but by sensations rumbling from under the earth. The Israelite army assembled early in Gilgal, so as the sun crested upon the horizon their voiceless march commenced once more into the valley. Noah's roommate was already awake. "Noah, come, we must go. The Sons of Israel are on the move."

Noah, dreary from the exhausting previous day, came to life faster than he would regularly back home. His bed nothing more than straw stacked atop the floor allowed him to feel the intensity of the vibration grow as the soldiers neared the city walls. Thankfully, he was still fully dressed from the night before. He was shocked morning was already here for he could not remember falling into slumber. Noah swallowed a drink of water from the leather skin and tore away a small piece of bread left out by Rahab. The refreshing water was like a shot of espresso to his soul. The boys rushed out the back of the inn, trying to keep a low profile in case a nosey soldier spotted them. However, a careful exit wasn't necessary this morning.

The hustle and bustle of Jericho from just days before was lost, replaced by a people stricken with terror. The faces of the crowd said it all. *Was this the day? Would the onslaught on Jericho's way of life commence?* Up ahead, Noah heard a soldier high above in the northern tower call out. Below the tower, a group of Jericho soldiers scurried to an area nearby and began striking a metal dish what sounded like a gong. The noise from the instrument rang in the ears of every citizen in Jericho. If they weren't awake yet, they were now.

From all around the city, the pagan soldiers of Jericho rushed to position. Many were caught off guard still dressing their armor and fixing weapons into place. They moved with haste, barreling over any pedestrian who dare cross their path. Up the ladders and ramps onto the wood scaffolding surrounding the interior lip of the massive walls, each soldier positioned themselves in their designated points assigned by an officer.

As the soldiers scurried forth, the conversation amongst the citizens focused on fear. Their worried ramblings increased as Israel advanced ever closer. The intensity of the vibration from the marching Israelites was at crescendo, each step shaking Noah's insides. *Thump...thump...thump.* The ground of Jericho trembled. The atmosphere was thick with worry and angst.

At this point, Noah watched in amazement as the citizenry, full of anxiety, moved needlessly in all directions. *Confusion* was the only word to describe it. Noah observed the elderly women cover their heads with shawls and quickly move indoors. Young mothers rushed to gather their small children and pushed them to safety. The laymen of the city, those not amongst the soldier's ranks, gathered their own make-shift weapons for a possible breach. Fires were left burning from breakfast, no time to cover the flames. Food burnt to a crisp left unattended. Goblets of water and wine cups were spilled on the ground.

Noah moved closer to the wall with Ashem. The faces of the people contorted with impending doom. Noah peered through a small window in the wall. The sheer numbers of the Hebrews blacked out the valley before them, the dust from the march filling the air with a cloud of sand. These men of Jericho knew in open battle they would stand no chance against this superior force. Their only hope of existence was behind these formidable walls.

A soft morning breeze blew by Noah, and with it the smell of death. Even though he had traversed the horrendous northern swamp, crawled through the bowels of the city tunnel, the aroma where he stood was not much better. Jericho was a festering sore busting at the seams with the sudden influx in population. An order was decreed a few days past which affected the city's sanitation demands. Unless otherwise notified by Governor Natsa, no one was to needlessly waste water any longer for bathing or cleaning the streets. No one knew how long the siege would last. Conservation in the early days could be critical for survival.

Without water, excrement and filth were already beginning to accumulate on the streets. Jericho was decaying from within. Survival mattered, cleanliness did not. Bugs multiplied, flies, mosquitoes, and of course rodents took to the streets. Flea-infested dogs roamed the marketplace, leaving their business on the ground as well. Areas formerly used for relieving one's self overflowed from the rise in population. The city had become one gigantic latrine. The smell of cat urine and thick stale sulfur wafted in the air. Fires had been set ablaze to burn away as much of the feces as possible.

The aroma of smoking dung choked any who stood nearby. The cobblestone roads and large boulders used for construction of the city were discolored from lack of water. When the smell became too much for the people, nausea overtook them, and vomit spewed forth joining the general disgust found on the floor. It was only a matter of time before bacterial sickness spread from poor hygiene. None of the people had a bother to care now. Their very lives were in jeopardy. Their focus was solely outside the walls, shaking not only the city they resided in but their future.

Along with the influx of people came livestock. Food supply was extremely important during a siege like this. Months upon months could pass quickly, and with it their stores of provisions. Starvation was an eventual fear that had to be protected against or at least planned for. The addition of thousands of animals did not help the overall stench and wellness of the city. The people continued to press hard against each other to get a glance at the marching enemy. Sweat poured from each person, body odor now taking its spot in the city aroma.

Noah took a step away from the window. His senses could take no more. His eyes filled with water from the repugnant smell. There were simply no words to describe the rancid environment, an adrenaline-pumping, sweat-pouring, poor hygiene concoction of refuse.

Ashem made a motion to get Noah's attention, and he followed. The boys continued on the outskirts of the ruckus, careful not to be spotted. They quickly determined that their presence was of little concern to anyone, all eyes focusing outside the walls. Rahab tried to stop the two earlier from leaving the inn, but the boys were persistent. Observing the march was a primary reason for Noah reentering the city after all. Suddenly, in front of Noah maybe thirty yards ahead, a loud clanging bell rang. The sound was followed by the noise of a heavy metal chain being rolled away by a pulley like a large anchor being dropped from an aircraft carrier. Then, like the drawbridge of a medieval castle, the massive doors leading to the upper portion of Jericho swung open.

Ashem grabbed Noah by the shoulder and forced him into cover behind a cart loaded with hay. Noah was perplexed by Ashem's cautiousness, but he soon realized from his vantage point why his accomplice rushed him away. There, walking not more than twenty yards from the cart, was the wicked governor of Jericho. Surrounded by his elite bodyguard, he stood dressed from head to toe in full military regalia. Golden armor glistening in the sun, his magnificent sword sheathed at his side, Natsa carried his helmet beneath his right arm. Laying atop the golden breast plate of the governor, Noah identified the object of his pursuit: the necklace! The massive green emerald swayed as Natsa strolled, ricocheting melodically upon his armor.

There it was! The object of his affection, the end of the veritable rainbow. If he was more heroic, he would have broken cover and charged the governor whose attention lay elsewhere. Perhaps he could grab the jewel and rush the outer wall. The Israelite soldiers would surely protect him! Noah's heart raced at the thought, adrenaline shooting rapidly into his bloodstream. But this wasn't the movies or some fantasy comic come alive. This was his very life, and Natsa knew better than to allow something so important to be taken so easily. His bodyguard would seize him before he could even get close anyhow. Stealth was key to his success on the mission. *Focus, Noah...*

Natsa paraded forth like a pompous peacock, flashing his colors for all his fearful admirers. His bodyguards created a moving barrier amongst the onlooking crowd. The people bowed in reverence as he passed on either side. Natsa demanded respect from the citizens but gave none in return. He had no time for these lowly slugs clogging up his path. He barked orders to his officers on the wall who passed them hastily on to the soldiers under their command.

It was clear to Noah that the fear that wrapped the city was nowhere in his demeanor. There was no fear of God in his heart; a thick veil of arrogance blinded him.

Natsa spoke slow and loud like an orator in an outdoor amphitheater, "Again, they march! And again, they will retreat! Be calm, my people! Morgotha has prophesied! You shall bear witness!" As he walked arrogantly around the interior walls, his bodyguards pushed the people back. But this is when Noah noticed something. With the spectacle of Natsa drawing the attention of the citizens and the soldiers focusing on the marching Hebrews, the gates to the upper portion of Jericho were unguarded and open for any to enter. The lowly people of Jericho dared not advance. Of course, they knew better. Noah was not a citizen with the same worry. He broke from cover to get a closer look, Ashem following nearby. As Noah neared the entrance, he looked up the stairs, and just as he suspected, no guards were on duty.

Everything in Noah was ready to charge forth with or without a plan. In fact, he took a few steps toward the opening. It was Ashem's hand on his shoulder that gave him pause. Noah turned to see Ashem shake his head in disagreement.

Noah knew Ashem was right. They needed to devise a proper plan for tomorrow. Besides, the focus of his pursuit was around Natsa's neck, dangling in the sunlight before him. *There is no rush. I have time.* Noah followed Ashem back to their hiding place behind the hay-filled cart and a good thing he did because within a few seconds, there was movement once more from the massive gate. Laba and Nomed came forth with their gang of thugs. Had Ashem not pulled Noah back, an entirely different ending to this story would have befell him.

Noah's attention shifted suddenly from the governor's sons. There was a commotion coming from atop the walls nearby. With growing excitement, the people clamored forth, edging for a view. Without breaking cover, Noah knew what was happening. The Ark of God was moving into position for its procession around the walls. Like chickens roused by a fox, the people screamed and shrieked, the old men shook their heads in agony, the elderly women cried. The soldiers were scared by its presence. Fatigue from terror caused some to fall to their knees. It was clear the people had heard stories throughout the years about the Ark of God. Confusion and worry spread amongst the citizenry, but Natsa stood unaffected. In fact, his arrogance swelled in the presence of the Ark.

Natsa could hold his wicked tongue no more. "Oh, now, come see the box of the Hebrews' god! Their priests dressed in white do not even blow their horns to honor its presence! So small and insignificant…a size perfect for burial, don't you think? Imagine our goddess Morgotha. She laughs at the infantile Hebrew god in a box! Hah! To think they wasted all that precious gold on it as well." He raised his arms in defiance. "To any citizen of Jericho, soldier or not, brave enough…bring me that Ark! And see that I will make you second in command to only me in this city! I so would love to melt it down and make a crown for my head!" The evil within Natsa glared like fire in his eyes as he spoke.

An uncomfortable laugh carried through the crowds surrounding the governor. The people feared the wrath of Natsa almost as much as the invading army of Israel and dared not deny respect. His pompous speech did little to assuage the fear growing ever thicker within Jericho. The city was now completely enveloped by the army of Israel, the march shaking the city to its core. *Thump…thump… thump*—the feet of the foreign army crashing again and again in unison.

Noah found it more difficult to hear anything within the walls. He and Ashem resorted to hand motions for communication. Noah felt something brush against his shoulder. A piece of stone the size of a quarter fell to his side. He looked at the wall he was leaning against as he hid behind the cart. Small cracks, superficial to the naked eye, opened and closed ever so slightly at the constant thumping of the march. Dust fell to the ground; another tiny piece of wall the size of a dime fell along with it. Noah watched as the pebble jumped off the floor in unison with the steps of the Israeli soldiers. The God of Israel was preparing their way, a small reminder of the ticking clock Noah was up against.

— ·❖· 38 ·❖· —

Unable to move because of the presence of Natsa and knowing Laba and Nomed roamed close by, Noah and Ashem were forced to stay in hiding until the morning's episode was complete. Once more, the silent march dissipated. The Hebrew soldiers exited the valley of Jericho and returned to Gilgal. No sword was drawn for defense, no arrows shot or stones hurled from the walls, no death to mourn, but the chance at another day of life in Jericho breathed a small slice of hope into the citizenry. The loud shout of an officer atop the wall woke the city from its terror-stricken stupor. It took about ten minutes for the ringing in his ears to stop and Noah's hearing to normalize. He felt as if he had attended a rock concert inside a packed football arena. The city slowly returned to life, the hypnotizing episode ended, but the fear lingered.

Mothers released their small children from hiding, running around, causing the general mayhem little ones are known to create. The elderly gingerly came forth as well to discuss the drama of the day. The lowly marketplace reopened for morning commerce, selling their food and wares to all the new people of the city. A large portion of the soldiers standing in defense descended from the scaffolding around the inner lip of the wall in order to rest until their individual watch shifts began.

Natsa spoke with his commanding officers briefly. He made a motion to his men, and his elite bodyguards surrounded him as they returned to the upper portion of the city. The echoing sound of metal against metal shrieked as the large gate slammed shut. There was a collective relief amongst the people in Natsa's absence. Ashem and

Noah waited a few more minutes before they left their hiding place, fully aware Laba and Nomed lurked in the lower recesses of Jericho.

More confident now to speak, Noah whispered, "There are two ways in and two ways out. Good to know."

Ashem was not as convinced in his friend's logic. "No, the gate is not a good option, Noah. Far too many eyes. Surely, we will be found out. Stick to the shadows, we must."

The boys broke from cover. Cautiously, they made their way along the wall out of sight of roaming soldiers. At times, they slowed and hid in case they were followed. Few paid any attention to the boys. The talk of the town was Israel and Israel alone.

Noah listened in as he followed Ashem to the general fear and confusion of the people. It was about the silence of the marching soldiers, the coming and going, the lack of aggressiveness, and seeing no ladders or ramps. Some spoke of mythical events in faraway lands about the Hebrew God. Armies were laid to rest on the battlefields before Israel without a Hebrew man dying. Many spoke of the river waters dividing. Some even heard about the plagues that struck Egypt.

Hysteria spread like a virus inside Jericho. No one was immune, young or old. The confidence Jericho once held situated behind the massive walls, built hundreds of years ago, melted like ice in a fire. The foreign people camped in Gilgal were different than the other kingdoms who came to challenge their way of life. These people were calm and confident. They were organized and clearly blessed by observing their overwhelming numbers. Noah heard others speak of their goddess, Morgotha. Her priests cast curses and sacrifices for protection. They screamed and writhed as they prognosticated victory to the people. It was clear by what Noah heard the people of Jericho were not buying their proclamations.

As they rounded the corner... "Someone is in the inn!" Ashem whispered, stopping Noah in his place.

"How do you know?" Noah questioned.

"That rag in the window." Ashem pointed. "My mother puts it there to warn me." Ashem looked around, checking for onlookers. "Follow me."

Noah followed Ashem as they moved to the back of the market-place, out of sight of any nosey people. Ashem sat where he could see the front of the inn. Noah remained close by, watching as the people went about their affairs. Ashem broke the mood, "I do not know how much more mother can take. Each day brings new trouble. One would think Natsa could find better use of his time. She has such a difficult life, Noah, and it has not improved since we met."

"I am sorry your family is suffering because of me. You must see that there is more to your story than sorrow?"

"I am most thankful for your friendship, Noah. Otherwise, my family would be nothing more than one of them." Ashem pointed out to the people clamoring about in the marketplace. "What hope have they in the coming days? We have the word of your leader for our safety. Lest my mother give up, I know our future is bright."

"Have you told her anything of our plans?" Ashem stared at Noah. "You know, the necklace of Natsa—"

"No, it would shatter what peace remains in her. That I would risk so much in these days, we must keep it to ourselves. Look." Ashem nodded his head toward the inn.

Noah fixed his eyes as Laba exited the inn. He had a ceramic cup in his hand. He took a drink and threw it on the ground, shat-tering it to pieces. Commerce stopped at this presence. He looked at the people in the marketplace with disdain as he turned back toward the inn. "Nomed! Come!"

Nomed burst out of the entrance into the street, carrying some-thing in his hand. "Stupid woman!" he muttered loudly. Then look-ing to the crowd gathering, he screamed, "Let this be a lesson to all of you fleas! Do not dare stand in opposition to Governor Natsa!" He turned around toward the entrance. Rahab was escorted out by the boy's bodyguard. She stood resolute and stoic. The guards released their grasp and moved to flank the boys. Laba swiftly approached her and slapped her with such violence that she dropped to her knees to gather her balance. Ashem immediately lunged forward to aid his mother, but Noah grabbed him before he could be seen.

Laba's venomous words echoed the silent marketplace, "Your time is running out, Rahab! Bring us your wretched son or pay the penalty on his behalf! I care not for either of you. If it was up to me, I'd burn your home to ashes and slaughter your entire family! It is but a matter of time before we locate Ashem. And mark my word, I will never stop till I lay hands on him!" Laba turned to the people. "And the same goes for you all! If we find out you are hiding Ashem or helping this vile woman, the penalty of death shall fall on you and your entire household! At the very least, it will relieve some burden on our food supply." Nomed and the bodyguards chuckled at the statement.

Laba moved toward Rahab aggressively as if to strike her once more. Rahab flinched, bracing for another vicious blow. The boy was bluffing, however, and laughed uncontrollably at her meek defense. He repulsively gathered his saliva within his mouth and nose and spit the wet mucus on the helpless woman. The horrific escapade had ended. The governor's boys departed with their bodyguards, and the crowd that had accumulated slowly evaporated.

None helped Rahab; no woman came to comfort her. The children sneered at her and pointed their little fingers, the elderly lifted their noses in disgust. She truly was an outcast, no better than the flea-covered dog lapping up the drink spilt by Laba beside her.

Slowly, Rahab rose to her feet, and wiping off the spit and brushing the dust away from her clothes, she reentered her inn and shut the door quietly. Within moments, life resumed as normal in the bowels of Jericho. The people had more pressing matters to attend to than some lowly cast off of a woman. She was no more important than a homeless man in downtown Dallas begging for change along a busy intersection during rush hour traffic. Drivers stared ahead, hoping not to make eye contact, hoping to not have to care.

People can be so cold and so selfish, thought Noah. He too was guilty. All the while, anger and hate brewed silently within Ashem as the boys waited for an opportunity to move. And move they finally did to the back of the inn.

Noah and Ashem found Rahab inside the dining area, collapsed on the floor, tears pouring from her eyes. A small trickle of blood rolled down her cheek from where Laba struck her. Ashem rushed to her side. She embraced him tightly. Noah stood aside and waited until she was ready to speak. Rahab was stronger than she let on. Years of ridicule and judgment had made her tough. Her example was what made Ashem strong and brave living in the squalor and repulsion they dealt with every day. Noah was reminded how Ashem stood in defiance of Nomed and Laba just days ago in the alley behind the inn.

Rahab's voice was still shaking from the attack. "Look at this place." The evil brothers and their bodyguards had destroyed what was left of her place of business. The chairs and tables were tossed about the room. Utensils were thrown all over, cups and dishes shattered. The decorations that adorned the wall were torn down. "How are we to survive?" she sobbed quietly. "I cannot open like this. No money, no food. I fear we are more in danger of Natsa than the Israel soldiers outside Ashem. Oh! That your people would make haste and destroy this city once and for all, Noah." Rahab closed her eyes, tears washing over her cheeks.

"I am so sorry, Rahab. I cannot begin to—" Noah was interrupted by the woman standing up.

"We must work now. Come, you two, help me put this place together." Noah was taken aback by how this woman ignored the pain and her feelings. She knew what it was to be mistreated, but she chose to go on. As the three cleaned up, she spoke, "I have thought about what you said last night."

Noah looked at her, confused.

"Faith," she answered, "I will have faith. Ashem will have faith. We will choose to hope for that which we cannot see. Eliab's covenant is all I have now. There is little doubt that if there is a God in heaven, then He is with your people. Men like Natsa have no place in the land. May the God of your fathers give us strength today and each day forth until our deliverance. Come what may." Rahab gathered some trash and exited the inn in the back.

Noah was speechless by her words. She was not merely making small talk of difficulties in life. She was living through them. He and Ashem helped Rahab for the rest of the morning returning the inn back to operating position. When their labors were complete, they excused themselves to Ashem's room to wait out the day and discuss their plan for tomorrow. Rahab opened for business as if nothing had happened. People came and left per normal. They ate, drank, conversed, but there was no mention of Rahab's trouble, no friendship offered to a woman in need. She was as nothing. She knew it.

Noah peered out behind a curtain to watch her work the room. He was astonished to see a small smile etch her face. It was obvious the hope of God was giving her the fuel she needed to continue.

39

That same hope inside Rahab was filling Noah with courage that evening as he and Ashem talked into the night until they fell asleep. Over and over, they discussed and planned their route inside Upper Jericho and escape from it. How Noah would get his hands on the necklace was another issue in and of itself, if and when they got to that point. Noah believed that God would show him that part later. His first priority was to get there.

As his father, Solomon, would constantly repeat, "*Faith without works is dead.*" Noah knew as long as he did what he knew he was supposed to, God would meet him when he was ready.

Maybe it was the adrenaline or a mixture of nervous anxiety, but the next morning, Noah was awake before the march began, and he was thankful for it. The city was eerily quiet with a tension that squeezed the very hope out of the people. The blackness of night still covered the land, but the horizon was losing its battle to the burgeoning sun. Noah and Ashem had hoped to be fully prepared to move before the march of the soldiers entered the valley. They chose to sleep in their robes once again for this very reason. With one quick rub on his chest, Noah checked the medallion was in place. He grabbed the leather skin of water and off the two went. *How much easier will travel be now?* Noah thought.

Not surprisingly, Rahab was up and about already. She locked eyes with Ashem as he neared the exit. "And where are you two off to so early?" She was calmer, it seemed, as she spoke compared to how the boys left her yesterday.

Ashem thought quickly. "It is better for us to get ahead of the crowd, Mother, in case some unwelcomed guests arrive." His indication of another lashing from Laba and Nomed sent shivers down their collective spines.

"Of course. Right as usual you are, my son. Be well…be safe… and for goodness sake, take this. You will be famished in no time." She handed Ashem a small piece of day-old bread to share with Noah. And with that, she returned to work.

The boys exited quietly out the rear and into the dank alley behind the marketplace. Ashem tore the piece of the bread in half and handed part to Noah. As they chewed, each glanced around, making sure they were not being watched. The friends looked at each other, and without saying a word, they knew it was now or never.

The sun crested the horizon, spilling forth its vibrant colors into the valley of Jericho. The noise of the city grew in crescendo with the coming day. The sudden jolt of the gong was like a cardiac arrest to the otherwise peaceful beginning in Jericho. The reverberating clanging sound ricocheted off the walls, ringing in the ears of all the people, bringing with it a sense of impending doom. Much like the terrifying days previous, children were hurried inside dilapidated shelters, the elderly stumbled for protection. The city was in a frenzy once more, rushing forward to meet the Israelite army.

Officers screamed orders and reminders to the men under their command as they climbed the scaffolding into position. Soldiers bullishly pushed overwrought citizens away from the wall lest they start a war.

From the darkness of the alley, Ashem nudged his friend. "Now is our time, Noah."

Noah's heart rate quickened as they jogged swiftly down the alleyway and away from the people like salmon swimming upstream to spawn new young. The unpleasant odor of Jericho's underbelly was again thrust upon Noah. The pungent smell of stagnant human waste coated the very walls surrounding them. No matter the challenge, the boys continued their press forward deeper into the bowels of the city. The sound of the gong again shook their eardrums. The Israelite soldiers were entering the valley in battle formation. Noah could hear the murmuring of the people grow in excitement, no doubt filled with terrorizing wonder if today the war would commence.

Ashem reached the ladder inside the small room first. The boys froze in place, overcome by the rumbling from beneath their feet; the Israelites were upon the city walls already. Without a word spoken, Ashem made his move to mount the ladder, but Noah grabbed him to stop. Confused, Ashem turned and allowed Noah to take the lead. Ashem watched as Noah removed the leather skin from his neck, popped the cap, and carefully poured its contents onto the ladder rungs, the walls, and anything he could see that needed a good washing. Like warm water on an icy road, the filth melted away, leaving a pure environment for the boys to climb.

Noah looked down at his companion. No words were needed. Ashem's face spoke a thousand. The purifying water reminded Noah of who watched over them, who marked his path, who cleared the way.

It took them half the time to climb atop than it did a few days previous. Noah removed the grate covering the hole and peered out to see if the coast was clear. From his vantage point, the upper portion of Jericho lay desolate. All eyes were on the Israelite military approach. Safely out, Noah reached down and pulled Ashem from the hole and covered it once again with the grate. Habit moved Ashem as he walked over to retrieve the change of clothes nestled between the walls, but Noah halted his advance. Noah, without speaking, raised the skin of water up to his friend as a reminder and then poured an ample amount of its contents over each of them. The aroma of the alleyway, the dirt and slime, the acrid smelling filth was washed clean away.

The shock of the purifying scene was shattered by the overwhelming vibration caused by the Hebrew army. Now coiled tightly around the city from end to end, the true force of the march again trembled the earth under Jericho. Ashem smiled at Noah and nodded his head. With little hesitation, the boys were off once more, traversing the clean cobblestone streets. The upper portion of Jericho was like flying first-class. It wasn't just better surroundings; it was a better life entirely. The high-born people up top were not affected by overpopulation and decrepit living that came with it. They didn't struggle with rationed water for washing and cleaning and stale food along with human waste pooling in low-lying areas. There were no flea-bitten mangy dogs roaming the streets. They lived like kings while the lowly suffered the misery of being born in servitude. It was a veritable wasteland on this level. No people could be seen. Even the high citizens on this level were pressed against the walls, watching the oncoming advancement. Ashem was in the lead now, moving quickly, Noah following close behind.

Ashem was first to enter the presence of Morgotha, the Asherim pole. Unlike last time, the area was abandoned of worshippers. Candles were left burning, creating a circular barrier around the intimidating pagan idol. Withering flowers of all sorts of colors were left trampled afoot mixed in with miscellaneous animal bones strewn about. Colorful necklaces made of precious stones, wood, and pieces of metal were draped upon the hideous carving. The first time Noah laid eyes on Morgotha, she was surrounded by hundreds of citizens, but now, without anyone to block his view, he saw the idol was horrifically discolored with dried blood left to stream down over the structure and onto the stone street.

Ashem, unfazed by the scene, continued moving through the forum, but Noah was transfixed. Something in him beckoned him to come close and lay hands on the statue. As he stared, Morgotha seemed to ripple like a snake coiled around a tree, hypnotizing him. He scanned the area quickly to make sure he was alone and made his way closer to the Asherim pole.

It did not take long for Ashem to realize his friend was not following. Scared, he turned and rushed back into the forum. As he entered the area, his heart leapt when he saw his companion nearing the idol, "Noah, don't! You know not what you are doing—"

Noah ignored his friend's plea. Whatever was pulling him closer had its hooks so deep inside that Noah could do nothing but approach. It was at this helpless moment that Noah understood there was a good possibility he wasn't alone. His mind struggled against the urge, but his flesh kept walking ever forward. He felt helpless, but he could not resist. He wanted to get away, but it was no use. He was committed. So many thoughts raced in his head. *Why did you stop, Noah? Why? You've come so far. We made it. The palace is right there.*

He felt like a failure. Now within striking distance, he reached out to touch the pole.

His hand was halted inches from the structure by a shrill voice from behind him, "*Arrgghhh!* What are you doing here?" The rickety female voice sent shivers down Noah's spine. He spun around and made eye contact with a shriveled old woman coming out from her hovel. The haggle-toothed specimen lurched forward, wobbling back and forth, her hunched back pushing her down. In her boney hands, she grasped a walking stick for balance, digging it into the ground with every step as she approached. Her nose was long and sharp. She was missing most of her teeth. Her beady little eyes were on fire with anger as she stared Noah down.

"You!" She pointed a long thin finger at Noah. Her pace was deceivingly fast for her age. "You are *not* welcome here! How dare you stand in the presence of Morgotha!" She spat on the floor near Noah in repulsive fashion. The way she pronounced the name Morgotha was like a witch casting a spell. "Death, I say! Tsk, tsk, death to you and your house!"

Instinctively, Noah moved backward away from the statue and the nasty hag. She hissed, "Where do you think you're going?" Just feet away from the boy, she paused. A wicked smile stretched across her nasty face. From within her little old body, a scream of such magnitude rattled forth, "*Priest!*" The echo of her shriek reverberated like the gong under the northern tower. Like a flash-bang, Noah froze in place. Ashem tried to coax his friend to move, but it was no use.

Behind the old woman, an ornate door burst open, and the priest who was charged with the care of the idol entered the forum. He was still adjusting his robe but came fast to see what the commotion was about. He looked at the haggard woman shrieking for help as she pointed toward Noah. The priest squinted at the foreign boy, quickly wrapped his untied robe around his waist, and hastily approached. The tall lanky man was on him in a moment. "What is the meaning of all this, Shecariah?" He glared at Noah, his voice full of anger. "You insolent pest! Dare you stand in the presence of

Morgotha uninvited? Not on my watch!" He turned his attention to the decrepit woman, "My dear Shecariah, it looks like an offering has been provided after all. Our prayers are answered, are they not?" He grabbed Noah fiercely by the arm. The pain gripped him like a vice. In one deft move, the priest grabbed the leather skin of water and ripped it from Noah's neck. He threw it to the ground. Thankfully, he did not see the medallion beneath Noah's robe.

"Who are you, boy? I have not seen your face before." He turned to the old woman. "So many new faces with the Sons of Israel in our valley. No matter. You, boy…you shall bow to Morgotha and offer blood like everyone else…or you will die. The choice is yours." The priest spoke with a pompous, holier than thou art tone. He pulled Noah forcefully near the hideous statue. Noah could smell death. Then from beneath his robe, the priest pulled out a small wooden-handled carving knife. The two-inch blade glistened in the sunlight. He clutched Noah fiercely by the back of his neck and thrust him forth in front of the idol, mere inches from the wooden image. He handed Noah the small blade and demanded obedience.

"Give blood freely and bow to the goddess of our city! Do it now!" the priest spoke in a devilish tone, like this was a normal thing to do for penance. Seeing Noah's hesitation, he hissed in Noah's ear, "Dare not challenge me, boy!"

"*No!* I cannot and I will not!" Noah was extremely forthright in his tone.

"Oh! But you will, child…you will…whether you do it of your own free will or I take it forcefully, we all submit our blood-life to Morgotha." The wicked words oozed from his mouth as his face contorted, possessed by something evil. "Last chance!"

Noah spoke calm and firm, "I serve the Creator of heaven and earth, the one true God. You worship a carved piece of wood! My God created the tree yours was taken from." Noah could not believe the words he spoke. *Where were they coming from?* His heart calmed beneath his robe.

"Your god? Hah!" The priest spat upon the ground in front of Noah. "What fills you with such courage that you insult our goddess? I am surprised Morgotha has not struck you dead already…

all in due time, I suppose. Wait…are you one of them?" He pointed beyond the wall toward the ever-pounding march of Israel. "Tsk, tsk… I see. Oh! How you will regret that you came here. I have so desired a complete sacrifice, and the people need it. Oh, how they need to be lifted up and reminded. A sacrifice to goddess Morgotha shall provide relief from their fear caused by your wicked people. You who challenge our great city…these walls." The priest raised his hand. "Your men will break upon the walls of Morgotha's city like water upon a cliff." His eyes filled with rage as he glared at Noah.

Noah's heart began to race. He knew in challenging the priest of Morgotha he sealed his death warrant in Jericho. The nasty old woman circled him all the while, chanting some unknown gibberish as she wobbled to and fro. She wailed with crazed excitement at the mention of a blood sacrifice. She lunged forward and grabbed the small knife from Noah's hand and started to screech and wail even louder. She approached the graven image and slowly pulled her robe back, revealing the tattered flesh of her arm. There were hideous scars all over her skin from repeated abuse. She took the small blade and swiftly slid it across her thin skin, and blood trickled forth. She raised her arm to the statue and rubbed it upon the dry bloodstained wood. She continued to chant all the while. The sight was nauseating, the smell repulsive.

The priest gave approval to her actions and smiled at Noah. "If you only understood the mistake you have made. You should have never come here boy." He sneered at Noah and then filled his lungs before shouting, "Guards!" Within a few seconds, a group of soldiers entered the forum with a boy following close behind. As the soldiers entered, they spread apart, and the boy came in between them and stood resolute. Noah turned around to meet the soldiers, still held by the neck. "You!" Noah exclaimed.

Laba replied, "My, my, my… I suppose I have Morgotha to thank for this gift. What made you believe you could hide from us?" The boy smirked. "Father will be so pleased to see you again. All the while, we thought you were with Rahab. But how did you get up here?" Laba quickly answered his own question. "Ashem!" He turned to the soldiers. "Take him to the dungeon! And tell my father when he returns from this morning's march I have a gift for him." The soldiers moved forward and took hold of Noah from the priest.

Before Noah departed, Natsa's son yelled in agony, "This never-ending marching is driving me mad! Will it never end? Why will your people not attack?" He put his hands to his ears. Laba turned his anger to Shecariah. "Was he alone when you found him?"

"Yes, my little master. Just him. I watched him approach Morgotha to do wickedness, my Lord, in her presence!" She was frenzied with accusations. "Punished he must be, Laba, severely. Our goddess demands blood atonement!" The woman bowed lower than normal, her own blood still dripping to the ground.

"Interesting." Laba looked at Noah. "I believe you found him alone, Shecariah, but he does not know our city well enough to reach this place. And so close to the palace? Why come here is the question. I suspect Ashem is nearby. He is, is he not?" Laba glared at Noah then screamed loudly, "Guards! On me!" Within seconds, ten more armored men entered the forum of Morgotha. "There is another the same age as him!" Laba pointed at Noah. "Rahab the harlot's boy, he must be here! Search the area and bring him to me! Ten pieces of silver to whomever finds him!"

Noah said nothing in response to Laba's accusations, hoping his friend was far from there. The forum was in as much a frenzy as the never ceasing march outside the walls. Soldiers moved quickly down every alleyway, entrance, and exit of the forum in search of Noah's companion. They threw every piece of furniture and container about. They kicked in doors and shattered windows. While all the commotion was going on, Noah turned his head slightly and saw the leather skin of water on the ground. How he longed for a drink to refresh his weary body.

Just then, he saw motion in his periphery and looked up to see the priest staring at him. An evil countenance filled the priest's face. He could see that Noah desired the skin.

The priest moved toward Noah and reached for the leather bag. "Thirsty?" He smirked at Noah. "You won't be needing this any longer. What a beautiful leather skin. I hope it wasn't a gift. Such a shame to leave it lying here. I shall take it as my own. Would you mind?" He removed the plug from the skin and tilted it back, taking in a huge gulp of water. He swallowed hard and stared at Noah in a gloating manner, water running down his chin. Within seconds, a look of horror covered his face. He turned a shade of purple, then red, and the priest clutched his neck. He was choking, losing the ability to breathe. It was happening so fast. A yellowish foam vomited from his mouth as the man struggled for air. He dropped hard to his knees in agony and then flopped onto his back, grabbing for oxygen, his hands grasping at his throat. He was flailing like a fish out of water.

The soldiers and the old hag watched in horror, helpless to save him. Noah was in shock. And then, in a moment, the priest of Morgotha lay dead as a board, a nauseating fluid pouring from his mouth. The old woman shrieked at the loss of life. She rushed to his side.

Shecariah groaned in agony as she hugged the priest's lifeless body. Laba stood over the man in shock. He saw the leather bag lying beside the priest. The boy reached down and grabbed the skin, then turned and threw it as far as he could down the alleyway. Noah watched to see where it fell, confused by Laba's actions. All attention was on the lifeless body beneath Morgotha. But in the shadows of the alley, Noah saw a silhouette move swiftly to pick up the bag. Ashem was alive and well! Noah was filled with hope again.

"Get him out of here!" Laba screamed.

40

A man was dead. An evil man full of wickedness and hate for the one true God, sure, but he was dead nonetheless. And to his horror, Noah witnessed the beginning, middle, and end of it all. How could something so precious and wonderful, the miraculous leather skin of unlimited water, turn to poison in the priest's hands? And why had it not done the same to Noah or Ashem? After finding the scepter and meeting King Josiah who ultimately sent him on this incredible journey, Noah knew he was in store for some wondrous happenings. It started off with him being nearly trampled by an ox! But witnessing a death so up close was not one of the experiences he assumed would take place. *Was it even real? Did I really see a man die?* he thought as the soldiers pulled him along. *Of course, it's real, Noah. Jericho is clearly real, Joshua is real, the Israelites marching, Ashem, Rahab... I can smell and taste, I can communicate. I actually just saw a man die, and now I am being led away to who knows where to experience God knows what.*

Noah whispered, "God, please, Lord, I need you!"

A piece of mushy rotting vegetable pelted his arm rousing Noah from his inner dialogue. Suddenly, the muffled sounds of the city came to life around him. Jeers, sneers, and hissing from bystanders, who minutes ago were consumed by the Israelite army, had turned their focus on him. Witnessing the death of the priest of Morgotha had desensitized Noah to the world. He could hear the Israelite army was on their way out of the valley again. Now out of Morgotha's forum and onto the main road, the people of the city were closing in on his position. Their anger grew at his presence instigated all the more by Laba, inciting them toward the "Hebrew boy spy." He was spat on, yelled at, and continuously pelted with food and rocks.

The two soldiers escorting Noah through the crowd pushed forward against the mass of people. As they came near the open area in front of the palace, officers situated inside commanded the palace troops to block the oncoming advance of the populous. The two soldiers pulled Noah into the open square before the palace, leaving the mass of people screaming at their rear. Seeing the area again reminded Noah of his path shown by Moses just days before, still highlighted in his mind's eye amongst the stones. But that was no longer needed. He was going through the front door.

The high citizens of Jericho stood aside in the square and glared at the intrusion of the Israelite boy spy. Laba paraded in front of his prisoner in an arrogant fashion. The governor's son stopped his advance and stared up high upon the palace walls. Noah's eyes followed his captor's, focusing on the balcony protruding out over the city. Natsa's Headquarters.

To his shock, the governor of Jericho was already in the palace, staring down at his son and the prize he was so eager to present his father. A look of satisfaction and possibility etched the face of the evil leader of Jericho. Natsa raised his hand. "And what have we here?" His voice echoed in the sound chamber created by the square.

"Father, I found the spy near Morgotha. The priest, Father, he is dead."

Governor Natsa, unfazed by the passing of the priest, responded, "And Rahab's boy...where is he?"

Laba hesitated. "The men search now, Father, he is not found... yet."

Noah's heart leapt with hope at the report of their failure. Ashem was alive and well and most likely nearby. No one, not even the resourceful Ashem could have made it back underground unnoticed. With Ashem out here, Noah knew his friend would do whatever it took to help him escape. If only he could share with him the path that Moses illuminated.

Natsa was not pleased with the failure of his son. His face contorted with annoyance. "Bring the boy to me." Natsa looked out upon the people who listened to him in the forum and on the main road, "City of Jericho! Morgotha shines upon our city once more! Do not fear the Sons of Israel. Look out upon the valley and see, they depart again. And this spy, a mere child, captured within our very walls. This day shall yet be a turning point for our people. Prepare yourselves, Jericho. Now, return to your affairs and worry not. The walls are strong, and the Sons of Israel have shown themselves incapable of attack!" His arrogant words roused the citizenry. They cheered and chanted at the announcement of their leader. Slowly, the crowd dissipated.

Laba led the way as the guards pulled Noah inside the palace. It took Noah a moment or two to adjust to the darkness within. He expected opulence and gold ordained on everything, but what Noah witnessed was a cold, uninviting, ancient medieval-type castle. The dark discolored walls were bare but for a few torches lit here and there to show the way. Few tapestries hung upon the walls, dull in color and design. Most windows were situated high upon the walls, casting very little light into the palace.

Noah could care less about this empty cold building. Searing pain rocked his body, and fear of what lay ahead filled his thoughts. The bullish guards pulled Noah forcefully to the left of the entrance and into a tight stairwell that coiled upward like a snake wrapping around a tree. The passageway allowed for little air circulation.

Laba insisted on going first, then a soldier, followed by Noah, and tailed by the final guard. After climbing at least five stories up to their exit, Noah was panting for air. They entered a narrow hallway which was no more exquisite than the entrance to the palace and just as dark. Nomed met them at the top of the stairs. He said nothing but gave a deathly stare at the prisoner. The air was stuffy and stale until a large wooden door at the end of the hallway was opened, bringing with it a swath of rushing air and sunlight.

Laba entered with Nomed at his side. He made a motion to the soldiers escorting Noah. Together, the guards moved Noah inside and hurled him to the ground. His body slapped hard against the surface. There was no care taken, no basic human value given to him;

NOAH AND THE HOLY SCEPTER

he was trash. He was lower than trash. Noah was a prisoner with a sentence of certain death. The only question was when.

Natsa's elite bodyguards approached the group and moved to the rear of them and shut the heavy wooden door. They stood fierce to block any intruders. Noah was helpless and alone. He kept his face down so as not to draw unneeded attention.

The south wall of the room was almost completely open to the city below, besides a few supporting pillars. The bright morning sun beamed into the room causing Noah to squint. Fresh air filled his lungs. The middle of the opening allowed for a balcony that edged out over the palace square. A low two-foot-tall fence lined the outside of the balcony for some bit of safety to whomever walked out upon it. Natsa remained on the balcony, staring out over the city as Noah and his sons waited for him to speak. He was dressed as he was the day previous—full military armor, gold breastplate, the necklace around his neck.

Noah wondered why Natsa was still in the palace and not down with the people as he had been the day before. As he approached Laba and Nomed, Noah could see he was annoyed. "Another day of waiting," he postured with little care at the sight of his sons. He glared at Noah curled on the floor.

"My Lord, as you requested." Laba motioned toward his captive eager for his father's approval. "Behold, Rahab's guest."

Natsa's beady eyes closed in on his prey. A crooked grin appeared on his menacing face. "What is your name?"

Noah hesitated a response. A swift kick from one of Laba's soldiers beckoned an answer, "Ugghhh!" he gathered himself. "Noah."

"Why are you here, Noah? Why did you not leave the city with the spies? Were you with Rahab?" The words slithered out of Natsa's mouth, but Noah did not respond. The governor turned his attention to Laba. "Where did you find him?"

Like a frightened slave, Laba answered Natsa in quick succession, "Near Morgotha, Father. Shecariah found him in the forum. She said he was alone. The priest was there as well. He spoke of a blood offering, but he is dead. He drank from *his* skin of water and perished. It must have been poisoned."

Natsa squinted. "Poisoned! Why poisoned? Was it meant for someone else perhaps?" He looked at Noah. "Give me the skin you speak of."

Laba did not expect the request. "I threw it away, Father."

"You did what?" Natsa spun aggressively to his son.

"Stupid boy! Send a child to do a man's job, what should I expect but failure. Will you never learn?" Natsa turned his back on Laba and paced the room, gathering his thoughts. He looked at one of his bodyguards. "You, take Nomed and a few others and find this *skin* Laba speaks of. If you can't locate it, ask Shecariah. She may have recovered it already, knowing her. And take care of the priest's body. Perhaps we can use this to rouse the people." They left the room in haste.

Returning to his prisoner, "Morgotha you say?" Natsa approached Noah, his knees pulled to his chest, fearful on the ground. "What were you doing there? And how did you reach the top without being captured? We have guards everywhere!" The second part of his comment was directed more at the soldiers around him.

Before Noah could answer, a messenger entered the room. "My king."

"What is it?" Natsa snapped at the interruption.

"Forgive me for the intrusion, but the Israelites are out of the valley." He bowed his head and waited. "Your orders, sir?"

Natsa turned and walked to the balcony. He looked out at the rear guard of Israel as they exited the valley of Jericho. "March, retreat, march, retreat..." He looked at Noah. "Why?" He approached the boy on the floor with violent intentions. He reached down, grabbing Noah by the lapel of his robe and picked him up like a rag doll. He spewed all his hate and angst from the approaching invasion on the child. "What is it your people are doing? Why will they not attack?" Natsa threw him again to the ground. Noah let out a holler at the pain but said nothing.

The governor spoke to the messenger, "As before, rotating watch shifts until otherwise ordered."

The messenger turned to leave, but Natsa halted him. "Wait. I need to know how this petulant child was able to reach Morgotha unnoticed. No way he entered through the gates." The messenger bowed and exited as quickly as he entered.

41

So many thoughts raced in Noah's mind. The searing pain from being thrown to the ground pulsed throughout his body; so blinded by the feeling he did not realize that the medallion had fallen out from under his robe. Noah looked up to see Laba staring at it. Mesmerized by its beauty and workmanship, Laba rushed to him. Noah tried to hold him at bay, but the boy reared back and struck Noah in the face. He tore the medallion from his neck. "You won't be needing this anymore." Laba held the necklace in his hand like a hunter would a trophy.

Natsa continued to pace the room. He cared not for Noah's necklace. His anxious thoughts lay elsewhere. To the people, Natsa presented himself unaffected by the Hebrews and confident in the city's defenses, but it was clear that Joshua was bettering his adversary. "Your soldiers, they say nothing. They do not present their weapons. The men in white carrying the horns of your people do not sound them. Silence! The silence is driving me mad. Is this something your people do? I have never seen this tactic." Natsa stared at the boy laying on the ground, blood now protruding from his lip where Laba struck him.

"Speak, you rat!" Natsa moved quickly toward Noah. Noah curled into a ball, anticipating the assault. Natsa violently kicked him repeatedly. The frustration of Natsa boiled over with Noah's refusal to respond. He screamed at the boy to answer his questions. From behind Natsa, Noah caught the flash of a blade as Laba approached with dagger in hand. Laba closed in to strike a finishing blow, his demonic face seethed with rage as he raised the weapon. In all the chaos, Natsa saw his son's intentions and grabbed his arm. "Wait!" He shoved his son away. "Not yet."

Natsa was breathing heavy now. His garments were out of place. Sweat accumulated on his brow. He adjusted his armor and moved away from Noah. "We cannot let this gift go to waste. He will talk, given the proper *motivation*. Noah will tell me everything I want to know." The king looked at Noah. "Maybe I should speak with Rahab." The statement lingered in the governor's chamber.

"What do we do with him?" Laba questioned his father, still clutching his dagger.

Natsa looked over to his bodyguard. "Throw him in the dungeon."

Noah couldn't move. Even the act of breathing hurt. Two soldiers from behind Natsa pushed forward and picked him up from the floor. He groaned in agony, blood streaming down his chin. Though his feet touched the ground, he had no strength to walk. His ribs may be broken. The repeated kicks from Natsa had rendered him useless. His consciousness faded in and out like a slideshow. The soldiers carried him from the room and into the dark hallway. Noah felt them struggle as they carried him into and down the tight coiling stairwell. Blackness faded in and out. Each time Noah regained consciousness, he was in a new part of the palace. The deeper he moved into the palace, the colder and damper the atmosphere became.

Noah opened his eyes. The uninviting darkness of the dungeon surrounded him. A few small torches lit a path in this foreboding area. Noah saw a large iron door before him swing open. Its hinges groaned under the massive weight; the dank foul air inside rushed at Noah. The stagnant aroma felt heavy and moist. The guards moved him forward and unlatched a smaller weathered iron cell door. They carried him inside and tossed him to the ground. With no strength left, Noah couldn't brace for the impact. His body thumped upon the hard surface. Pain seared his limbs. He did not even attempt to move. He heard the cell door shut and then the larger outer door slam into place.

Dripping water echoed inside the cell chamber. The only other sound he could hear was his own struggling breath. Noah closed his eyes and fell into sleep.

*****

What finally woke Noah from his pain-induced coma was the repetitive unceasing march of the Israelite army. The thundering of the Hebrew soldiers shook the cell floor. A whole day was lost! One less day to lay hold of the green jewel around Natsa's neck. And now the medallion was in Laba's possession. Despair filled Noah's heart, not to mention the agony of the day-old pain in his limbs.

The memory of multiple blows from Natsa caused his body to twitch. Every small movement Noah attempted brought searing pain up and down his arms and legs starting from his belly. He could taste blood in his mouth. Noah turned and spit out a glop of it on the ground. As he shifted, a splitting headache made him close his eyes. He curled back into a ball, wrapping his hands around his knees. Words were lost on him. All he could muster were a few groans. The dark room was as he felt: hopeless. Alone in the thick blackness, Noah cried. The reverberating march lulled his mind and body back to sleep.

*****

The crackling sound of the large outer door opening followed by the creak of his cell door woke Noah from his coma. The sensation of the fifth day of the Israelite march he felt earlier was gone. Two soldiers entered his cell and carelessly wrestled him from the ground to bring him back to Natsa. Their course hands reminded him of the trauma he endured the previous day. Each touch sent pangs of pain like tortous waves over his skin. With every shift of his body, Noah released a groan of agony. He assumed he slept the morning through. Thoughts of what torture lay ahead jostled in his mind as the guards carried his lifeless body back to Natsa's quarters.

The large wooden door at the end of the dark hallway opened to Natsa's chamber. Laba and Nomed came walking out. Noah immediately noticed the medallion resting around Laba's neck. They laughed at their prisoner and continued past the guards on their way out. Inside the room, Natsa was already berating someone. "How many nights have we spent together? Have I not treated you and your family well in the past? Even though I should have left you to live in squalor! And when you decided to open the inn and serve the people of Jericho, did I not permit this? And yet you dare persist in lying to me?" Noah listened as Natsa screamed incessantly at a motionless woman whose back was to him.

"I am thankful for all you have done for me, my king. But I spoke the truth when I said the spies left the city." Rahab's calmness increased the king's rage.

Natsa looked behind her at his soldiers. Noah was hanging between the two men, unable to stand on his own. The king walked over and grabbed Noah by the ear. Noah let out a shrill of pain. He pulled the boy away from the guards and moved him near the woman. "Then how do you explain this?" He pushed Noah toward Rahab.

Noah winced, tears filling his eyes. He looked up, slowly making eye contact with Rahab. He cocked his head and shifted his eyes to communicate as much as he could without letting the others notice. He wanted to calm her, tell her not to speak, tell her to lie. Noah worried Ashem was in trouble. He wanted to warn her. Even if he had the words and the time, his body and the pain coursing through his veins wouldn't allow it. Rahab locked eyes with him.

Without expression. Without a change in demeanor, Noah could feel her sympathy and compassion. There was a twinkle in her eyes. She resolutely looked back to her king. "The boy means nothing to me. As I said before, I speak the truth."

"Nothing, you say?" Natsa was amused by her response. "Very well." Natsa clutched Noah by his arm and pulled him out onto the large balcony protruding from his headquarters' five stories above the palace square. "Bring the woman!" He ordered his bodyguard.

The morning sun blinded Noah after many hours spent inside the darkness of the dungeon. The warmth of the sun's rays enveloped him. Natsa marched the fragile boy to the edge and turned back to Rahab. "Speak a lie once more, and the boy dies!" He pushed Noah against the rail that wrapped the edge of the balcony. His body bent back by the waist, his torso dangling over the forum below. The only grip on life was Natsa's hold by his wrist. Noah was too weak to fight. The possibility of death stared Noah dead in the face. He closed his eyes. Tears poured out.

"What kind of…? Are you? Is this how you rally your people? Killing a mere child!" The boldness of Rahab shocked the governor and the men around her. She knew she overstepped her place by the reaction.

Natsa pulled Noah up and tossed him onto the balcony floor. The anger inside of him boiled over. "You piece of filth! You dare speak to me about how to lead *my* people. Who do *you* think you are? I should sacrifice your entire family to Morgotha!" Natsa was overcome by the insult. He removed the blade from his side and gripped it tightly in his hand. The look on his face was that of a rabid animal. He stalked toward his target.

Just then, a messenger burst through the large wooden door of Natsa's quarters. The commotion drew away the governor's attention. "My lord." Natsa, still fuming over Rahab's insurrection, did not answer. The messenger moved closer to the balcony. "My king." The man pleaded for Natsa's attention indicating its importance.

"What?" Natsa screamed at the servant.

"Your men found something that you need to see." The servant bowed his head.

Natsa stared at Rahab breathing heavily. "Your boy dies as soon as my men find him. If I see you again before then…you die in his place." Natsa screamed for his men, "Remove this *harlot* from my presence, and throw the boy back in the dungeon! His time with Morgotha will come soon enough."

The guards quickly picked up Noah from the ground. He realized he was brought for no other reason than to pressure Rahab into speaking. As they carried him away, he heard Natsa order, "Wait!"

The guards stopped abruptly and turned Noah around and saw why they were halted. In Natsa's hand lay the leather skin given to him by Thios. Thoughts rushed in Noah's head. Did they find Ashem? Surely, he had seen Ashem in the alleyway pick up the skin, or was his mind playing tricks on him? *God, I pray he is safe.*

"Bring the boy to me!" Natsa was clearly pleased to receive the gift.

The skin was full of water by the way it sloshed to and fro in the governor's hand. "Look familiar?" Natsa raised it to Noah's face with a menacing smile. Noah moved his eyes as if to acknowledge it was. Natsa shook his head in an agreeable motion. Noah could see the wicked man was considering his options. "I have a thought." Natsa paced the room as Noah surmised was his custom, and he orated his ideas like the egomaniac he clearly was.

"You won't speak. Nothing so far has prompted you to answer my questions. Clearly, you are in pain, so beating you more will do me no good. I could wait until my men locate Ashem or…" He moved the skin in his hands. "Tell me what I want to know…or you shall drink of this poison." Natsa was pleased with himself.

Noah was very careful not to express too much appreciation to his captor at the thought of drinking once more from the healing waters. His tormentor was offering breath to a drowning man. Noah kept his face as stoic and defiant as possible. He said nothing.

"What are the plans of Israel?" He waited, but no response.

"When do they plan to attack?"

Again, nothing.

"Last chance!" Natsa thought carefully. "Why did you return to the city?"

Noah said nothing, but his eyes unintentionally hovered over the necklace dangling upon the gold breastplate of Natsa. The governor noticed the look and quickly realized the intentions of his guest.

42

Natsa chuckled an evil laugh. "Hold him," he commanded his men. Natsa removed the plug from the leather skin and grabbed Noah under his jaw, forcing his mouth to open. He tipped the skin and poured the water into his mouth. Overwhelmed by the refreshing liquid, Noah swallowed as much as he could. Like a shot of pure adrenaline mixed with all the vitamins and nutrients a growing boy needs, the searing pain that coursed through his veins dissipated to a memory. His muscles twitched with excitement. Healing power spread over the length of his body. He felt more alive than ever. His captor was dumbfounded by the reaction.

Noah stood now by his own strength, his head held high, shoulders back. Natsa shook the leather bag in his hand. He thought of drinking from it himself, urged by this foreign boy's transition, but instead decided to use a guinea pig, "You! Drink!" The soldier close by hesitated until Natsa removed his blade and raised it to his throat. The soldier reluctantly swallowed the liquid, and just as the priest, he fell before the others to a horrific demise.

Dread filled the countenance of Natsa. He could see there was a power at work far beyond his understanding, a power his statue of Morgotha could not match. Terror spread inside the room amongst the soldiers. Natsa's throat went dry with cotton mouth. He swallowed hard. It took him a moment to gather his wits. "You think you are special, don't you, boy? You believe you know something we don't. Your people say they serve the true god. Well, let me tell you something! In all my days as ruler of Jericho, I have seen countless clans of men challenge our way of life, declaring they serve the one true god. And each time, their men fell upon our swords in defeat!

"Now, here your people march in our valley and disrupt our way of life. I don't know this witchcraft you practice, causing my men to die from poison that you clearly are immune to. But don't let this give you hope! In the end, you lose! Defeat is an outcome already decided, my boy. No one has ever successfully mounted our defenses. The only difference between you and the tribes that came before is you carry your god in a box." With that, Natsa motioned for Noah's removal. "Burn the skin," Natsa ordered as he was led away.

The blackness of the dungeon surrounded Noah once more. The water from the skin had awakened something that was dead inside. The pain that plagued him through the night was completely gone, the bruises, bleeding, and pounding inside his head along with it. He was ready to fight, ready to run, ready to live, but he was trapped and alone. He sat motionless against the damp wall. All he could hear was his breath. Suddenly, the cell door swung open, and a peasant woman entered. He knew it to be a woman by her voice answering the guards near the door. The door was shut behind her, yet she remained.

Noah moved toward the bars to get a better vantage point. She began to hum a tune as she toiled away. What shocked Noah was its familiarity. He knew the song's melody like an old hymn from church back home.

He moved closer and cleared his throat to broach a line of communication.

She responded without looking, "And how's the day finding you, little master?" The irony of the statement struck Noah.

"That song you were just humming…what is it?" Noah whispered.

She smiled through her words. "Think on it, and it will come to you soon enough." She scurried about with her brush and a bucket full of water. She fulfilled her duties diligently, leaving the bucket for Noah. "The bucket is for washing, if you desire, then for relieving yourself after." She pushed the object near the bars where he sat.

Noah could sense something was different about this woman. Her face was soft in the torchlight. Her amber hair pulled back in a bun surrounded by a small piece of cloth. Her light brown eyes twinkled compassionately as she looked the boy square in the face. Her entire countenance filled the dark dungeon with an unexplainable love. She spoke softly, "Rahab is a special woman." She took a step toward Noah. "You know, her story *gave* me hope when I was a young girl."

Her words did not fall on deaf ears. "Gave?" Noah questioned. "You said gave?"

"Smart boy... Noah." She smiled and came closer still. Her voice was soft so as not to draw unwanted attention.

"You know my name?" he was stunned.

"When I was around Rahab's age, I too was an outcast much like her, treated just the same. I made many, *many* mistakes. Not proud of what I did, no...but it did bring me here, so I can't complain too much." She made a matter-of-fact gesture, placing her hands on her hips. "People treated me poorer than a wild dog. None cared for my well-being, not one...not even my own family! Even so, I continued to make poor choices. Guess eventually I thought it was the best it would be for me. Ever feel that way? It got so bad at times that I could not even carry out basic duties women were called to do. Like fetching the day's water, for example. I had to wait until the heat of the day. It was awful! The women of my village wanted nothing to do with me like I was a leper and my disease would transfer to 'em. You know, one day, one burning hot summer day, I went out to the well and there was a man there unlike any I had known. Thing was, he was one of your people, a Jew."

There was a noise outside the door prompting her to return to her duties in case someone came in. Once she felt it was okay to continue, she moved closer to Noah and spoke softly. "Now in my time, the Hebrew people had nothing to do with us in Samaria, especially a woman. We were considered unclean, but this man took time to speak with me. It was He that changed my life. He spoke of grace and salvation."

Noah knew who she was without another word spoken, "You're the Samaritan woman…at the well?" His excited words echoed the dungeon.

She raised her hand not to speak so loudly. "Hush." The window on the massive outer door slid open. The woman moved to the side, back to her duties. The eyes behind the door scanned the room, then the window slammed shut. Feeling it safe to talk again, Noah whispered, "How are you here? And *why* are you here?"

"Since Christ met me, I do what He calls of me. And He called me to you." She winked at him. "Rahab is a very special woman as you know. Her lot in life was decided before she was in her mother's womb. Much like Ashem and you as well, of course. The path for all of us is written and ordained by our heavenly Father. So let me ask, Noah, why are *you* in this dungeon?"

"Because I was stupid. I should have never approached that dumb pole." He lowered his face. "I beat myself up when I think on it. I got a man killed too. How could I be so dumb? All I had to do was follow Ashem, but something came over me. I can't explain it. I want to do right, you know. My dad tells me what I'm supposed to do, and I know the stories in the Bible, but something in me makes me want to break the rules. I hate it."

The woman's face filled with compassion as Noah beat himself up. "You know, when I was a child, not much older than you, my mother told me something that never left me. In my day as I said, it was the duty of the women to go to the well and gather the water needed for her family each day. Mother would say, 'What's down in the well comes up in the bucket.' I thought she spoke of dirty water, but what she said spoke of was what was in a person's heart." She paused to let her words linger, "Noah, the only reason you are in this place is because God wanted you here. So what's coming up in your bucket?"

The dungeon door creaked behind her and opened abruptly. A menacing soldier moved inside. Noah knew the man to be Laba's right-hand bodyguard. He grunted at the servant woman. She collected her things and glanced at Noah as she was led out. She pointed

NOAH AND THE HOLY SCEPTER

toward the ground, "Remember the bucket." The door quickly slammed shut, echoing the silence left behind.

Noah sat in utter shock at her words and the mere fact he just met the woman at the well! He repeated her words, "God put me here? What in the world was she getting at?" He slunk again to the ground. Emotional exhaustion swept over him. The afternoon was in full circuit by the sounds the city made. Sudden pangs of hunger stroked his gut. It had been hours since he ate something. The ominous darkness wrapped Noah in hopelessness as he sat still on the cold stone floor in his private cell. A small stream of sunlight cast a ray like a flashlight above his head. He held his knees to his chest and replayed the crazy morning in his head.

43

Like an eight-year-old boy sitting at his elementary school desk counting the seconds as they ticked down until recess, fresh air, soccer, and freedom, Noah felt desperately trapped in the dungeon. Even though his body was miraculously rejuvenated from the liquid, he was a prisoner, and time was running out. Five days down, two more to come; Jericho's market and city was in full swing.

Governor Natsa, desensitized already to the invading forces tactic, was no longer leaving the palace, which could make matters more difficult for him. Thio's gifted medallion was out of his possession, the worst situation in Noah's estimation. If he had the amulet, he could call for help as before. Double duty now once he was freed of his captivity. First the green jewel, then the medallion, or maybe the later first. Did he have enough time though? How could he locate both? *Did God really put me in here? Calm down, Noah.*

In the stillness of the cell, Noah's mind drifted to his Texas home, a thought forgotten with all that transpired in the previous twenty-four hours. He wished he could be back with his buddies, shooting hoops and playing games or watching a movie with a greasy slice of pepperoni pizza at his fingertips. At this point, he'd even take a day at the blistering hot dig site with Arham, waiting for his father to find something interesting in the ground. His father... Oh, how Noah missed seeing him and listening to his stories! He longed for his advice and leadership. What would he tell Noah to do?

"Buck up, sailor! You got this, bud! Believe in yourself. Pull yourself up by the bootstraps?" Noah smiled. He never wore boots, a silly idea for a boy who was born and raised in the south but grew up more city than country.

In the silence, alone, the song hummed by the Samaritan woman carried its tune in his head. Coincidentally, a song many know and love. A melody that he had not sung since he was a child. The last song, in fact, he heard his mother sing. Noah moved slightly and began to whisper the tune, "Jesus...loves me...this... I know." He felt tears gather behind his eyes. "For the... Bible...tells me sooooo. Little ones...to Him belong. They are weak...but He...is strong."

A tear rolled down Noah's cheek. He thought of his mother. Oh, how he missed her. He thought of his father's strong arms around him. "Yes," he moaned, "Jesus loves me." Another tear fell to the floor. "Yes, Jesus loves me. Yes... Jesus loves me...the Bible tells me so."

Noah wiped the tears from his cheeks and sat isolated in clouded memory. Then, a sound. Was it the scurrying of a rat? No, a noise like someone shifting in their sleep sounded from deep inside his cell where light was defeated by utter darkness. The entire time, he thought he was alone. From yesterday till today, being forced into and out of the prison cell, he saw nothing when the light pressed against the black. Not that he inclined to investigate beforehand. Noah merely assumed he was the only guest. *Had someone been spying on him? Did he reveal anything when he spoke aloud?* He held his breath, waiting for another shuffle.

Muscle memory from many weekends spent hunting in East Texas came to bare. Sitting in a cold, weathered deer blind next to his father in complete silence, maintaining breathing kicked in. The slightest shift of body or rifle could scare away an animal. He waited a few good minutes, but nothing. Maybe it was in his head, he thought. Maybe he made the noise as he sang. Then he heard the faint sound of a muffled cough. And again. The cough was weak and gargled. An elderly man he assumed by the struggle.

Noah braced himself and scooted near the light of the entrance. He pressed his back against the wall in order to see if the stranger inside the cell approached. Again, he waited for another noise. Noah's muscles twitched. His body rushed with adrenaline, anticipating the stranger being unfriendly. Filled with courage, Noah rose up, planting his legs firmly on the ground. Keeping his body against the wall, he peered into the darkness. Another cough echoed from the deep interior of the cell. *How large is this place?*

Delaying was no use. Noah decided the stranger could clearly see him in the light. He threw caution to the wind, "Hello?" He waited for a response. Again, "Hello?"

Once again, he heard movement. The stranger acknowledged the boy was speaking to him. The sound of a man clearing his throat, and then, "Peace be upon you."

And there was peace in Noah! A miraculous undoing of fear. Noah knew there was no threat within his hidden roommate. God made it undoubtedly clear. Noah waited a moment and questioned, "Who are you?"

Slowly, the unseen man shimmied toward Noah, his mangled body dragging on the ground as he crawled forward. Noah stared into the darkness, desperate for a glance at his roommate. A gray silhouette of an elderly man entered the faded light of the cell. Noah studied the stranger with each movement. By his odor and the general wear of his clothing, he was a resident of Natsa for many days. His once clean white robe was torn to pieces, large gaping holes eaten through by rats and discolored by a multitude of liquids. His skin was painted with soot and dirt. His white thinning hair was disheveled and gnarled like a wild dog. His thick beard unkempt and racing in all directions. His receding hairline left only the sides to grow, and grow they did past his shoulders. The man was frail and starving, his bones protruding under his emaciated skin.

The man's voice shivered from lack of use as he spoke, "I enjoyed your song. Did you write it yourself?"

Noah shook his head.

"Many days since I have seen another. Many." The weakness of his voice filled Noah with compassion. The mere use of words was a struggle for his frail roommate. "Although you are far too young to be in here." Noah could see his concern.

"How long have you been here?" Noah questioned.

"I lost count many days past." He chuckled. "Darkness has that effect on men. It is no easy task living in isolation. Man was not meant to be alone." There was a matter-of-factness to his tone. His words were chosen carefully. He was obviously a learned man, educated, and teeming with wisdom.

"Why are you here?" Noah questioned.

The man stopped moving and leaned against a wall opposite Noah. "Said the wrong thing to the wrong person at the wrong time." He paused. "Now…the real question is why are *you* here?" A broken smile appeared on his wrinkled face.

Noah dropped his head overcome. Other than the brief interlude with the Samaritan woman, it had been days since he had a real conversation with someone. The emotion of the last twenty-four hours welled up inside. His roommate was not here by accident. Noah could see that immediately. Tears began to stream again. There were no words to speak.

"My boy, it is okay to be afraid. One cannot be brave or courageous without fear," the stranger whispered. "So be strong and courageous. Hope is not lost."

Noah jerked his head up. The tears ceased. "What did you say?" He could not believe the timing of the statement.

The two were interrupted suddenly by a tremor. Dust fell from the ceiling, and small pebbles on the floor of the cell jostled about. The old man whispered, "Here we go again." He scurried into the darkness of the cell from whence he came. Noah waited a moment, confused by what was happening. The Israelite army was gone. The messenger told Natsa of their exit while he was with Rahab. He looked up high to the window situated near the ceiling. "What's happening?"

"Aftershocks," the voice of the old man answered from somewhere deep in the recesses of the dungeon. "Jericho knows not of this nor Natsa and his men. You and I are low to the earth, lower than they. We feel everything down here." More dust fell from the ceiling onto Noah. "The tremors are getting stronger with each passing day."

For the next thirty minutes, Noah listened to the crackling city settling into place. From within his cell, he could hear no commotion or reaction from the guards or people outside the palace. They were deaf to the subterranean destruction, convinced that all was well within their walls. Noah remembered a verse his dad mentioned in one of his many lessons: "The wealth of the rich man was his stronghold." That was the people of Jericho and their leadership, this false sense of security, veiled to the impending decimation. It was more than confusion and fear that would overthrow these people. It was coupled with arrogance and unpreparedness.

From deep in the darkness, in the lull of crippling noises, the old man whispered, "You are not here by accident, Noah." The statement sent a shiver up Noah's spine. "The words of the woman speak truth. God put you here."

44

Noah jumped when he heard the creak of the foreboding outer door to dungeon open. He turned to see a soldier entering his cell, holding a filthy plate containing a piece of crusty days' old bread. Then from behind the soldier, Noah noticed the silhouette of a man push through. Natsa grabbed the plate and held it out just far enough away from Noah's grasp. In the few hours since his departure, he had grown impatient with the boy's refusal to speak.

"Hungry?" his words seethed with hate.

Noah didn't move. Whether it was from shock or fear, he kept his back against the wall. Natsa surveyed the cell with disgust then back to his captive. By his facial expression, Noah could see he was still angry at his newfound strength from drinking the miraculous waters of the leather bag.

"You will be glad to hear that your *skin* was destroyed." He paced the room, still portraying himself unaffected with the army at his doorsteps. "The high priest of Morgotha is to be celebrated tomorrow morning for his many years of service. I do so thank you for the opportunity to bring my people together. A festival is good for morale, don't you think?"

Noah did not respond.

"Still not speaking, I see." He bobbed his head and breathed deep through his nose. "We shall see how long your silence lasts. It is a matter of time until my men find Rahab's boy. Do you desire *his* sacrifice in your place? Because that is where this leads, Noah!

However, answer my questions, and I give you my word you both shall live."

Noah calmly looked at Natsa, but he was not scared. He knew he should be. The man was wicked to the core, and his life appeared to be in his hands, but Noah knew who was in control.

Unpleased with the silence Natsa continued, "Very well. I have all the time in the world. You, on the other hand…another night without food." He made an evil face and exited the cell. The soldier slammed the door. As Natsa walked away, he announced, "If you change your mind, ask for the guard."

Noah remained motionless as the sound of his host's departure echoed into silence. Alone again. Once more, the voice of his new-found roommate called out from the darkness, "It was good of you not to speak." Noah listened as the elderly stranger scurried toward him again. "Sometimes, holding your tongue is the best option." He reached out and touched Noah's arm in friendship. "I learned that truth when I was much older than you."

The old man breathed deep and pondered, "Don't know how much more this city can take of that marching, though. Come with me. I must show you something." The old man crawled away into the sprawling darkness. Noah hesitated a moment, then followed suit, staying close to his guide. It took a moment for Noah's eyes to adjust to the darkness. The two moved to the farthest corner of the dungeon. The old man whispered, "I have been imprisoned for quite some time now. Many…*many* days. Trying to pass the time is more a practice of finding purpose than fighting boredom. I have counted these stones, the cracks, the pebbles even, virtually everything to keep my mind operating in solitude. But once *your* people began their march on the city, let's just say my numbers are no longer accurate… especially the cracks." There was an excitement in his voice.

Noah watched as the old man took a deep breath and blew away some loose dirt in the corner of the cell. He used his boney fingers to brush away the larger debris. In a moment, piercing the darkness was a small ray of light trickling through a crack in the floor. Noah waved his palm in the light, allowing it to dance across his hands. "Cracks like this showing up more each day. All the marching and trembling

NOAH AND THE HOLY SCEPTER

of the earth and aftershocks like the ones from earlier… I think this city is crumbling beneath us." Noah was stunned at the sight. "Even the dungeon doors, when I arrived, they made no noise at all. Can't tell you how many times those guards snuck up on me. Now, that painful creak it makes wakens me from my sleep! Hinges bending from the weight of the walls collapsing is my guess. One or two more days… I think we may just have an exit large enough for escape!"

Ironically, a sound of the outer door to the dungeon opening once more scared the pair. The man motioned for Noah to move. "Quickly! They mustn't know we have spoken. When the time is good, I will come to you." Noah refused at first but relented, knowing that the man knew better than he. He crawled back near the cell door and returned to his position near the light. Silence again. The small peep door slid open. Noah glanced up at the dark black eyes staring back. The slide shut fast and hard, echoing in the chamber.

Noah did not hear from his guest until much later that evening. In the meantime, he sat and listened to the sounds of the city. The people of Jericho mindlessly continued in vain the labors that kept the city operating, trying to ignore their impending destruction. He recalled the faces of the people watching from inside the walls a few days before, terror-stricken by the sound of the Israelites marching. The false rally of courage from the soldiers and empty bravery of their governor. Noah was amazed how clear his thoughts had become when not being constantly bombarded by electronics, to-do lists, or pestering people. So many questions for the elderly man listed in his head he desired to have answered. The only thing that did not make sense was why Moses showed the path to him. If God had put him in prison, why that escapade?

Noah thought about the magnificent green emerald the size of a golf ball, his entire purpose for being there. He guessed its location on escape would be in Natsa's headquarters, but what about the medallion? Where was Laba's room? He hoped his friend, Ashem, was okay. If he could get a message to him it would be to keep him and Rahab as far away from the palace as possible. *She truly is an exceptional woman created for an exceptional time,* he thought. *No wonder she found her story in the Bible.* All the while, the song hummed by the

Samaritan women played in the background of his mind, reminding him of his purpose, his protection, and his mighty God who watched over him. In the quiet of the evening, as the sounds of the city lowered in preparation for supper and bedtime, Noah heard his roommate once more scurry toward him. He handed Noah a piece of stale bread.

The man smiled at Noah's reaction. "It's not much, so take your time. Think we are safe to speak now."

"Oh my! Thank you, sir. I have not eaten in days."

The man waited a moment as Noah swallowed the hard bread. "I was once a great man." He smiled a little as he spoke, eyes tearing at the memory. "Beautiful wife, sons, a precious daughter and a great house. Oh, you should have seen it! Rolling hills, a hewn cistern full of pure water, livestock covering the horizon. My daughter was highly sought after, my little girl. You could say I had it all. Yahweh is so good."

"Yahweh?" Noah was shocked to hear the man speak of the Israelite God in this evil city. "You are not Hebrew?"

The man nodded his head. "No, I am not." He paused for a moment. "From the time I was a boy, I knew there was something greater than myself. Something was missing in my life, like a hole in my heart. How else can you explain all of this? When I came of age, I decided that life was not worth living until I found who it is my worship belonged to. My father thought me crazy." The old man laughed. "But he loved me and I him. I had a wonderful father. How about you?"

Noah nodded his head, tears gathering in his eyes. He knew he was blessed to call Solomon his daddy. "The best." Noah choked as he said the words.

Noah admired the man as he reminisced his life. He continued, "My father prepared camels with supplies for many days, all that I needed, and sent me on my way. I traveled months heading west, then south through unknown lands. When my supplies ran low, I found work on farms, sometimes tending livestock. Nation upon nation and tribe by tribe, I searched for many years, speaking to many *wise* men. Found a wife to love, and she bore me beautiful children. Earned enough to purchase a property of my own. And the hand of God was upon me before even I found Him.

"Yet…with all I was given, my heart was still restless to find God. It is hard to explain the emptiness of my life even when I had so much to be thankful for. So once my boys were old enough to care for my wife and property, I decided to attempt one final journey to Egypt. I had heard it said the wisest of men reside in Pharaoh's court. Surely, they would have the answer…no?" The man was getting excited and exclaimed, "Pardon, I never introduced myself, did I?" He chuckled. "Far too long have I been alone. My name is Urriel, son of Jephthah."

"Nice to meet you. My name's Noah…son of Solomon." Noah wiped his face.

"Noah," he continued. "Good name. Well, Noah, Egypt was quite the place, a land teeming with a multitude of people from all over the world. I did not know men could build such things. Buildings of stone reaching high into the blue skies. How men could lift these massive boulders, I cannot fathom. Granite statues of animals and past pharaohs lining the cobblestone streets. Oh! And the pyramids! My boy, they are man-made mountains to honor their past leaders! And gold everywhere. Gold statues and figurines, gold cups to drink from, women dressed in the finest clothes and jewels. My eyes were overwhelmed with such excess.

"I was finally hopeful that the quest of my life's path was at an end. Surely an answer was here. The question on the tip of my tongue for near thirty years, 'Who is the One that deserves my worship?' I lost little time seeking out and speaking with many of the temple priests throughout the land. But alas, it was more of the same. I spoke with mystics and mediums, sorcerers and magis. Scholars who dribbled endless words, scribes who argued their preference, and priests practicing their magic or reading the stars. All of it was empty. All utterly useless. All failed attempts of men trying to control others."

The old man shifted his body. A look of peace washed over him. "My heart was downcast within me. I decided then and there that my journey was at an end. It was time for me to give up this vain pursuit of my Creator, return home to my loving wife and family, then die. Perhaps even it was time to return to my father's homeland. That night, as I prepared for bed, exhausted in my old tired body, I overheard a man speaking. *His words…* Something inside of me stirred in my cynical heart and told me to get up and investigate. I left my tent and walked outside to join a large group of people gathering, some sitting, others standing around a man speaking truth. I listened, Noah. My very life hung on every word rolling across his lips. Words of love and hope. How the God of Abraham, Isaac, and Jacob had sent him to bring His people out of Egypt. The longer I listened, the more my heart overflowed.

"Noah, there was something about his words. A power behind them. He was older than me and was not the most eloquent speaker either. The people followed and trusted him. The people called him Moishe."

Noah's skin immediately covered in goosebumps. He interrupted, "You mean Moses?"

Startled that Noah knew who he spoke of, the elderly stranger locked eyes, "That is correct! How did you—"

"He is well-known amongst my people. All my life I have heard stories about Moses."

"I spoke with him, Noah. That night, when the others left, I stayed. I could not let him leave until he told me. Till he told me all that my heart desired. Who is worthy to be praised?" The old man's eyes were filling with tears like Noah. "You see, Noah," his voice cracked, "what else matters in this forsaken world than eternity? We are nothing without God. We are dust."

Noah was overwhelmed by Urriel's testimony. "I know exactly how you feel." Noah waited and then questioned, "What did Moses tell you that night?"

Urriel moved closer to Noah. The shared love of God brought these two time-displaced strangers together. "He told me *my* story. A tale of a man born in privilege. A boy blessed with food and shelter and a family who loved him. A boy who grew into a man and found that all the world could offer would never be enough."

Noah remembered the conversation with his father at the airport and interrupted, "Like Job."

"I do not know this Job you speak of."

"Sorry, Urriel, please continue."

"It was all meaningless. Moses told me of his banishment to the desert, his time in isolation. And how one day, when all the trappings of the world had worn away and all that was left was a broken man, God came to him. Yahweh found him where he was and spoke life into his body. How God filled him with His spirit and gave him purpose and a plan. And how now God had something for him to complete. He called it his *path*."

Goosebumps rippled across Noah's arms as he listened to the elderly man. *The path...* "What is your path?" Noah asked.

The elderly man scooted closer to Noah. He reached his aged hand out to Noah, palm up, and waited for Noah to give his hand in return. Noah reached back, and the man squeezed his hand shut. He looked at Noah a moment and whispered, "Isn't it obvious?" He smiled with comfort, "It's you."

A shockwave of emotion ran through Noah's body. "What?"

"I know why I am imprisoned, and I am at peace with it, my boy. Besides, I was more in a prison of despair when I was outside these walls. Now that I know the one true God, freedom has filled me with hope in the darkest days of my life. My salvation is close at hand, but you have known this truth since you were a child. Noah, I would give up everything I ever had or have ever known to be with Yahweh." The man pointed above.

"You must know who you are, Noah, whose you are. Remember the power of the One you serve. Like your father, Solomon, God loves you more than you know. So...be strong and courageous."

Noah looked away. "Easier said than done. You are older, you have lived your life and seen things. I'm just a kid."

Urriel chuckled. "Yes, but most people, in their limited days on earth, never learn. They grow up seeking and pursuing and worshipping all the wrong things. Blinded by the gifts of God and the riches He provides, their lustful eyes keep their minds full of waste and despair. It amazes me when I see man worship the creation rather than the Creator. But this is not you, Noah. That singing servant woman yesterday, the one you spoke with, she speaks more truth than you understand."

"How so?"

"Her words…she asked 'Who put you in this dungeon?' Your answer was the mistake *you* made."

Noah became argumentative. "It was my fault…and Laba, Natsa's son."

"You underestimate your God still. The only reason you are in prison is because *He* put you here. Eventually, He puts us all in a 'prison of choice.' The only question you need to ask is *why* He did. Stop beating yourself up for something out of your control." The old man yawned. Jericho was silently sleeping now. Noah could hear the soldier outside the dungeon snoring. The old man smiled and nodded his head. He turned from Noah and crawled into the darkness of the cell, leaving Noah to his thoughts.

The elderly man whispered into the night, "Noah…"

"Yes, Urriel."

"God is our refuge and strength. Not walls, not armies, not swords. He is a very present help in trouble. When the time comes and your path is laid before you, remember who your stronghold is. Until morning…"

45

The metal hinges shrieked under the massive weight of the dungeon door outside Noah's cell. Noah was already awake upon sunrise, listening to the Israelite army march at Jericho once more. "Day six," he whispered to himself. He did not anticipate so early a visit, at least until the Hebrew army left the valley. Needless to say, he was unprepared. Dust fell from the ceiling, clogging the air like smoke. The walls shook against the drumming footsteps of a few hundred thousand Israeli soldiers outside. Urriel remained silent and motionless somewhere in the deep recesses of the prison, no doubt monitoring the ever-growing cracks. From behind Noah, the cell door swung open and with it entered an aroma of death.

The two sentries who monitored the jail burst into the cell, grabbed Noah, and stood him to his feet, pressing him hard up against the wall. Once Noah was restrained, an extremely large man lumbered into the cell and stood near the entrance. This giant of a man's presence was foreboding. His head and neck completely covered by a black veil. Large leather straps crisscrossed his torso and arms pressing into his intimidating muscles. In his hands, he wielded a gigantic ax, the head of which shimmered in the torchlight. The shaft of the weapon was at least five feet long. Natsa entered behind the giant, apparently annoyed, having to start the day once more listening to the Sons of Israel march. Noah steadied himself for another onslaught of abuse.

Noah thought it odd Natsa was no longer wearing his military regalia from days before. No gold armor, no sword, not even the necklace dangling from around his neck. His outfit instead was more ceremonial looking, a soft white linen robe stretching the length of his body with a purple sash, a few pieces of green emeralds studded the gold jewelry, and a small simple crown of leaves. An army more than fifty times the population of Jericho was wrapping around the city like a python around its prey at this very moment, and he was tending to other affairs. The governor, the leader, the king of Jericho was no longer worried, no longer preparing. He had all but become immune to the disturbance. His desensitized heart blinded him.

The same sort of hypnotizing effect happened throughout the whole city. The people no longer rushed the walls or feared attack. Their senses dulled to the impending doom. None knew what Noah did, that tomorrow would be different. Tomorrow, the march would not cease with one revolution. Tomorrow, the Israelites were coming in and over. And somewhere in the chaos, Noah would find a way out and lay hands on the jewel of Jericho.

Noah's thoughts were chased away at the sight of Laba and Nomed slithering into the cell behind their father. They both were wearing similar ceremonial garments like Natsa. Regal deep purple robes with white linen sewn throughout. Their appearance was clean, hair situated with purpose, a small thin piece of gold wrapped each of their heads like a halo sitting behind their ears. Noah carefully studied Laba to see if he wore the stolen medallion, but he was not. Yet another piece of useful information gathered for Noah.

Natsa gave an order, and a group of four or five soldiers, his personal bodyguards, rushed into the cell, carrying torches. The flames lit up the darkness, illumining the area his roommate had called home for more days than he could count. The squalid environment was covered in filth and garbage. Pieces of cloth, dead animals, broken cups, rotting bones littered the ground. Huddled in the corner in tattered garments was Urriel, his emaciated aged body wasting away from starvation. The light from the torches blinded his virgin eyes. Too many days in darkness overwhelmed his senses. His disheveled greasy hair covered his face. The bodyguards brushed past Noah, and the sentries and took hold of Urriel. "Seems my time has come, Noah."

Natsa's men picked up his frail body.

"I told you my purpose was you."

"I see you two have met," Natsa mused.

Urriel confronted Natsa, "Do what you came for. I care not for myself for I know who I serve and where my eternal rest shall be. You, on the other hand, have an entirely different end. A place of weeping and gnashing of teeth." He pointed at the boys, "For you and your hell spawn!"

"Still dribbling on about the afterlife? You shall be there soon enough, old man! Remove him from my presence!" Natsa commanded.

Noah watched as the bodyguards forcefully removed the frail man from the cell. He wanted to scream, but he knew it was no use. Tears filled his eyes. He lowered his head and closed his eyes. Slowly he shook his head back and forth in unbelief. An empty feeling filled his stomach. He was helpless, alone, incapable of defending himself. He was a prisoner of God. No power, no freedom, no friends. His captors despised everything about him and desired nothing more than elimination. The only reason he was still alive in their eyes was leverage against Rahab. At that moment, all he could see in his mind was the calm face of his father looking at him square in the eyes. He watched as Solomon's face shifted ever so slightly and a peaceful grin etched his lips.

Natsa took a deep breath and exhaled loudly. "You hear the marching of your soldiers this morning, I am sure. Oh! How long will they waste their time and mine as well! What are your people doing? I can understand an approach and retreat for a day, maybe two. Reconnaissance, measure your opponent's response, watch their positions. But it has been six days! *Six!* Do they plan on boring us to death?" Natsa stared at the boy being restrained against the cell wall. "Speak!"

Noah said nothing. He had nothing to say. Any words he spoke would do nothing to quell the rage of Natsa. The governor bent down and picked up a thin rock and slung it at Noah. The stone barely missed its mark, striking the wall, ricocheting to the rear of the prison. "For years I heard the rumors of a nomadic people that plundered powerful Egypt. Numbers so great they blot out the land like locusts. They move without any challenge, their god leading their path. Stories of food falling from heaven. But if your people are so great and your god so near, why do they refuse to draw their swords and attack? Even after what I heard about their battle with Og, king of Bashan? Or maybe the stories are false, mere myths to strike fear into my people." Natsa stared at Noah and shook his head. "Your time here is quickly coming to an end, Noah. That is, unless you would like to answer my questions... Rahab has been warned. I am sure she has spoken with her boy."

"Where are you taking him?" Noah whispered.

"Urriel? To your favorite place of course... Morgotha's Forum. The people desire a blood sacrifice in honor of our fallen priest that you saw fit to poison. Oh, and tomorrow, we offer another to bless our battle ahead. You or Ashem will suffice. It matters not. You had better pray to your god in a box its Rahab's boy." Natsa and his sons laughed as they exited the cell, followed by the massive ax-wielding man and the two sentries. Noah collapsed to the floor as soon as the door shut behind them.

Weak from lack of food, overwhelmed with fear and sadness, he sat exhausted on the cold damp floor. Noah moaned in agony. "What now, God? I am so tired and hungry... Lord, please watch over Urriel and thank you for sending him," Noah whimpered to himself. He sat in silence for a while gathering his thoughts.

The kind old man was gone, his last friend in this wretched place, this vile sore of a city. Noah was thankful for the brief companionship. The Samaritan woman never returned either. She played her part ordained by God. The people of Jericho clamored inside the walls unaware of the looming destruction. He could hear their cheers as his roommate was led outside the palace gate into their gnashing teeth. The citizens demanded sacrifice, blood for blood. Their sole hope lay in a carved statue, its horrific façade stained crimson with anything they could lay a knife's blade to.

Clearly, Natsa had lost all sense of the danger swarming outside Jericho's massive walls. God had desensitized the pagan leader to the danger at his doorsteps. He didn't even bother to dress for the occasion! A veil of stupidity blinded the leader of Jericho like Pharaoh of Egypt with Moses. He was bored of the incessant marching and arrogant in his position of power, a combination which would soon determine the end of his people's way of life. His hell-spawned children would join their father, bringing a much-needed finality to the family line.

Dust fell from the ceiling as a small aftershock vibrated his cell. Noah crawled to where Urriel had pointed out the cracks yesterday. He was shocked at how much larger they had grown in so little time. Urriel was a godsend. An example of a life well-lived, a life of privilege and love, a life of growing wisdom; he searched and found, and he finished strong. God was pulling Urriel ever closer.

Something about Urriel reminded Noah of his conversation with his father in the airport on his travels over from the States. Sitting at a diner in Chicago, discussing the story of Job, a story of a man who had it all and lost it in a day. A man full of all life could offer but only desired one thing: to be near his Creator. Though God allowed Satan to take all he loved away, he could never sever the love Job had for God. To Noah, Urriel was Job.

Noah wished he could have a few moments with his father. He wanted his father to see and know what he had experienced, but he knew it wasn't possible. And even though Solomon was not there, Noah knew his faith in the one true God outweighed even his own. His father had a magical way of bringing the Bible to life and an even more powerful ability to show his boy enough love to drown away the yearning for a departed mother. *What a man to call my dad!*

In the stillness of the dungeon, alone, surrounded in shadow, Noah recalled the dig site and his wandering hike. A fall into the hidden cave and the hollow path to the scepter of Judah. The rebellious impulse to hide his "find" from the others. The yearning to be alone and study the treasure. The pull and power of the ancient relic. Then darkness. Darkness thicker and more pressing than he felt in the loneliness of the dungeon. The mysterious boy king approaching. His invitation and explanation of all that lay ahead. The path! A path many had traveled before. The majestic meeting place between Noah's home and heaven. The bounding, joyful Thios Lypri, his personal guide, riding upon the powerful cat leaping about the room.

A rainbow wormhole and a medallion adorning his neck. Then the two-thousand-pound hulking beast that almost trampled him! An elderly couple with hearts and home large enough for any lost soul. The caress of a barren mother, the wisdom of a man of many years. A majestic midnight meeting in the wilderness with the spokesman of God. Then the introduction to the military genius, Joshua, only bettered by his genuine love and faith in his Creator. The promise held that bestowed on him long life with a trusted friend, Caleb. And how could he forget Adonai, captain of the Lord of Hosts? The path held out looking for one courageous enough to undertake. Two anchors to flank him in battle, Enud and Eliab. A second river divided, another dry riverbed to cross.

Rahab, an amazing and despised woman along with her son to give him love and support through a pagan city. Ashem, a child warrior with no sword. A rejected and bullied boy willing to give his life for a stranger with a purpose far exceeding any he had known. Salvation for his new friend, faith explained. Then an encounter with the humblest man to ever grace creation, Moses, Urriel's teacher. A palace path illuminated. Oh! And the skin of water for a parched child hiding in the shadows of a boulder by the most disgusting swamp known to man.

Noah giggled as he reminisced the crossing. The plan, the meeting, the watching, and waiting. Witness to the terror of God on a lost people hiding behind a wall. A people mesmerized by the Ark and spitting hate at the same time.

And then his Morgothian capture, the brevity of hope and the entrance to hopelessness. The fork in the road and the torture to follow. A gift lost, the goal within arm's reach, yet farther away than when he arrived. The cleansing waters and refreshing rush of liquid to restore a weary sinner washed pure as snow. Hope restored. Even in the darkest prison, a visitor from time lost, a story of a woman come to life. A bucket, and then an old friend. A choice and silence. And now time to converse with His Lord. Noah whispered, "*God* put me here. *God* gave me friends. He has supported me through it all. He showed me the way in, the way out… All I need is to *trust*. Be strong and courageous Noah!"

Noah leaned back against the wall of the cell for one last evening in the city of Jericho. A peaceful calming overtook him as never before. No hunger pangs quaked in his gut.

— ⋄ 46 ⋄ —

fter the departure of Natsa and his entourage, Noah was left to himself for the rest of the day. A lingering fear remained that someone may come for him, but nothing. There were a few periodic cell-checks from the sentries; the peep window on the cell door would slide open, black beady eyes stared to make sure he was alive, and then slam shut. Noah heard no news of Rahab, no visit from the Samaritan woman, and not a mention of Urriel. Although the sound of the crowd cheering of what Noah assumed was the presentation of Urriel as sacrifice to Morgotha sent shivers over his body.

The day was spent mostly drifting in and out of short naps and fighting off the never-ending hunger pangs poking his insides like a jagged knife. Never in his life did he think he could go this long without food. It felt as if his stomach was eating itself. After many hours in solitude, he could hear Jericho's marketplace shuttering for the night. The smell of supper wafting in the air made his starvation all the worst. The sunset spread amber hues across the land and through the elevated window in the cell. He could hear the guards outside his cell, snoring again.

Noah pressed himself against the filthy wall, sitting up knees to chest. He dropped his head and closed his eyes to rest once more. He nearly had a heart attack when he looked up to find a stranger standing across from him not more than five feet away. He jumped to his feet and rushed to the corner of the cell nearest the door. He could hardly catch his breath from the shock.

"Fear not," the powerful voice of the stranger, clear as crystal, echoed in the cell. "Peace be upon you, Noah."

Noah's heart rate slowed as did his breathing. He cautiously approached the shadowy figure. The man was wrapped in a dark robe, his face hidden by a hood. Noah glanced at the cell door locked fast in place. He heard no noise of entry. The guard continued his snoring outside. "Who are you?" Noah demanded.

"A messenger sent by the Most High." The stranger handed Noah a package wrapped in linen.

The smell of the gift hit Noah before he had it in his grasp. He unwrapped the cloth quickly like a child on Christmas morning. A fresh warm loaf of bread! The soft moist sustenance met every need in his body. He scarfed down as much as he could as fast as his body could take. The soft flaky morsel went down easy, satisfying every craving and desire. With his mouth full, he questioned, "Thank you…but why are you here?"

The messenger calmly replied, "Comfort."

Noah was confused. "How did you get past the guards?"

The stranger ignored the question. "May I read something to you…as you eat?"

"You want to read to me?"

"Man shall not live on bread alone, Noah"—the messenger pointed at the loaf in Noah's hand—"but on every word that comes from the mouth of God."

Noah sat down with bread in hand to listen while the messenger remained standing. He continued, "A prayer of King David." Noah's skin immediately covered in goosebumps just as happened at times when his father would read to him.

> I cry aloud with my voice to the Lord;
> I make supplication with my voice to the Lord.
> I pour out my complaint before Him;
> I declare my trouble before Him.
> When my spirit is overwhelmed within me,
> You knew my *path* in the way where I walk.
> *They* have hidden a trap for me.
> Look to the right and see;
> For there is no one who regards me;

No one cares for my soul.
I cried out to You, O Lord;
I said, "*You* are my refuge,
My portion in the land of the living."
Give heed to my cry,
For I am brought very low;
Deliver me from my *persecutors*,
For *they* are too strong for me.
Bring my soul out of *prison*,
So that I may give thanks to Your name;
The righteous will surround me,
For You will deal bountifully with me.
—Psalm 142

Noah hung on every word the stranger read. Words written by King David many years ago. Words that described his very situation. Words of helplessness, words of imprisonment, words of prayer and hope. For the last few days, all Noah had done was cry aloud, pray, and complain to God about his imprisonment. His spirit was overwhelmed with fear; fear of Natsa, fear of pain, fear for his friends. But God did know his path just like He knew David's. Noah just did not realize it would take him to prison.

Noah was alone in Natsa's trap with no one to regard or help him. As for escape, the odds looked bleak. But God was his refuge, his strength. Time and again over the last few weeks. Noah watched the power of God stretch out before him. *Why would this be any different?* Noah's only hope was deliverance, a miraculous escape from prison and his persecutors. Though outnumbered, Noah knew that all the men under Natsa's command were no match against the Most High God.

The messenger interrupted Noah's thoughts, "Blessed be the Word of the Lord."

"I never heard that prayer of David," Noah whispered in shock. "He wrote like he was sitting beside me for the last few days."

The messenger remained standing, his face hidden beneath the robe. "You are here because God wants you to be. Our Father in heaven uses suffering to increase the faith of all who love Him. When one is alone, as you find yourself, when your best-laid plans fail, God provides mercy. Through many trials, you will enter heaven. Your path is just beginning, Noah."

"So what now?" Noah asked.

"Rest," the figure proposed, "and prayer. For tomorrow approaches to test your strength and courage."

Noah took a deep breath. The bread was gone. His belly was full. He bowed his head in thought to ponder the stranger's words. When he looked up, the messenger was gone. He entered without a sound and exited all the same.

47

Before the night had given way to the morning sun, Noah's cell door burst open. Two of Natsa's soldiers rushed in and grabbed Noah, still groggy from the intrusion. He must have passed out soon after the stranger departed. The words read seemed like a dream, but the taste of the warm bread still lingered in his stomach proving otherwise. The guards said nothing as they moved their captive. Their grip on his arms held tight, causing him to wince a few times. They moved with haste out of the dungeon, across the palace foray, and into the winding staircase up to Natsa's chambers. The torches were the only light in the early morning hours, but Noah knew the path well.

The large wooden door to Natsa's office was already ajar. The soldiers escorting Noah moved inside and tossed him in the corner. The sound of his body slapping the ground grabbed the attention of the governor who glared momentarily at the boy and then returned to what preoccupied his mind. He half-listened as his commanding officers reported the news of yesterday, updates on provision stores, and the movements of the Israelites. Natsa devoured his breakfast while the men spoke, giving little to no respect to those he hand-selected to report to him on the comings and goings of the city. The annoyance of Natsa listening to the tedious reports was not lost on the officers.

The cold mood shifted when a Jericho soldier in full armor entered the room. "My king," the soldier bowed, "the Israelites are on the move."

Natsa studied the soldier before turning to look out upon the valley. "Aw... Yes... I see..."

The officers ceased their report. Natsa rubbed his temples in frustration. "Day seven, a week of this incessant marching?" His words lingered in the air. Natsa rose to his feet and walked toward the balcony protruding from his headquarters. He was clearly aggravated. "The Israelites march." He shook his head. "Every morning, they march and march and *march!*" He breathed heavy, his hands clenched in fists at his side. "But nothing else! I care not of their parade anymore." He returned his attention to the messenger. "Order the soldiers to the wall. Tell them not to fear. The Sons of Israel have no way inside. Now...leave me!"

The messenger bowed and departed without saying another word. Natsa glared at Noah briefly sitting quietly in the corner. Noah could see the hate Natsa bore him through his dead eyes. Noah remained motionless as the governor stared. *Not much longer*, he encouraged himself. He only wished he had the medallion already around his neck to call out for help. Noah took a deep breath of relief as Natsa returned his attention to the officer's morning report.

Thirty minutes later, Noah could hear the palace coming alive around him along with the city. The marching Israelites were wrapping their forces around the city as before, their thunderous footsteps shaking the core of Jericho. Occasionally, Natsa would glance back over his shoulders for a view of the mass of soldiers circling like vultures. His meeting was interrupted only by the sound of Laba and Nomed arguing down the hall over breakfast. Even they had found no reason to leave the palace. However, the morning mood shifted when the huge gong inside Jericho rattled an echoing blow. Something was different. Momentary fear gripped the room along with the entire city.

Once more, Noah heard the footsteps of the messenger soldier approach the governor's chambers. He rushed inside with a terrified look on his face. "My lord... They are—"

"Speak!" Natsa screamed.

"The Sons of Israel, my Lord...they are not leaving!"

"What do you mean not leaving?"

"Sir, they continue their march—"

Oxygen left the room. Everyone froze in fear. The officers stared in dismay at their leader. Natsa said nothing. He slowly rose to his feet and turned around toward the opening. He watched as the Sons of Israel began to circle Jericho for a second time. The dust from their movement creating a massive cloud. Unlike the previous days, there was no exiting force. "Get me my armor," Natsa whispered, his voice crackling in shock.

"My lord?" one of his bodyguards spoke from behind Natsa, unable to hear.

"My armor! Now!" The terror in his voice resonated the chambers.

"Sir!" the intimidated soldier replied. He bowed his head and rushed out of the room.

Noah sat in disbelief as he watched these powerful men who moments ago thought themselves immune to attack wrestling with fear so palpable he could feel it. All the officers looked defeated as they stared at one another and then at their confused leader. Natsa screamed commands, but the terror-stricken men struggled to regain their steady hands. Natsa slapped one of them hard in the face to rouse him from his stupor. One by one, they regained some semblance of courage. Natsa ordered the officers to their individual posts with instructions for a possible breach.

"Prepare the men as before!" Natsa turned and stared at the invading army. "Wait!" Natsa raised his hand to halt his commanders. "I see no ladders, no garrisons, no ram for the gate. The valley is empty! The entire force of Israel surrounds the city, but they have nothing to mount an attack. Nothing to climb our walls. What are they planning? Go now and report back if you see anything unusual." The governor's attention turned to Noah, and the officers left.

His fury raged at Noah's demeanor. Noah could not hold back his facial expression declaring, "I know something you don't know… and I'm not going to tell you." A feeling of satisfaction filled Noah with the thought that once and for all, this heinous leader of this decrepit pagan people was about to receive their comeuppance. He knew he needed to be careful lest he feel the fierce brunt of his rage.

The officers silently exited the room at their leader's commands to prepare for battle. Before Natsa could question Noah, the clumsy soldier tasked with retrieving his armor came barreling in along with the remainder of his bodyguards. The foreboding men who once carried an air of superiority were stumbling and falling into one another still dressing for battle. How could these elite soldiers be caught so ill prepared? It was as if Natsa had given them the day off and they were responding to a fire drill. The whole scene was surreal as Noah watched on from the corner. Laba and Nomed came rushing into the chambers as well. Their attire was similar to the day before, dressed in ceremonial robes for Urriel's sacrifice.

Natsa hastily moved around barking commands at anyone in earshot.

"Father, what is happening?" Nomed questioned.

"You two…get dressed! Now! Something is different this morning," Natsa spoke as the soldier who was sent to gather his armor dressed the disorganized king of Jericho. The clumsy soldier shimmied up and around Natsa's outstretched arms, tying strings and clasping metal snaps. "Hurry, you fool!"

Laba looked down at Noah in the corner with a demonic expression. "What about him?" He pointed at the boy.

Noah immediately noticed he was not wearing the medallion.

Natsa looked over at Noah. "You two." He nodded at the Sentries tasked with bringing him up earlier from the dungeon. "Take him back and then join the other men on the wall. Morgotha's blood sacrifice will have to wait."

The sentries quickly moved toward Noah and grabbed him. They raised him to his feet and forced him out of the governor's chambers. Before they reached the stairs, Noah overheard Natsa scream at the soldier responsible for retrieving his armor, "*Fool!* Where is the necklace, you imbecile?" In all the confusion, the soldier had forgotten the most important piece to the leader of Jericho! "Guards!" Natsa was now moving so quickly he was knocking things to the ground as he tried to fasten his armor. "Just forget it," was the last thing Noah heard as the sentries hurried him down the stairs.

48

Within a few minutes, Noah was thrown into the all-familiar dungeon. The sentries hurriedly slammed the door shut and returned to their commander. Noah listened as they hurried back until silence. The only noise now was the all-encompassing pounding of footsteps from the ever-circling army outside the walls. Noah knew Eliab and Enud were amongst the men. He imagined Joshua at the helm, urging his men on. Surely, they had not forgotten him. The orders from Joshua were already given. On the seventh circuit, the trumpets would blow, followed by a shout from the soldiers, and into the city they would rush. No ladders were needed as Natsa had postured. God would provide the way in.

Noah could feel the spy's prayers for his safety. Suddenly, he heard the ringing of the large gong inside Jericho. The third circuit of the city was beginning...four more before his time was done! *Time is running out! Think, Noah!*

By Noah's estimation, the time it took for the soldiers to wrap once around the city was close to fifteen minutes. The third circuit had begun, so he had about an hour remaining before the chaos of war consumed Jericho. Three main objectives marked his path. First, to break free of the dungeon. Second, locate and apprehend the medallion along with the green jewel of Jericho. And finally, if God be for him, escape to Rahab's inn. The city of Jericho quaked by the force of the marching. The walls to the dungeon felt as if they were swaying with every pounding step.

Dust fell from the ceiling along with larger pieces of rock. He stared at the iron door barring him from freedom. The hinges were clearly loosening with every passing minute. He could see light from the torches outside peeking through slightly. Noah bowed his head and closed his eyes, "Lord God, I know that You brought me here. You guide me and protect me, and now I need You, Lord…please… give me the strength. All I have heard since leaving the dig site is to have courage. I now know that my courage and strength is in You and You alone. One opportunity is all I need, Lord. Guide my steps. My life is yours. Amen."

Noah backed away from the door to the rear wall of the cell. He lowered himself like an Olympic runner placing themselves into blocks before the starting pistol cracked and the race began. He took a deep breath and burst forth. As he neared the door, he lowered his right shoulder, and with all his strength, he slammed sideways into the door. His body crashing against the heavy door echoed loudly throughout the dungeon. Had a sentry been within a hundred yards, they would have come running…but nothing. Noah scanned the door. The hinges had separated substantially from the wall. One more solid hit, possibly two, and his freedom was at hand. Noah gathered himself and quickly moved to the rear of the room to charge again. He felt the wind press against his face as he rushed forward and *slam!* He could now reach his arm through an opening but still not enough to press his body entirely through.

"One more time!" Noah coaxed himself to ignore the pain screaming on this right side. He rubbed it aggressively, hoping the friction would numb the sting. He paused one final time to make sure no one approached. A deep breath, and then he was off and running…*slam!* The door hinges released completely, allowing him to fall into the hallway! Freedom was his. He lay for a moment in shock from what had happened before rising up.

"Now to Laba's room." He ran quickly to the outer dungeon door, released the lever, and slowly opened it to scan the hallway. Nothing. Not a soul in sight. The entire palace dungeon was eerily empty.

As he left the dungeon area and entered the main portion of the palace, he heard Natsa screaming at his men still. By the approaching sound of the group, he assumed they were descending the stairs from his headquarters. Noah hid behind a large vase near the rear of the great hall of the palace. Noah listened as random horns blew throughout Jericho, sounding alarm. He heard the tandem steps of Natsa's soldiers, their weapons clanging against their armor. As Natsa and his bodyguards exited the stairwell, the governor was met by another messenger.

"What now?" Natsa barked.

"My Lord, the Israelites are beginning their third rotation of the city. They say nothing and their weapons are not drawn. Their priests refuse to blow their trumpets. And the Ark is amongst them still."

"And what of our men?"

The soldier hesitated, increasing Natsa's agitation. "Answer me!"

"They are scared, my lord." The messenger spilled everything, the overwhelming fear causing him to near hyperventilate. "Some refuse to take their positions on the wall, choosing to stay with their families. Others fight against one another like something has possessed them. The captains shout orders that make no sense. All the while, my lord, the cloud of dust created by the marching Hebrews thickens by the minute." Natsa stared at the messenger, angered by the report.

"I see." Natsa rubbed his hand along his jawbone to his chin. His face contorted with a wickedness Noah had never seen before. "Go to the captains immediately and tell them from this moment forward…any man who refuses to stand their post is to be slaughtered in the streets without hesitation! That should solve the problem." The messenger stood motionless. His face turned pale. The command was not what he expected to hear.

"What has changed?" Natsa pompously mused as he turned to the officers and bodyguards following him. "Something is amiss!" Natsa paused momentarily to listen to the marching force outside his city. "This whole routine has become wearisome to me. The wretched Hebrews' intentions must be different this day, do you not think?" His attention returned to the messenger still motionless from the command. "You…before you go, is there any sign of ropes or ladders?"

"None, my Lord," he whispered, daring not to raise his eyes to the governor.

"Well, then, if they cannot mount our walls…we have nothing to fear." Natsa smirked. He turned to the commanders following him. "You three, go now. Prepare for battle. Order all men to the walls. And if they refuse, you know what to do. Now…leave me!"

The commanders bowed to Natsa and rushed out of the palace. The shell-shocked messenger was dismissed as well to pass on the orders. Natsa anxiously paraded about in thought near the entrance to the palace, contemplating his options. By his actions and words, it was clear he was confident Jericho's defenses would hold, no matter how large the opposing force, especially one with no ramparts to mount a siege. Arrogance oozed from his face, but inside, his heart was overcome with fear, and Noah knew it. His bodyguards waited in formation for orders, Nomed and Laba near his side, watching their dad pace. Natsa turned suddenly toward his men with a demonic expression, but all Noah could see was what was missing! Noah's heart leapt inside his chest. Natsa took one last look around the palace and spoke, "Very well…we move." And with that, the group departed to join Jericho's people.

49

Noah remained hidden for a minute or two just to ensure no one was near to spot him break cover. All the while, he hoped that if Natsa was careless enough to leave the necklace, the jewel representing who holds the power and key to the city, Laba would do likewise with the medallion. "God, give me a path," he asked beneath his breath.

The palace walls swayed to and fro from the man-made earthquake churning outside the city. Suddenly, like an explosion thundering from inside the palace, the wall near Noah split apart. The shifting weight of the massive boulders used to construct the palace were too much for the beams to bear. The constant jostling overwhelmed this section of the palace. The snaking crack moved from the top left corner of the wall across to the opposite end.

Noah listened as the stones shattered and shifted. Dust fell from the gaping wound, and the stones slid and slammed into each other, looking for a place to rest. The smashing and cracking sounded like a fireworks show inside the great hall. Surely, someone would hear and respond. But alas, the palace was vacant of soldiers, servants, anyone that would care. All the people of the city were outside, preparing to defend their homes with their lives. Like God dividing the waters of the Jordan, He created safe passage for Noah inside the palace. Even the Sentries charged with guarding him hadn't bothered with one last look.

"This is it," Noah whispered. He broke cover and moved stealthily across the great hall toward the stairs. Just as he did, a massive chunk of wall fell and smashed the vase he had used for shelter. The shock of the destruction reminded him of his vulnerable position. He shuddered at the thought of what just happened but chose to not hesitate any longer. Laba and Nomed's room was near their father's headquarters. He wrapped the stairwell quickly, being careful not to make unnecessary noise.

His first objective was the medallion. He felt confident once he had that in hand, finding the green jewel would be much simpler. In the early morning chaos, the soldiers and servants had left the entire palace in disrepair. Articles of tremendous value, treasures collected over the course of centuries, and furniture had been knocked over and pushed around. Broken glass from goblets, vases, and mirrors littered the floor. Food was abandoned, half-eaten; stew was left burning over open flame which gave Noah an idea. *Fire could be a useful diversion.*

As he exited the stairwell into the long hallway, Noah turned into the first room he came to on the right. By the looks of the place, it had to be Laba and Nomed's quarters. The room was in shambles. It was hard to tell if it was from the morning tumult or just the way the two slobs lived. Their bedroom was as horrid as the lower level of Jericho. As he carefully searched the chamber, the sound of the gong near the gate of Jericho sounded once more…

"Four! Already!" Noah's heart leapt in his chest. The clock was ticking away, the minutes faster than he desired! He aggressively tore through the boys' room, earnestly searching for the Medallion. "It must be here!" Noah screamed in desperation. He opened their drawers and dumped out the contents, ripped everything off the shelves, looked under all their clothes…but nothing. There was a window overlooking the palace grounds. For whatever reason, ignoring the urgency of the moment, he felt pulled to have a look. He knew it better to resist the urge but decided to comply. What he saw overwhelmed all his imagination could ever muster.

The Israelite army was in full battle array. The tribal banners of Israel swayed in the wind, guiding the soldiers. Dust was circling high over the city. The marching soldiers stared straight ahead, silent and steady as they went, ignoring the screaming people on the wall. In the distance, Noah could see Joshua and the elders watching on as the soldiers marched. The people of Jericho had taken their positions once more on the wall in defense. Fear had gripped them all. Their faces were white—pale white.

Women screamed, and children hid behind anything they could find. Men jostled about, running into each other in complete confusion. Fires burned throughout the city, casting smoke that melted into the dust cloud. The smell of burning food swirled amongst the aroma of manure, mixing with the fear circling inside the walls. Officers screamed at their men while horns blew in the distance.

Noah watched as a soldier on the wall turned and vomited over a group of workers piling weapons for defense below. Noah was hypnotized by his vantage point. A scene so shocking, in fact, that he failed at first to notice Laba and Nomed in the courtyard arguing with their father.

It was clear Natsa had no intention of allowing his boys near the battle, and by their reaction, they were not pleased. Though they rebelled, their soldiers answered to Natsa's orders alone. The king quickly left them each with a few guards for added protection. From Noah's vantage point, he could see the massive gate to the lower level opened and guarded by a few men. Noah glanced to the left of the palace square into the alley he and Ashem had used a few days before. "Where is he?" Noah whispered.

Noah was confident he would find his buddy nearby, and there behind a few wicker baskets was the silhouette of a boy doing his utmost to avoid detection. "Ashem!" Noah knew his friend would not give up on him. He motioned aggressively to get Ashem's attention to no avail. Noah opened the window of Laba's room to allow for better movement. He leaned out and waved his arms to get Ashem's attention. After a few seconds, he saw the hand of Ashem wave back. Noah's heart was filled with courage.

Then the shrill voice of Laba echoed in the vacant palace square, "You!" Noah looked down to see Laba and Nomed staring up at him. The demonic eyes of the brothers glared at him as they made their way back into the palace, their soldiers following close behind. Noah turned, his heart pounding within his chest, adrenaline pumping through his veins. He scanned the ransacked room. Where was it? Where had he not looked? "Lord, help me!" Noah begged.

Something caught the corner of his eye. Suddenly, there underneath the covers and pillows on a bed, a light came beaming through. He moved quickly to the bed, tossing the covers off. He picked up the pillow, reaching inside the case. He removed the Medallion. The necklace vibrated in his hands. He quickly took the relic and hung it around his neck. A feeling of relief overcame his senses. He took a deep breath. "Now, the jewel!"

Noah needed a diversion, some way of slowing Laba and Nomed along with their guards. "The fire!" he remembered. He quickly gathered some of the boys' possessions and tossed them in the hall near the entrance to the stairwell. He grabbed a piece of wood burning beneath a pot boiling stew near their bedroom. He tossed the burning ember, lighting the pile aflame and moved up the hall toward Natsa's office.

Like a gazelle evading a cheetah, Noah burst down the hallway. He could hear the echoing footsteps of his enemy approaching from below. He moved swiftly and carefully, sidestepping the debris that had fallen from the walls and the broken glass left by the early morning chaos. He flung open the doors to Natsa's chambers, thankful to find it empty. From behind him, he could hear the boys and their soldiers zeroing in on his location. Laba screamed, "Bring water! Hurry!" Noah had bought himself a few minutes.

Like a magnet pulling on his chest, the medallion lifted forward, floating in the air, guiding him right where to look. He followed to the corner of Natsa's room and opened a beautifully hand-carved wooden armoire. Inside this magnificent piece of craftsmanship was a mountain of treasure. There before him was a pile of gold coins, jewels of all shapes and colors, silver bricks, royal crowns, necklaces and bracelets—more than one man needed. Noah ignored the luster of these empty riches. All he wanted, all he needed, his whole purpose of entering the pagan city again was the green jewel of Jericho.

And then he saw it, hanging innocently behind a wall of papers, isolated from the other treasures, the most valuable stone in all of Jericho. Noah was transfixed by the beauty of the sparkling green emerald. He was within reach of the sole reason he was sent to this time and this place. *How could Natsa have been so stupid to abandon this precious stone?* The miraculous confusion of God created by the Israelites had clouded his judgment. Noah reached out and clutched the precious stone. Ignoring all around him, he stared at the necklace. He pushed against the green rock and felt it give a little. He pushed again, trying to break it free from the gold setting, but it was no use. He took the necklace and threw it around his neck. He placed the stone under his robe next to the medallion.

Just as he turned, another loud, resonating shiver reverberated throughout the city. The gong of Jericho announced another Israelite circuit. "Five!" Noah's heart began to beat fast again. "Thirty minutes!" Escape from the palace was his goal now. If he could just get to Ashem, he knew he had a chance. "I can't go back the way I came. Laba and Nomed are coming." He scanned Natsa's office for some hope of an exit. "Lord, show me the way."

The medallion vibrated like a smart phone beneath his robe. Noah blinked, and as soon as he opened his eyes, the room was black and white. It was just like when Moses met him in the palace square to illumine the path. Noah looked down at his feet, and a golden path lit up! It all made sense now. Moses was not showing Noah the way in, he was showing Noah the way out! "Of course!" Noah exclaimed. "Moses showed the Israelites the way out of Egypt, not the way in!"

The golden path at his feet led to the balcony, protruding from Natsa's headquarters. Noah moved fast. He could hear the sound of enemy footsteps in the hallway. "They must have made it past the fire," he surmised.

The dust from the marching Israelites surrounded Noah, blotting out the morning sunlight. The golden path illumined by the medallion crossed over the balcony, bringing him to the edge. Nearly fifty feet up. Noah had never been too fond of heights. But courage was what was expected. No way was he going to stop now. He carefully mounted the railing wrapping the balcony. He shimmied along the edge of the structure, keeping as close to Moses's path as possible.

Noah was conscious of the danger, but adrenaline pushed him on. Just as his body was out of view, he heard Nomed and a few of his soldiers burst into Natsa's office. They were all breathing heavy from climbing the stairs and tearing through the palace. "You, search there! You…over there!" he heard Nomed screaming at the soldiers to scour the surroundings.

Noah continued on, carefully scaling the narrow edge across the ledge to another smaller balcony extending from an adjacent room. When he reached the new platform, he looked down and knew exactly where he was! Below him was the small storage area he crawled into days before where the path of Moses guided! The climbing apparatus to descend the platform was barely visible. The ladder-like rungs were hidden within the stone setting designed specifically for the king to escape in case of attack.

Noah heard a scream of frustration come from Natsa's headquarters. Laba and his cohort of soldiers had joined with Nomed in their search. As the group scoured the top floor of the palace, Laba lashed out at anyone in earshot, "Where is he? Find him!"

Noah listened as the soldiers threw aside anything large enough to hide a boy his size and smashed whatever blocked their way. If it wasn't for the marching Israelites, everyone in the city would have heard the commotion. It was now or never! Noah peered over the side of the ledge. The drop was near forty feet from where he was. If he slipped, it didn't matter if the gong sounded for the seventh time, he would die from the fall.

The words of Joshua resonated in Noah's head, the same words he heard repeatedly since leaving Josiah, "Be strong and courageous…be strong and courageous." With one last prayer for bravery, he carefully lowered his body, one leg at a time over the edge. Now completely hanging from the wall, he froze momentarily from fear. Thankfully, he heard the whisper of a familiar voice below. "Hurry, Noah!" It was Ashem! He must have seen Laba and Nomed racing inside with their soldiers and made a move for the storage room once he saw Noah on the balcony.

"Noah, come, please…we have little time," Ashem begged him down. "The soldiers have abandoned the palace for the wall. Our escape is open, but you must move quickly."

Noah descended carefully, making sure he had good footing before making a move. Once he reached the bottom, Ashem shoved him fiercely against the wall. The unexpected jolt sent shockwaves of worry through Noah. *Was he being set up?* Ashem pressed his finger to his lips and pointed to the balcony of Natsa's chambers. Noah glanced up to see Nomed and Laba looking over the palace grounds. A moment later, they were gone. Noah heard Nomed screaming, "He must be here! Where is he hiding? *Find him!*"

—·✧· 50 ·✧·—

Noah hugged his friend, thankful Ashem had not given up on him, an embrace that enveloped all the feelings and words that they had no time to share. "Noah, come...this way." Ashem scurried ahead out of the storage room and across the palace square.

Noah watched from the crawlspace and waited a moment to make sure his friend crossed successfully. Watching Ashem run, knowing he was outside of the palace with both the medallion and the necklace of Jericho filled him with a feeling of elation. All this time, the planning, the struggles—he was almost to the finish line. The city of Jericho was on high alert, monitoring the marching soldiers circling their walls. Natsa had abandoned upper Jericho with his bodyguards. And Noah had successfully evaded capture. Just minutes ago, he was a sitting inside the royal dungeon awaiting his imminent sacrifice to Morgotha.

Ashem made it across the courtyard to the dark alley unimpeded. He turned back to Noah, surveyed the palace grounds and the balcony to make sure the coast was clear, and waved for Noah to advance. *Just need to get to Rahab's and wait for Enud and Eliab to find me.* As the thought finished in his mind, a shattering ring from the gong of Jericho shook the city, "*Six!* Oh no!"

Noah's heart burst in his chest, pounding at the lack of time. "Fifteen minutes!" *Was it enough?* Noah loosened his body with a quick stretch and burst out of the shadows of the storage room. He ran as fast as he could across the palace square, his eyes focused on his friend. The cool morning breeze hit his body, invigorating his senses. Freedom was nearly at hand. Then from behind, he heard the screeching cry of the sons of Natsa. "There he is!" Laba yelled. "Stop him!" Noah didn't even bother looking back. Ashem urged him on. "Noah, hurry!"

As Noah reached the entrance to the alley, he saw a Jericho soldier closing in from behind Ashem. In all the commotion inside the palace, this soldier must have returned from patrol on orders from Natsa to check on the governor's boys. But this was not some average soldier on patrol! Noah knew the man. It was Natsa's trusted bodyguard, his personal attendant, the man responsible for checking on Noah while imprisoned, the man who was to be his ultimate end at Morgotha. At the sight of Noah, the soldier began to rush in his direction. Noah pointed behind his friend, "Ashem, watch out!"

Ashem turned and walked slowly back toward Noah as the soldier approached. By the time Noah reached his friend, the bodyguard was twenty-five yards away and closing. "He cannot grab us both." Ashem winked with a smile and took off running full speed directly at the intimidating soldier. The alley was narrow, the shoulders of the bodyguard nearly able to touch each wall. Like a three hundred-pound NFL linebacker bearing down on the opposing teams running back, his silhouette blotted out the sun.

The armor of the bodyguard glistened in the morning light, his sword clanging against the metal of his armor with each approaching step. The pounding steps of the Israelites echoed in the narrow alleyway. Noah gathered his courage, took another deep breath, and ran right straight in behind Ashem. The soldier obliged the charge and picked up his pace, barreling toward them. Like a scene from a movie, two high-speed vehicles racing head-on in a game of chicken, Noah and his friend prepared for the collision.

Ashem moved to the left of the alley, Noah stayed center. The massive soldier jockeyed for position to cut off Ashem's escape. As he moved to block, Ashem made himself small and jumped in a Superman-type pose, his body sliding against the alley wall and right under the outstretched right arm of the soldier. Noah, seeing his opening, dropped to the ground and slid under the soldier's legs like a runner stealing second base. The swift coordinated movement of the boys and the awkward reach of the bodyguard caused him to fall under the weight of his armor.

Natsa's henchman slammed to the ground, the metal sound echoing loudly. The maneuver was a success. Freedom was before them. "The sewer! This way, Noah!" The boys ran as fast as their legs could carry them. The city was creaking and crackling. Noah heard loud snaps as boulders split along the wall. A few people of the city were still in upper Jericho. They ignored them as they ran past. Two servant boys mattered not against the never ceasing marching of the Israelites. Noah watched as the high citizens of Jericho scurried about for protection, seeking shelter wherever they could find it. He knew in less than ten minutes, there would be no hiding place left!

It did not take long for them to reach the Forum of Morgotha. The horrific statue no longer stood perfectly erect. The constant Earth-shaking march of the Israelites had detached a portion of the base from its foundation. The bloodstained idol leaned to its side, its weight begging at any moment to succumb to gravity. From across the forum, the familiar screeching voice of Shecariah screamed. Like nails against a chalkboard, she hollered for the palace guards, but none came. All had been called to the defense of the city. But Noah feared because he knew Laba and Nomed were in pursuit. The woman hurled a clay goblet filled halfway with wine in her hand at the boys as they left the forum. The cup smashed against the wall between the two, spilling the blood-colored liquid over the cobblestone street.

Noah slowed a moment and glanced at the decrepit woman. He smiled at the haggle-toothed beast, increasing her rage even more. She waved a silver dagger in her hand, wishing for an opportunity to thrust it into his gut.

And then she was gone. Ashem was well ahead of Noah. He was already at the hidden passageway working on the grate that barred their exit. Noah felt a sense of relief. They made it! As Noah came upon Ashem, he could see something was wrong. Ashem struggled to lift the metal covering. It was no use! He motioned for Noah to help. The two of them grabbed an iron bar they found leaning against the wall, and on the count of three pulled. But the grate would not budge. The shifting city of Jericho had locked the grate in place. The massive weight of the stones had sealed it permanently in place. It would take a tractor and three full-grown men to pry it loose. Nothing was going to dislodge it.

A thunderous sound filled the city. Noah and Ashem looked up, the buildings inside Jericho were literally swaying now. Dust filled the air. Small pieces of the walls fell into the alleyway.

"Ashem…what do we do?" Noah questioned. "We're running out of time!"

"It is no use! The passage is blocked." Ashem thought for a moment. "We must leave as everyone else."

"What do you mean?"

"Come!" Ashem ran past Noah back toward Morgotha.

"Ashem, no! We cannot go back!" Noah screamed as he raced after his friend. Noah's heart was pounding. At any moment, he expected to round the corner and see Laba and Nomed. Adrenaline was pumping through his body allowing him to sprint at top speed.

"Ashem!" Noah breathed heavy, trying to keep pace. "Where are we going?"

"The main gate," Ashem spoke in a matter-of-fact tone. His decision was made; no point in arguing now. The only way to Rahab's inn was through the main area, guards and all. Whether they liked it or not, that was where their path was headed.

"Quickly, Noah, we must be inside my mother's house!" Just as he said that, the horns from within the city sounded. The Jericho soldiers were prepping for an assault. Surely the focus of the city would be on the Israelites with God's protection the two boys will speed right through the gate unnoticed.

Noah, of course, knew what his friend meant. Rahab's inn was like home base in a video game. Invincibility from any weapon of war. A cloak of protection.

The screams of the citizens of Jericho surrounded him, the noise increasing all the more the closer they got to the gate. Jericho's people knew war was at their doorsteps. The two raced back into Morgotha's Forum, but this time, Ashem took a different side path out of it. Shecariah was nowhere to be seen. As they exited the forum,

Noah heard a crackling noise from behind him. He turned around, peering back, assuming they were being followed. To his pleasure, he watched as the pagan statue of Morgotha met its ultimate end, giving way to the vibrations. It collapsed to the ground. "What a god," Noah snickered sarcastically.

— ❖ 51 ❖ —

shem knew the area well from his many visits over the years. He did not so much as hesitate one second as he bobbed and weaved in and out of alleyways and back pathways. Noah kept on his heels the best he could. Some of the alleys were so tight only one person could pass at a time. The blessing of God guided each step, each turn, each fleeting second. The people of Jericho paid little attention to the two peasant boys. Then as Noah exited the final street, the road opened into a large area teeming with hundreds of people—the main gate!

Terror and panic consumed the city. People were bumping, pushing, and wailing as they moved about in chaotic fashion. Women were screaming, children crying. Men were yelling and waving, trying to communicate to each other over the deafening sound. Soldiers were pushing against the crowds to move away from the walls. Officers barked orders which went unheard in the madness. All the while, the incessant pounding steps of the Israelites shook the city to its core. The walls were creaking and cracking, pieces of stone pelting the people as they fell. The overwhelming dust cloud made visibility near impossible at distances over ten yards, and the closer you moved to the wall, the worse it became. Like a scene from a movie, anarchy had gripped Jericho.

Then Noah caught sight of Natsa and his men. The vibrant golden armor of the king of Jericho ricocheted the light of the morning sun through the dust bowl. Noah watched as he motioned and screamed for the people to follow orders, but it was useless. At the very least, Noah need not worry of being spotted by the governor. In all the chaos, Noah believed he was going to be all right. A sense of peace enveloped him. He knew outside the walls Joshua was at the helm. He had successfully escaped the palace with the necklace and medallion and was a few hundred yards from Rahab's inn.

The once heavily fortified main gate was now manned by a few soldiers. Their attention was on the marching Israelites, so two boys racing through raised little notice. People were pouring through the area by the hundreds, some racing toward the walls, others scurrying away for respite. All of this went unnoticed and unchecked by the guards. Once free of the alleyway, Ashem never stopped running. Noah followed behind as best he could. Ashem cleared the gate first. Seeing it was clear, Noah made his move. He stared at the soldiers begging them not to look and just as he was about to pass completely through, a horn blew violently behind him, so loud that anyone close by stopped in place. Noah froze and turned. "Laba!" They had been in pursuit the whole time.

"Stop him!" Laba screamed at the gate soldiers to grab him. Noah watched as the guards turned their attention to him. Why the boy was important they did not ask. The son of the king wanted Noah, and it was their duty to comply. The soldiers jumped down from their perch and advanced toward Noah, weapons in hand. He was locked in place like a deer in headlights. Everything in him screamed to run, but his body was like stone.

Ashem screamed, "Noah! Run!" which jostled Noah awake.

Noah looked at his friend. Ashem waved then turned and ran, hoping that Noah would follow suit. "Be strong and courageous," the words of Josiah whispered in his ear. Like a rabbit evading a fox, Noah burst from his stance. It was as if he was freed from quicksand! He ran at a pace he never thought his body could muster. The gate soldiers and Laba along with his private bodyguards gave chase.

His goal was to make it to the crowd. Ashem had already disappeared into the mosh pit of people. Noah made himself small and squeezed through their ranks. The soldiers were right on his heels. They tried to follow, but their size forbade passage. Noah heard as people screamed from the soldiers violently pressing into the crowd tossing and punching the people who would not comply. The citizens of Jericho were lost in the mix of anarchy, air was thin from the pressing weight of the mass.

Noah dropped down low, at points crawling to make his way through. A large man stepped on his hand, another unknowingly kicked him in the side. In the pursuit, Noah had lost sight of Ashem, but he knew where he was headed. *Keep pushing, Noah.* He was a few hundred yards away from Rahab's and protection.

Suddenly, time froze, the men of Israel stopped marching. In response, a deafening silence inside Jericho spread like a virus. Time stood still. Terror covered the faces of the people as they stared at each other. Nothing could have prepared them for what came next. The panic in their eyes said it all. In the distance, the familiar booming voice of Joshua called out, "Shout! For the Lord has given you the city!" The battle cry was followed by the blowing tune of Israel's trumpets. The instruments note ignited an earth-shattering scream from every Hebrew soldier surrounding the city.

Noah had attended sporting events with his father a few times back home. The largest venue and the loudest was in Arlington, Texas, for a Dallas Cowboys football game. Over one hundred thousand people screaming, music blaring. But that was nothing compared to the nation of Israel shouting as loud as their lungs could muster, a sound so overwhelming, Noah lost his vision. His head split with a pain he never thought imaginable. He collapsed to his knees and squeezed his eyes shut, his hands pressed hard against his ears to protect himself from the noise. All the people of Jericho did the same; young and old, men, women, and children, soldiers, and peasants dropped to the ground in agony.

Even though Noah had read the story of Jericho in the book of Joshua and heard many sermons recounting its meaning, nothing could have prepared him for the indescribable experience. Jericho's towering walls, walls that had stood for hundreds of years, walls that protected the people of the land from countless attacks trembled like a tree in a tornado. The gigantic barrier loomed menacingly above the people. A people now writhing in pain on the ground trying to recover from the Israeli battle cry.

And with a snap of God's finger, a massive piece of wall, a chunk the size of a mid-sized SUV weighing hundreds upon thousands of pounds fell. Gravity brought it down like a missile. When it met the ground, it sounded like an explosion. That one section took out twenty or more people. The days of protection being hidden behind the walls of Jericho was over. Like dominos, section by section and boulder by boulder, the massive structure gave way. The people of Jericho screamed and pushed and pulled and yanked, trying to get out of the way. With each collapse, the road Noah stood upon lurched and shifted.

Another gigantic rock from the wall he stood next to fell on the road before him. Then another, and then another. Noah looked around him. The city was caving in. The soldiers situated high upon the wall for the defense of Jericho had no chance. Most came down with the wall, others took a chance and jumped—neither fared well. With each passing second, chaos and confusion grew and grew. Everyone was running for their lives. No one cared for anyone but themselves. Some men fought violently against each other. Mothers abandoned their children. No one stopped to help the animals. The soldiers of Israel continued to scream.

Behind Noah erupted a sound unlike any he had heard. The largest piece yet, nearly the entirety of the wall fell in. As it hit the ground, a humungous cloud of debris blinded everyone nearby. As the cloud dissipated, Noah witnessed the end of Jericho. The first Hebrew soldiers were entering the city, pouring in like water through a broken dam. Noah stood hypnotized, watching the utter anarchy of war. The Israelites continued to shout from beyond the walls and the horns continued to bellow throughout the city. Surprisingly, amongst all the carnage, Noah heard Ashem scream at the top of his lungs. He rushed to Noah's side and grabbed him by the arm, shaking him to wake up. "Noah, we must go now!" Ashem pulled on his friend, begging him to follow.

They were near the market. From behind, Noah heard Laba's soldiers closing in. Beckoning them on was Laba. "Get him!" the evil boy hissed. Noah turned to see Laba pointing in his direction. There was no retreat. He had to move now!

Noah burst forth like a rocket. His path was hindered unlike before. People and boulders filled the road. He bobbed and weaved like a sprinter in the race of his life. He dug his feet into the ground and plowed ahead. People were flying in front of him in all directions with nowhere to hide. The walls were caving in all around. The force of the wall hitting the road caused sections of the road to jut forth. Noah jumped over them. He kept his eyes straight ahead on the back of his friend. Each step was more difficult than the next. His friend was fading in and out of the crowd and the dust. "Oh…no…" Noah worried he had lost his way.

The medallion under his robe started to vibrate. The environment around him continued its chaotic collapse, but the colors changed. Everything turned black and white, just like when Moses visited. The deafening sounds faded away. Just quiet. Below his feet, a golden path led the way. The path of Moses! "Be strong and courageous," the voice of Thios announced in Noah's ears.

He zeroed in on the path, his heart pumping, his breath labored. Anywhere the golden streak led, he followed. It moved left then darted right, around rocks on the ground, under pieces of clutter, through groups of people. Without the path, Noah would have been crushed or trampled by the onslaught of destruction and sea of people. Every now and then, he would catch a glimpse of Ashem running. He was in the marketplace, the surroundings a bit more familiar. They were getting close! A lapse of judgment overtook Noah. He made the mistake of taking his eyes off the path and looking back at his pursuers. The scene of destruction mesmerized him. He watched as a massive stone fell and crushed the lead soldier. The other soldiers ignored the horrific demise and continued their pursuit led by the venomous sons of Natsa.

Noah's penalty for peering back was a severe tumble into a pile of rocks. The pain from the stumble shot up his legs, blood rushing from his knee. *No time to baby the wound…* Noah jumped to his feet and limped into a semi-sprint once more. The glowing path was still there to follow. *No more looking back, Noah.* He picked up his pace, knowing that Laba and Nomed were closing in. Suddenly, to his right, the outer wall completely gave way and collapsed, causing a huge cloud of dust to fill the area. Noah covered his eyes as best he could to keep the debris out. All the while, he struggled to keep visual on the golden road. As the dust settled, he stared at the gaping hole in the wall of Jericho. Silence fell on the people around him as they cowered in fear. Their defense had failed!

The Sons of Israel came pouring in, swords drawn. The timing could not have been better. Like crossing a train track, the Hebrews created a barrier between him and his pursuers. The citizens of the Jericho were helpless. They screamed a blood curdling cry. The Israelites fell on the enemy soldiers. Noah heard Natsa barking orders for a counterattack, but it was no use. The sheer numbers of Israeli soldiers overpowered Natsa's best men.

"Noah!" Ashem screamed. Noah looked up to see his friend make the left turn down the back alley to his mother's inn.

Just then, he felt the grip of someone from behind. "Got you!" Noah turned and twisted with all his strength to break free from Laba's hand. He shifted to gather his balance and then pushed the boy to the ground. He looked up to see Nomed and five of his soldiers closing in. Noah felt a lump in his throat as he swallowed. They were advancing full charge. He was standing still. There was no way he could escape. "God, help—" Noah whispered under his breath.

Then, like a tidal wave of salvation, the army of Israel came pouring over the wall on Nomed's right, tackling the boy and his soldiers into submission. Swords were swinging violently, the sun dancing on their iron blades. Noah whipped around, not wanting to witness the slaughter, but the screams he could not hide from. He sprinted forth, leaving Laba with his brother on the ground to whatever vicious fate God had ordained. He quickly traversed the marketplace, following the path of Moses into the back alley. As he turned the final corner, the golden path disappeared. No matter, he knew where he was. The walls on either side were breaking to pieces; their end was inevitable. The tight area was littered with small to mid-sized boulders. He climbed and dodged them as he ran.

Ahead, he could see Rahab begging the boys on. She stood in the doorway of the inn, arms wide open, screaming for her son. The whole of Jericho in chaos, every structure collapsing, everyone except

343

for hers. The inn was nestled against the wall, yet by the grace of God, her section stood resolute. Noah was thirty yards behind his friend. With a giant leap, Ashem bounded into his mother's arms. She embraced him tightly, the only possession she truly cared for. Ashem immediately removed himself from her clutch and turned to cheer Noah on. "Come, Noah! Hurry!"

Noah ran as hard and as fast as his little legs could take him. Blood continued to pour from his wounded knee, the red stain covering his left leg down to his ankle. He ignored the pulsating pain. His heart pounded beneath his chest yearning for rest, but the adrenaline gave him the juice to keep moving. His lungs burned for oxygen, sweat drenching his robe. His arms were tiring, shoulders aching with every volley over a boulder. Twenty yards away... *I can do this!*

Suddenly, an ominous thundering boom crackled over his head. Noah stopped as did Ashem, along with anyone in earshot, and they each looked up. The top portion of the wall that Rahab's house was built against was about to give way. Noah clutched the medallion desperately looking at the ground to find the path of Moses...there was nothing. He took a step forward toward Ashem, and once more, the menacing sound echoed, casting a warning to anyone nearby. Noah looked at Ashem. Ashem looked back. Time froze. The boys shared a moment of clarity. Ashem waved to Noah, begging him to move. Noah, throwing caution to the wind, leapt forward over a hundred-pound boulder in his path. Another deafening noise came from above as the humungous piece of wall came tumbling down upon his position. Noah closed his eyes. Ashem screamed.

52

Silence.

Deafening silence.

A silence that reminded Noah of sitting in the abyss before being approached by King Josiah. Surely, he was dead. No more screams, no pounding footsteps, no horns blowing or gongs ringing. The smells of Jericho no longer filled his nostrils. His heavy breathing had subsided. His body was dry from sweat. Even the pain in his knee was gone. There was quiet and coolness about him.

Noah opened his eyes. It took a moment for his vision to come into focus. He felt something wet on his face and moved his hand to wipe the drool away. "What? Where am I?" He scanned the dark room. A lamp flickered in the corner. A groggy confusion filled his mind. He was spread eagle on the floor, but not in Jericho, not with his friend, Ashem. There were no menacing boulders collapsing around him, no Jericho soldiers in hot pursuit, no women screaming, no thunderous rumbles. Just silence.

He stared at his arms, then his clothes. He was back! He was inside his camping tent again! Lying on the floor, gathering his strength, he stared at the lamp, it's light cascading an amber hue to his environment. Noah sat up. It was night.

"Was I asleep this whole time?" he whispered. "A dream?"

He looked at the ground around him and found his Bible opened nearby. He replayed the day; travel, the dig site, the late dinner—he must have passed out as soon as his father left him. He rose to his feet and moved toward the tent entrance. He unzipped the covering and looked out. All of Solomon's men had turned in for the evening. He heard a few workers in the main tent cleaning up supper, but that was all. The fire was still burning.

His first instinct was to fetch his father and tell him of his adventure but decided against it. "Was it really a dream?" Noah spoke aloud to himself. "There is no way." He could not believe how real it all felt. He zipped the tent and moved back inside

He rubbed his chest with his hands, hoping that just maybe the medallion was there…but it was not. He looked on the ground, hoping to find the scepter of Judah. "I know I left it here." Remembering the last he saw the relic was when he read the Bible in search of its history, he scanned his cot—nothing. He went to the chest containing his possessions—not there. He dropped to his knees and scanned the room. Something in him coaxed him to kneel low and peer under his cot. There nestled in the back was the iron relic. He flattened his body to the ground and reached out to take hold of it.

"Must have kicked it back there in my sleep," Noah whispered.

He rubbed his hand over the scepter as he held it up to the light. He studied the piece carefully, thinking about his dream, how King Josiah spoke of its power. He chuckled at the silliness of it all. God choosing him, a boy of little regard, sending him of all people back in time. Meeting Joshua and Eleazar, making friends with a boy in Jericho, Thios, an angel of God—for goodness sake. As he turned the rod in the light, a sparkle hit his eyes, causing him to blink.

"That's new."

He looked intently at the crown of the scepter. There, nestled in the side, in one of the carved fittings, like it was there the whole time, was a green jewel the size of a walnut.

Noah's heart skipped. He held his breath in silent shock. He clutched the scepter tightly in his hands, so many thoughts racing in his mind. "There's no way!" He rose to his feet, trying to stay calm. He paced the inside of the tent. "It was real…" Noah shook his head. "Come on, get it together, Noah. If it was real, then Ashem!" Noah looked at the ground to the Bible still open. He quickly turned to the book of Joshua. "Come on…where is it?" He scanned chapter 6 of Joshua. He read the events, each one making his heart beat faster. He read of Joshua, son of Nun, the sending of the spies who befriended

Rahab the harlot and stayed at her inn. Noah got goosebumps recollecting his time with Eliab and Enud. He read of the captain of the Lord of Hosts meeting with Joshua, the marching around the city walls for seven days, culminating with Joshua shouting for attack.

"Here it is." Noah found what he was looking for.

Joshua chapter 6, verse 22 and following:

> Joshua said to the two men who had spied out the land, "Go into the harlot's house and bring the woman and all she has out of there as you have sworn to her." So the young men who were spies went in and brought out Rahab and her father and her mother and her brothers and all she had; they also brought out all her relatives and placed them outside the camp of Israel. They burned the city with fire and all that was in it. However, Rahab the harlot and her father's household and all she had, Joshua spared; and she has lived in the midst of Israel to this day, for she hid the messengers who Joshua sent to spy out Jericho."

"Is that all?" Noah scanned quickly ahead. "There must be more." He turned the Bible to the back once more to the Concordance. The pages flipped to R, "Rahab... Rahab..." Noah whispered. "There she is." Noah guided his hand over the verses. "Matthew chapter 1, verse 5." Noah turned in the Bible. It read:

> Salmon was the father of Boaz by Rahab, Boaz was the father of Obed by Ruth, and Obed the father of Jesse. Jesse was the father of David, the king.

The words sent a shiver up Noah's back, a good shiver. "So Rahab is the great-great-grandmother of King David?" The thought of her meeting a good man and starting a family which would later beget King David made Noah happy. He was assured Ashem had a great life. What a reward for choosing God over her city. The words of Joshua whispered in his head, "Be strong and courageous."

Noah thought about his friend, Ashem, and whether he would ever see him again and, for that matter, Mathius and Hani. He thought about Josiah and the majestic meeting hall. Was he going to tell his dad all this? Would he even understand? And Thios…how he longed to speak with Thios once more.

Noah sat up in the middle of the tent the lamp still flickering. The scepter of Judah lay across his lap. His Bible opened before him on the floor. He spoke to God, "Thank you, Lord. Thank you for giving me this opportunity. Tha—" Noah was interrupted by a rustling from behind him. He paused and listened. It sounded more like a vibrating cell phone. He located it coming from his cot beneath the sheets.

He took a breath and pulled back the covers. As he did, a brilliant orange light filled the room. "The medallion!"

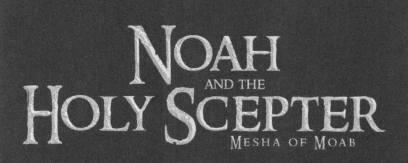

NOAH
AND THE
HOLY
SCEPTER

OAK OF OPHRAH

COMING SOON

About the Author

Luke Andrew Elliott was born and raised in Irving, Texas, a suburb of Dallas, the youngest of three boys, followed by his baby sister. Raised in a Christian home, he accepted Jesus as his Lord and Savior during a Wednesday night youth group meeting in seventh grade. His fire was lit, and he was filled with a passion for the gospel of Christ. Luke was a burgeoning eighteen-year-old college student when God placed the idea of *Noah and the Holy Scepter* in his curious and creative mind. Over the coming years, ideas for this seven-part novel series poured into his thoughts. He would diligently jot them down on pieces of scratch paper and place them in a folder for future use. The folder went untouched for almost twenty years! During that time, he married the love of his life, Tammy, and became a proud daddy to his daughter, Trinity Elaine, and his son, Ethan Andrew. He is now a small business owner, working in the field of health insurance. A disciple of men, a teacher to youth, he devotes his free time to family and friends…and writing of course! With a desire to serve God more, his thoughts always came back to *Noah and the Scepter*. In 2019, he opened the neglected folder, read through his jumbled-up notes, and began to write the adventure that awaits you. The first offering, *Noah and the Holy Scepter: The Walls of Jericho*, was released in October 2021. FB Luke Elliott

CPSIA information can be obtained
at www.ICGtesting.com
Printed in the USA
BVHW090744040123
655464BV00002B/90